Paparazzi

Want to get more FREE from Erika?

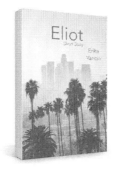

Sign up for the author's New Releases mailing list and get a free copy of the short story "Eliot." You will periodically receive free short stories and unique chapters.

Click here to get started:
https://www.erikavanzin.com/newsletter.html

To my father, who taught me to love the silences.

PRESS *Review*

We'll Soon Be Hearing More about the Jailbirds!

Hi, Roadies!

How are you? Did you have a fabulous Thanksgiving? I'm still in a food-induced coma from the big, delicious meal my friend prepared yesterday, but luckily, I was able to roll up to the computer to give you this news. Almost five months after the tour has ended—which featured our Jailbirds and their opening act, the Red Velvet Curtains—we have an album coming soon!

Apparently, the Jailbirds are in the studio laying down the final touches (we know what a perfectionist Damian is), but all the songs for the album have been recorded. According to the label's official press release, an EP with three radio singles will soon be released, but we will have to wait a little longer for the full album. There is no official date, but we know how fast the press and marketing offices move when they get started.

We're keeping our eyes and ears wide open for any news coming soon.

Be kind and Rock'n'Roll,

Iris

15230 Likes 12694 Tweets 11598 Shares 3622 Comments

CHAPTER 1

Thomas

Returning from the bathroom, I find Damian and Lilly making out in front of the stove, passionately kissing like two teenagers held hostage by their hormones, ignoring the fact that I'm in the room.

"For God's sake! Do you two ever stop fondling each other like two teenagers?"

Since we returned from the tour, they haven't been separated for more than five minutes, even going so far as to move in together to a much bigger apartment than Damian's previous one. They built a classic love nest. They spend their evenings on the sofa, under the blanket, trying to watch a movie but never seeing the end of it because, after twenty minutes, they've already ripped their clothes off and become a tangle of limbs, sweat, and moans of pleasure.

I know this because they once invited me to a pizza and Netflix night, as they call it, and I went to make some microwave popcorn before staring at a show I didn't want to watch. Two and a half minutes later, I returned to find my shirtless friend lying beneath Lilly as her tongue worked its way across every inch of his skin. I had to walk to the front door with my eyes closed before bolting out of the apartment and getting into the elevator at light speed.

Lilly glances up from their make-out session and giggles, giving me one of her contagious smiles that light up her eyes, then pushes Damian away, her hands on his chest. In response, my friend lets out a guttural grunt. Maybe I should have accepted Simon's invitation to relax in his Connecticut home, reading books and looking at the greenhouse filled with bonsai and other plants whose names I don't know.

"You only say that because you're jealous." Damian goes to the fridge and hands me a beer after uncorking it. His face is enlightened by an amused smile, making fun of me. He's been doing this a lot lately since this woman came into his life and made him so happy.

I sit at the kitchen counter and sip from the bottle, watching Lilly manage the stove. She's a fantastic musician, but she could burn a precooked dish in the microwave. She's using a metal spatula to peel off the chicken breast she forgot to check—it's so burnt I doubt it's healthy to eat. I hope my friend comes to the rescue of our dinner and prepares something edible.

I glance at Damian and find him looking at her with adoring eyes. I had no idea how much a woman could change a man until I hung around these two. The stubbornness of this girl has capitulated even an unrepentant womanizer like my best friend. It's a rare relationship, theirs. I've only seen it in a handful of couples, and I've come to the conclusion that love is an endangered experience. It exists here and there, I'm sure, but few are lucky enough to find it in a world full of masks and fake smiles, opportunism, and stabs in the back.

"No, not jealous. I have my share of sex. It's not like I've become a priest," I boast, even though the number of women coming on to me has been fewer lately.

The Jailbirds are eighty percent Damian, fifteen percent Michael—who with his brazenness and beauty manages to earn his space—and the remaining five percent I share with Simon. The groupies always want the damn front man who exudes sensuality and slams waves of testosterone in their faces. They don't look at the drummer hidden behind a wall of instruments. When we walk into a club, the girls recognize Damian and Michael, while Simon and I have to be introduced as "the other bandmates." Not that this prevents us from getting girls, but they usually settle for us because Damian chooses someone else.

"Don't you miss having a steady companion?" Lilly's question is as simple as it is complicated.

"Not exactly. With the life we have, it's not easy to tell what women want from you. And since we don't stay in the same place long enough to go out with someone more than three months in a row, my only option is the sex without strings attached." It's only a half-truth. Even if I didn't have the tour, I still wouldn't want anyone by my side. From the way he's looking at me, I know Damian understands my reasoning.

"You've been here for a few months now," says Lilly, who seems worried I won't find a woman.

"Look, the right one should literally fall into my arms." I chuckle while I sip my beer and pull out my cigarettes. I need to cut this conversation short before it completely spoils my evening. I'd rather not visit memories of a past that should just stay buried.

"Not in here!" Lilly glares at me and points her finger at the door.

Damian chuckles and shrugs his shoulders.

"I know, don't get your panties in a twist. I'm going out to smoke." I roll my eyes and stroll toward the front door.

The late November night is way too cold, even by New York standards. The smell of Manhattan is like a fog that seeps into your bones these days: a mixture of smog, ethnic cuisines, and dust. It's not a bad smell. It's what sets this city I love apart from any other. Simon loves to take refuge in his Connecticut home in the middle of nature as soon as he's free from work commitments. I tried it too, really, but to me, it feels like something is missing there, that the air doesn't smell of anything, even if it is healthier. And this time of year, this city is a sparkling feast of Christmas decorations that light up the streets. Every corner of this place is transformed into a world of magic and hope. On December first, the tree lights will light up in Rockefeller Center, officially kicking off the festivities. Tourists will invade the streets, with their eyes shining and their mouths open, enraptured by the decorations so realistic that they seem alive. Noses pointing upwards, they'll wait impatiently for the snow that whitewashes everything and muffles the hustle and bustle of the city that never sleeps, making this corner of the world even more magical.

I can't help but smile in this alley, hidden by empty trash cans, thinking about the city that adopted me and makes me feel at home. Illuminated by two street lights, this spot feels less sinister than the rest of the city. When I come to visit Damian and Lilly, I often take refuge in this alley. I don't like to smoke in front of their apartment because sometimes people recognize me, take pictures, and I find myself in some gossip newspaper just for smoking in peace.

Here in the back alley, though, I'm always alone—or at least that's what I thought until a metallic noise above my head makes me look upwards. I don't even have time to figure out what's going on before I find myself lying on the ground, some unknown person in my arms.

"What the hell..."

A mane of long, red, wavy hair moves above me, trying to get back on its feet with some difficulty. It takes me a few seconds to catch my breath and get up; my back is killing me.

"I'm so sorry! I slipped." A woman's sweet voice brings me back to reality.

I watch her swab her bloody knee with a napkin she's pulled out of a bag emblazoned with the name "Iris" in giant bold letters. Probably written with a marker when she was a teenager, since it's a little faded. There's no doubt that this girl with legs for days, wrapped in a pair of tight black jeans and a figure-hugging jacket, is no longer a teenager. I stare at her like she's an alien who's came down to earth, swooping on me straight from the sky.

"Are you hurt?" I ask her, looking at the blood dripping from her knee.

She looks up at me and my breath catches in my throat. Two huge, green, fawn eyes stare at me, wide-eyed. Her face is covered in freckles, her pink-perfect lips slightly open in surprise. She has that familiar look of someone who recognizes me—but this time, I'm the one paralyzed by the breathtaking view in front of me.

"No, just a scratch..." Her voice comes out a little uncertain, but the smile on her lips is confident. She is not intimidated by my presence.

"How the hell did you fall from the sky?" I'm curious to know what she was doing up there, on the fire escape.

"Are you going to ask if I'm an angel now? And if I got hurt when I fell? Like one of those movie pick-up lines? You don't seem like the type who needs jokes to pick up girls," she teases as she finishes cleaning the blood from her knee and tosses her napkin into the trash can next to us.

I burst out in unexpected laughter. Clearly, she's not fooled by the charm of a "famous" musician. "Apart from the fact that I already asked if you got hurt, no, I wasn't going to hit on you. I don't use those pick-up lines to impress women," I admit, laughing and lighting another cigarette, as the first one ended up on the ground with my butt.

"Yes, I guess you have no difficulty with women. Do they usually let you to talk, or do they take off their panties as soon as they realize who they're with? I've never been able to tell."

The laugh spontaneously arises in my chest again. This girl doesn't walk on eggshells. I like her bluntness, that she doesn't go into respiratory crisis when she tries to put two words together. I love the fans who recognize me and surround me, but sometimes it's too damn difficult to relate when they squeal, blush, freak out or ask me where Damian is. It's a breath of fresh air to talk to a woman who's not jumping on me or using me to get to my friend.

"If they're brazen enough, they stick their tongues in my mouth without any talking. Or they ask to see the hands I hold the drumsticks with, or the strong shoulders that beat the drums," I admit. Embarrassed, I take a deep draw from the cigarette, trying to hide my discomfort.

Her brow furrows for a few seconds, as though trying to figure out whether I'm kidding or not. Unfortunately, I'm not. My relationships are a continuous "What strong arms you have," like I'm the big bad wolf in "The Little Red Riding Hood."

"Are you serious? They really ask you those things?" It's clear she's holding back a laugh.

What a twisted irony of the universe: this beautiful girl who takes my breath away is also the only one who isn't melting at my musician's charm. I get the feeling a killer smile and two beefy biceps are not enough with her.

"Serious as death." I rub the back of my neck, trying to drive away the embarrassment.

This conversation makes me look idiotic and, for some crazy reason, it annoys me to be seen like this by her. She's a smart girl. Am I just an arrogant womanizer—or worse, a loser who can only get a woman because he's a musician? I feel ridiculous, intimidated by the opinion of a perfect stranger.

"It's a shame they miss everything you could say, just to have a trophy to add to their famous fuck shelf. You seem like someone who's had more experience than most ordinary mortals on this earth."

Her response, accompanied by a sincere smile, floors me. The women I've met have never treated me like more than a checkmark on a list of celebrities to brag about with their friends—and not even their first choice. I smile like a kid, looking down at my shoes—a feeling I haven't experienced since fifth grade.

"Thank you. I take that as a compliment." I take another drag from the cigarette to keep my lips busy, to prevent a frown from forming on my face.

The girl shrugs and smiles. "I don't know if it's a compliment, but for what it's worth, I don't think you're just a pretty face. You're a phenomenal drummer, and I'd give anything to know the story behind that time you took the stage wearing a pair of jeans with one leg ripped off." She laughs and I join her. Out of my entire musical career, the only thing people remember is the time I looked like a complete fool.

"Why the hell does everyone ask me about that? Damian took the stage in a much worse state than me, but all anyone remembers is my mishap," I say with a laugh.

"Because you looked like someone out of an '80s pop video. All that was missing was a flowy wig, and you'd be perfect."

"Aren't you tired of hearing that same old story?" I reproach her good-naturedly, but I can tell she's dying to know.

"I don't think so...and most importantly, I don't think that's all you have to say about that."

I nod and take another drag, trying to gather my thoughts before appearing to be a total moron as I tell the official version for the umpteenth time.

"We were at the festival, backstage waiting for the group before us to finish playing. A group of girls approached with their expensive all-access passes hanging around their necks. They wanted an autograph from the whole band, along with something that they could bring home as a trophy. Damian took off his shirt, Simon gave them four guitar picks, Michael...no, better you don't know about him. They wanted my pants. Since I couldn't get on stage in my underwear, I tore off a leg of my jeans. At the time, it seemed like a good idea; later, I realized I looked like a moron." I still giggle at the memory I've told so many times to the press that reality and fiction are now forever confused in a foggy haze.

"I don't believe you."

Her affirmation is solemn. I didn't think her green eyes could get any bigger, but here she is, proving me wrong, with two irises that seem to want to nail me for my lies. She really doesn't believe the pre-approved PR bullshit I tell the press.

"That's what happened that day...that's what happens when you're part of a world-famous band. Women just want to take a trophy home. Sometimes it's a t-shirt; other times it's something physical in another way."

She smiles and shakes her head. "You're lucky you're a fantastic drummer because if you had to act to survive, you'd be starving." She nails me in my bullshit without beating around the bush.

"I'm lucky I met those three idiots I've been hanging around with for years, I suppose." I smile at her, hoping I didn't ruin this strange connection between us.

The girl studies me for a few seconds. Her head is slightly tilted. "They're the ones who are lucky to have met you. The Jailbirds wouldn't be the same without their drummer."

For the first time, she openly admits that she knows who I am, and I appreciate her straightforwardness. I smile at her and take another drag of my cigarette. My heart starts pumping against my chest when I see her wave and take a few steps away from me.

"Where are you going?" The words leave my lips before I realize what I'm saying. Anxiety assaults my stomach.

"It's not like I usually spend my evenings in the alleys surrounded by garbage, even if the company is pleasant." She nods at me, gesturing to the environment around us.

I look around and remember where we are. Talking to her transported me to another reality.

"Iris! Can I at least ask for your number?"

"So you can tell me another pre-approved story about how you ripped off your pants?" She smiles at my inability to answer coherently. She raises her hand, waves at me, and disappears through the streets and traffic of Manhattan, leaving me with a myriad of questions.

Is her real name Iris? Does she live nearby? And most importantly, why the hell did she fall from the fire escape? For the first time, I've met a woman I would like to talk to for hours, and I can't come up with a convincing excuse to persuade her to stay. I hate feeling so unprepared, so inept at reading someone who intrigues me. I'd like to get lost again in her teasing smile and her curious, questioning eyes. I'd like to know everything about the only woman in years who has attracted my curiosity so much I'd give anything to talk to her—not just sleep with her.

CHAPTER 2

Iris

Twelve blocks on foot, and I still can't stop shaking. I'm shocked that I slipped down that ladder—I thought I was going to break my neck. And I'm shaken that I literally ended up in the arms of Thomas Simons, drummer of the Jailbirds. That boy has blue eyes that leave you completely naked. I can't calm the agitated trembling in my stomach and hands.

I've been sitting at my usual table in my favorite coffee shop for at least ten minutes, holding my hot cappuccino with the peppermint stick the barista slipped into it. I can't afford one of those expensive sweetened seasonal drinks they make at Christmas time, so he made me a plain cappuccino and added a twist. The familiar red brick walls, covered in chalkboards with pastel-colored writing, twinkle with Christmas lights strung up everywhere, from shelves to walls, that lead to a fake Christmas tree they have yet to finish decorating. This place always relaxes me, with its warm colors, rustic tables, baskets filled with fresh-baked sweets, and the aroma of coffee that penetrates your nostrils. It feels like home and warms my heart. At Christmas time, the magic practically envelops me like a warm blanket in winter.

My encounter with Thomas seems surreal. From afar, he

comes across as a classic famous, out-of-reach type you'd never even get close to. But face to face, he's just a normal man, even a little shy. He maintains that rock-star façade imposed on him by the media, but his eyes betray him. I enjoyed listening to his voice; it's rare to hear it even in official interviews. Everyone focuses on Damian because he's the leader of the band, charismatic and sometimes a boaster, or Michael because he always manages to attract attention.

Thomas, however, is the beating heart of the band. They would not have the same success without his passion for the drums. I consider myself lucky to have met him and spent some time alone with him. Even if he did try and feed me the pre-approved PR version of the pants story. I don't care, because I know all too well how to get through life by telling lies so often that reality and fiction get confused. The nuances of embarrassment in his attitude intrigued me—it made him seem more human and less celebrity. For a moment, I felt so comfortable that I almost forgot the guilt I felt when I realized who he was.

"Why the hell are you shaking so much?"

Ron's annoying voice brings me back to reality. I look up from my cappuccino and meet the slimy gaze of the man standing in front of me—forty years old, blonde hair, gray eyes, athletic physique, successful. On paper, an ideal man if it weren't for the fact that he makes his living speculating on people's misfortunes, stopping at nothing. If you asked me to describe someone who's lacking a moral compass, slimy, unreliable, and a double-agent, I would show you Ron's picture without hesitation.

"It's nothing. I had a little accident on the way here."

I learned early on that lies don't work with Ron. He sees right through them, as if he has a radar tuned to my heartbeat. Half-truths are more acceptable. I really did slip and fall from the second floor of a building. He doesn't need to know I landed on someone he would kill to have pictures of. Ron is the worst editor of the worst gossip magazine on the planet. No one digs into people's pasts like he does, and above all, no one is as unscrupulous in selling others' suffering to make money.

Unfortunately, I work for him too.

"I hope at least you got some good shots out of it." The mischievous smile he gives me as he sits down gives me the shivers.

The thing is, I called him here because I was hoping to get some pictures of Lilly and Damian—that's why I was hanging out around their house. Nothing outrageous, I was just hoping to see their faces outside the bubble they live in. But when I saw Thomas enter the building, I realized they had no public appearance planned, and I was disappointed. I waited for hours, hoping he had come to pick them up and they'd all go out together, but it was just wishful thinking on my part.

The irony is, if any of my colleagues had been lurking around, a picture of Thomas and me talking in the alley would have made them a lot of money. Unfortunately for me, my day was fruitless, and now I have to hustle up the money to pay my bills, or this time they're really going to cut my electricity off.

"I'm fine, Ron. Thank you for asking," I reply sarcastically. Waiting for a shot didn't seem like such a bad idea—I even went so far as to climb the fire escape next to Damian and

Lilly's apartment to see if I could get something that could tide me over for a while. I felt disgusted with myself for trying to capture something salacious, but I had to decide whether I wanted to eat or have a clear conscience.

"Don't waste my time. You know I don't like people playing around. If you have decent shots, I pay you more than generously. If you don't, go back to the shabby apartment you crawled out of." His tone is annoyed, and he's irritating me too.

I tighten my fingers around the cup to avoid punching him right in his perfect teeth. If he dragged me into court, I couldn't pay for it. Unfortunately, the golden years ended a while ago. Back then, paparazzi earned five thousand to fifteen thousand dollars for a photo of, say, Britney Spears fleeing a photographer in her car, her children on her lap. Or Lindsay Lohan collapsed on a garden wall after a wild night. Now, the tabloids rely on the agencies that collect these shots and, with the growth of gossip sites, they sell through a subscription: you pay a monthly fee and download as many photos as you want. Paparazzi are paid based on the number of downloads of a picture, so we take and upload as many shots as possible, focusing on quantity more than quality.

Although newspapers have taken a step back in an attempt to follow a moral publishing ethic, Ron continues under the table, demanding shots that cause an uproar. The more outrageous, the better. He doesn't care if you've done something illegal to get them. He just wants a front-page story that will sell hundreds of thousands of copies, which has become more difficult for the print edition. While many paparazzi have to settle for a second job, keeping their distance from publishers like him, some, like myself, can't afford to give up a well-paid photo, even if it harms the person who makes the front page. Ron exploits the desperate, both paparazzi and celebrities. He doesn't care what you have to do to please him. His only aim is profit.

"I have shots of Logan Preston lying on the ground drunk and covered in pigeons, if you want."

I feel guilty about proposing something like this, but to silence my conscience I tell myself that Logan Preston is asking for it. He's an old Hollywood star who won a couple of Oscars back in the day who's since ruined his life with alcohol and drugs, and now he's no longer in his right mind. He drags himself, drunk and high, through the streets of New York like a zombie, fainting in ridiculous places like the middle of Union Square, covered by pigeons, holding a bag of popcorn. It happens so often these days it no longer makes the news. Not that this justifies my shots, but it is an excuse I use to live with my dirty conscience.

"If I want Logan photos, I can go to the Instagram profile of any loser tourist here in Manhattan. That man has become a tourist attraction." His words are harsh, sharp. If we weren't in a public place, I'd feel a little threatened by his attitude.

"I have nothing for you, okay?" The anger begins to rise, and I can't keep it at bay.

"Damian and Lilly have been a couple for months, and you haven't brought me a single decent shot yet. What the hell are you doing instead of working?"

I have several shots of them in intimate poses while they walk down the street or go shopping. The problem is they're too personal, and I hoped to shoot something that could feed me, but not put them in hot water. I don't want to throw them at Ron because I know he'd make a crappy case with them.

It wouldn't be the first time he's taken something extraordinary and turned it into an infamous scoop. I've seen this for myself in the past, unfortunately, with a couple of very young actors. In the end, given the pressure, they broke up. He went so far as to imply that the guy was a rapist because the girl was only fifteen and he was seventeen, the legal age for consenting to sexual intercourse in New York State. The photo I gave him captured the two eating ice cream in Central Park, holding hands. I delivered two teenagers in their first crush, and he turned them into the sex scandal of the year. Ron can turn everything rotten in order to enrich himself at the expense of others. Handing over a picture of Damian and Lilly kissing in the supermarket—including tongues and hands tucked under the other's waistband—could quickly turn into sex in a public place. Which would then need clarifying by their press offices.

"They are cautious and reserved. They're always on high guard and aren't easily tricked in public. Do you think they don't know how we work?" The words coming from my lips are poisonous, and I hope my contempt reaches him.

"Bullshit! They don't live like hermits in that house, and you know it. Your colleagues discovered the new address two days after they moved in, and you didn't bring those shots to me."

It's true, I didn't take them to him, but not because I don't know where they live. I found out right away because I've been following the Jailbirds and Damian for years, since the beginning of their careers. I know I'm stuck in this crappy job, but being a music journalist is what I wanted to do when I grew up. I just don't know yet when I can afford to make the leap to grown-up, considering I can barely survive, and this is the only job that brings me decent earnings. I have other income, like everyone else who does this work, but it's not enough for my situation.

"I haven't figured out if you've lost your knack or if you're fucking with me. Either way, I don't need you if you keep this up. I have a line of people who can sell me what you can't give me," he spits out more and more angrily.

"So why are you wasting your time here with me, on a Sunday night, if you have all these people giving you wonderful shots?" I openly challenge him, even though he has all the power—in this conversation and my whole life. If he decides I can no longer work as a paparazzo, he just has to make a couple of phone calls and I'll never sell a photo in this city again.

Ron's nostrils almost seem to vibrate; his jaw tightens into a look that could kill. "Do you really think there's no one who brings me pictures this time of year? Your colleagues understand this is the time when you sell the most. Sure, everyone loves Christmas, but do you know how much better you'd feel if your favorite Hollywood star made the covers of the gossip magazines by sticking his fingers up his nose or, better yet, arguing with his sweetheart? We're all kind and loving as long as we feel superior to others. Why not give people something to talk about during the holidays while they eat their turkey, or talk with the sister-in-law they only see once a year? Don't make me lose my patience, kid. You know I can crush you whenever I want."

He's right, he can, but I'm not afraid. Showing weakness is not in my blood, and it would not help my case. To be weak in front of a person like him means having your throat slit. He feasts on easy and helpless prey. "But you haven't done it yet because you know I'm the best."

It's true. My investigative ability, combined with my intuition and the ability to take excellent photos, makes me particularly good at what I do. I'm incomparable when I'm following my prey and shooting in burst mode.

Luckily, Ron decides not to answer me, gets up annoyed, and walks out of the cafe without even turning around. The pleasant adrenaline rush I felt when meeting Thomas slips away, leaving only guilt. I'm not so naïve as to delude myself into thinking this is an honest job, not from an ethical point of view. I take pieces of other people's private lives and hand them over to people who have no scruples. I have to admit my own share of guilt. One fragment of my soul at a time, I'm selling my dignity for a piece of bread. I'm afraid if I keep shoving down all that guilt that weighs down my heart, over time, there won't be any goodness left in me, only the rottenness this business has created.

"Wow. That man can sure suck the happiness out of a room." Emily's sweet voice brings my attention back to reality and the smile back to my lips. Her large dark eyes and ponytailed hair welcome me as she sits down with a cappuccino and a cupcake. I met Emily a few years ago when I was trying to sneak into a journalism class at NYU that I wasn't enrolled in but that she attended. She helped me get books and notes from all the classes and, in the end, we became friends. I can say she's the only person I trust blindly in this town.

"I don't know if he has a soul or if he's possessed by Satan himself." I smile at her as she cuts a cupcake with icing in the shape of a tiny Santa hat and hands me half of it.

"Is everything okay? Do you need money?" she asks with disarming calm. She is the only one who is aware of my distressing economic situation.

"No, don't worry. I'm not that desperate. I have pictures I could sell to Ron, but I only keep them in case I'm really desperate." I smile at her and taste the cupcake. "Have you finished your shift?" I ask, trying to deflect the subject.

Emily's always been the one who helps me make ends meet. She introduces me to her classmates who pay me to do their class papers, and I'm glad she decided to continue with her specialization and master's degree here in New York. I don't know what I'd do without these rich kids who can't even tie their own shoes.

"Yes, now I have to go home and start studying," she whines almost desperately, making me smile. Sometimes I don't know how she holds down two jobs while also studying for her thesis. I respect her for that.

"Do you have time for juicy gossip?" I whisper conspiratorially.

Her eyes light up, and a smile appears on her lips. She scoots closer to me on the bench so the conversation stays between us. "Studying can wait."

I look around to make sure the tables next to us are free from prying ears. In my line of work, I've become paranoid about my private life.

"I literally fell into the arms of Thomas Simons." I smile and wait for the news to settle in. I talk to her so much about the Jailbirds, and my obsession with their music, she's come to love them as well.

"Thomas, the sexiest drummer on earth? Don't look at me like that—those are your words, not mine. By now, I know the shoes size of every member of that band!" She squeals quietly, like a little girl trying not to be heard.

I giggle, amused at her reaction, and nod vigorously. My stomach does flip flops again as memories of less than an hour ago make their way into my mind.

"I want to know every single detail. In particular, I want a play-by-play of 'literally falling' into his arms. Were you dressed or naked?"

Her enthusiasm is contagious, and I start rattling off my story like a 15-year-old with her first crush. It's nice to have someone to talk to about these things without being judged, even if she does know what my job is.

"And he doesn't know why you were there?" she asks when I'm done.

"No. I tried to act cool, but I felt the guilt crawling up my stomach. After what happened, I was afraid he'd find out who I am."

"Stop feeling guilty about that old story. I've told you a thousand times, you're not the only person who's responsible. It's all over, and everyone is fine. You can't keep punishing yourself."

"That doesn't mean I didn't do wrong."

I feel my cheeks heating up with embarrassment when I think back to what I did, but Emily throws me a look that keeps me from basking in my guilt again.

"And how does he look up close? Is he gorgeous, like you see in the papers?" She knows the previous subject is difficult for me, and I appreciate her attempt to focus on the sweet part of the encounter.

"He's gorgeous. I think he's physically perfect, with those dark curls and blue eyes... And then those arms. You have no idea what arms that man has!" I hide my face behind my hands in embarrassment. I have to admit, I've had lustful thoughts about all those muscles. Over and over again.

Emily bursts out laughing. "You didn't ask him to show you his biceps, did you?"

"No, I'm not like his fans. And it was obvious he was embarrassed about that. He's so sweet when he's embarrassed," I confess candidly.

Emily smiles excitedly, as though she were there. "From the way the papers paint him, he looks like a heartless womanizer—like everyone in that band, by the way."

"I am living proof that you don't have to listen to gossip newspapers. They print a lot of bullshit to sell. You see Damian, since he met Lilly, he's become another person. Maybe he wasn't that bad before either."

I almost feel compelled to defend them. I have no idea what's true about what they write about them, but I know that ninety percent of what you read is fake news slapped onto photos that have no context.

"Do you think you'll see him again? Why the hell didn't

the week leading up to the festivity, we would start preparing what could be stored until Christmas Day, when we got up early to unwrap the presents and bake the turkey. I mashed the potatoes, my sister made cranberry sauce, my dad helped by basting the turkey while it cooked. It was a string of small rituals that culminated in the joy of that day. Now, you find yourself celebrating from the beginning of the month: the record company party, the charity gala, guest of honor at the fundraiser. It's a continuous toast to a Christmas that, on December tenth, still seems far away, and when you finally get to the twenty-fifth, you're too exhausted to celebrate because of all the events leading up to it.

"Why the hell are you walking like you have a pole up your butt?" Michael asks me.

"I slipped in the shower and slammed my back."

"Jesus, you're older than my grandpa."

"Drop it, please. Did you see the waitress? How about those reindeer horns," I laugh, trying to move the conversation from my bruise and Iris, if that's really her name, to something Michael loves: sex.

For some stupid reason, I don't want to talk about the redhead I met this afternoon. He would transform the conversation into something sexual and, for the first time in my life, I don't want to. I haven't had a decent conversation with a woman for I don't know how long, and I'm a little protective of the moment we shared. I don't want those few minutes to be dumbed down, making them seem like foreplay for sex.

"I hate Christmas in this city," Michael complains. "You barely have time to get rid of the turkeys and pumpkins before you find sparkly trees and ornaments on every corner. Not to mention the damn songs. It's a nightmare!" He slumps down on the sofa, sipping from his glass.

I burst out laughing and nod. I understand his aversion to the songs. It's okay to hear them once, twice, even a week I can stand them, but thirty days in a row becomes a nightmare. A couple of years ago, a famous mall chain asked us to do a rock version of Mariah Carey's song to revamp their repertoire in every store. We were so stunned we immediately thought it was a joke. Needless to say, we kindly declined the offer.

"Really? You hate Christmas?"

A blonde from a nearby table sits next to Michael with a pouty face. The tables are way too close in this place if you ask me; it's too easy to eavesdrop on other people's conversations. On the other hand, her friend sits next to me, so close she's almost in my lap. I wanted a relaxed night with my friend—I don't think this place was the right choice.

"I hate Christmas songs in November. It's different," Michael points out, stretching out his arm and making her sit on his lap.

One glance in their direction and I know I'm not going to spend this evening with him.

"Do you hate Christmas too?" the brunette asks me, still glued at my side.

I'd like to reply with a joke, just to be funny, but I notice her gaze wanders everywhere except my face. I don't think she's too involved. I sip from my glass and stare at her without hiding the irritation. I've already figured out what question will come next.

"Are you here alone, or will Damian join you two?"

Like clockwork, women's attention is always directed at

my best friend, even when he's not physically in the room.

"He's home with his woman. You know, the one he's been living with in a steady relationship for months? The love of his life?" I reply, annoyed as I get up, ignoring her offended gaze. "But Michael will be more than happy to keep both you and your friend company." I extend a hand toward my bandmate, who has already stuck his tongue in the blonde's mouth.

"Where the hell are you going?" he asks when I catch his attention.

"Home. I don't feel like spending the evening looking at you sticking your hands in places I don't want to see."

"What about her?" He nods toward the pouting brunette.

"She's waiting for Damian, but I'm sure you'll be able to make her forget about him." I roll my eyes when a sly smile crosses his face.

"Come here, darling. There's enough for both of you." He pulls her in and, without wasting time, sticks his tongue in her mouth while her friend dives into his neck.

There's one thing we're all sure of: sooner or later, Michael's dick will fall off if he keeps using it with every woman he lays eyes on. I leave the club without feeling too guilty. Iris's cascade of red hair and smart mouth has filled my thoughts since I laid eyes on her.

*

I sip my hot coffee while watching the city wake up beyond the window of my apartment. From the sixty-second floor, it looks so peaceful it's hard to believe there are people down there who have been working for hours, who may not have gone to sleep yet, who keep the "city that never sleeps" alive. There's always something open, something to do even at night, someone getting up when others go to sleep.

I didn't sleep last night either, but not because of the club or the wild night I actually didn't have. Nor is it the pain in my tailbone, where a purple bruise is spreading. No, I think what kept me awake is the fact that I can't get my mind off a pair of sweet green eyes and a mass of red hair I'd like to stick my hands into. Never in my life have I spent a sleepless night over a woman, especially one who's not even slipped into my bed.

I hope the coffee will wake me up soon, or they'll have to punch me in the face to keep me awake in the studio today. Luckily, all I have to do is hang out with Damian while he finishes the vocals on a couple of songs. I go with him because I get bored staying at home. After the tour and recording the album, the drop in adrenaline leaves me bored and restless. I should find myself a hobby, but I never even had one as a kid. I ended up in prison too young to find out what I really liked. My adolescence was not like most kids' and, despite coming out of it okay, I missed out on some things, like discovering what I like besides music.

The only passion I still have from childhood is decorating cookies, like I did with my mother when I was a kid. I get my artistic side from her, although I never told anyone—we still make fun of Michael for his passion for carving wood. I don't want them to start with me too. This, however, is something I'm protective of and continue to carry on because it reminds me of my mother's generosity. When I was a kid, we churned out huge batches of cookies during the holidays to give to those who couldn't afford them. A tradition I continue, in the tranquility of my apartment, because the donations are still undoubtedly needed, but mostly for the gesture of giving to someone who does not expect it and cannot afford it. It puts a smile on the face of those who have nothing, and that makes me happy.

I finish my coffee and place the cup in the dishwasher of the ultramodern kitchen in my apartment. Everything in this place is brand new, high-tech, and a little sterile, to be honest, but I didn't choose it. I bought this place sight unseen, and I didn't have time to try to furnish it properly. Despite the fact that I'm always complaining about making this apartment a little more personal, when I sit down and think about it, I don't have the energy to do it. Instead, I do everything *but* remodel.

The hot shower calms my nerves and relieves the tension headache hammering my head since last night. When I get dressed, bending down to put on my jeans, my back pain stops me in my tracks.

"This is a joke, right?" I whisper in a low voice, clenching my teeth and giggling like an idiot. I need to lean on my dresser just to slip on these damn pants. Walking around Manhattan in my underwear, as much as people are used to anything, including giving money to the half-naked cowboy in Times Square, is still not socially acceptable. I grit my teeth and take a deep breath. I'm a man, not a kid. Something like this can't stop me. Or at least that's what I keep repeating to myself to feel less like a decrepit wreck at twenty-six.

I call Max, our driver, to take me to the studio, and when I get in the car, I notice he is a little perplexed at of my inability to move. "I know, I can't sit down. I swear if it doesn't go away by tomorrow, I'll go to the doctor," I say when he notices that I'm all tilted in the seat to avoid putting weight on my tailbone.

Max looks at me for a few seconds before entering Manhattan traffic with his usual angelic calm. "My wife, when she gave birth, had hemorrhoids. If you want, I can lend you the donut pillow she sat on to relieve the pain," he suggests out of the blue after a few minutes.

I look at him through the rearview mirror to see if he's kidding, but his face is pretty damn serious. "Please don't say the word hemorrhoids in my presence again. It hurts to hear you say it. And also, do I look like a woman who just gave birth?"

Max has been accompanying us everywhere like a shadow for years now; he's become part of the family, but that doesn't mean I want to talk to him about this.

"Can you sit your ass down or not? It seems to me you can't, so maybe you shouldn't be so picky about that pillow. Can you imagine the press photos of you walking with your legs all spread out or sitting all crooked?" he teases good-naturedly, as he usually does.

"Okay, all right, bring me the damn thing but don't tell the others or they'll drive me nuts with their jokes," I mutter.

Max chuckles but says nothing. He's a good guy, and I know that not a single word will come out of his lips about this conversation. He's seen so many stupid things driving for us that he would have every right to judge, but he never has. Not only because he's professional, but because in the end, he loves us as much as we love him, and he protects us like family.

"Do you think you can get out of the car, or do I have to help you?" he asks earnestly as he parks in the basement of the recording studio.

"No, I'm going to get out of here alone...or I hope so, anyway."

The walk through the hallways to the recording room goes quickly, despite my pain. When I arrive, I am surprised to find the sound technician and Lilly sitting in a corner writing on her laptop.

"Good morning!" She looks up from the keyboard and smiles at me as soon as she sees me coming in.

"Good morning. Did Damian drag you out of bed this morning too?" I look for a fairly comfortable chair to sit on without attracting attention; my friends are oblivious to my encounter yesterday because my back didn't hurt so bad when I went back to their apartment. They were so busy kissing they didn't even notice my presence. After a quick dinner, it's normal for me to run to Michael's. This is one of the problems you have when your best friend is in the "honeymoon" phase.

"I had nothing to do this morning, so I thought I'd come here and do some work for the band. There are thousands of fan emails." Her eyes widen in disbelief.

Lilly insists on wanting to reply to the messages herself because she wants to be more in touch with fans, but she will soon realize that they're becoming so famous they're going to need press offices and assistants.

"How's the album going?" I ask.

"We're almost finished. I'm meeting with the others this afternoon to decide whether or not to include a couple of songs we're not sure about."

"If you need another opinion, you can always count on us," I offer sincerely.

The friendship that grew with these guys started when Damian screwed up, requiring us to announce a contest which they ended up winning. But I think it was the best mistake my friend ever made. It's nice to have someone around who's still excited about the novelty of this business, who's not jaded by fame and money.

"I know, thank you. If we're still stuck this afternoon, we'll call you for sure."

"Don't tell me he's still recording 'Rise,'" I whisper when I hear the song's first notes.

Lilly rolled her eyes desperately. "He doesn't like the way the chorus came out. He says he's not gritty enough and blames me for softening him."

I burst into hysterical laughter. "For Christ's Sake, it's getting worse than 'Jude,' which we've heard a million times too many."

"Imagine having to deal with this at home too."

Arthur turns to us and smiles, clearly desperate. He's our sound engineer for the album. Even Adam, our producer, doesn't want to see us in the studio anymore.

"How many times have you heard it?" I ask him when the expression on his face looks halfway between amused and desperate.

"Let's just say I've never had more bass tracks than an entire fifteen-song album," Arthur replies diplomatically before returning to focus on my friend on the other side of the glass.

"Simon ordered a whole truck of new bonsai plants just to relax after Damian slaughtered him with this song," I laugh with Lilly and Arthur.

When you record an album, the various tracks are usually done separately: vocals, bass, guitar, and drums. Everyone does their part, and then the multiple tracks are mixed together, cleaned up, enriched with effects, if necessary, and perfected to create the song that will then be recorded on the album, the one that everyone will eventually listen to. Each track can be recorded multiple times, so you get the best possible result. When you work with Damian, this process can be murder. I don't think I've ever met more of a perfectionist than he is. Simon wasn't able to play the bass part Damian had in mind and he made us stay in the studio late into the night for weeks. One day Simon didn't show up at the studio, and Evan, our manager, told us that he had been spending time in Connecticut, relaxing before he ended up in jail for murder. Simon, the man who has the patience of a saint, ran away so as not to kill my best friend. Michael and I probably would have helped him hide the body.

"Should I get out of here before he makes me do the chorus again?" I ask worriedly.

"Don't even joke like that!" Lilly threatens me before she gets back to work.

When she goes back to what she was doing, and on the other side of the glass Damian keeps recording, I open my laptop and do something I've never done in my life. I type in the Google search field 'Iris' and 'redhead.' I don't even know if that's her name or if the bag she was wearing belonged to a little sister or a friend. I don't even know why I'm looking for an excuse to tell myself, maybe because I realize that I look like a crazy maniac.

The number of photos that appear on the screen is over-whelming—from flowers to women dressed in skimpy clothes—so I narrow the research with keywords like 'New York,' realizing that I know so little about her that I could put in completely different terms and receive the same results.

"Are you looking for an escort?" Damian's voice behind me almost blows me off the chair.

When I turn around, he's smiling like an idiot and my heart is pumping hard in my chest. He caught me like a kid watching porn. When the hell did he get out of that room? I was so focused I didn't even realize it.

"No, are you kidding?" My lack of explanation makes me appear even more guilty, and Lilly gets up from her seat and leans behind Damian's big shoulders to snoop. I feel like a kid getting caught sneaking on the internet with his father's password.

"You're looking for 'Iris' and 'redhead.' You must have a great explanation that I can't wait to hear," my friend teases me with a raised eyebrow. Lilly is quivering with curiosity next to him, and I can't avoid explaining what happened yesterday afternoon.

"What the hell was she doing on a fire escape?" Damian's expression is both perplexed and amused.

"I don't know...she didn't say," I confess with embarrassment.

"And her name is Iris?" asks Lilly.

I feel like a kid getting questioned in class. "I assume so. It was written on her bag."

"Didn't you even ask what her name was?" Damian is increasingly amused.

"I asked for her name and number, but she was very good at glossing over the answer." I'm a little nervous.

"And does your butt hurt from the fall? Is that why you've been sitting all wrong in that chair since this morning?" asks Lilly, giggling.

"I knew if I told you, you'd make fun of me. I'm going to go get a coffee while you keep squealing behind me." I wink at her and leave the room before the embarrassment makes me blush, giving them one more reason to keep it up.

*

I've been sitting at one of the tables for a few minutes when Lilly comes in and, seeing me, orders a coffee and sits next to me.

"Are you offended by our teasing?" she asks bluntly.

"No, I don't know. Not that I'm offended, but... For Christ's sake, I don't even know," I confess.

Lilly smiles and sips some of her coffee. "When you told us that the right woman had to fall into your arms, I didn't think you meant it literally," she says, trying to play it down.

I burst out laughing, covering my mouth to avoid attention from the few customers inside this small cafe. I like this place because it's intimate, nestled between rows of offices that no one knows about. It's not the usual tourist trap you find in Manhattan; here I can relax without putting a thousand layers of clothes on to hide.

"Now let's not overdo it. She's not the woman of my life."

"But she intrigues you. I've never seen you so fascinated by a woman."

It's not an accusation, just a simple observation that points out evidence I have decided to ignore. "I don't know. I do think it's different this time, but not because she's different. I don't know her enough to tell if that's the case. But she's one of the rare women who didn't ask me about Damian, who seemed really interested in what I had to say. For the first time in a long time, I was just Thomas Simons, drummer of the Jailbirds and not 'The Drummer of Damian's Band.' She caught my attention because of it. Does that make sense, or do I sound like a fool?"

"She didn't ask you about Damian. I already like this Iris."

I look her in the eye, and she's smiling. The first time I met her, I thought she was just a kid full of insecurities. Instead, I found a true friend. Not just because she's my best friend's girlfriend, but because I feel comfortable with Lilly.

"Thomas, I must congratulate you. You have officially become an adult. You got your act together," she announces solemnly.

I bump shoulders with her slightly. "Do you know you're more idiotic than Damian sometimes?"

"That's why we're so good together."

I smile and shake my head. These two will drive me crazy.

"Seriously, maybe this girl got your attention because she doesn't treat you like a superstar. The way you described her, she seems like a smart girl, not jumping on you as soon as she recognized you. Maybe that's what enthralls you about her."

"That doesn't justify me being glued to the internet like a maniac looking for her."

"Or maybe you're just helping fate since they're the only clues you have, and it's not that easy to find someone in a city like New York. She could be anywhere."

Lilly's words don't help me. Knowing the chances of us meeting again by accident are so slim shatters all my hopes. What disturbs me, however, is precisely the fact that I'm hoping for it. I haven't invested so much energy in someone since I was a teenager. At the time, I didn't understand anything.

"I don't believe in destiny," I reply. "I believe that life is just a series of choices and consequences."

"Please, don't abandon your cynicism. You might actually become a human being capable of loving!" Lilly teases, raising her hands as a sign of surrender.

I like how straightforward she is. Daily, it amazes me how she can stand all our bullshit without falling for a second for the moronic things we say. She must really be a saint, or she's crazier than all of us together.

"A couple of years in this business, and you'll see—you're going to agree with me," I chuckle as I finish my coffee.

"Probably, but I'll never admit it. I'd rather tear my vocal cords apart than give you the satisfaction," she says, rising.

I laugh heartily and follow her out of the cafe and onto Manhattan's busy streets. "Do you think Damian is finished laughing at what I told you two?"

Lilly looks at me like I've grown a second head. "Do you know Damian? Do you think it's possible that he could let go of something like this? He's probably already called Michael and Simon to tell them the details, adding some of his own, and they'll all make fun of you until you're old."

Her words confirm my fears. I've known these guys all my life, they'll never miss an opportunity like this, and I laugh a little because I would do precisely the same if I were in their situation. I open the back door to the recording studio and let Lilly in before following her. It's going to be a long day.

CHAPTER 4
Iris

I reluctantly wake up when Dexter begins to tap my face with his paw, meowing as if I haven't fed him in weeks. I look at the clock. It's only five-thirty.

"I hope you've finished every single piece of dry food inside your bowl, or I swear this time I'll use your tail as a candle wick."

The meow of protest is more of a mockery than a real moan of terror at my vain threats. I could never lay a finger on him, and he takes advantage of it by waking me up at impossible times and making me do whatever he wants. I've never accepted anyone running my life or giving me orders, and here I am, succumbing to a cat I love who doesn't reciprocate. He is the only male who commands me simply by putting his nose to my face and rubbing himself, giving me some love, five minutes at a time, one day a month, only during leap years. And I'm cleaning his litter box morning and night.

I put the dry food in the bowl, which, as I already knew, is full on the sides but empty in the middle. I give Dexter the stink eye, but he looks at me with those huge, sweet eyes that make me speechless.

"Betrayer," I whisper as I put water inside the coffee machine and half the amount of usual coffee, since I don't have much left and I have to survive until the next time I get paid.

I turn on my laptop while I wait for it to brew, scrolling through email alerts about famous people in New York, and immediately notice that today's hot news is about the Jailbirds. A week ago, they launched a new competition for their fans, and the winners will get to listen to the three unreleased songs from their upcoming album. Officially, the first release date is next week, but the luckiest fans on earth were airlifted, first-class, and put up in one of New York's most luxurious hotels to listen to the three songs this morning.

I confess that I enrolled in that contest, so I could have written the review today on my blog, but my luck ran out two weeks ago when I swooped into Thomas' arms. I've never been a finalist for any competition, let alone win one. The embarrassing thing, though, is that I'm not entirely sure I enrolled in that contest for the review or because I was hoping to see Thomas and his blue eyes again. Since bumping into him, he has become my obsession, awakening the sixteen-year-old in me, fantasies included. He brought to life again that crush that I had long dismissed as irrational and typical of teenagers who fall in love with their idols. I'll really start to worry when I start sticking the band's posters on my walls.

I decide to show up in front of the record company building, regardless. There will undoubtedly be a lot of photographers there. It's one of those classic over-advertised events, with a final press conference included, almost an official invitation for the paparazzi in the area. I'll take some pictures of the winners, who will have their five minutes of fame. I'll try and take a few shots of the Jailbirds, and then I'll go home and continue my life as usual: looking for the unlucky star to be photographed in some awkward situation.

When the coffee machine starts bubbling and the glass carafe is filled, I pour a cup. I'd like to add some creamer, but I remember finishing it a few days ago. Dexter climbs to the kitchen counter, smells my mug, and looks at me disgusted.

"You better save the dry food in your bowl because we're poor, and we need to ration." Not that I've ever left my cat without food, but lately, I can't afford to buy him too many of the treats that he loves so much.

I go back to my computer and take advantage of the early morning to finish a manual for one of my older clients. Their company produces cardboard packaging and needs to update internal manuals for employees at least a couple of times a year. It's a job I hate—it's boring and requires a massive effort of concentration, but they pay a few hundred dollars for a few hours of work, so every time they call, I accept without thinking twice.

"Admit it, you woke me up so early because you knew I had to finish this document today."

Dexter meows as he rubs his nose against the corner of my laptop.

"You're afraid to be left without food, aren't you?" I almost challenge him with half a smile.

I have so few friends, beyond Emily, that often, the only conversations I have during the day are with my cat, and I'm not even sure he pays attention to what I say. In fact, he turns around, shows me his backside, and jumps from the coffee table to go to snuggle between the sheets.

*

As I predicted, the mob of photographers in front of the

record company is impressive. I'm surprised the police aren't already here to get us out of the way of traffic. With all the tourists in New York City during this festive time, a gathering like this is immediately kept an eye on by law enforcement to prevent someone ending up under a car. The barricades have already been placed, confirming that all this staging has been prepared for some time. There's even a banner with the record company's logo, sponsors, and a couple of big clothing brands, so winners can take selfies in front of it and post their photos on Instagram. I'm surprised they haven't thought of a hashtag for the occasion. I should write to their press office and remind them of the basic rules of marketing.

"Hi Jack, how are you doing? How is Annabelle?"

Jack is a married man of over sixty with two grown children. At night, he works in a warehouse as a security guard, and during the day, he sleeps a few hours and then hangs out on the streets of New York to be a paparazzo. We often find ourselves at events like this, and, over time, I have gotten to know him better. Not that it's his greatest aspiration to be out here photographing celebrities, but his wife Annabelle fell ill with cancer a few years ago, and to cover the expenses the insurance company refused to pay, he had to find a second job.

I first met him in front of a barricade, alone, looking like a lost puppy. I felt so bad for him, I introduced him to my narrow circle of trusted colleagues. There are so many places to cover, to take good shots, that we come together in small groups and divide into different areas. We let the others know when we spot a celebrity. Working alone becomes too complicated and expensive, in terms of energy and money, to think about surviving doing this job. Jack wouldn't go far, so I tried to teach him as quickly as possible how to move. Over time, he's become something like a friend.

"Baby Doll! What a pleasure to see you here. Annabelle's fine. I took her for her check-up last week, and the cancer still doesn't show up. It's been two years now." He tells me this with the happiness that only a person who has risked losing what is dearest in life can have. Now he can devote himself with less concern to paying off the debts that her illness incurred.

"I'm so glad! One of these days, I'll come by and bring her that lemon cake Emily makes that she likes so much." I'm barely able to tell him this before being swallowed up by the noise and turmoil rising among us. Apparently, a limousine with the lucky winners inside has just stopped in front of the red carpet and is letting the occupants out; they're mostly teenage girls dressed like they're at the Oscars, their phones ready in hand to document every single second. This event is more fake than my worst expectations. I imagined it would be a waste of time, but I didn't think they would arrange something so far from the authentic, almost rough, image of the Jailbirds.

I take some photos; the kids parade practically all in a group. Within five minutes, the show is over, and it is clear the Jailbirds will never walk this carpet. They are already inside enjoying the show from some window upstairs.

"Quick and painless," Jack laughs as we move away from the mob.

I already know this morning's shots are entirely useless. No newspaper will pay for an agency picture when you just have to be here with a cellphone or fish from the winning kids' social networks to find better photos than ours. It was still worth a try. If, out of a hundred tries, ninety-nine are bad, but one gives you the shot of the century, it will always be worth it.

"At least you can go home and spend some time with Annabelle. Did you sleep a few hours last night?" I ask him worriedly, taking in the deep, dark circles around his eyes and his hollowed-out face.

Jack smiles softly and rests his hand on my shoulder, and then pulls me into a hug. "We're fine, Baby Doll, don't worry, okay?"

I nod and watch him walk away to the nearest subway stop, among pedestrians who bump him without caring for the expensive camera inside his crossbody bag. They're oblivious to the fact that this is actually one of his livelihoods and the reason Annabelle is still alive. I'd like to shout at them to be careful, not to break it.

I enter one of the alleys behind the record company, an area of Manhattan where you can breathe a little more, far from tourists. The difference between visitors and people working here, in the center of the world, is all in the walking. Tourists stroll, looking around with their noses up among the enormous skyscrapers, stopping suddenly in the middle of the sidewalk to look at the map on their cell phones or take a picture. The festively decorated shop windows create annoying traffic jams, with everyone stopping to immortalize the engineering masterpieces that fly the reindeer of Santa's sleigh or run trains laden with presents inside fake tunnels, artificial snow descending at an almost hypnotic pace.

The people who live and work in Manhattan, on the other hand, walk fast without ever turning around, looking at people in front of them, unconsciously calculating trajectories and traffic light times. Months of trampling the same sidewalk make them experts on the subway-office journey, where even a single second can change the entire working day. If you have a job in this city, among these skyscrapers, they expect you to be available twenty-four hours a day, seven days a week, three hundred and sixty-five days a year. You can never pull the plug, and even that miserable minute between the subway car and the office is a minute you could use to do something constructive. Whether it's Christmas, New Year's Eve, or the middle of summer, the people who work here don't care how beautiful and magical this city is. They don't have the time.

That's why I love this café nestled between the walls of the offices, practically invisible. They are efficient, quick to serve you. You are in line behind people who know exactly what they want and do not even look at the price list on the wall behind the counter. Christmas decorations are also few and essential: a tree with warm lights and some garlands hanging on the walls. Some call it minimalist. I just see something simple and quick to set up, so as not to waste too much employees' time. I'm pleased when I order my black coffee. I sit at one of the ample modern white counters next to the entrance and start working on my new blog post.

"So, you can survive even with your feet on the ground. You don't have to be suspended over other people's heads."

A voice I recognize makes me raise my head. Next to me, holding a tray with four cups in his hand, Thomas is looking at me as if I were his favorite dish. I don't know if I'm flattered or intimidated. He's looking at me curiously, lingering on every inch of my face, like a photograph he wants to imprint in his memory, freckles included. It is not a lustful look. On the contrary, he seems genuinely happy to see me again, making my legs tremble and my stomach tighten.

"I thought one of the perks of being rich and famous was that you had an assistant who gets your coffee," I reply, pointing at the tray.

He bursts out laughing, closing those blue eyes that choke my breath in my throat every time, and showing his perfect pearly whites. He grabs the stool next to me with a smooth gesture, sits, and rests the tray next to my laptop.

"I volunteered to come and get them. If they had forced me to smile for another selfie, I would have risked paralysis," he explains, amused.

"Your working day must be really hard, all those smiles, the cameras. A real ordeal." It's so natural to talk to him that I become brazen in making fun of him. Of course, I don't typically restrain myself when it comes to being ironic and sarcastic, but I do it with Emily, a person I've known for years, not a stranger.

Luckily for me, Thomas laughs. He seems really comfortable staying here chatting with me, and I can't help but gloat a little bit.

"Don't get me wrong, I like it, just sometimes I don't know if these people are here to take a picture with us or to really listen to our music. Every time we release a new song, I get a lump in my stomach because I think, 'What if people think it sucks?' Having an idea of the public's reaction before being thrown into the lion's den helps me to be more prepared, that's all."

"You're a perfectionist."

Thomas crinkles his nose. "Not exactly. I like to be aware

of things to solve problems when they arise. Having some of the information in advance helps me better cope with what life throws at me."

I smile at his response. It's clear that he wants to have things under control, and I honestly understand. It must not be easy to live at his level of fame. Something gets out of hand, and everything is immediately magnified to the point of crushing you.

"If I had won the contest, you could have read the review on my blog. Too bad I didn't win." The words slip from my lips before I can connect my tongue to my brain. I don't want him to know what I write. But it's too late to pretend I said nothing. His eyes seem to light up.

"You have a blog?"

There was no chance he would miss that part. "Yes, I like music, so I thought I'd take advantage of living in a city where I can find it until I get tired and write about what I like. Concerts I go to, up-and-coming bands, album reviews...nothing different from what everyone else does." I try to downplay it. I don't want to make a big fuss about a successful blog; it's certainly not comparable to an industry magazine.

He nods, looking me in the eye as if he really cares about what I'm saying. "Are you a journalist? Who do you work for?'

"No, I'm not a journalist. I'm a simple music lover who was lucky enough to build a following online, that's all."

He nods, and, luckily for me, he doesn't investigate any further. "And have you tried to enroll in the contest?"

I look down, a little ashamed. Why did I say anything? Looks like I'm whimpering because I didn't get what I wanted. "Yes, but I'm not worried about it. I'm going to write a blog post about the event. I came here to take some pictures, so I could put out original content instead of the usual old photos from the internet."

"What's the name of the blog?"

"*Rocking in New York*, why?"

He pulls out his cellphone, and I watch him type something on the screen. "Man, you've got a lot of followers. Are you sure you're not a journalist?"

I burst out laughing and shake my head. "I am not, trust me. I don't earn anything from that blog."

Thomas looks at me, puzzled. "Really? With that following, you should be able to monetize."

"I decided to keep it without ads or affiliations. I don't want to feel tied up because someone pays me to review a certain product or band. It was born out of my need to talk about music, and I want to have the freedom to say what I think."

Thomas nods and smiles. He seems to think about it. He looks at his cell phone, scrolling in search of something. He motions for me to stay where I am. And why would I move? I don't think my legs would hold me for two steps. I'll have to sit here for the rest of the day to recover from this second meeting. If I was thrilled to see him in the first place, I'm on cloud nine for sharing something so personal with him. This goes way beyond knowing things about him through his public image: this feels profound.

A few seconds later, a smile brightens his face, highlighting two small dimples covered with a few days' beard scruff. He grabs his earphones from his pants pocket and hands them to me. I stay still, puzzled for a few seconds at his gesture.

"Do you or don't you want to write the review of these singles?"

It takes several seconds, staring at him like a complete idiot, before I realize he's actually proposing I listen to their music. "Are you serious? Look, my blog isn't a magazine. I don't have any credibility in the industry... I'm not someone who can give you visibility or anything...I mean, you don't get anything out of what I write... I'm just a loser who has a blog and zero social life."

Thomas's thunderous laugh makes me stop my inconclusive blabbering and utterly embarrassing stuttering. "We don't need publicity, trust me, for that we have legions of agencies. But it would be nice to have an opinion from someone who listens to music out of passion and not just for work."

"Considering that I liked 'Sunshine' from your very first album, I may be biased when it comes to your music."

Thomas looks at me wide-eyed, with such surprise he almost seems speechless. "But we didn't even put that song on the album for the label. It was part of a demo we recorded in the beginning so Evan could represent us!" he exclaims, stunned.

I raise my shoulders and smile at him. "I've been following you for a while."

He shakes his head with an incredulous smile and invites me to listen to the new pieces. I grab his earphone with trembling hands, take the notebook and pen from the bag, open them, and motion for him to hit play.

The first one out of the earphones is so overwhelming I find it hard to sit back and take notes. I want to get off this stool, move to the beat, and sing along—even if I don't know the words. It's a rhythm that overwhelms in every sense, and it shows how much they've grown and matured musically since the last album. It's hard rock, sometimes a bit dirty. Damian's voice is dreary and scratchy. It gets into your gut and holds you in a grip. The rhythm is hectic, overwhelming, does not let you breathe. It's that classic concert song that gets you up, jumping frantically and falling, exhausted, at the end, burned of all the energy in your body. I can't wait to hear it played from a stage, with Thomas's arms frantically beating on the drums, sweat dripping from his forehead and gluing those dark curls to his face. I want to see Simon and Michael's fingers flying all over their instruments in the frenzy of the moment, setting and breaking the rules with every refrain. I want to see Damian wriggle on that stage as if possessed, unleashing a hormonal storm in every single woman in the stadium.

The second song is slower than the first. Still, it vibrates inside you, dragging you to the underworld with low tones, and leaving you there to agonize under the lashes of Damian's voice accompanied by dry, almost violent drum shots. It's a march that guides you into the darkest corners of the soul and brings out agonizing emotions. I have never heard Simon go so violently on the strings of that bass; he's usually the quiet one, the one who almost softens the rough sound of their music. Not this time. He seems to want to destroy the instrument, to emphasize the rawness of the lyrics of this song. It's a song of revenge, of payback, almost of hatred toward those who hurt you.

The third song is the one that surprises me the most—a slow ballad. The lyrics unfold into a story about a violent, suffocating, toxic love. The sweetness of the music clashes with Damian's rough voice; the words envelop your heart and tighten until it stops. With the last verse, you feel your heart stop like the woman's life between those lines. *Red as the love you desired, red as blood on your grave.* I have to swallow a couple of times before I can knock down the knot in my throat.

They've come a long way from the first album full of passion and anger. In moments that seem all too short, the three songs end and Thomas stops the music, takes back his earphones, and looks at me as if my opinion alone will decree whether this album will be a success or not. They are a world-famous band, with this album they will ascend the Olympus of music, becoming part of the history of the greats, of legends.

"So?" he asks me hopefully.

"So, you're going to wait for my review like everyone else," I say, unfazed, as if this were a respectable professional meeting. The reality is my heart and mind are so distressed with emotions I would not be able to formulate a coherent sentence, let alone a sensible opinion.

Thomas widens his eyes and looks at me as if horns had grown in my forehead. "Are you serious?"

"Of course I am. Do you think I pulled out this notebook to give you a ridiculous, incomplete review on the spot?"

He furrows his brows and seems almost disappointed by my answer, or perhaps even frightened.

"I knew you were serious, but I was hoping you'd give me at least a general idea... Look, it doesn't matter, I still have to bring this coffee to those three before they think someone kidnapped me," he says, standing up and making me feel terribly guilty.

He really expected to hear my opinion, and I didn't dare to

give it to him. The smile he gives me before standing up never reaches his eyes.

"Thomas," I call before he leaves. "If I were you, I wouldn't be anxious about my opinion. It's definitely positive, I just don't have anyone read my articles before they're finished... you know, I'm a perfectionist too." This time his eyes light up with his smile, and what looks like a weight rising from his chest. "You have to give me the song titles if you want the article to be complete."

"If you give me your phone number, I can send you a text," he smiles slyly.

I burst out laughing at his attempt, and then hand him my pen and paper. "Or you can write them here. What do you say?"

"And you'd miss the chance to hear the story of how I took the stage with my pants ripped in half?"

"Do you mean that what I heard from your own lips is not the real one?"

He pretends to think about it, scratching his chin. "I told you the one where—during a spiritual session—my pants caught fire on a candle, and I had to cut off the leg of the jeans just before I took the stage, right?"

I burst into amused laughter. "Those were not the words, but I get the feeling I'll never have the real version of that story. Or am I wrong?"

"You can give me your number and find out," he tries again.

"Or you can write the titles of those songs here and keep that aura of mystery a rock star needs to survive." I push the notepad toward him again.

He says nothing, nods a couple of times as if he wants to

say something, but then stops. He grabs the paper and writes down the titles. "Will you ever tell me why you don't want to give me your number? Do I scare you or something?"

"You meet a lot of women. How do I know you don't ask for all of their numbers? After all, you didn't tell me why you want it." I smile at him, but I don't add anything else. The truth is, I'm beyond nervous about this whole situation and making excuses is the only possible solution I can see.

As before, Thomas seems to hold back a thought, picks up the now lukewarm coffees, and makes his way to the door. He throws me one last look and a smile, then waves and disappears into the streets of Manhattan carrying with him all the air I had in my lungs.

CHAPTER 5

Thomas

It's been a whole day, and Iris hasn't posted her review yet. By now, I'm sure her name is Iris because once I discovered her blog, I read every single article she's posted in recent years, all really great pieces, all signed with her name. There is no doubt this woman is a journalist, even if she says otherwise, and one of the good ones, competent both in her subject and her style. I can't believe she never studied journalism.

Locked up in my apartment all day, sitting on the white leather sofa next to the window overlooking Central Park, reading and rereading the same articles, was not a great idea. I was so nervous that at one point, I gave in and cooked almost two hundred cookies and started decorating about fifty of them. Even though I had promised Claire, the assistant Evan found me, that I would never cook anything again—at least until Christmas. There was a time, right after the tour, when she spent whole days contacting associations that help the homeless to donate the decorated cookies I churned out in industrial quantities. At one point, she threatened to tell Evan and my friends if I didn't stop immediately. She's not going to be happy about helping me pack dozens of cookies to give to some good cause. But I was too anxious waiting for the verdict—I had to release some tension this way.

It didn't help. My nervousness is still skyrocketing. I feel like a caged, chained lion who would bite its own paw off to get out of here. But I can't run away, not from myself, at least. The truth is I'm terrified of the review she might write. Maybe she didn't like the songs, and that's why she doesn't post anything. She's playing for time. And yet yesterday, she reassured me before I walked out of that damn café. I'm paranoid. That girl got so under my skin I can't have one rational thought anymore. It's ridiculous!

I get up from the sofa and head to the kitchen to turn on the coffee machine. Maybe caffeine isn't a great idea, considering how nervous I am. I'll risk pulling an all-nighter. On the other hand, I've never been famous for my brilliant choices. I pour a steaming cup and go back to the couch where I left my laptop. I reload the blog page for the millionth time, and my heart almost stops.

The new post is there, with the name of our band clearly written in the title. I put down the laptop, grab the cup and go to the window to sip my coffee, trying to calm down. I don't dare read it. It's what I've been waiting for with trepidation all day, and now I can't bring myself to read those lines. The problem is that I care too much about her opinion, and even the possibility that she didn't like the songs scares me. If one of the kids in the room yesterday for the listening group wrote a bad review, I'd be displeased for sure, but it would only last a short time. It won't be so easy to forget if she blasts it. I laugh at my total inability to be rational at something that is a non-problem.

I breathe deeply and take courage. I go back to the post and start reading it. At first, I feel so eager to get to the end that my brain can't process the lines I'm reading. Then the words 'magical,' 'higher level,' 'incredible quality' enter my visual field. When I reread the article for the third time, I finally realize it's praising our music. Every word is designed to emphasize the musical quality and the improvements we've made with this album.

When we sat down and started writing the new songs, we set out to satisfy our fans and take the next step, take what we've built so far and improve it, grow our artistry and not just our fame. Apparently, according to Iris and her article, we succeeded.

I'm so caught up in the enthusiastic comments starting to appear in the post that I share the link on Twitter without thinking twice.

@Thomas_Jailbirds
She likes the new songs! Read the *Rocking in New York* blog review!

Not even a minute goes by before the phone rings and Evan's face appears on the screen. The euphoria I felt reading the post and sharing it is replaced by a cold shower.

"Can you tell me why the hell you tweeted that link?" His tone is unbelievably angry. I can almost see his red face and neck veins about to explode.

"Because it's a good review?" I wish I was more sure of myself, but my voice comes out trembling.

Our manager expects such impulsive gestures from Michael or Damian, not from me, and I realize that I didn't think for one second about whether what I was doing was right. I took it for granted that this article was excellent, and didn't consider that it might not be approved by our press office.

"First, explain to me how the hell that blogger got to hear the singles. Second, explain to me how the hell you found that post. Third, explain to me why the hell you shared it without first consulting the press office!" He's so angry his shouting sounds like he's on speakerphone. It scares me.

Our public life is controlled by legions of press offices and marketers who scrutinize everything we post. Such an impulsive gesture will have triggered at least twenty alarms on the cell phones of those who take care of our image. It's an excellent review, enthusiastic, precise, professional...but it was not authorized. Only now do I realize my mistake.

"What the hell did you think? What if that blogger puts the songs online?" he continues scolding me.

"It's not possible. She only listened to them once from my phone."

The silence that follows almost makes my blood freeze.

"You're screwing this journalist and letting her write what she wants? Are you crazy? Thomas, what the hell are you up to? I expect to be called out of business hours for Michael's bullshit, not yours." The last few words come out so shrill that I'm afraid he's ripped out his vocal cords.

"I'm not screwing her! And she's not a journalist... It's just, she has an excellent blog, and she's a fan of ours." I try to justify myself.

"Thomas, shut up. You're digging your own grave," he hisses.

I follow his advice and curl up in the couch cushions hoping this outburst will end soon.

"For Christ's sake, now that Damian settled down, are you the one starting to screw up? Give me a break, guys, or I won't live to see my forties. Is it at least a good review?" The tone of voice is calmer, but I know he is still angry.

Evan is the one who's been watching our backs since the beginning, and when we mess up, he makes us pay for it. He's not one to let things slip past him, especially when it comes to us. We were his first band, we grew up together, and he took charge of our past as if it were his. He'd do anything to protect us.

"It's great."

Yet another interminable silence.

"Evan?"

"Don't post anything else about her. Don't follow her on social media. Don't do anything. And, Thomas, be careful. She's still a journalist."

His last words settle in my chest like a boulder. I know what he's afraid of: it's become increasingly difficult to keep our secrete from the world—that we've been in prison. Exposing ourselves to those who make a living doing research is not a good idea. When curiosity takes over, lies become unmanageable. But Iris is not a journalist, she is a blogger, or at least this is the lie I tell myself to indulge my obsession with her.

"Don't worry, she's not a journalist. She has this blog for passion. If you look at it, she doesn't have ads on the site because she doesn't care about the money. It just has reviews, no gossip. There's only one post about Damian and Lilly when the tour scandal broke. She demanded her readers to leave them alone because she doesn't want gossip about their private lives on her blog."

"You've scrutinized her site well." Evan's observation is cautious, as if he wants to test what my connection is to Iris.

"I wanted to be sure she was a good person before I let her hear the songs," I lie to my friend, something I never do.

Evan seems to think about it for a long time, then inhales thoroughly. "Okay, but be careful," he tells me before hanging up.

The adrenaline I felt reading the article is a distant memory, and now I find myself back on the sofa scrolling through Iris's Instagram photos. She's very active in the music scene, and I'm surprised I've never noticed her before. At the end of the day, we frequent the same places, and suddenly I realize how different our worlds are. Although we both deal in music, we're on different sides of the barricade. I move in the world of celebrities, the famous and glossy ones. She moves on the sidelines but perhaps it's a more authentic world—one of genuine feelings and opinions, not filtered by the unwritten laws of this business.

I find myself scrolling through every single photo, and when I'm done, I put my finger on the screen and start Instagram stories. Her writing an article, the subway doors opening onto the Broadway-Lafayette station, her entering "The Bitter End" in Greenwich Village to listen to a band, her ordering a beer at the bar counter. The pictures keep flowing and, as if in a delirium, I grab my jacket and the black cap I wear to keep from being recognized, and slip into the private elevator before I can think twice about the bullshit I'm about to get into.

*

I look out the taxi window when we arrive in front of the club and realize that I look like a perfect idiot. The guy at the entrance is letting in the last people who stayed in line, and I'm pondering whether or not to get out.

"Have you decided what to do?" the taxi driver asks me in a slightly irritated tone, turning to me and staring, bored, from behind the plastic divider.

"Yes, sorry man, keep the change," I tell him, handing him fifty dollars, which immediately alleviates his irritation, earning me an almost sincere smile.

I get out of the car and approach the entrance to the place, leaving some space between the people in front and me. When he sees me, the bouncer beckons me with his head to go in, and I find myself at the entrance, in front of a middle-aged woman inside the ticket office that is precisely the size of her person. I wonder how she can move or even just breathe in that space with a miserable little window she's locked in.

"Who did you come to listen to?" she asks me with little enthusiasm, as if she has no desire to be in there and I can understand why.

I look at the poster for the evening and notice that there are three bands, all similarly unknown to me, so I shake my head. "None in particular."

The woman marks something on a sheet of paper and then fastens a plastic paper bracelet on my wrist that serves as an entrance ticket. I feel sorry I didn't give a name. If I had said one at random, they would have given the boys the percentage of the income instead of dividing it between the three groups and giving them a few pennies. We used to play like this, barely surviving. Things have changed radically for us, and I sometimes forget how hard it is to come up in this business. I take a picture of the poster so I don't forget to check out their sites and buy t-shirts directly from them.

The place is dark and crowded so I approach the counter and order a beer. I look around and realize I have nothing in common with the people in here. They all look like hipsters in their perfect clothes that cost hundreds of dollars, and are eco-friendly and tailored in countries where there is no exploitation of child labor. I'm like a seal hunter in the middle of a PETA demonstration with my leather jacket and boots. I feel ridiculous with my cap down over my eyes and my head tucked into my shoulders, trying to blend with the dark wallpaper behind me.

"What the hell am I doing here?" I think as I grab the beer and approach the darkest corner of the room, away from the soft light of the lamps attached to the ceiling. On the small stage in front of me are several instruments, including double basses and trumpets. I don't even have any idea what kind of music they're playing here tonight.

I'm a crazy man for running out of my house, following the Instagram stories of a woman who has never given me a sign that she's interested in me. She never told me her name, she didn't give me her phone number, and most importantly, she didn't invite me here tonight. I must have gone completely crazy if I think such idiotic behavior is normal. I'm usually the one who plans the outings with the others, so there are no problems with paparazzi; the one who reminds Damian to call the professional accounting firm that deals with his investments to manage his donations. For Christ's sake! I'm the one who, when we were nobody, had a notebook to keep track of the group's income and expenses and manage the money to be sure we could survive—because if it was up to the others, we would have starved to death.

I wouldn't be surprised if a documentary came out on Netflix in a few years about me, with all those creepy stalkers I'm acting like right now. More ashamed of myself than I've been in a long time, I decide to drink my beer and leave before Iris realizes I'm here and runs for the hills.

Needless to say, luck isn't on my side tonight. I look up and she's there, at the bar counter, staring at me like she's seeing an alien.

PRESS *Review*

I Thought the Jailbirds Couldn't Surprise Me More, But I Was Wrong...

Hi Roadies,

How are you? I have a big surprise for you! Yesterday, in a massive stroke of luck, I listened to the three, brand-new singles from the Jailbirds. You know when you think a band can no longer surprise you because they've surpassed your expectations already? Well, the Jailbirds will always amaze me. With this album, they have stepped up to yet another level.

But let's get to the singles you can download next week. There are three songs, very different from each other, but all of them will get way down into your belly and stir up the anger inside you.

"Running Fast" is one of those concert songs that's going to blow up every stadium in the world. Imagine a crazy, chaotic rhythm that makes you jump, dance, shout with all the breath you have in your body. Rarely have I heard such an overwhelming beat and this time, Thomas and Simon seem to be coming from another planet. It's not humanly possible to play at that tempo for almost five minutes. They're unbeatable.

"Don't Mess with Me" is entirely different. It's slower than the previous one, but the lyrics and the title leave no doubt: you don't want to mess with the Jailbirds. Have you ever felt anger at someone who has done you wrong or hurt you? Listening to this song, you'll have no doubt about how that feels. Damian has masterfully channeled so much rage and resentment that his powerful voice seeps into your veins, like poison running through your body.

But let's move on to the last song: "Bloody Love." If the slow pace brings to mind a romantic ballad, you're so wrong. This is the rawest song of the three. The gentle, slow tempo contrasts with the lyrical images of sick and violent love. Maybe Damian took inspiration from the bad experience he had on the last tour? We don't know yet, but from this song we certainly know his condemnation of those who use force against a person they should protect.

Are you curious to listen to these singles too? Are you quivering and counting the days that separate you from next week? Drop your opinion in the comments below.

Be kind and Rock'n'Roll,
Iris

72270 Likes 69312 Tweets 30502 Shares 9484 Comments

@jailfreakingbirds How do you stay focused on the songs when you have four rock stars staring at you? Asking for a friend!

@jailbirds_groupie Forget the songs, I think I got pregnant when Damian looked at me and smiled.

@wannabe_rockstar I want to be as famous as Damian and have the women drooling over me. I'd even settle for being like Thomas or Simon. Oh I almost forgot: I liked the songs!

CHAPTER 6
Iris

"Is that Thomas Simons?" Emily asks me incredulously.

I've been staring at him for so long that it became awkward. "Yes, it's him." My voice is trembling. What the hell is he doing here?

"I have to admit, you've been meeting a lot lately."

I turn away from Thomas to face her, and panic grips my stomach. "Can you ask the others not to say a word about my job? I don't know why he's here, but I don't want him to find out, please." I'm so confused I forgot I came to this club for my blog, not to shoot compromising photos of unfortunate celebrities.

Emily smiles and hugs me, then puts her hands over my shoulders and looks at me straight in the eyes. "You're becoming paranoid. The others won't say anything, don't worry, but you'll have to tell him sooner or later. I have no idea why he's here tonight, but it's clear that these encounters aren't random. He'll find out sooner or later."

My conscience materializes in front of me in the form of Emily. She's sweet, she's not scolding me, but she makes me face the cold, hard reality. Should I just pretend I haven't seen him and continue my night, thus ending this unhealthy game I'm playing with him? But then I remember the lost expression on my face and the ginormous surprise when our eyes met, and I realize I can't ignore him. It would be immature and cruel, especially after he was so sweet to retweet my blog post.

I turn around again to meet Thomas's lost and slightly embarrassed look. Maybe he expected me to confidently walk to him, not turn my back on him and talk to my friend. I take a deep breath, raise the corners of my mouth in a sincere smile, and approach him.

"Hi! It seems we meet a lot lately." I smile, and he reciprocates with one of those expressions that lights up his face, even if he does still look awkward.

"Yes, Manhattan seems to have become a small suburban village where everyone knows everyone and bumps into each other..." He stops himself. "I'm just talking bullshit, right?" His insecurity makes him adorable, and I find myself smiling like a teenager in love.

"No, I agree. It's a fact that I've never met you before, and then we've bumped into each other three times in two weeks." I wanted it to sound like a joke, but it comes out more solemn than I intended, and I notice him tense slightly.

Why did it get so hard to talk to him? We were in perfect harmony until yesterday. What the hell changed in such a few hours? I know he's not here by accident. The truth is, I'm flattered by his attention but also terrified. I'm afraid the 16-year-old in me—the one who's always been in love with him—is under the illusion that there may be something real between us. My heart is split in two: one part beats excitedly at the idea that my teenage crush has noticed me, but the other is terrified to indulge in emotions that could crush me. Life has taught me that dreams are impractical. They're beautiful fantasies that help you live in a much less fascinating reality. What are the odds that my dreams about Thomas will come true?

"Are you here to listen to the bands? Do you know them?" I venture when he doesn't say a word. He lowers his head and looks at the floor. I didn't know he was this fidgety. They all seem like boasters with huge egos, but the guy in front of me now is sweet, sensitive, and all too attentive to how he appears in public. He doesn't like to seem vulnerable and gets defensive when his emotions take over. Maybe I'm wrong. Maybe it's just a pickup trick to appear to be a regular guy.

"Actually, no... I saw on your Instagram you were here, and I wanted to come and thank you in person for the article you wrote. It's an excellent piece. Is that creepy? Because now that I'm saying it out loud, I feel like a crazy stalker," he chuckles, rubbing his hand behind his neck.

I smile, amused and some of my tension goes away. To be honest, I'm ecstatic. As much as I'm afraid this situation will become complicated, I would be a hypocrite not to admit, at least to myself, that I am flattered by his attention. The part of my heart that beats excitedly is taking over the terrified part.

"No, it would have been creepy if you had had no reason to come here, but thanking me for the article seems to be a more than honest motive to do so." As the tension slips away, my voice becomes playful.

"You make my behavior seem almost decent. Thank you!" Thomas laughs, much more relaxed than before.

"No, I have to thank you, tweeting the link of my article literally blew up my phone with notifications from people who started following me and writing to me. I have to keep it constantly connected to the power outlet, or else it shuts down." I point to a spot behind the bar counter where my cellphone sits.

"Sorry?" he asks me uncertainly. I don't think he understands that this is a good thing.

I laugh out loud and lay my hand on his arm, immediately realizing what I'm doing, how close I am to him, and distance myself again. A mixture of fear and excitement squeezes my stomach: I'd like to be even closer, and at the same time I'd like to put a wall between us before he hurts me. "Don't apologize. It's a good thing."

The first band takes the stage and starts playing.

"I'm sorry, but I have to work tonight," I say with a grimace. The truth is, I have no desire to do that. I would like to stay here and talk to him all night about music and their new single, tell him how much I liked the old albums and how much they stepped it up on the new songs. But when I turn to Emily, Albert and Jasper, I find myself catapulted into reality. My friends are open-mouthed at our interaction and remind me that our two worlds are so far apart we might as well live in two different galaxies, and this encounter is pure illusion.

"Can I follow you, or do I bother you?" As soon as the words leave his lips, he seems to regret the question. It gives me the impression that this situation, this way of approaching me, is new to him too. He doesn't seem comfortable. I have a feeling that it is women who usually chase him and not the other way around. My hesitation at his attempts makes him insecure.

I smile and beckon him with my head to follow me, without ruining this moment with awkward words.

We approach the stage with some difficulty. The place is chock-full but, either because of the cap he's wearing or the dim lights, no one gives Thomas a second glance. I wouldn't be able to handle it if people started freaking out about his presence and took pictures. I know what it's like to be on the other side of the camera, and I don't want to end up on all the Google searches because I've been photographed with one of the most famous drummers in the world. Ron would immediately pressure me for some juicy gossip and ruin my life.

"They're not bad at all." Thomas's warm voice in my ear brings me back to reality, and a pleasant shiver runs down my back.

At this distance, I can smell his scent. It's not very strong, as though he put a little on in the morning and then let it soak into his skin. It's not as aggressive and masculine as I usually imagine on men. It's almost sweet, a delicate fragrance that makes me think of freshly baked cookies. And he's like a cookie: good, sweet, irresistible. He's that sin you gladly indulge in when you're on a diet, but regret later. A sweet, pleasant torture you don't know how to resist.

"Yes, they're really good even if they are so young. They maybe need some experience on stage, but they're not bad. I came here to interview them when they're done. Do you want to come with me?" I propose without overthinking about the consequences. Being with him makes me almost reckless, as if this perfect bubble we're in protects us from the outside world. Thomas has this incredible ability to turn off the rational part of my brain that warns me from getting too attached to him.

"Gladly." I notice that he opens his mouth to say something else but then closes it immediately.

People start dancing, and Thomas's chest ends up pressing against my back. The shock that comes to life along my spine makes my hair stand up on my neck. It takes considerable effort not to lay my head back onto his shoulder. People move to the beat, and we're almost forced to follow the flow. Thomas's hands rest on my hips, and when he slips his fingers under my shirt, stroking my skin, I almost struggle to breathe. My hands wrap his, dragging them to the front, on my belly, inviting him in a hug that tastes of forbidden intimacy. His head drops and touches mine. His lips taste my neck with kisses so light I'm afraid I'm just imagining them. His arms hold me, his fingers search for my skin. His tongue gets bold, reaching that spot just below my ear that makes me moan with pleasure. The warmth invading my body intoxicates my senses so much I forget everything around us.

"Get a room!" Albert's voice falls on us like a cold shower.

I move away from Thomas just enough to get back to reality, to the concert, to Emily smirking, looking at us. Jasper's mouth is wide open, and Albert looks disgusted. I turn slightly toward Thomas to try to understand what he's thinking. His eyes are glued to mine, and I can read in them all the passion and frustration he's feeling right now, reflecting my own. Confirmation that my teenage crush is more than alive. In fact, it's grown to the point that it's become a physical necessity. My brain, telling me to run away, is alone in this fight. The rest of my body wants him.

The concert continues in a sequence of songs I find challenging to follow. My senses keep searching for Thomas, who is still behind me but has not come any closer than before. I, who am usually famous for my rigorous attention to the band I'm reviewing, find my mind wandering to those few intimate moments with Thomas earlier. Finally, the band greets the audience and gets off the stage. I wait for them all to get to the green room backstage, then I catch up with them to do the interview.

"Iris!" Seb, the guitarist and leader of the band, welcomes me with a hug.

I met him during the classes I sat in on at the university, and I found him to be a cheerful guy, full of enthusiasm for his own music. I'm happy to spend time with him and talk about what he does with his band.

"You were great up there," I say, pointing to the door behind me where the stage is.

Seb bursts out laughing and puts his hand on his chest in an almost theatrical way. "Whew! I must admit, I was afraid you might rip us. You're very technical and detailed when you have to review something you don't like."

Everyone laughs, including Thomas, who's on the sidelines.

"That's not true!" I pretend to be offended, but I know I'm a bit of a pain in the butt in that regard. I just can't lie if I didn't like something; I can do it calmly, giving my reasons without tearing down other people's work, but I certainly can't shut up or write something that's not true.

Some of the guys look over at Thomas, who I almost forgot was in the room. I introduce him, finally addressing his presence.

"This is Thomas, my...friend," I say, choking on the last word because I don't know if he considers it an exaggeration. I glance at him and he smiles, reaching out his hand, first toward Seb, then to everyone else who shakes it, and unceremoniously introduces himself.

They recognize him, of course, but they're all professional enough, or perhaps intimidated enough, not to comment. I mentally thank them because I want this to be their moment, their interview, their space.

"Shall we begin? Do you mind if I also take some pictures for the blog?" I ask before sitting on one of the sofas in the room and pulling out my camera and notebook with the questions I prepared in advance for the occasion.

Out of the corner of my eye, I notice Thomas leaning against a table scattered with takeout containers and water bottles, crossing his arms and watching my every move. He's discreet about it so it doesn't bother me. On the contrary, I like that he witnesses what I consider my actual work. Maybe I'm looking for justifications for my lies. I'm hoping that when he finds out I'm a paparazzo, he can tell the difference between what I do for the sake of music and what I do just to survive.

*

"Do you want a beer?" he asks when we leave the green room. The second band has almost finished playing.

"Yes, I do."

We both sit at a tall table away from the stage. It's sticky with old liquor. Thomas nods to the waitress, gives her his credit card, and invites me to order first. I'd rather him not pay for my beer, but I have no choice, since my credit card is at the limit this month and I don't have enough cash in my pocket. When I accepted, I didn't know Manhattan bars prefer credit cards and don't like cash.

When our orders arrive, I pull out my wallet, but he glares at me. "Don't even think about it. I asked you if you wanted a beer, and I intend to pay for it."

His voice is calm but firm. He wants to make a nice gesture.

I bite my tongue and put aside my eternal battle about equality. Women and men should be free to pay their own way on dates without the unwritten obligation that the guy should pay for the whole night. But this isn't a date, right?

"Thank you."

Thomas smiles and sips from his beer. "You're very professional when you do interviews. I hardly ever see journalists pulling out a prepared list of questions. They usually use the standard ones they've memorized without doing research on the band they're interviewing."

His words make me blush. It's nice that he realizes I put commitment and passion into what I do. I'm proud of how I run my blog. "I like my job, I like music and, honestly, the most beautiful part of the interview is just getting to know the story of the people behind the songs. When I ask them questions, I want it to be like talking to a friend because I'm really interested in what they have to say. I don't want it to be just a simple sterile question and answer, without any human contact, without emotions. After all, music is emotion. Why shouldn't I put it in my articles when I talk about it?"

Thomas looks me straight in the eye, nailing me to my stool with those ocean-blue eyes. A smile forms on his lips, and his gaze lights up when he glances at my mouth. I didn't realize I was so close to him until I feel his breath caressing my face. Thanks to the darkness of this corner, it feels like we're alone. People crowd around the stage listening to the third band, but I don't even care. All I can look at right now are Thomas's eyes, loaded with desire, and his face inching toward me. His lips crush mine in a kiss so perfect it makes my toes curl. His hands slip into my hair, grab me tightly, and pull me toward him in a kiss full of desire and despair. It's like he's been waiting for this moment for a lifetime.

His tongue caresses mine in a mixture of frenzy and sweetness, releasing those butterflies in my stomach I thought I'd managed to numb when I was sixteen. In fact, I thought this entire moment was just the impossible dream of a little girl in her first crush. My hands slip under his jacket, pulling his shirt until he gets off his stool. He presses his hot body against mine, letting out a little groan when my fingers slip under his shirt, caressing his skin, the muscles flexing under my touch. He takes a moment to catch his breath, but then his lips pounce desperately again on mine as he intensifies his grip on my hair. I groan into his mouth.

"Iris, we're going. We'll leave you here if you don't move your ass now!" For the second time tonight, Albert's voice interrupts us, and I'd like to kill him.

We're still panting when we separate. Thomas can't take his eyes off mine. I reluctantly look at my friend, and reality hits me like a landslide crushing my heart. The disgust on Albert's face brings me back to the truth of who I am and what I do for a living. I grab my bag and jacket and, without one last look at Thomas, I walk away quickly. Thomas's voice calling me sounds almost like a mirage.

We reach the others in the parking lot in silence, Albert pouting like a child, and I with the most conflicting feelings in my chest.

"What the hell happened?" asks Emily as soon as she sees us.

I look at her begging her to let it go, but Albert jumps right in. "God, I didn't think you would become the groupie of the first rock star you met. How low can you stoop?"

His words hurt, but I try not to show it. "What the hell is your problem?"

"You stuck your tongue in the mouth of the first jerk you meet who has a little fame."

"Did you kiss Thomas?" Emily's incredulous voice makes me turn toward her to find a smirk painted plainly on her face.

I nod with half a smile, but I don't tell her anything. I don't want Albert to ruin this moment by making me feel guilty.

"He was practically fucking her on the table."

"That is not true!"

"Really? When will you see him again?" Emily asks.

I give her the stink eye. "No, it's not true, and I won't see him again."

"Did you give him your number?"

"No, I didn't give him my number. It's bad enough that I kissed him."

Emily rolls her eyes and walks away from the parking lot.

"Where the hell are you going?" We all look at her perplexed.

"I forgot something inside. I'll be right back." She runs away and doesn't give us time to call her back or follow her.

"So, are you fucking the rock star?" chuckles Jasper.

"No, no one's fucking him." I smile.

"Of course not. If I hadn't arrived, he'd already have his hands between your legs," Albert mumbles.

I turn to him, annoyed. "That's not true. We kissed. Period. Don't exaggerate things just to prove you're a jerk," I attack him a little too harshly.

The truth is, I'm not mad at my friend. I'm mad at myself

for completely losing control with the only person I should stay away from. And what worries me the most is the whole time it never crossed my mind that I was doing something wrong. Everything about that kiss and his hands on me seemed right. But my fantasy is based entirely on my lies; if Thomas knew what I've done in the past, he'd be disgusted with me.

CHAPTER 7
Thomas

Idiot. I feel like a complete idiot out here at this café, looking at her through the window while she's working on her computer, for God's sake! I woke up this morning with last night still burned in my mind: her lips bending slightly upwards when she talks about music, the way she gets angry when people don't understand certain songs, her persistence in defending some albums that, for the rest of the world, are really awful. I still feel her taste on my tongue, her hair in my fingers, her hands on my skin. The distance between us almost hurts.

She sucked me into her world, captured me with her big green eyes, and made my legs tremble like a kid. I look around as people passing by on their way to the office cast strange glances at me. They're right. I'm here in the middle of the sidewalk in Alphabet City. The café in front of me is all painted in bright tones with graffiti. It's a splash of color in the middle of the tall, gray, and dilapidated buildings in this area. It's one of Manhattan's less wealthy and popular neighborhoods, where the streets would be glum and bare without these vibrant spots. It's certainly not as Christmassy as Fifth Avenue and its twinkling lights. Still, some decorations have appeared on the windows, giving glimpses of the festive atmosphere inside those spaces. And Iris is a splash of life amid those spirals of colors. Her red hair, gathered in a messy bun held together by a pencil. In the daylight, it almost seems to catch fire. She's focused on her laptop, her lips pouting in concentration that makes her adorable and her forehead wrinkled as if she's writing the next Pulitzer-winning piece.

A middle-aged man with graying hair and a suit at least two sizes too big walks past, bumping me slightly with his shoulder while looking at his cell phone and muttering an apology. That's just what I need to wake up from my daydream. I take a deep breath and decide to go into the café and make myself look ridiculous for the umpteenth time.

I look around and get lost for a second at the endless list of items written in colored chalk on the huge menu attached to the wall behind the counter. The shelf in front of me is cluttered with glass vases containing various biscuits from a local pastry shop. Around me, the tables, sofas, and chairs are mismatched, as though taken from some flea market, giving it a quirky vibe. What may seem like a nonsensical jumble of furniture is actually an explosion of color that elicits a feeling of joy.

"Finally, you decided to come in. I thought you'd cut and run after you finished your cigarette and were about to light a third. You could still dash out if you want, because she's so focused on her work, she didn't even notice you coming in." Emily teases me from behind the counter, although her infectious smile doesn't embarrass me at all. I get the impression she's like Iris: very straightforward and sincere in dealing with people.

"Are you suggesting I should avoid being an idiot and leave before she notices?" I ask with a laugh, but the truth is, I'm tempted to actually do it.

"Are you kidding? I didn't run back to the club last night and tell you where she would be this morning because I needed the exercise. She's a woman. How many have you had in your life? This is no different!" Her rebuke makes me smile but also feel like an idiot. "Do you want anything in the meantime?"

I study her for a few seconds. "I'm sorry, I'm lost," I confess, a little embarrassed.

The girl smiles at me, and her brown eyes light up. "Do you want to order?"

"A black coffee," I say without thinking about it, ordering what I usually get when I go out, avoiding the endless menus and the pressure of the cashiers who want to take your order and quickly dispose of the line behind you.

This is not the case with Emily; she looks at me almost disappointed. "A black coffee? Are you sure?" she asks, nodding to the wall behind her that's crowded with dozens of different types of coffee, as well as herbal teas and a list of sweet and salty sandwiches so long it makes me anxious. Does anyone really need to order a decaffeinated latte with cream and sprinkles of caramelized hazelnuts? Can a person even drink something like that?

"And a double granola?" It's more of a question than a statement, given my insecurity as I'm pointing a finger at the first jar in front of me. I basically have no idea what I ordered.

"Great choice. It's one of my favorites."

I have the vague impression that she's good-naturedly making fun of me, but I can't make any decent jokes to escape this awkwardness. Ever since meeting Iris, I've been piling up an almost embarrassing list of blunders. My awkward moments are evolving from bad to worse.

"Thank you, that's reassuring to know." The statement comes out so serious and solemn that Emily can't hold back a chuckle.

"Do you want to pay, or do you want anything else?" Her kind smile reassures me she's not making fun of me at all.

"I'll pay." I smile at her shaking my head. I already know these two aren't going to make my life easy.

When I finally grab my coffee and a very inviting looking cookie, I turn to Iris and find her staring at me with the same wide eyes as last night—like an alien just landed in front of her.

"What the hell are you doing here?" she asks aloud, making half the people in here turn and look. I feel almost undressed, and not in a pleasant way.

Iris realizes she's raised her voice too much. She beckons me to sit next to her with a smile that seems sincere. "I'm sorry, I didn't mean to be rude. It's just that I'm surprised to see you around here. It's not where you hang out, is it?"

She's trying to apologize, and it makes me feel terribly guilty. I should be the one to apologize for popping into her life so urgently I look almost psychotic.

"No, you're absolutely right. The truth is, I wanted to see you and, since I don't have your number, but I knew you were going to be here this morning, I came in person." I hope my confession is not so honest it scares her. Although, by now, she should have run like hell.

"You could have contacted me on Instagram or on my blog. You didn't have to go to the trouble of coming all this way to talk to me." She smiles, but I notice she's a little embarrassed. Maybe she regretted last night's kiss, and now she doesn't know how to tell me to stay away. On the other hand, I'd like to repeat the experience a thousand more times because, after tasting her sweetness, I can't think of anything else.

I was wrong to come here without telling her. It's clear that I've crossed more than one line with her lately, and it's getting a little weird and embarrassing for both of us.

"Or, if I had your number, I could text you that I'm coming by to say hi, and not look like the perverted maniac who follows you," I venture and immediately regret it, seeing her grimace. "I'm sorry, I shouldn't have asked you, and I certainly shouldn't have come here," I stammer uncertainly, standing up, ready to run out of this place like a one hundred-meter runner in the race of his life.

A hand grabs my wrist before I can walk outside. When I turn around again, I find Iris's almost confused eyes. "No, please. We got off on the wrong foot this morning," she reassures me, motioning for me to sit next to her again. "So would you like my number so you can tell me about that time you took the stage with half your pants?" The mischievous smile on her face tells me she's not mad at me.

I burst out laughing. I like how this story has become our inside joke to break the ice. "The time I was attacked by a dog that ripped off my jeans? Yes, I really should tell you that story."

Now it's Iris who bursts out laughing. "Really? A dog? I didn't remember it that way."

"I swear." The tension slips away with this private joke only the two of us share.

"So, what did you get for breakfast?"

"A black coffee and...I don't know, I think it's called double granola." I look at the two cereal cookies with cream in the middle, holding them together.

"A black coffee? Seriously?" Her raised eyebrow tells me she doesn't believe it.

"Don't make me feel guilty like Emily did. I always order a black coffee when I'm out."

She chuckles, leans on the sofa, and looks at me with an interested smile. "Are you one of those rock stars who survive on black coffee and cigarettes?"

I laugh out loud, forgetting my manners. "No, definitely not. I order black coffee because it's easy. Everyone has it, and I can play it safe without losing my mind with these crazy menus. I'm a person who likes to have the situation under control. I like to plan, find solutions and try to anticipate any problems. The unexpected annoys me. Having a line of people behind me in a hurry to order makes me nervous. I feel the pressure and, in the end, I never get to read the whole menu. So I order the black coffee and clear the line in less than five seconds."

I know it sounds like a fool's speech, but it's not like I can make a worse impression than the one I've already made. I might as well be honest.

"So you can face concerts in stadiums with thousands of people in front of you, but you feel pressured to order a coffee?" she asks me incredulously, and I burst out laughing.

"Exactly. For the concerts we prepare for months, everything is planned. I know what will happen, the timing, the set list we'll play. Over time, I also learned to predict which unforeseen events are statistically more likely to happen and have somehow become part of my routine. But if you make me order a coffee in front of someone who's fussing because he has a meeting he's going to be late to, I'm going to freak out." Iris looks at me, and I see understanding in her eyes, not someone trying to comprehend the rantings of a madman. Right now, the people sitting around us seem light years away, as if glass walls surrounded us, cutting out the rest of the world, giving this conversation special relevance.

"It's not your fault that the person behind you is late for his job. He could always get up five minutes earlier, take an earlier train or decide not to have breakfast out," she points out.

"I've learned that my actions have consequences for others, whether I like it or not. I prefer to be as less of an obstacle as possible for the people around me," I respond with a half-smile.

Iris studies me for a few seconds, then perhaps realizes the topic makes me uncomfortable and decides to bail me out of my embarrassment. "So, the fact that I don't do things like you expect, like giving you my phone number, is upsetting you." It's a straightforward observation, but I hear almost satisfaction in her voice, as if she understands that she has a power over me that she did not expect.

"The truth? You're freaking me out. I'm acting like a teenager who makes a series of bad decisions but doesn't know how to snap out of it. I spent ten minutes outside this café this morning convincing myself to go home because I look like a lunatic, but here I am, with a black coffee and a cream-filled cookie that I ordered just because Emily pressured me. I have no idea what's inside this damn cookie!" I laugh, and she does the same, covering her mouth with her hand, but I still see those amused green eyes peeking out from above her fingers. I feel like a kid at Christmas for making her laugh.

"It's hazelnut cream, and it's Emily's favorite cookie. You must have made her really happy after ordering only a black coffee," she teases me a little.

I look at Emily, who is still watching us, smiling and waving her hand. "So, you're very social, but you don't have Facebook?" I move the focus of this conversation to her again.

Iris shakes her head as she sips from her cup. "You checked." The satisfied smile on her lips almost makes me want to lean in and take it off with a kiss, like last night's. But now it is daylight. There is no darkness to hide from prying eyes.

"I at least wanted to know if you're 'in a relationship' before asking for your phone number for the umpteenth time, and Facebook is the best source for this kind of news," I admit without beating around the bush.

"I have a feeling this is information you will add to your not-able-to-control list and it will drive you crazy."

The way she deflects my questions is one of the things I find most intriguing about this woman. Is it possible that when I talk to her I leave more confused, and with more questions, than I had at the beginning of the conversation? Right now, I have absolute certainty that this woman is putting me under her thumb, and I have no idea how to get away without hurting myself.

"It means I will have to take you home to see if you live with someone. You know, I've been good at stalking people lately."

Iris laughs, and my day lights up a little more. "You go from my phone number to my home address. You're leveling up."

It's my turn to burst out laughing, and in an impulsive move,

I stretch my arm out and draw her to me to kiss her head. I feel her stiffen for a moment but then let go of a long breath and relax. For a moment, I forget we're in a crowded coffee shop.

"If you really want to find out where I live, this is your chance," she tells me, stuffing the computer in her bag and putting on her jacket. I'm almost surprised. I thought she was going to skate over this like she did with the phone number. It takes a moment before I rush up and follow her out into the cold Manhattan morning.

"Your coffee and cookie? Don't you want them?"

I smile, embarrassed because I completely forgot I put them on the table in front of us. "Emily won't be offended if I leave them there, will she?"

Iris smiles amusedly. "She'll remind you for the next six years, but then she'll forget about it."

"Only six years? I can handle that."

We walk a couple of blocks in comforting silence, with our hands in our pockets so as not to feel the bitter cold. The air is charged like it's about to snow, and the gray sky makes this city even more magical usual. Iris stops in front of a building that has seen better times, with peeling plaster, the chipped steps leading up to the slightly open door, and a row of garbage cans occupying the sidewalk. Christmas magic is nowhere in sight on this desolate corner. I hope this thought doesn't translate into a grimace on my face.

"Will you promise to close your eyes as we go up?" she asks, a little embarrassed.

"Do I have to worry?"

"Let's just say this place isn't like the luxury hotels you're used to," she admits, looking down.

"Trust me, my life has not been all luxury and glitz." After prison, any place can feel like home to me.

Iris inhales deeply and eventually seems to convince herself. She beckons me with her head to the stairs, and I follow her. She pushes the door slightly and as soon as I take a step inside the small and dark entrance, the pungent smell of urine forces me to cover my mouth to keep from vomiting. I glance down the three steps that descend into the basement and find a filthy blanket in the corner where, I'm guessing, the homeless take refuge at night. For a moment, I imagine Iris coming home late, with some drunks here bothering her as she takes the stairs to her apartment. Nausea almost makes me falter. The sense of disorientation destabilizes me. I have never felt such strong feelings of protection toward anyone but my bandmates and it confuses me.

I follow her up stairs that are worn and chipped and covered in so much dirt you can't even tell what the original color was. It's so narrow here that two people trying to pass at the same time would have trouble. The hallway walls are bare, there are no Christmas decorations on the doors—a stark contrast to the luxurious buildings in Manhattan. In the building where I live, the lobby is decorated with a ten-foot tree, every single free space is filled with poinsettias, and each door is decked out with Christmas garland or a custom arrangement made by a trusted florist. Even I had Claire get one, so as not to be out of place. Here, it seems the magic of Christmas disappeared at the entrance.

The third-floor hallway Iris enters is better. The dark gray plaster is peeled in some spots, but at least the place is clean, and at the entrances to the various apartments a few doormats decorate the otherwise bland surroundings. When we arrive in front of her apartment, the lamp's dim light next to her door illuminates her carpet, and I find it difficult to hold back a laugh. The black lettering on the brownish bristles reads, 'If you're the pizza guy, you're welcome.' I imagine her standing in a store in front of such a carpet and smiling, satisfied as she puts it in the cart.

"Congratulations. You've survived the valley of tears without running away. Not many of them arrive at the door." She tries to play it down with a joke, but I see in her eyes that she is embarrassed by the desolation of this place.

"Because they didn't realize that to get the prize, they have to overcome the obstacles first," I smile.

"Let's hear it—what would this prize be?" Her gaze challenges me.

I bend down and kiss her without giving her time to think about it. I sink my fingers into her hair and draw her to me to savor her tongue that gently caresses mine. She grabs my jacket to pull me closer and I gently push her against the door jamb. I press against her body, and she feels a little more mine. Iris has a tendency to slip between my fingers, but with this kiss I want to feel every part of her, caress the skin of her face, inhale her sweet scent. Since last night I've wanted to do this, take a moment to savor her without rushing, without witnesses, without interruptions. When I step away from her, she looks at me perplexed and perhaps even a little disappointed.

"Don't you want to come in and see if I have a boyfriend?" She smiles.

"If you really lived with someone, you wouldn't have let me up here and risked being discovered."

When she sees me moving away from her, she's taken back. She's still panting from the kiss, with a dazed and dreamy look and red cheeks. She's so beautiful, I'd like to go back and kiss her again, without giving her time to breathe, but I don't. It's my turn to confuse her, to leave her gasping in front of that threshold that divides my sanity from pure desire. If I cross that door, nothing will be the same, and the emotions I feel scare me too much to be able to deal with them. I need to distance myself before I cross that fine line that I won't be able to go back from.

I walk down the stairs, this time with a smile planted on my face. I couldn't get her phone number, but at least now I know where she lives.

PRESS *Review*

A Band You Can't Miss!

Hi Roadies!

Have you seen my Instagram stories from last night? If you have, you'd already know that I was at "The Bitter End" for The Revolver concert and interview. This band surprised me in a good way because, despite everyone being very young, they have an enviable stage presence. Their second album came out recently, and we noticed a vast improvement over their debut record.

Q: On your first album, you experimented a lot with genres. You covered a wide range on the spectrum. However, in your latest work, the funk turn is the common thread from the first to the last song. How did you make that decision?

A: The truth is much less poetic than you can imagine. On the first album, we were looking for our identity. We wanted to do something that might please everyone a little bit. In the second, we were more selfish and played only what we like, what amuses us, and what makes us remember why we started making music.

Q: So, should we expect this direction on the next albums

as well?

A: We can't be sure because people grow, mature, tastes change, but unless it takes fifteen years to release the next one, I'm pretty sure it's going to be something down this line.

Q: In the spring, you start an overseas tour with twelve concerts around Europe. There are many venues planned but also two big festivals. What should fans who come to hear you expect?

A: Yes, we still can't believe we're finally going to visit Europe. We have a loyal fan base over there and decided to go and meet them. Some of them came to the US to follow us on tour here. They're a blast. It's time for us to reward them for their support. What they can expect is an energetic tour like the concert you saw tonight. We're going to make them dance and sweat at every show!

To read the full Revolver interview and find out what else they told me last night, go to their website.

Be kind and Rock'n'Roll,
Iris

35480 Likes 17842 Tweets 17458 Shares 3592 Comments

CHAPTER 8

Iris

"Do you think you're going to tell him what you do for a living?" Emily's question hits me as soon as I open the door.

I let her into the house after her shift at the café. I knew she'd ask. When Thomas followed me to my apartment, she watched us leave, half happy and half worried. She's concerned about me, and knowing this makes me feel even more guilty about the turn my life has taken.

"It would be much easier if he forgets I exist."

A little laugh escapes her lips. "Are you serious? He kissed you in a crowded place, then he came to the café to find you, accompanied you home... To make him forget you exist you'd have to remove part of his brain." She sits next to me at the kitchen table. Her smile is sweet and understanding.

I know she's right; this situation is anything but simple. I should have walked away the moment I fell into his arms and recognized him. I should have run and not gotten involved. Any attempt at approaching him, at this point, is a lie. It's not just because of my job. It's the way we met, why I was there in that alley, and the fact that I've lied to him all this time despite having more than one chance to tell him the truth. It's no longer an omission. It became a straight-up lie when I kept meeting him and hid the truth about myself.

"I know," I agree with Emily. "I refused to give him my number again, but he stayed anyway. I didn't seek him out—I made sure I was nowhere near him when I knew he'd be out in public somewhere. I avoided him in every way, but he always found me. I don't know what to do anymore. By the way, you told him I was going to be at the café this morning, didn't you?"

My scolding glare doesn't seem to affect her. She just shrugs and smiles. "Sometimes you have to help fate."

"I don't want to help it, Emily. I'm walking into something I already know will hurt me. I like him a lot. Right now, the love-sick teenager in me is delighted at finally having my dream come true. But I'm afraid to encourage something I already know will backfire. How do you think he'll react when he finds out I'm a paparazzo?"

"If he finds out by accident, he'll be mad for sure, but if *you* tell him and explain why you do it, maybe he can forgive you." She echoes my conscience while she strokes Dexter's fur. He has climbed onto the table to be cuddled.

"Let's say that it's true, that he is more understanding than a saint and that he forgives me. How do you think he'll react when he finds out I was the one who sold the photos that almost destroyed their career four years ago?"

Emily's eyes get compassionate, and it makes my heart tighten in my chest. She knows I've made too many mistakes in my life to not deserve that forgiveness. But I'm not in a position to forgive myself. Why should I expect others to?

"You were desperate, you needed money, and it was the only solution. Don't condemn yourself. You had no choice."

"That's not true. I could have prostituted myself, but I

didn't. Instead of selling a piece of me, I sold them. And the thing that makes me feel the most guilty is that, despite everything, I'm so selfish I can't stay away from him."

"Who could resist him? He's so gorgeous he takes your breath away—sensual, cute, and so shy you want to hug him. He's the perfect mix of cute and sexy every woman desires. Like he's been custom-made to set you on fire just being near him. I understand why you can't stay away from him: on paper, he's the perfect man for you." She says out loud what I don't dare say.

Dexter complains a little while Emily holds him in a hug but shows no sign of getting off the table.

"You are not helping."

"I don't want to help. He's the first decent man you've met and you literally fell into his arms. You can't keep punishing yourself for the rest of your life for the choices you've made. Life has been a bitch to you. You've faced difficulties people your age can't even imagine. Give yourself a few moments of happiness. You can't keep carrying the burden of the whole world. It's unfair to you."

Her words shut me up and assuage a little bit of my guilt. I always thought I didn't have time to be happy; there was always something more urgent and vital than my happiness. Hell, sometimes I had to put aside basic necessities like a meal because I had no choice. I never paused to think for a second about myself. Even the relationships I've had never brought me much pleasure because my situation has always been too complicated to have a carefree dating life. All my dreams have ended—I can no longer enjoy life like an ordinary twenty-four-year-old.

The phone rings in my pocket. A message from Ron tells me that Alicia Pinker—the famous Hollywood star—is in one of Manhattan's most prestigious restaurants with her new flame who's twenty years younger. Her husband dumped her for a guy he met on set.

"See? I've allowed myself to think I have a normal life, and here reality knocks at my door. Ron asked me to go to the Mandalay to photograph Alicia. This is my work, and it will never be compatible with his life. I'm the one he hates and avoids and wears horrible caps to keep from being recognized by. He travels in cars with darkened glass to confuse people like me...to protect himself from people like me. I'll never have any other job than this. Do you understand why this story is going to end badly?"

"Better to be hurt by an intense love story than to barely survive in a sterile life, don't you think?" She raises an eyebrow.

I don't dare answer her question even for myself, let alone utter it out loud. "Can I call you when I get back?" I ask, going to get the camera from under my bed.

"Yes, though I don't think your cat will let me go. He's so sweet and cuddly."

I roll my eyes because Dexter is everything but those things. Sometimes I get the distinct impression he wants to kill me in my sleep. "I'm almost sure he loves you more than me. The only contact we have is in the morning when he puts his paws on my face to be fed," I admit with some disappointment mixed with humor.

*

There are only five of us here in front of the restaurant.

This time Ron got the tip from someone well connected, someone who knows the magazines that will run the story. In most cases, this type of information comes straight from the star's manager or from his press office, especially when the fame around his client is fading. In Alicia's case, she had the misfortune of being dumped by her husband for a man. The news was spiced up with a sex scandal that surfaced on the movie's set they were filming together. It was a nasty blow. She was the victim in that situation, but that was irrelevant compared to the fact that her husband—a two-generation sex symbol—turned out to be a gay man who never came out. Unfortunately, in modern, progressive Hollywood, it's more scandalous to be gay and come out than to betray the wife you've been with for more than fifteen years.

The excuse I give myself for being out here making money off someone else's misfortune is that most likely that same person is paying me to be here. Our wait doesn't last long. After not even twenty minutes, Alicia comes out walking hand in hand with Peter Rayan, a young actor who has made more news for his dating life than for his high-profile roles. But he's only twenty-three years old and has a life ahead of him to prove his worth in Hollywood.

The flashes of five cameras go wild as they try to cover their faces, even if they're not putting much effort into it, confirming my theory that it was them who called us. The noise is like a round of machine guns. It takes forever to call their driver, who arrives five minutes later, despite coming from the garage of this same place. When they finally get into the car, I wave to my colleagues who are already walking toward the subway. It was a quick, painless job that will earn me a few hundred dollars. It could have been worse.

I put the camera in my bag and walk to the alley behind the restaurant that cuts through the entire block to Fifth Avenue. I'll have to walk down it to get home. As soon as I turn the corner, my heart stops: Thomas is there, smoking his cigarette, his gaze fixed on the asphalt. He's within walking distance, and as soon as he hears me, he looks up, and his eyes go wide. Did he see me in front of the restaurant?

"I swear I didn't follow you this time!" He raises his hands and shakes his head.

I smile, but I'm nervous. If he'd seen me in front of the restaurant, he wouldn't try to justify himself for our meeting, but I can't be sure. "I believe it, but what the hell are you doing out here in the dark?"

He shows me the cigarette he's holding. "I had to walk out the back door because there are jackals with cameras in front of the restaurant."

It hurts to be called that, but it's not his fault. That's who we really are. "Are you here for dinner?" I try to move the topic away from the paparazzi.

"Yes, I'm with Damian, Lilly, and Michael. But what are you doing around here?"

Good question. "I came to see a friend. I'm on my way home." It feels like the nervousness is palpable in my words.

"Can I walk you home?"

"Aren't you having dinner with your friends?" I laugh.

Thomas shrugs and puts out the cigarette, stepping on it. "They'll survive without me."

"Okay."

We walk silently side by side until we reach Fifth Avenue, where a cascade of light from a shop window decorated for Christmas showers us. Behind the glass, a sleigh pulled by white horses makes its way through the snow and trees adorned with red ornaments. Every year, the shops compete for the most beautiful and dramatic decorations. Elves, Christmas trees, ice sculptures, and real-looking snowfall take turns showing off during one of the most beautiful seasons of the year. Millions of tourists trample over these sidewalks, filling their eyes and hearts with the magic that these windows, and this city as a whole, manage to convey. And every year at this time, I remember how lonely I am in a place where millions of people gather to celebrate.

"Are you going to spend Christmas with someone?" he asks, as if reading my mind, when we have been walking silently for five minutes.

"With my mother, as usual. You?"

"I think we'll all be at Lilly and Damian's house. Since they started living together, those two have become more domestic than a retired old couple."

I laugh and feel a little honored. It's not everyone who gets this kind of inside information about their favorite band, which makes me realize how comfortable he is with me. His barriers are slowly collapsing, and mine are starting to creak, too.

We don't even notice when we arrive at my apartment, alternating moments of silence and small conversations about our daily life.

"I blew your dinner."

Thomas shrugs and smiles, his hands shoved into his pockets. "It's not like you get fed enough in that place. It's the classic upscale restaurant where portions are tiny and cost a ridiculous amount of money. Did you already eat?"

"No. I haven't had time yet." And I don't have much in the fridge to put on the table.

"Shall we order a pizza and have it delivered to your place? Or is that too brazen of a proposal?" His question is almost timid.

My heart goes crazy in my chest, shouting yes, while my brain tells me I should end the evening here. "Okay, but I warn you, I have nothing to offer you upstairs, apart from tap water... I haven't had time to shop these days."

"Okay, you go up and order the pizza you like. I'll go to the store down the street and buy something to drink."

As I climb the stairs to my apartment, my heart explodes in my chest and agitation grips my stomach. As soon as I enter, I pull out my camera and computer and, before ordering pizza, send the photos to Ron. A sense of unease fills me when I think of Thomas being here in a few minutes, and I'm hiding the real reason I crossed paths with him in that alley.

A slight knock on the door almost makes me drop the camera I'm putting in the closet. Dexter precedes me, and when I open the door to let Thomas in, my cat rubs between his legs as if he's known him for a lifetime. Thomas seems pleasantly surprised by the meeting.

"So, you do live with someone," he says amusedly.

"Yes, his name is Dexter, and he loves everyone but me." I approach the kitchen cabinet to get two glasses while Thomas picks up that traitor that is my cat. He starts to purr.

"What did you do to make him hate you so much?"

"Nothing! I feed him when he meows, I clean his litter box twice a day, I give him the best space on the bed to sleep in."

Thomas bursts out laughing, and I scowl at him. "I understand now. He basically considers you his human slave. You'll never get cuddles from him. You're just around to give him a comfortable life," he teases me as he puts the red hairball on the ground and opens the bottle.

I watch him, almost holding my breath. It seems impossible for Thomas of the Jailbirds to be here in my tiny Manhattan apartment. When he offers me the glass and slightly touches my hand, an electric charge runs through me until it explodes inside my stomach. I look up, and I'm sure he felt it too. His eyes, full of desire, don't lie. I sip from my glass without ever taking my eyes off his. Maybe alcohol isn't the best choice when I'm in a room alone with a man I've dreamed of having since I was a teenager, and who I'm sure reciprocates my attraction. Someone knocking on the door reminds us of reality, breaking our tension and letting me catch my breath.

"Here's the pizza and the parmesan bread." The delivery guy rests the two boxes in my hand without glancing at Thomas behind me.

"Thank you. Can you give the box of bread to Charlie down the stairs as usual?"

"No problem." He takes back one of the two boxes and waves at me.

"Who is Charlie?" my guest asks me, intrigued, when I close the door and place the pizza on the table.

"The homeless man living down the stairs."

When I look up at Thomas, his eyes glisten, and he's hiding a smile. He seems to want to say something, but then he closes his mouth. He approaches me slowly, takes my face in his hands, and draws me in for a kiss that makes my knees tremble. He is sweet and, at the same time, intense. His tongue caresses mine with frenzy and desire as if he wants to own everything about me, body and soul. When he walks away, my head is spinning, and it's not because of the wine.

"The more I'm around you, the more you surprise me. The first time I walked into this building, I thought you needed someone to protect you from the drunk down there. It never entered my mind that you were actually taking care of him."

"Don't make me out to be a heroine. I'm a long way from it, trust me."

Thomas shakes his head and smiles. "You know you're making it hard for me to keep being a gentleman and not take those clothes you're wearing off of you, right?" he confesses in a whisper. "Every time you surprise me with something I like about you, you make it impossible for me to stay away."

"I know. I'm not having much success keeping you away either," I admit.

Thomas smiles before sinking his fingers into my hair and pulling me in for a new kiss. His tongue caresses mine at a slow, almost hesitant pace. Then it becomes more and more frenetic, full of passion, invigorated by my hands that slip under his sweater and caress his smooth skin. A groan escapes his lips and my reason—the one that tells me to stop and send him away—goes out the window. We forget about the pizza and the wine. Right now, the only thing we both seem to need is skin on skin, and his breath mixed with his kiss makes a shiver of pleasure run along my back.

It's as if, since the beginning, a force has lured us toward each other with no chance of escaping it. It wasn't enough to avoid giving him my phone number because, one way or another, we found the way that led us to this moment, with a desire to make love we can no longer control.

His hands follow my hair down my back to my hips and lure me in with a force that leaves no doubt about how much he wants me. His erection presses against my belly, making me surrender and press into his body as if I could merge with him. Thomas pulls back just enough to sit on the bed and draw me to straddle him without ever taking his lips off mine. His fingers slip under the fabric of my shirt, caress the skin of my back, making me groan.

I leave his lips panting, grab the sleeves of his jacket and slip it off. His eyes are full of desire and scrutinize my every movement with lust. His sweater slips on the floor along with the jacket, and my heart leaps into my throat. The toned physique and muscular arms with their raised veins drive me crazy. I want everything about him, every single inch of skin that covers this statuesque physique. I want to kiss his body and caress it with my hands until I memorize every single muscle, tendon, vein I can reach.

For years, I dreamed of how this moment would be, and my imagination did not even remotely conceive of the beauty of the man I am facing. I stop to admire his desire-laden blue eyes, the dark hair that falls across his cheekbones like the first time I met him, his solid arms and sculpted abs. His hands tighten around my hips, pushing me toward his erection, giving me a shiver of pleasure that rises from my lower belly up to my stomach. I close my eyes and moan.

I can't resist. I go down to taste that inviting skin, deeply inhaling the sweet scent that always seems to accompany him. I can feel him holding his breath when I taste his abs with my tongue and, as I climb back to his chest with light kisses, his hand slips into my hair, clutching it in a light grip at the back of my neck. He's losing control faster and faster, kiss after kiss, bite after bite, as I approach his neck like it's all I need to survive for the rest of my life.

I go back to his lips, but Thomas pushes me away gently. He grabs my shirt and lifts it over my head in a quick gesture. With one hand, he unhooks my bra and leaves me naked. He opens his eyes wide, inhales deeply, and holds his breath. When he comes back to look me in the eyes, I know there's no turning back from here. We've crossed the point of no return. I get up, slipping off my pants and panties as I watch him get rid of his clothes and stick a condom on his erection.

I go back to riding him slowly but without stopping. I become one with the man I have dreamed of for a lifetime. His tongue teases my breasts, his firm hands grip my hips and dictate the rhythm of my movements as I sink my fingers into his hair and pull it hard. I moan with an orgasm that makes my legs tremble while he thrusts under me, getting more intense, fast. The guttural sound filling the room when he reaches his peak of pleasure is the sexiest sound I've ever heard.

I collapse on him, panting, while his arms wrap me in a heat I haven't felt in a long time. I hear him giggling, and I look up just enough to meet his gaze. "I think the pizza is cold."

"Apparently, you're supposed to skip dinner tonight." I smile at him without turning away.

"We could always tuck under the blankets and eat it in bed."

His proposal floors me. It's the only thing I'd like to do for the rest of my life, and I don't know if there's ever going to be anything beyond tonight. However, I decide not to spoil this moment. I get up, move the blankets and slide him between the sheets, then I go grab the bottle of wine and the pizza and return to snuggle up next to him.

"I confess that when I realized you were a fan, I thought you'd have posters of us over your bed," Thomas chuckles, looking around for the first time since he walked in.

I smile, chewing a piece of pizza I pounced on. "I did. I took them off the walls of the bedroom when I moved into this apartment, but I never hung them again... You know, when you pretend to be an adult and decorate the apartment decently?"

Thomas laughs and sips from the glass of wine. "I'm glad you grew up. But I would have liked peeking into the life of one of our fans. I've always wondered if they have posters on their walls, our albums on their shelves...I mean, all those things girls do when they love bands."

"Like this?"

Thomas watches me curiously as I stretch out and stick my arm under the bed in search of the tin box I guard with my life. I pull it out and watch Thomas smile at the container a little bigger than a shoebox, pink with blue bows. My heart explodes as I open it to reveal its contents. I see him frowning and concentrating as I pull out the newspaper clippings and give them to him.

"I've kept all the articles about you that I've been able to find in the newspapers," I say, a little concerned that he'll consider it childish.

Thomas seems absorbed in his own thoughts as he calmly browses the pages concerning him.

"These articles are years old. Some are from when we weren't even famous!" He looks at me, surprised and maybe even a little excited.

"I told you I'd been following you for a while."

"Yes, but this stuff is something you'd find in a museum!"

"Look," I tell him, rummaging to the bottom of the box where I keep their first flyer. "This is my first historical find regarding the Jailbirds. One day, I was with my dad doing local alcohol deliveries, and we stopped at a place...I think the bar was called 'Joe's.' Anyway, you were playing and I stayed for a few songs while my dad finished unloading the crates. That was the first time I listened to you—my first ever Jailbirds concert. You weren't famous yet. You became famous maybe nine or ten months later, signing with the record company." I smile at the memory of that day.

Thomas is staring at me, wide-eyed.

"What?" I ask, almost fearing that my confession makes me look crazy.

"It was you!" He bursts out laughing, but I don't understand. When he finally calms down, he explains: "We had just started playing around, and there was never anyone to hear us, just a few drunks that hated our music. Joe only let us play there because we stopped after closing time to clean the place. That day, when you walked in, you were the first one to ever to stop and listen to us. We were euphoric. When we finished, we wanted to come and talk to you, but your dad came for you, and we never saw you again. Two days later, Evan randomly entered the venue because he had the wrong address, and it was the day he discovered us. We've always seen you as a bit of a lucky charm—as if you started our career."

I look at him, stunned. "Do you really remember that day?"

"Impossible to forget. But I have to admit, I didn't recognize you. We hoped to meet you again at some of our concerts, but you literally disappeared. You've become like a memory, like you were just a figment of our imagination."

My heart hammers in my chest furiously. "I was sixteen years old. I was too young to sneak into clubs. But that's when I started the blog. I was blown away by your music."

Thomas looks at me in disbelief. Then, without saying another word, he pulls me in and holds me in a hug. I thought that day was a one-way fantasy of a teenager, but finding out that my emotions were reciprocated makes the butterflies in my stomach flutter. My connection to this guy has deep roots all the way back to my adolescence. Which is why I feel even more guilty for all the lies I've been telling him.

PRESS *Review*

People:

Alicia Pinker steps out with her new flame, Peter Rayan, twenty-five years her junior. Last night, after a romantic dinner at Mandalay in New York City, the new couple took refuge in the hotel and didn't leave until early the next morning. How will her ex-husband—who now lives in France with his new boyfriend—take it? Certainly, Alicia has a habit of choosing men with whom she risks not going very far in a relationship. Is she afraid to commit?

Gossip Now!

Wild night for Alicia Pinker and her new flame, Peter Rayan. After having an intimate dinner at the Mandalay in New York, the two lovebirds holed up in the hotel and never left. Witnesses in the restaurant confirmed that the two could not stay away from each other, and rushed back to the hotel after a hasty meal. First, she marries a man who prefers male company, then she dates a boy twenty-five years her junior. Certainly, Alicia doesn't like easy relationships. How long will the new couple last? One piece of advice we can give her? Don't introduce the new boytoy to your ex if you don't want to be single again.

CHAPTER 9
Thomas

I'm riding in the elevator alone, heading to the new recording studio. My instinct is to press the button to the ground floor and go home. After untangling myself from Iris's arms and finally checking my phone last night, I found several messages and calls from my friends. I left the restaurant sending a quick text to not worry about my non-return, but apparently it triggered a series of questions I have yet to answer.

Talking with her and listening to her confessions about when she was a teenager, between a piece of pizza and a glass of wine, were the best moments I've had in years. It wasn't just the sex, though that was exceptional. It was waking up with her body cuddled in my arms, the sweet scent of her hair tickling my nose, her deep breathing, one hand resting on my chest as she felt comfortable enough to fall asleep next to me. It was realizing that I loved the feelings creeping into my chest. I've only always looked for sex from women, but Iris has given me a whole other world that I can't forget. Because as much as I don't want to think about it, as much as I keep telling myself a serious future will never be there for me, the hours I spent hugging her, sleeping by her side all night, have been my happiest in a very long time. What will I say to my friends when they ask me who I spent the night with? Because just the thought that they might make jokes even remotely vulgar about it annoys me. It's going to rob me of the serenity I've been carrying with me since last night.

As soon as I open the door to the recording studio, I find three pairs of eyes peering at me: Damian, Michael, and Lilly, with smiles printed on their faces.

"Are you waiting on me for the recording?"

They burst out laughing, and I know my attempt to buy time has failed miserably.

"Where were you last night? After diner, we walked to your apartment, but you weren't there." Damian says out loud what everyone is thinking.

"I got a pizza."

"Alone?" asks Lilly with a smile on her face. It's always gossipy when she picks up something we try to hide.

"With a friend."

"Red hair and nice ass?" Michael gets straight to the point.

"Red hair, nice, smart, and an amazing blogger." I get a little annoyed, making all three of them laugh.

"Don't be pissed, don't worry. No one touches your Iris."

I sit in my chair, my mood drastically worsening. "She's not mine, and I don't know why you're making it a big deal."

They all stare at me like I'm crazy.

"Are you serious?" Lilly scrutinizes me. "Since she swooped into your arms, you seem crazy. You share posts without asking the press office, go into Manhattan clubs without someone from security accompanying you, go outside to smoke a cigarette and disappear for a whole night. You're the one who usually plans everything down to the minute. This is a big deal!"

My bandmates stare at me, and I'm aware that Lilly is speaking the truth. At times I don't recognize myself either. Sometimes I've gone so far as to convince myself that I do it out of boredom, because this down time between the end of the album and the beginning of the tour hit me hard. The apathy that assaults me makes me do strange things, but lately I've been thinking that if I can't bring Iris on our tour bus, I don't even want to go.

"Don't you think you're exaggerating just a bit? I'm getting bored, that's all. And—I don't have sex with her. I just hang out with her and then leave."

"Exactly! This is even worse," Michael says emphatically. "You don't 'hang out' with anyone. You fuck a different girl every night and move on. You don't chase one girl, you don't eat pizza together, you don't do boyfriend things."

I burst out laughing and look at each of their faces. Underneath the teasing, they're worried about me. "If I were you, I wouldn't start sending out wedding invitations. Nothing happened."

Their questioning is annoying me because talking about it diminishes what happened between us. It wasn't just a great fuck. It was nice to eat pizza tucked naked under the blankets while watching a movie, make love again before we even got to the ending titles, realize it was five in the morning and we hadn't slept a single minute yet.

"No, of course not." Michael stands up and pushes his chair until it slams into the wall, then leaves the room.

I look at the others and notice the same perplexity that I feel on their faces. It's not like Michael cares about women, especially if the woman isn't even his.

"I'm going to go talk to him."

I get up to follow him out of the recording room and find him in the small break room on this floor. It's the one least frequented by the staff because it only has a couple of sofas and a coffee machine, and no vending machines full of every snack you could want. It's where we usually take refuge when we don't feel like making small talk with people we know little about.

"Do you want to talk about it?" I ask when I see that he doesn't look up from his coffee.

He shrugs but doesn't answer.

"Did I do something wrong? Have I offended you in any way?" I have the impression that his irritation is directed at me.

Michael leans back on the sofa, releasing an almost re-signed long breath, passes his hand over his face, and then looks me straight into the eyes. "No, you didn't do anything wrong...at least not to me."

"So, what? Don't make me come over there and punch you."

Michael bursts out laughing. "Don't get upset. I don't know what's happening to me either. You're all finding yourself a woman, and I feel cut off. Lilly's in the rehearsal room on a permanent basis. You disappear to eat pizza with the redhead... Sometimes, it seems like the only solution is to go prune plants with Simon in Connecticut. It's depressing."

His words hit harder than I would have liked. I'm caught up in this bubble of bliss, excitement, and happiness, and didn't realize I was leaving behind a friend at the worst moment of my life. I feel guilty.

"It's not like I have to get married to this girl. There's nothing serious about it." I don't know if I'm reassuring him or myself.

"Really? When was the last time you chased a woman like this?"

I was a teenager, and at that time, it didn't go well at all. I look down without saying a word.

"Are you going to tell her that you've been in prison?" His question is direct and leaves no interpretations for the answer.

"We haven't reached that point yet." My voice sounds agitated, expressing all the tumult that runs in my chest.

Michael bursts out laughing and looks at me with an almost paternal gaze, not his usual look. Michael is the most brazen party-goer of all. His only desire is to go out and live life to the fullest. The truth is, he's afraid to stop, to awaken his demons.

"Really? The problem is, you're not really thinking. Ever since you met this girl, you've been behaving completely irrationally, completely out of character. Which can be a good thing. See how Damian has changed. But going out, fucking a different girl every night and forgetting about them the next morning avoids the problem of having to lie about where we've been. We've been to jail, Thomas. Nothing will ever change that and, if you really care about her, sooner or later, you'll have to tell her, and it's not going to be a pleasant conversation."

Michael's words are as sincere as they are brutal. I know he's not trying to scold me, but it still makes me feel guilty. "Don't worry, Michael, we really didn't get to that point, and we'll never get there. You know relationships aren't for me either. I tried once. I'm not going to repeat the same mistake."

So, what the hell am I doing?

Michael smiles and looks down, looking like he wants to say something, then thinks again. "The important thing is that you're convinced of it. But if you ever realize you've lost control, know that I'm here. Damian and Lilly are in their honeymoon phase. Sometimes they're not the most rational people to ask for advice. If you feel lost, I'm here."

He gets off the couch and puts his hand on my shoulder before returning to the studio, leaving me with a thousand more thoughts than I had when I walked into this room.

CHAPTER 10

Iris

"Dexter, I swear if you stick your paw in my eye again, I'll use your fur to clean the windows," I grumble angrily, realizing that the sun has yet to peep through the buildings. It's way too early.

My cat emits an annoyed meow, standing next to the bowl. He clearly understands he gets everything he wants. "You're the most annoying cat I've ever met," I mutter, filling his bowl.

I head to the bathroom and as soon as I turn on the light and look in the mirror, a sigh escapes my lips. "Do I really have dark circles under my eyes?" I wonder aloud, seeing the two shadows that contrast with the pale skin of my face.

Considering the cat wakes me up at unacceptable hours, and Thomas kept me up all night a couple of days ago, my face looks like a battleground of sleeplessness. Memories from the other night come back to my mind, and I blush like a teenager. His lips and hands have left an indelible impression that even guilt can't erase. The other night it was like my world flipped, and now I'm inside a snow globe where everything is magical. All the bright, sparkling feelings have yet to settle at the bottom. And sooner or later, they will. They're going to settle at the bottom of my heart when I realize this isn't going anywhere.

When I told Emily what happened, with my heart in my throat, she was in seventh heaven thinking this is finally my chance to be happy. But how can I be happy if the whole relationship is based on my lies? I built a house of cards, and when he finds out, everything will collapse and my heart will be buried under a pile of rubble. Sure, I could enjoy this whole great adventure without thinking about the consequences, but it's impossible to tell my heart not to invest too much energy because it won't last. The magic of waking up next to him, making love to him in the morning, and then seeing him feed Dexter as if he'd always done it was like opening a door to a future that's not real. It left a bittersweet taste in my mouth that made my heart plummet a little lower. I keep telling myself we don't have a real relationship, but is it true? He went to the corner café to get breakfast and brought it back to bed, using the keys to my apartment while I took a shower. Isn't that a relationship? Those are the intimate actions of a couple who aren't afraid to admit what they are, and when trust comes crumbling down because of my lies, that door on the future will close and crush my heart in the process.

When I get out of the bathroom, I make a cup of coffee as Dexter approaches and rubs himself against my ankles. "Now that you have a full belly, you're quite the brown-noser, aren't you?" I scold him as I pick him up. His moment of affection lasts precisely four seconds, enough time to pull out his nails and scratch them on my arm, then run over to the bed to lick his fur as if I had just soiled it with jam.

"You don't love me. That's the truth," I whisper as I grab my hot cup and approach the window.

I watch people walking quickly on the sidewalk in front of

me. The tall building with the black fire escape obstructs the view of the city I love so much. Sometimes I wonder what it's like to live in one of the apartments in those tall buildings made of glass and steel scattered around Manhattan. It must be like standing forever on top of the Empire State Building and dominating the city. What a powerful feeling to be able to do that, a feeling I'll never taste since I can barely survive week to week.

I shake off my daydream and return to my apartment, furnished with pieces I found in dumpsters and restored with a lot of love. An apartment with a room and a bathroom, and I'm lucky there's a door that divides the two. I smile at the idea and open my laptop to check my email. Since Thomas tweeted my article, new visits to my blog have exploded, as have the recurrent readers. Emails for interviews or requests for album reviews are piling up in my inbox like snow in winter. Maybe I could consider making some money from this blog, even without allowing the advertising I hate so much. I need to talk to Emily and figure out how to take advantage of this sudden rise in popularity and translate it into revenue that might make me feel a little more relaxed about money.

I start with the comments on my last interview, checking to see if there are insults—which I delete immediately—then answering questions and suggesting that those who ask for interviews contact me by email. Then I go to the old articles, and I see there is more engagement, more comments, more shares there too.

"Of course, Thomas gave this blog a pretty good boost," I whisper to no one in particular. Not even my cat listens to what I have to say anymore. "Besides being super-sexy and a god in bed, he brought in more activity than an entire marketing department."

It's at least two hours before I can finish making it to the bottom of all the post comments and messages on Instagram. When I start with the hundreds of emails, I'm already into my second coffee of the day. If Dexter continues to wake me up so early, I'll be addicted to caffeine. After deleting all the spam, I realize that another hundred and fifty emails are waiting for me. How the hell have I gone from five to a hundred and fifty? Have all these people really only discovered my existence now?

Someone even invites me to a record-launch party in Las Vegas. It doesn't look like a scam, and I put it among those to check later and do more in-depth research on the group. When I get halfway through, my heart skips a beat. What seemed like a normal request for an interview turns out to be the email every music journalist dreams of getting: the Red Velvet Curtains ask for an exclusive in-depth interview for the launch of their new album. It's signed by Lilly herself, and I have to reread it three times before I realize it's not a joke.

I stand up, pour a third cup of coffee, walk around the table, sit down, get up again, look out the window, watch passers-by for a few minutes, then sit back at the computer. The email's still where I left it. It didn't disappear, I didn't dream about it, the computer didn't burst into flames. If this is the reward for sleeping with Thomas, I'll do it again more than willingly. Just thinking about it makes me feel guilty. I'm not sure he asked them to contact me, but I have the impression that he's behind it. Why would they have noticed my existence otherwise?

It seems, however, that the email is genuine, professional,

but also very kind. And there's no sign that Thomas put a word in it. The problem is, I don't understand why she sent it to me. I'm not a magazine. I have no professional authority as a blogger. Despite Thomas's trust, I am not considered an industry insider. They're the emerging band of the year. They have the most prominent news media vying for a story from them. They're considered the heirs of the Jailbirds, and I'm just a blogger. Thomas is the only explanation for this interview, and it annoys me a little: I don't love favoritism and especially not unasked favors. If I need help, I ask. I don't need Prince Charming intervening on his white horse. In fact, to be honest, I've always hated those fairy-tale princes. As if the princesses were all brainless and unable to figure things out on their own. My mother always laughed at my protests to change the fairy tales she read me.

I don't know how to feel about this email: flattered because they chose me or angry because they didn't choose me on merit. While I have the opportunity of a lifetime for a blog like mine, I wish I'd gotten this job honestly, not because I opened my legs.

Guilt strangles me and makes me choke. I need to clear my head by getting out of my apartment and going to the only other place where my problems can take on a better perspective. So, I close my laptop without replying, grab the keys to my apartment, and head out without a second thought.

*

The garden in front of the entrance, with its perfectly cut grass and pruned trees with sinuous shapes, is surrounded by high brick walls. If I hadn't taken two subway lines that I'm sure are in New York City, it would almost seem like I ended up in another state. The white clinic and its large windows that illuminate the hallways and rooms is as bright as ever. I set foot inside and the scent of vanilla barely disguises the smell of the floor disinfectant, reminding me that this is still a clinic despite looking like a luxury hotel. Even if she is always smiling when she sees me, the nurse behind the counter is not a bearer of good news. On the contrary, those who enter are here because they have no hope of getting out.

I approach the counter, and Eleonor's blonde bob turns to me. "Good morning, Iris! How are you today? Did you rest? You look tired."

Her sweetness always leaves me breathless. I admire the people who work here, the way they manage to keep a smile in a place with so much suffering and despair. "I'm fine, thank you, I just worked late. How are you? How are the kids?"

At the mention of her children, the woman in her forties makes a grimace that makes me smile. "I just got back. I stayed home for two weeks because first Livy then Rita got bronchitis. I swear, I thought I was going crazy with those two rascals sick and locked in the house all day," she whispers almost exasperatedly.

I smile as I sign the visitor log. "I guess it's less tiring to do the double shift in here."

"You have no idea how true that is." She waves a hand in front of her face.

I wave as I walk away toward the hallway that takes me to the room that has brought me here for the last five years, at least four days a week. Walking in, I find Liberty preparing the brush to comb my mother's hair.

"How is she?" I ask when she turns to me.

The nurse in her thirties smiles at me and beckons me toward the window where my mother sits in the cream-colored armchair that mirrors the entire room's color. She's looking out the window with the same vacuous look I've seen for years. At first, I was floored by what I saw. I had no words when I first came to see her; then, over time, it became routine, and I began to have long conversations with her, even though I knew it was rare for her to answer me or even recognize my presence. I gave up trying to make her remember that I am her daughter a long time ago. She often doesn't recognize me overnight, sometimes from one hour to the next. Now, the moments when she seems to regain some clarity of mind have become really sporadic. She hasn't uttered my name for at least three years.

"Today is a good day. She spoke a little bit when she woke up. Do you want to comb it yourself?"

I nod and grab the brush she hands me before she leaves me alone with my mother, with her long coppery hair streaked with white. My mother isn't old. She's only fifty, has red hair the same shade as mine, and freckles on her nose that make her look younger. She also has green eyes like mine, but there isn't a spark any more to light them up like when I was a child and she read me fairy tales before going to bed.

"Hi, Mom, how are you? Today I have a little more time to be with you. I don't have to work." Or, I don't want to go back to that apartment and torture myself again over the meaning of the email.

"Guess what? I met a guy... He's cute. He's nice and also smart—very. The problem is, I told him a few lies, and when he finds out, I'm afraid he'll get mad at me. Now, a friend of his wants an interview on my blog. You remember I told you I have a music blog, right? The thing is, she asked me after this guy and I met, and I don't know why she asked. I'm afraid she's just going to want to meet me to do her friend a favor, not because she really appreciates my work." Or worse, because she discovered my lies and wants to tell me to stay away from Thomas, but I don't want to tell my mother about it. I don't want to say to her that I'm afraid Lilly contacted me to say that she will ruin my reputation here in New York. Or that she wants to get a restraining order against me. It would be the end of my career that, disgusting as it is, I need to help pay for this clinic.

"I don't know whether to agree to do that interview," I continue while gently brushing her long hair, "but if I don't, I risk missing an opportunity that could launch my blog like never before."

The reasoning becomes clear to me as soon as I say it out loud. If I don't accept, they'll continue with their lives while I'll have missed an opportunity that won't come around again. My guilt about lying to Thomas, and the fear of being discovered, haven't allowed me to think clearly. Add to that my chronic refusal to ask for help, and I've totally lost sight of what's important.

I don't know if Thomas did orchestrate this whole thing. But if I do the interview, I can ask Lilly directly and then tell Thomas not to get involved if that's the case. Interviewing them means being noticed by the most prominent press outlets and, perhaps, using it as a resume when I submit articles as a freelance journalist. Until now, the big news organizations have always rejected my pitches, but getting an interview that others have been struggling to land for months could be a great calling card. After this interview, even A-list artists will be more willing to give me a chance. I could request press passes to the biggest events and write articles like a real journalist.

In theory, what I have to do is obvious; but in reality, the fear of being crucified for lying to Thomas makes my stomach tighten in a vice.

"Do you want me to read you a book?" I ask my mother when I realize I've been silent for a while, thinking about my problems instead of paying attention to the dearest person I have in the world.

I get up, take her copy of *The Great Gatsby* from the night-stand, and settle into the other chair. I open to the bookmark, realizing I haven't taken the time to read her something for a few days. I'm always too busy chasing temporary distractions and overlook what's really important to me.

"Did she fall asleep?" asks Liberty when she enters the room a few hours later.

"She's been dozing off for a few minutes. Do you want me to help you put her to bed?" I offer her my support, since I know from experience what a strenuous job it is to move a sleeping adult from an armchair to the bed.

Liberty smiles at me but shakes her head. "No, leave her there. It doesn't hurt her to sit a little instead of lying down. I'm still going to have to feed her in a while, and it's best if she wakes up already sitting down."

My heart clenches thinking that she is the same woman who used to bring me to the beach, piggy-back ride me, and play with me in the water. Now she can't even hold a fork in her hand or clean her mouth after eating.

"Do you want to stay and feed her?" she asks when she sees

the sadness taking over me.

I nod and smile, watching the woman who gave birth to me dozing in front of me. "Yes, I'm in no hurry to get back to my job today."

Liberty smiles back at me, and her blue eyes light up. "You should consider your own life too. I don't need to say it every time, do I? You can't be alone looking after her for the rest of your life."

I know she's just worried about me. My mother was one of her first patients, and she saw me grow up here, basically. But I don't want to have this discussion, not today.

"I come with too much baggage not to scare guys my age to death."

For a moment, my mind goes to the only person older than me who seems to have experienced even more than I have, and I wonder how he'd react if I told him about my mom. With Thomas, everything is a thrill, a rollercoaster ride, but only because reality hasn't reached us yet. We're in a bubble where only the two of us exist, without the lies and the mundane things of everyday life.

What Thomas and I have isn't real. It's a fantasy built by decisions that were made based on false information. A beautiful movie, a love story that will end in tragedy. After the credits, the two actors will go their own ways and never meet again. I wrote a script and put Thomas in the starring role without his knowledge. I've erased facts from the past about us. I've invented an Iris that doesn't exist. I show him what he likes and hide what I don't want him to see. He called paparazzi jackals outside the restaurant that night. I can't imagine him forgiving me when he finds out I was one of them.

Rocking in
New York

PRESS *Review*

News!

Hi, Roadies!

How are you today? I'm popping in to announce that I'll be attending several concerts and events during the Christmas season, so don't miss my Instagram posts to discover new bands.

The juiciest news today, however, is that I've been contacted by the Red Velvet Curtains for an exclusive interview! You got that right. I have an opportunity to meet and interview the rising stars of rock face to face. Remember I told you they would make it big after winning that contest that took them on tour? Apparently, I was right! I can't wait to be able to tell their story.

Be kind and Rock'n'Roll,
Iris

37630 Likes 20874 Tweets 12458 Shares 3762 Comments

CHAPTER 11
Thomas

I stand for ten minutes in front of her apartment door before I decide to knock. In a normal relationship, I'd call before I showed up at her house in the middle of the afternoon, but she hasn't given me her number yet. This might suggest she doesn't particularly want to see me again, which should make me think twice about showing up at her door, but I couldn't wait any longer. It's been two days since I ended up in her bed, and I miss her so much I'm in physical agony. The guy in the apartment next door opens the door a few inches to scrutinize me from head to toe then he quickly closes it. He must think I'm a fool, and I certainly can't deny it. I'd be thinking the same thing.

I inhale deeply and raise my hand to knock when it suddenly opens, and I find myself facing Iris's perplexed face. "How long have you been here?"

"I just arrived," I'm ashamed to lie to her.

"Strange, Dexter's been restless for ten minutes. He usually gets agitated when there's someone in the hallway."

I forgot the nosy cat. "I don't know..." my voice falters while she moves aside and lets me in.

I look around, focusing on details I didn't see the first time because I was too absorbed in the woman who lives here. It's like stepping into an alternate universe, compared to the rest of the building. The apartment is tiny. To my right is a pastel blue kitchen and on the left, a small loft with a double wrought iron bed, separated by a low wooden railing and a bar-sized table with two stools, I suspect from a bar in the area. What strikes me, though, is how much personality this room has. The red brick walls contrast with the pastel blue of most of the furniture and the green plants crammed along the two large windows on the wall in front of me. The furniture is clearly salvaged from around the neighborhood. Still, it's all decorated and painted with so much creativity the room feels like a DIY Pinterest page that's one of a kind.

"Why are you here?" She doesn't sound disappointed, but I can't see her face because her hairball cat is stuck between my legs and won't let me go on if I don't offer him a few scratches on the back. After a couple, he gets annoyed and walks away. I smile because clearly, he is the boss of this house.

"If I tell you I wanted to see you, does it make me sound cheesy, mushy…basically, like a loser?"

"You're asking me? Don't you have to keep the rock star facade up? Never show your tender side?" she teases with a laugh and motions to a cup of coffee she's filling for me.

I gladly accept and sit at the only table in this small apartment. "No, actually, my behavior is swinging dangerously between a boy in love and a crazy stalker. Which do you prefer?"

"Boy in love? Aren't you going a bit too fast?" She laughs amusedly.

"Look, the way a rock star's life works, seeing a person three times in a row is like a marriage proposal for a normal person. Don't underestimate the speed of this business."

"Do you count the years in the same way you count a dog's age?" She raises an eyebrow as she tries to hide an amused smile behind the cup.

I grab her gently by the arm and pull her toward me, making her settle between my legs. The contact with her slender physique short-circuits my brain, and I have a hard time controlling my body's reaction. Her smooth, soft skin makes me want to kiss her endlessly. I want to worship her body until I bring her to orgasm and then start over again and take her back to the peak. The scent of her coconut shower gel almost makes my head spin. It's as sweet as the cookies my mother used to bake, and right now, I'd like to undress her and taste it. It's hard to stay focused on a conversation when my erection wakes up in my pants.

"Are you enjoying making fun of me?"

"I'd say yes," she admits with a candor that makes her look even sexier.

"Okay, I wish I had a reply like something you'd read in those novels you love: super smart, sarcastic, and utterly captivating. But having you so close is confusing my brain. The blood flowing down to other parts of my body is not helping any."

She bursts out laughing and gently kisses me on the lips, sending me into even more confusion. "So...why are you here?"

"I told you, I wanted to see you. After basking in the feeling of waking up with you, I can't stay away anymore." I look her straight in the eye and watch as embarrassment makes its way over her face. She's adorable when she can't hide her response to my directness. She's used to being tough and sarcastic, but

I'm starting to realize it's a defense mechanism for protection.

"You tell that to all the women you sleep with." It's a statement, but I can see she's looking for reassurance.

"I assure you, there's never a second time with a woman. Nor do I go looking for a woman after having sex. And most of all, I don't wake up next to her. I rarely even fall asleep next to a girl I've had sex with...let alone feed her demanding cat the next morning." I smile seeing her blush. "I mean, I don't know if you understand, but since you fell into my arms, I've been acting like a lunatic. Not even my friends recognize me."

Her face darkens for a moment before lowering her eyes and letting her hair fall on them. As if to protect herself from her surroundings, from me. "What if I'm not the person you imagine? What if you were acting like a fool for a woman who doesn't actually exist?"

I shrug and think about it for a while. If only she knew what I'm hiding. "Do you think I was born a famous rock star? Everyone has parts of themselves that aren't visible to others, but that doesn't mean that the part the person shows you isn't real."

A smile spreads over her face, and her arms tighten around my neck in a hug. Her lips rest on the skin of my cheek and then move toward my lips and stun me with a kiss full of a feeling I can't decipher. I wrap my arms around her narrow waist and plunge my face into the hollow of her shoulder, into her shampoo-scented hair. I inhale deeply and get her sweet smell into my brain and chest, responding to my body's need to have her.

I cover her pale skin with my lips, from her shoulder to behind her ear, savoring with my tongue what I've missed like air. She shudders under my touch, and when I stick my fingers under her shirt to undress her, she lifts her arms, leaving me breathless in front of her round breasts, which rest perfectly on the palms of my hands. I lower to kiss them, grabbing between my lips a pink nipple that reacts under the touch of my tongue. I can hear her moaning as she sinks her fingers into my hair, drawing me against her chest so I can't escape. I lower my hands to her jeans and unbutton them, then tuck two fingers under the waistband, pulling them down with her panties.

I kneel in front of her, grab her leg and put it over my shoulder. As I sink into her with my tongue and explore her intimate parts with my fingers, I look up and find her looking at me, her cascade of red hair hiding her slightly reddened cheeks, open lips, and green eyes fixed on mine. She's always beautiful enough to take your breath away, but when she comes whispering my name, dropping her head back, she's almost a heavenly vision.

I get up and smile at her. She reciprocates by fastening her arms behind my neck and kissing me as if she wants to steal my oxygen. Her tongue slips between my lips, stroking mine in a kiss laden with an eroticism that makes the erection hurt inside my pants. She seems to notice it. She lowers herself, kneeling in the same space that I occupied a few minutes ago with a mischievous smile. She unbuttons my pants and slides them, with my boxers, down to mid-thigh without ever taking her eyes off mine for a second. She's so sexy and innocent when she kneels in front of me, I could die of desire right now. How the hell did I last two days without her?

When she wraps her lips around my erection, grabbing it with her pale fingers at the base, I'm about to come like a kid for the first time. Her tongue moves sinuously, stimulating the spots that drive me crazy. Watching her head move to give me pleasure is an almost hypnotic dance, those lips slipping up and down my flesh, dictating a rhythm I can't control. She accelerates, taking me to my limit, but then slows down to prolong the agony of so much pleasure it makes my legs tremble. I can't resist. I close my eyes and lose myself in her soft lips, her tongue that caresses my erection, her throat I press against with every plunge. I can't take it anymore, and Iris lets me come inside her, the feeling so intense I almost fall over and have to lean on the stool behind me. I never want this feeling to end. I wish I could lock myself in this apartment and make love to her every day of my life, losing myself in the emotions she stirs in me—like a junkie getting his fix. I can't get enough of her. I want more of her, again and again, until I'm totally intoxicated.

I find it difficult to catch my breath, and when I open my eyes, I see her two immense green irises welcoming me. Her expression is almost curious, a half-smile on her lips that catches me by surprise. She's pleased at her control over me.

I look behind her and find Dexter staring at us with what looks like a disgusted face. "I think we just shocked the cat." I completely forgot the hairball was here watching us every single moment.

Iris giggles as she turns around and throws him an amused glance. "He'll get over it...or tonight, he'll kill me in my sleep."

"The second hypothesis is more likely." I hold her in my arms and kiss her on the forehead as we drag ourselves to sit on the bed. She's so beautiful I'd like to make her orgasm again, this time between these sheets.

"Anyway, he's going to have to get used to it, because now that I've found out what it's like to have you naked in my arms, I'm going to spend a lot more time around here making you moan my name." I kiss the tip of her nose as a mischievous smile forms on her lips.

"I don't say your name when we're in bed." She laughs amusedly.

"Yes, you do, even if you don't realize it. And it's the sexiest sound a woman can make."

"I'll have to be careful not to say the names of the other lovers then."

I turn to her and feel my heart clench. It never crossed my mind that she might have someone else, but it's not like she's my property. She can sleep with anyone she likes, and I can't really stop her. But it hurts just thinking about it.

Iris bursts out laughing. "I'm joking, don't worry. You should see your face. It looks like you swallowed a lemon."

I hug her tight and start to breathe again. "Don't joke about something like that."

Iris gets out of bed and looks at me with a smile. She doesn't seem floored by my reaction to the idea of seeing other people. "Not that I mind having you here, really, but don't you have a super busy life? I mean, is it normal that in the middle of the afternoon of a working day, you show up at someone's house?" She slips on her shirt again, leaving her pale, perfect butt uncovered and it makes me want to do anything but answer her.

"Damian and Lilly invited Michael and me to their house for dinner tonight. I'm wondering if you wanted to come too."

"No." Her answer is so sudden that a punch in the stomach

would have hurt less. Her face is a mix of concern and terror—as if I'd asked her to go to war. Her jaw clenches and her eyes lower without meeting mine, making me realize her answer was not impulsive after all.

"Wow, I expected having to convince you a little, but your answer seems pretty final," I admit, not hiding my disappointment. "Can I at least know why?"

I see her blush, slip on her panties, and I feel embarrassed with my pants still mid-thigh. How the hell have we gone from unrestrained orgasms to this total awkwardness?

"I don't think it's a good idea."

"If it's because they didn't invite you directly, I can assure you it's not a problem. In fact, if you want, I'll call Lilly right now to let her know."

"No, I'm busy," she replies dryly, and I can tell it's a lie. But I don't go any further. I have the feeling that insisting would make the situation worse.

The silence in the room suddenly got even more awkward. She steels herself against me, giving me her back, while she fiddles with something in the pantry that doesn't need to be fixed. I pull up my jeans, watching her for a few minutes. I don't know what I did wrong, but it's clear from her demeanor she doesn't want me around.

"I guess I should go..."

"Okay, bye." She doesn't even turn around.

I watch her for a few more seconds, the temptation to walk to her, turn her around and ask her why she's angry is strong, but I feel hurt. I don't expose myself like that to anyone, and her dry rejection stings. I go out the door and close it behind me without turning around, walking down the hallway until I get out into the open air and inhale thoroughly. It's not enough to relax the grip on my stomach that's almost making me vomit. I approach a side street, busier than where Iris's building is located, and stop a taxi, ready to go home with my tail between my legs.

The sense of disappointment that grips my chest is almost heartbreaking. I thought I was more than just a celebrity fuck. Her body language, the way she asks about my job, I thought she was really interested in me. That we could take a step beyond just the random encounters. Am I seeing more than what's really here? Because she didn't give me the impression she was looking for a famous fuck. I was convinced she was really into part of my life that she's loved from the start. She's the one who managed to find our first demos on eBay. She should be ecstatic at the opportunity to get to know the band that's made her passionate about music since she was a kid. I assumed that her fan spirit would win over the nervousness of a dinner with me.

I don't think even baking cookies all afternoon can help ease the pain of her confusing, hurtful behavior.

*

"Can you tell us what the hell is going on?" Michael stares at me across the table, chewing on a piece of meat he just picked up from his plate, which, unlike mine, is now empty.

"It's true. You're particularly quiet tonight. Is something bothering you?" Lilly, next to me, rests her hand on my arm, her expression concerned.

I try to muster a genuine smile, but I realize I can't do it when my jaw muscles tighten. "No, I'm just a little tired. There's nothing to worry about."

"We have nothing to do these days. How the hell can you be tired?" Damian points out amusedly while Lilly gives him the side-eye.

"He's right. And besides, you don't get this cranky when you're tired," Michael says.

I realize there's no escaping their interrogation, so I put down my fork and let this evening take a turn that annoys me. "I asked Iris to come to dinner with me tonight, and she said no in a rather brutal way," I admit.

The silence that descends over the table is unexpected. Everyone is looking at me with wide eyes and open mouths.

"I didn't kill anyone, don't look at me like that!"

"Excuse us, but you can't drop a bomb like that and expect us not to be stunned." Lilly smiles at me, but I see she is worried.

"What bomb? It's a dinner, which I don't know if you noticed, but she said no. I didn't ask her to marry me." The nervous laughter coming from my chest makes me think it would have been better if I hadn't come tonight.

"Honestly, it's like you did." The smirk on Michael's face floors me.

"It's just a damn dinner!" I snap, annoyed.

"It's a dinner with the only people you consider family. It's like you asked to introduce her to your parents without even taking her out on a date." Damian's voice is calm, but it doesn't hurt any less to hear the mention of my parents.

"You're reading way too much into something that really doesn't matter." I try to defend myself. I never took anyone out to dinner. I never felt the desire. This is new for me too, and it scares me to death because without realizing it, I have reached the point where I am thinking about the future and haven't noticed it.

"Look, there's nothing wrong with falling in love." Lilly's voice is sweet, and she has all good intentions, but I don't want to hear that word.

"I'm not in love, and I have no intention of being so in the future."

She looks at me with a creased forehead and an irritated look. "What the hell is wrong with growing up and settling down with a family? It's not so bad being in a relationship, you know?" She's scolding all of us.

I look up at Damian and Michael and see that they're putting as much thought as I am into her question. "I can't speak for them, but I have my reasons for not being in one."

"What are they? What could possibly be the reasons why you categorically refuse to open your heart to a woman? If it's because you've been in prison, I can assure you that that's something you get over in a relationship. You're not criminals."

I appreciate her optimism and stubbornness, but my story has nothing to do with Iris and the fear of losing her. It has to do with me and my past with women. I didn't want this dinner to get so depressing. "It's hard to trust again when the only woman you've ever fallen in love with is also the one who destroyed your life. Do you know how I ended up in prison?"

Lilly shakes her head, and I can see from her expression that she's preparing for a painful story. After Damian's story, she knows our past was anything but easy.

"I was thirteen when I met Rita. She was a beautiful girl, two years older than me, and she had her eyes on the loser boy with pimples, me. It was a dream come true, she French kissed me, let me feel her up...Christ, I wasn't even fourteen, and she fucked me in her bunk bed one afternoon after school. I was in love with her, I felt invincible. I would do anything to keep her and literally did everything...including handing over drugs to drug dealers on behalf of her brother. I wasn't even fourteen, and I became a drug mule. I'd carry packages of cocaine and heroin in my backpack and come back with wads of money the size of an encyclopedia. I did it for her because I thought she loved me for doing it. She made me feel important, indispensable to her life.

"Until they caught me, two years later, at an age when I could go to juvie. And you know what I found out when they locked me up? She had four other kids around, all my age. She made us so crazy over her so we'd do anything for her. I loved her. I trusted her completely, I put my life in her hands, and she made me into a criminal." I look up at Lilly, tearing up, feeling my pain. "That's why I find it hard to imagine I'll ever fall in love again."

Lilly moves toward me and hugs me hard. I feel the love she pours into the gesture, causing the knot in my throat to melt a little.

"Well, at least you didn't ask her to come to the Metropolitan Museum's Christmas fundraiser with you," Michael blurts out, laughing and trying to lighten the tension.

I turn to him, and my embarrassed face betrays me.

Lilly's eyes grow as big as the plate in front of her. "Don't tell me you did. That's a huge step— it would mean making your relationship official to the whole world. The paparazzi will be all over you."

Events like Christmas at the Met are the hunting ground for gossip. Officially, you show up for an evening dedicated to a particular charitable cause. There's endless small talk, toasts so fake they sound like movie quotes, and you give an avalanche of money to help someone you'll never meet, making only your accountant happy because he can deduct it from the pile of taxes you have to pay. These are events advertised to exhaustion, where everything has to be perfect, from the way you're dressed to the person you decide to take. Inviting Iris would have meant saying to the world, 'Look, this is my girlfriend, and she's beautiful as hell.'

"No, I didn't invite her." I chuckle nervously.

"But you wanted to do it, didn't you?" Damian says, laughing.

"I thought I'd do it after this dinner..." I admit with incredible embarrassment.

"Christ, we lost him too," Michael teases me amid everyone's laughter.

"Stop, you two! You're bad friends. Can't you see how much he's taken with this girl?" Lilly scolds them. "Maybe she felt embarrassed because I offered her the interview with the Red Velvet Curtains, and she doesn't know how to manage the relationship outside the workplace. Or maybe she just felt floored by your proposal, you haven't known each other for a long time... Or she was afraid to make you look bad with your friends, girls sometimes become so paranoid. You have to consider that you're rich and famous and she's a normal girl. Maybe she thinks that we're used to glitzy dinners or something, and she feared feeling out of place." She tries to cheer me up while my two friends just go on laughing.

"Lilly, don't worry about me. She said no to dinner. It's not a tragedy. And you arranged that interview because you're as curious as a monkey and you can't wait to meet her, so you're going to ask her yourself why she refused. Don't think I believed your 'we have to reach out to fans who don't read traditional newspapers' story." I laugh and try to calm her down.

"But you're hurt. I can tell!"

"I'm just a little disappointed with her answer, but she didn't stab me in my back. I'll survive!" I smile.

"But it bothers you that she didn't give you a chance." Michael's observation and careful scrutinization of the situation are out of character.

I think about it, trying to formulate an answer that doesn't make me look crazy. "No one likes rejection. Yes, I was hurt, because I had assumed that she'd accept. It's my fault."

Damian frowns. "And she didn't give you any explanation?"

"She said she had something to do, but I know it was a lie to get out of going... She seemed almost angry, and I can't understand what the hell I said to set her off."

"You have to ask her to clarify. Contrary to what men think, women do not get angry for no reason. Maybe you didn't notice, but you did something that bothered her."

I think about the conversation with Iris. "No, I'm sure I didn't do anything wrong."

"All the more reason you should go and clarify with her." Lilly seems determined on this point.

"And tell her what? Sorry I set you off, but I don't know where I went wrong?"

"Well, would you rather leave it like it is, without some

explanation?"

"It's not like I can go knock on her door every freaking day like some kind of madman. I'm already ridiculous!"

Lilly rolls her eyes and shakes her head disappointedly as my friends burst out laughing yet again.

I, on the other hand, can't relax. This evening opened my eyes to one thing: I put my heart in Iris's hands when I started pursuing her and didn't even realize it. I'm terrified that one day she might crush it and throw it away, leaving me broken hearted. I couldn't stand it, not again.

CHAPTER 12
Thomas

Literally twenty-four hours ago I left this exact apartment, and now here I am, a perfect idiot, holding two coffees, home-made cookies, and a supermarket bag filled with any food I could find. I hate it when Lilly gets all caught up in 'things have to be solved.' Easy for her to say—she's not the one who had to come up with an idiotic excuse to show up here today, having no idea where to start. Iris might yell at me, kick me out of the house, tell me never to show up here again. Hell, she could call the police to escort me to the nearest asylum, but I don't care. Yesterday I wanted to take her out to dinner, today I'm demanding a meal with her.

I breathe deeply and knock, and it takes longer than usual for her to open it. When she finally does, I'm half turned toward the hallway, ready to change my mind.

"Okay, I see you more than my best friend lately," she says with a smile, giving me room to enter.

Her face is smiling, not tense. She's not doing a happy dance seeing me, but she doesn't seem to want to tear my eyes out either. She's not mad at me anymore, which gives me hope. I immediately find myself with the cat between my feet and almost trip to the floor. She smiles and raises her hands in a completely innocent way.

"You're the one who attracts animals. He doesn't do this with me."

"I suspect this is all a scheme to kill me and make it look like an accident. Maybe he's taking revenge for the show he had to watch yesterday," I observe, puzzled as he walks through my legs rubbing his muzzle.

Iris giggles and I look up just in time to see her eyes shine, and a sincere smile. I could watch her for hours. "Probably."

I raise the bag in my hand and put it on the kitchen counter while she looks at me curiously. "Before you start freaking out like you did for yesterday's dinner invitation, let me explain, okay?"

Iris lowers her eyes, blushing, and nods. Perhaps she's regretting the way she reacted at invitation. "Okay, but I didn't freak out. Let's be clear."

"You didn't even turn around when I left. You were so focused on an empty shelf you wouldn't talk to me."

She rolls her eyes and crosses her arms over her chest. "Of course, you're touchy. You take everything personally."

I laugh, but I avoid fighting back.

She continues: "However, I want to apologize for my reaction yesterday. You took me by surprise, and I felt overwhelmed with feelings. I'm not used to certain invitations, and I got scared."

"I swear, I replayed the conversation in my head a thousand times, and I couldn't understand why I pissed you off," I confess.

"I wasn't angry, I was overwhelmed with emotion, and when that happens, I keep people at a distance because I don't know how to handle it. I'm not good with people, especially people I don't know very well."

I nod, understanding her point. "So, you weren't mad at me."

"No. I was pretty mad at myself because I wanted you to stay, but I didn't know how to tell you I didn't feel like coming to dinner."

I nod and smile, reassuring her I'm not angry. "I went to the supermarket to get you something. Last night I wanted to take you out to dinner, but you didn't want to. I understand. My friends scolded me and told me I acted like a lunatic. But I really want to have dinner with you. So I went to the supermarket and, not knowing what you particularly liked, I grabbed more or less what I saw here in the house...plus, I added some things I like and would like you to try."

I hope she understands my explanation for the groceries. I actually noticed she doesn't have much to eat in the house. I get the impression she's struggling to make ends meet.

Iris looks at me surprised, opens her mouth a couple of times, trying to find the words, but then closes it. She peeks inside the bag and then looks up in disbelief. "You went to the grocery store for me?" she asks, like it's a heroic gesture.

I swear I don't understand this girl. I invite her out to dinner, and she practically freaks out and shuts me out. I show up at her house with groceries, and she almost starts crying with gratitude.

"Well, I don't know...I mean, not knowing what you like, I just bought some random stuff," I admit nervously.

Suddenly, I'm afraid she hates everything I put in that bag, but she surprises me and takes me by the hand, guiding me to the fridge. The shock of touching her skin is so thrilling I almost smile like a goofy kid in his first crush. When she opens the fridge, I see completely empty shelves, aside from half a lemon, and some off-brand of ketchup that's been out of production for five years.

"You practically saved my life," she says with a half-smile, then blushes, embarrassed. Her reaction makes me realize something I haven't considered. Maybe she thinks I'm mooching off of her. When she made coffee yesterday, I noticed she hesitated before doubling the grounds she put in the filter. I got the impression she normally used half that amount. When I offered her a drink at the club, I saw her covertly counting the money inside her wallet, grimacing with concern. I recognize those signals—in my family, there were many times we struggled to make ends meet. Even with the Jailbirds, when we were nobodies, we'd split a coffee in fourths. I wouldn't want her to take my intrusion the wrong way, reading a message I don't want to send.

"I'm glad I did something good," I smile as she closes the fridge and approaches the bag.

She peeks into it and smiles as she starts pulling out what's inside, studying everything. I watch her, gripping my hands on the kitchen counter to keep myself from moving her hair away from her face to see it more clearly.

"I love these cookies," she smiles as she pulls out the package and puts it on a shelf. "And how did you know I like Froot Loops?" she wonders out loud.

I point to one of the two windows where there's an empty box of cereal in which she stores paint brushes.

"Oh." She smiles awkwardly. Maybe she didn't expect me to notice so much about her apartment since we've been busy with other things. She doesn't know that everything about her attracts my attention, like a kid in a playground.

"Santa Claus cupcakes and bagels in a reindeer bag?" She looks at me amusedly.

"You know everything is Christmas themed right now. It's impossible to find normal packaging. Even the mayonnaise looks festive. I know because I bought it without looking at the label, thinking it was ketchup. Who the hell puts mayonnaise in a red container?"

Iris bursts out laughing as she puts the blueberry jam and a can of crab and potato soup on the shelf. "You've also thought of coffee. You're my hero. I finished it. I love this! Cream cheese on bagels always drives me crazy. But when you order it in coffee shops, you get those tiny packages that only give you a thin layer of cheese. I like to slather it all over that hot bagel!"

"Me too. Have you tried the veggie cream cheese?"

Iris shakes her head.

"Then I'll bring it next time I see you!"

"Gnocchi and pesto?" she asks with a puzzled expression then an amused smile. "I understand you're a rock star, but do you really have someone who cooks Italian at home? It wouldn't even cross my mind of buying something like this."

I laugh at her confusion. "First of all, when I'm home, I do the cooking. I've been living alone long enough to know how to cook a fair number of dishes and not starve," I say, feeling proud when I see she looks pleasantly surprised. "Second, I don't usually cook Italian. It's a dish my mother always made on Sundays for lunch—the 'Sunday meal'—and every time I cook it, it reminds me of when I was a child." I can't hide the bit of melancholy in my voice.

Looking at her face, I think she understands how I feel. She smiles. "Does your mother have Italian roots?"

She's intrigued, there's no malice in her question, and I'm a little bewildered because I usually never get to talk about my family. "No, absolutely nothing can connect her to Italy. I don't think she's ever left her home town, actually, so no travels to the other side of the globe. She fell in love with her neighbor, they got married and lived two houses away from where they grew up." I say this with a bit of hesitation, biting my lower lip to force me to stop. Even Damian doesn't know this story.

Luckily, she is smart enough to understand that the topic makes me uncomfortable and finds a way to lighten it without interrupting the conversation. "So no Italian origins, but I hope you know how to cook it because I don't even know where to start."

I take the packet of gnocchi in one hand and the pesto sauce in the other. "Now? I was hoping you'd say yes, but I thought you'd already eaten."

"Why not? Do you have anything against gnocchi at two in the afternoon?" she asks me with a raised eyebrow, and I wonder how long she's gone without eating. This girl didn't even see the shadow of a lunch.

"Absolutely not. Tell me where I can find a deep pot," I reply, despite still being full from the salmon and avocado I ate for lunch.

She points to a lower cabinet, and I pull out the pot, fill it with water, and put it on the stove.

"Do you have salt?" I ask her, and she looks insecure about

what to do.

"Isn't there salt in the sauce already?" she asks, handing me the jar.

I smile with the bravado of someone about to show off their heavy artillery in front of a woman. And for once, surprisingly, I'm still dressed. It's pleasant surprise I've never experienced before. "It's used to salt the water for the gnocchi, so they get more flavor."

She looks at me like I'm a Michelin-starred chef.

"Don't make that face. It's not like I'm sending the Space Shuttle into orbit," I protest when her admiring eyes embarrass me.

She passes me salt and takes one of the two cups of coffee I brought her "This isn't black coffee, is it?" she asks before sipping it.

I smile at her while I pull out a sauce pan and dump the pesto in, too runny for my taste, and start to thicken it by lighting the low heat under the pot "To be honest, they're both the same. I asked your friend to give me two of what you like."

I look at her furtively while I take the cup of coffee and sip some of it. It's surprisingly good.

"Did you regret it?" she studies me to see my reaction.

"It's good. I like the vanilla taste, even if it's not my favorite," I admit honestly. I'm not one to keep quiet about what I really like to make people happy. It isn't fair to them.

"And what do you really like?"

"The caramel macchiato, even though your friend looked at me horrified when I ordered it and told me that the best she could do was an organic latte with a splash of caramel. So, I opted for what you get."

Iris bursts out laughing, one of those belly laughs that makes her throw her head back and turn my whole world upside down. "Emily hates coffee chains where all drinks are the same. It's a miracle she let you order, and hasn't kicked you out of the cafè."

I smile at her and finish my coffee. "I probably intimidated her with my fame." I pose like the rock star I am not, just to see her smile.

"Emily? No, trust me. You may be a god who fell to the earth, but you will never have that effect on her. That's why I like to go to concerts with her. She won't squeal for anyone."

Her explanation gives me a pretty clear idea of what their friendship is like—they're perfect for each other.

"What are you doing now?" she asks when I put the gnocchi in the boiling water after salting it.

"I cook the gnocchi. You have to leave them in until they float."

"No timer?" she asks, scandalized.

I laugh at her horrified face and shake my head. "No. But trust me, it's simple. I didn't understand it at first either, but then I saw my mother do it dozens of times, and I learned."

She nods, frowning and observing the water starting to boil again. "It's true! They're floating!" she exclaims, like a little girl who sees snow for the first time.

I laugh again, her naivety making her look even younger. "See? It's not that complicated."

"You're a chef, as well as a decent drummer," she teases me.

"Decent, you say?" I raise an eyebrow in defiance, though the sly smile doesn't leave my face.

I drain the gnocchi and add them to the pan with the pesto and stir, then I put them on the two plates she pulled out.

"Come on, you're good! I'll give you that."

"Wait till you taste the pesto gnocchi. You will be ecstatic at my skills."

She smiles as she pulls a bottle of wine from a kitchen shelf. "I don't know if red wine goes with pesto gnocchi, but I have nothing but water to drink. I think Emily brought me this bottle. I never buy wine."

I nod and set up the bar table in the middle of the room, rummaging through the drawers to look for things like it's my house. It's weird how she lets me do it, and I don't feel particularly embarrassed. It's like we've been doing this routine for years, and haven't only known each other for a handful of days. This is what scares me the most: with her, everything is so natural and simple I'm afraid it's just a beautiful fantasy that will hurt when I wake up.

"I confess that I never understood the wine-food pairings. Usually, when I go out, I'm lazy. The restaurants I go to have someone who chooses wines as a job, so I let them do everything," I candidly admit.

"You're right. After all, you can't be an expert on anything. For example, I like photography and music. It's not like I start taking a cooking class just because I have to feed myself." She shrugs and sits next to me as I open the bottle of wine and pour it.

I look around and focus on the black-and-white photos of New York City that I've already noticed hanging on the walls. People walking, others dancing, a piano in Central Park, and children playing around it while an elderly gentleman is sitting on the bench, are all life shots of a city full of electricity, life, movement.

"Did you take them?"

"Yes, I've been living in Manhattan since I was born, and the camera is something I've always had with me." Her explanation is as simple as it is intriguing. I would like to ask her more about her, her family, her friends, but I know that these questions would lead to questions about me that I'm not yet ready to deal with.

"They're gorgeous. Have you ever thought about selling photos for a living? Someone would pay a lot of money for those. They're stunning. I'm not just saying that."

I see her blanch and cough and realize I'm staring at her. She regains some composure and sips her wine to cover an embarrassed smile. "Not really. To do that you have to be connected with art galleries. I tried to go to the most famous ones, but they just said: 'We'll let you know' and then disappeared. I needed a job that paid the bills. I can't count on the slim chance that someone will walk into a gallery and buy my shots."

"It's a shame because these photos should be shared with the world."

Iris smiles, and I feel something melt inside me, like a teenager in love. "Have you always wanted to be a musician? Or do you have any other passions from when you were a kid?"

"As a child, I wanted to be a lawyer."

"Really?"

I smile at the memory as I sip to wash down a bite. "One day, an insurance lawyer came to our house to ask my father for something. I remember he parked his shiny black car in front of the house. I was maybe seven or eight years old, I didn't know what kind of car it was, but I clearly remember thinking it was expensive. Our family never had much money, and for a while, I believed being a lawyer was the way to buy things for my family, not just a car."

"Then you started playing and discovered your calling?"

"No, my mother told me I would have to memorize a lot of laws to be a lawyer, and I wouldn't see a courtroom or the real money before I was thirty. My passion for that profession died there."

Iris laughs. "Can't say you're not honest."

I smile, scared at how easy it is to talk about my family with her. A dangerous subject that I'm dealing with too lightly. "Then I found out I'm good on drums, and I make more money than a lawyer," I joke.

"But you didn't buy the luxury car! Or did you?" she asks, puzzled.

"No, living in New York, I don't even think about buying my own car. Do you know any New Yorkers who have one?"

"I actually know several who don't even have a driver's license."

"See?"

"But from what you tell me, you haven't always lived in New York... did you have one before?"

This is the question I was hoping wouldn't come. Iris is brilliant. She doesn't miss a detail. "I started this job so young that I didn't need it." I'm so comfortable with her, I don't feel the same nervousness I normally do when giving answers about my past to strangers. "You, on the other hand, had some childhood dreams? What did you want to do be when you grew up?"

Iris smiles and shakes her head. "A ballerina. I started in dance class, but I found out very quickly that God gave me the coordination and grace of a person with two left feet. My dreams of glory and joining Juilliard were shattered at an early age," she says with humor, and I laugh with her.

What's so great about this girl is that she's down to earth and grounded and, at the same time, she knows how to laugh at herself. For a moment, it almost crossed my mind to tell her about my past. Stupid idea, since it would not only be my story, but my friends' whose trust I could never betray.

For the first time in my adult life, I find myself spending an afternoon in complete harmony with a woman, with clothes on and stomach in a turmoil of excitement. It's not so much her clothes I want to strip off in these moments, but rather the protective layers she carries around her heart. Sharing glimpses of my life, I find that she opens up about hers, and I treasure this information like gold. Minute by minute, I find myself lost in a maze of emotions from which I no longer want to escape.

CHAPTER 13
Iris

I've pulled a box of photos out of the closet that I had put aside when the reality of life required all my attention. Thomas is flipping through them, taking an infinite time between photos, and I'm watching him with my heart in my throat, fearing his judgment. In this moment, my passion for photography doesn't disgust me like it usually does when I work as a paparazzo, and the feeling is so pleasant I can't stop smiling. Snuggled up on my bed, he analyzes every composition, questions me, marvels, makes me feel like the center of his attention, of his world, and I find it difficult to get used to it.

"Wow, this one of the Romeo and Juliet statue in Central Park is amazing. How the hell did you find a moment when there were no snow prints on the ground? Did you cover them?"

His expression is so incredulous it makes me laugh. "No, actually, this picture was taken at seven o'clock on a Sunday morning in December, after a snowstorm. It was dawn and the snow had stopped falling for less than half an hour. An hour later, the prints were already there. There wasn't much light, but a tripod and long exposure can work wonders."

He's about to say something, but we are interrupted by a knocking on the door. "Are you waiting for someone?" he asks, intrigued.

I cover my face with my hands and curse. Wrapped in this bubble of happiness this afternoon, I completely spaced out on my plans for the evening. "I forgot about dinner with Emily and Albert."

Thomas pulls his phone out of his pocket. His eyes go wide. "It's already eight o'clock."

Emily knocks again violently.

"I'd better go open before the neighbors call the police."

He giggles behind me as I get out of bed and catch up with Dexter, who's already in front of the door. When I open it, I find Emily with a huge pizza in her hands and Albert right behind her with two bottles of wine, one tequila, and six beers. I raise a perplexed eyebrow. I wasn't going to get drunk tonight.

"Finally!" my friend yells as she enters. "Were you getting off staring at a picture of Thomas? Oh! I see you have the real deal right here." She admires Thomas, who is fastening his shoes sitting on my bed.

"Emily!" I scold her, certain my cheeks are burning with embarrassment.

"Look, it's not my fault you take a lifetime to open the door. One can only imagine what's going on behind closed doors."

"Emily, stop it!" I try to sound stern, but it comes out shrill and desperate.

Meanwhile, behind me, Thomas laughs, and I don't dare look him in the face, at least until he encircles my waist with his arms and kisses me on the cheek.

"So, you like to masturbate to my photos. Do you use the ones you find online or the posters they sell on the record company's website?" he teases me as Albert looks at us disgusted and goes to put the drinks in the fridge.

"I don't do that!" I say more embarrassed than indignant.

"Look, there's nothing wrong with it." Emily sides with him, laughing.

"I'm going now before I discover any more secrets that might shock me." He kisses me on the nose.

"You have no idea how many there are," mumbles Albert, annoyed while Emily punches his side and he grunts. Thomas doesn't seem to notice his comment, but my heart jumps in my throat.

"Hey, you can stay for dinner," Emily proposes with a smile from ear to ear.

"Thank you, but I leave you to the evening you have planned. I've already had the pleasure of her company all afternoon." He turns to me and says softly, "Look...I know it didn't go very well with the dinner invitation, but there is this Christmas event at the Met...I don't need you to give me an answer now...I mean, but I'd love it if you came with me."

I'm staring at him like he's a mirage. Did he really just invite me to the most famous event of the winter season? This is a surprise of epic proportions. I open and close my mouth a couple of times without being able to formulate a coherent answer.

"Think about it?" He turns around to leave—smart move to drop the bomb when he's already on his way out. He opens the front door, turns around with a smile, and gently kisses my lips. Before he goes out and closes it behind him, he winks, and I smile like a sixteen-year-old on cloud nine.

"Look at the two lovebirds." Emily's voice is a mixture of teasing and dreamy sighs.

"Not lovebirds. And do you think it's a good call to embarrass me like that in front of him?"

"I swear, I had no idea he was here. Otherwise, I would have said worse!" She bursts out laughing as I throw a pillow at her in response.

"Are you fucking him? Christ, you've stooped low," Albert says bluntly.

Emily rolls her eyes, exasperated, and I don't know what to say. Albert asked me out once and I said no. Since then, he's become a plague every time I have a guy interested in me, whether or not I actually date him. We all go out together, we have fun at concerts, and he often helps me with extensive research and systems I don't have access to. He works for a newspaper; he verifies that facts and sources are accurate and reliable on behalf of the journalists who then put the paper's signature on their articles. He has access to means and sources, sometimes legal, much more often illegal, that I'll never have. Every now and then, I feel guilty for taking advantage of him, but he always offers to help, and sometimes I give in to temptation.

"What do you want me to tell you? It's not true?" I snap, annoyed. I don't like to answer him so meanly, but sometimes frustration outweighs my determination to respond nicely.

Albert gives me the side-eye and offers me a piece of pizza without answering my questions. Luckily, it's Emily who comes to my rescue, breaking the tense silence between us. "Do you realize that Thomas had the arrogance to come and ask me for a caramel macchiato today? To me, who works in a place that doesn't serve that junk."

She's outraged. I laugh, amused. "I know, he told me. You

terrified him."

"I wanted him to learn his lesson. You have to train them, or they'll keep ordering caramel macchiatos!"

Emily jumps into her invective against the chains that transform people into robots, and Albert and I are forced to grab the alcohol out of the fridge to turn the evening into a more cheerful one. A pizza, a bottle of wine, and six cans of beer later, we're sprawled on the bed with my laptop on Albert's legs googling stupid things like what penguins smell like while Emily opens the bottle of tequila.

"Do you realize that you slept with the rock star you've had a crush on since you were sixteen?" she asks me in a tone that is a mixture of conspiratorial and dreamy.

We're all a bit tipsy, and maybe more than that. Unfortunately, when Emily is drunk, she tends to focus obsessively on a topic, and this time she chooses Thomas.

"Don't talk about it. It seems absurd." I cover my face with my hands, a little ashamed. I don't know if I'm blushing about the turmoil of emotions that affect me or because I'm drunk.

"Really absurd if you consider you've slept with someone you don't know anything about," says Albert.

"Can you explain what your problem is?" Emily glares daggers at him.

Albert blushes but doesn't give up. "It's true! If he was any other guy, you'd never have ended up in bed without knowing anything about him. Doesn't it seem odd that there's no information out there about that band's past? They seem to have materialized out of nowhere," he says, agitated.

"He's right. They have that halo of mystery that makes them to-die-for sexy, but, if you think about it, zero personal information," Emily admits.

Not that I didn't think about it. It's true what she says, and maybe Albert is also slightly right: if he was any other guy I met at a club, I'd never be having sex with him without knowing anything about him. When you look at famous people, at the glossy life their press offices put out, you feel like you know them like friends, but that's not true. We only know what they want the public to know about them, superficial things that satisfy the curiosity of their readers, but not what really matters. I know Thomas's shoe size because I read it in a fashion magazine, but not where he's lived his whole life.

"It's not true that I don't know him. Today he opened up a lot with me!" The need to justify my actions mingles with the guilt that's been gripping me for days, making my voice sound shrill like a whiney little girl.

"If it's true that he opened up so much with you, prove it," Albert challenges me as Emily passes me the bottle.

I throw down a generous swig of tequila, trying to wash away the nervousness Albert stirs up, when in fact, this was a perfect day. I've never had such a wonderful afternoon just staying in the house talking to a guy. Albert's words threaten to destroy the bubble I've built around myself to keep away the lies that try to crush me. I want to nip that negativity in the bud, drown it with so much alcohol it can never resurface.

"Indulge him. Otherwise, he won't give up."

"If what I say tonight leaves this room, you two are dead. No matter who talks. Do you understand me?"

"Who do you think we're going to tell? We're all drunk! Tomorrow morning, we won't remember this conversation. We'll only have a big headache to remind us of this night,"

Emily mumbles as she pours another drink.

"Okay. Let me see... Well, he's not from New York but a small town around here whose name I don't know."

"Really?" Emily is wide-eyed.

"That's not news. Everyone suspected this because no schools in New York City remember them. Without the name of the town, it's not even information, it's a random guess," Albert complains as the blood begins to boil in my veins.

"You want names? His mother's name is Susan and his father Arthur," I snap, annoyed, as a half-smile appears on his lips.

"Now, this is what I want. Start talking." He leans on my shoulder and hands me the bottle of tequila after smelling it and wrinkling his nose without touching it.

I drink again, feeling my throat and stomach burning like I've swallowed lava. I pass the bottle to Emily, who takes a sip and makes a disgusted face. It's not our favorite alcohol, but it's doing the job—driving away that feeling of heaviness brought on by Albert's insistence.

"Anything else you want to confess to Uncle Albert?" he jokes.

Emily passes me the bottle of tequila again, and I take another sip. The evening took a strange turn: I feel my head spin, and I have to squeeze my eyes a couple of times to focus on Albert. On the other hand, the lightness filling my chest feels good.

"Come on, spill some more secrets while I go get the salt. Tequila alone sucks." Emily crawls off the bed and drags herself to the kitchen cabinet to grab the blue container I keep on the top shelf.

"He doesn't have a car..." I realize I'm slurring, and Albert's smile is getting blurry.

"What the hell kind of information is that? Most people who live in this city don't have a car," he groans, and I'd like to punch him.

"I don't think he even has a driver's license, because he said he didn't need one where he spent his teenage years."

"Really? A kid in a small town who doesn't have a driver's license? They make you get it when you go to high school. You don't even have to leave the building to take the class!"

I take another sip from the bottle, and Emily sticks a slice of lime in my mouth after smearing my lips with salt. I almost throw up and take another drink of the tequila to rinse my mouth of the horrible taste of salt.

"Where did he go to high school?" Albert pushes.

"I don't think he went because he told me he didn't have many friends his age."

The words come out drowsy, and my eyes close until Emily gives me a shove to wake me up. I study her, and her face is blank, without expressions. For a moment, it seems to me that she doesn't even have eyes.

Albert is talking to me, but I respond with difficulty, slowly, like I have a potato in my mouth and can't form the words properly. Sometimes I nod with my head, sometimes I don't. Albert gets close to my face and doesn't stop asking questions. Then I close my eyes, and even his voice slowly disappears into oblivion.

CHAPTER 14

Iris

The cat begins to meow, and my head throbs with every sound from his throat.

"If you don't shut up, I'm going to choke you," I whisper to Dexter, who's at my feet and whining, disappointed because he knows his breakfast is delayed this morning.

I open an eye to see what time it is. My mouth feels like sandpaper, and my head starts to throb so hard I almost throw up. And then I do. Clinging to any surface that can support me, I barely make it to the bathroom. How much did I drink last night?

When I get up and grip the sink to brush my teeth and wash my face, I find a note from Emily attached to the mirror.

'I had to go to class. I have no idea where Albert is. Maybe Dexter killed him and buried the body. Let's pretend nothing happened.'

I laugh and immediately regret it. The pain hammering my head is unbearable. When I finally get out of the bathroom, I run into an agonized Dexter lying on the ground and emitting an excruciating lament.

"Stop looking at me like I killed someone. I know it's late, but meowing like this won't make me go any faster." Dexter jumps on the table and stares at me like I'm a murderer. Sooner or later, I'm sure, he'll kill me in my sleep. When I pour his food and he doesn't even come near the bowl, I give him the stink eye. Is he trying to make me pay for drinking last night?

While I prepare coffee, I look around, searching for my laptop, and, after a moment of panic, I find it sticking out from under one of the pillows. I open it and approach the table to charge it. When I open my email, I notice that some messages dated last night have been opened. I try to recollect what happened and a series of confusing images of a bottle of tequila and some heated conversation with Albert come back to my memory, but that's all.

One thing, though, I remember distinctly: Albert had my computer on his lap all evening, doing moronic searches on Google. It bothers me to think he read my emails. They're mostly work-related articles I've written, concerts I've been invited to. I have nothing to hide, but they're still private. I don't want to share them with anyone, let alone Albert. I check the browser history and am surprised when I find it empty. Before Thomas arrived, I remember working. Is it possible I didn't open any internet pages? I grab my phone and text Emily. 'What the hell did Albert do last night with my computer?'

She answers almost immediately. 'Nothing, I think. He was looking for stupid videos of penguins, as far as I can remember. Is there a problem?'

'My browser history of the last twenty-four hours is gone.'

'He must have watched porn while we were drunk. It's Albert. I wouldn't be surprised if he downloaded some naughty videos.'

The mere thought makes me search the download folder, and, luckily, it's empty. I go back to look at my emails and realize that not only were a couple opened, but those that contained some concert tickets were forwarded.

I furiously text Emily: 'That asshole went through my email to get into some concerts with my tickets! That's why he deleted the history, so I couldn't see which links he clicked on!' I curse between my teeth. Did he think I wouldn't notice? He was so drunk he didn't even delete all the outgoing emails to his address. I swear that's the last time I invite him to my house.

Something else occurs to me. 'Albert didn't ask me to give him those pictures of the Jailbirds I secretly took, did he?'

'I don't remember exactly what we talked about, but it wasn't really about the band. He asked you a few questions about Thomas but nothing special.'

My heart pumps into my chest. 'Questions like what?'

'If you know where he lives or if you've ever been to his house, I think. But he was disappointed when you said no.'

Some of the tension that knots my stomach disappears. Just to be sure, I check some folders where I keep the photos I send to Ron. I hope he didn't snoop in those too. But they're all protected by password, and he'd have to go deep into my computer to find them because I don't keep them in plain sight.

I'm so focused on checking my computer that I almost jump out of my chair when my phone starts ringing. I look at the name flashing on the screen, and anger sends a wave of bile up my throat. Apparently, Albert is the lesser of two evils today.

"Ron, what a pleasure."

"Can we meet at the usual café?"

Whenever I talk to him, in person or on the phone, I'm always surprised at how rude he is and how little consideration he has for me. Does he not know he's supposed to say hello to people when he calls them? Then I remember how much of a crook he is, and realize there's probably no part of his brain that understands these kinds of feelings.

"Are you offering me lunch?"

I hear him hesitate for a few moments, and my anger grows. I bring him photos worth thousands of dollars. I shoot at his command every time he snaps his fingers. I spend hours in the worst places in Manhattan in the sun, rain, or snow. I think I deserve at least a lunch.

"Coffee?" he tries to bargain, and I almost laugh in his ear.

I hang up without even considering answering him. Less than thirty seconds later, his name flashes on the screen again.

"I think the line went dead," he tells me as soon as I pick up the call.

"No, Ron, I hung up on you. I don't leave my apartment for less than a lunch." I say this more because of my headache and not wanting to cook a decent lunch than because I want to see him.

"Okay, all right. In half an hour at the café," he demands without waiting for an answer.

He must have something vital on his hands if he caved on lunch and called me twice. I'm dying of curiosity, but I wait in my apartment doing absolutely nothing for exactly half an hour, just to piss him off and arrive twenty minutes late.

*

The coffee shop doorbell rings and Ron's head immediately snaps in my direction. I'm wrapped in a huge jacket over a heavy sweater, a scarf pulled up to my nose, and a cap dropped over my eyes to protect me from the freezing cold and snow-threatening gray sky, but Ron's eyes immediately find me. I can hide under endless layers of clothing, but that man will always find my face in the middle of a thousand others. His gloomy expression tells me he's mad at me, and I can't hold back a satisfied half-smile when I see him. I may need him, but I don't want him to think I'm his lapdog, running wagging every time he whistles.

"Punctuality is not your forté," he complains when I sit down.

"No, Ron, it's that you have a bad habit of demanding things without asking. I arrived when my schedule allowed me to do so," I calmly tell him, reaching out my hand with my palm facing upwards. He looks at my fingers stretched out, and frowns trying to figure out what I want.

"Your credit card. First lunch, then we talk."

He looks at me wide-eyed, like I've just told him I want to see him dance naked on the table.

"Are you serious?"

"As death."

"You're unbelievable," he hisses between his teeth.

"Thank you." I wink at him as I grab his card and go get food.

I load the tray with a salad with eggs and chicken, a pastrami sandwich, fruit salad, a lemon cake, a bottle of fruit juice, and a bottle of water. I have every intention of pissing him off properly.

"Hi, Iris." The guy behind the counter greets me with a sincere smile.

"Hi, Ian. Can you tell me if there's anything really expensive on the menu?" He looks at me, puzzled for a few seconds.

"He's paying." I beckon my head toward Ron.

Ian smiles and nods. "I can give you the specialty of the day, the puff pastry stuffed with beef and potatoes." He winks at me. "Do you want me to warm it up?"

"Yes, thank you, you're very kind," I tell him as I pay sixty-four dollars for a meal that could easily feed four people.

I go back to the table with my packed tray and give the credit card to Ron, who looks at me horrified. "How long have you been starving?" He shakes his head with a disgusted expression as I open the salad box and nibble something. My stomach's still shaken from last night. The truth is, I don't need a meal like this, but I wanted to spite him.

"What do you want, Ron? Why did you call me?" I get straight to the point.

"I've seen from your blog that you're on very good terms with the Jailbirds, especially Thomas and the Red Velvet Curtains. I want you to sneak into their private lives and get me the scandal I've been waiting on for years."

I maintain an impassive facade even though I am bubbling with rage inside. I linger to look at his eyes shining with victory, and I take all the time to come up with an answer. I don't want to slip on anything that puts Thomas or me under the microscope of this vicious bastard.

"I'm sorry, but I don't have any particular contacts. I simply got an email from their press office to do the interview. And my work as a blogger doesn't concern you. I bring you the photos I have, but our collaboration ends there. If you called me here to get information about that interview, you came out for nothing because you'll read it like everyone else when it comes out on my blog. And for the record, the Red Velvet Curtains and the Jailbirds have separate press offices. They're two different bands. You know that, don't you?" The sarcastic tone in my voice covers the discomfort I feel right now.

Ron bursts out laughing, and a shiver, not at all pleasant, runs down my back. "First, Thomas shares your blog post on Twitter, when you wrote that preview review of their album, then you get an exclusive interview with the up-and-coming band of the moment, which, coincidentally, is linked to the most famous one in the world. Rumors tell me that a car with darkened glass often roams your neighborhood. You really want me to believe you don't have any contact with them? They're so heavily guarded that even *Rolling Stone* journalists have to wait months before doing an interview." He spits all this out at me angrily.

As much as the man in front of me is a real bastard, revolting and arrogant, there's one thing I have to admit he can do well: his job. He finds malice in everything, and ninety percent of the time, he's right. Plus, he has zero ethics, which leads him to dig into the darkest ravines in people's closets to bring out the most hidden and dusty skeletons: even ones the owners don't remember.

"That's right, I don't have any contact with them. I won the contest and heard the singles before they came out, that's all. I was with nine other people," I shamelessly lie, looking him in the eye and chewing my salad as if the subject doesn't bother me.

But in reality? My panic is growing because this man has already framed the situation, and I wouldn't be surprised if he put one of his lapdogs at my house. I'm not the only one working for him. There are dozens of desperate people like me who need money. I carefully avoid getting close to the subject of the car in my neighborhood. For the first time in my life, I regret that I don't have Thomas's number. I could warn him to stay away, at least for a while. I don't know how I'd explain to him how I know paparazzi follow him, but at least I could keep the situation from getting out of hand.

"You didn't win the contest. I checked the names when I saw your article. Do you think I'm an idiot?" He raises his voice slightly and then immediately composes himself when he realizes that the people around us have begun to stare.

"No, Ron, but I don't really know what to tell you. I don't know them." I shrug and look at him with indifference.

Ron studies me for a while with his jaw rhythmically twitching. He's furious. "Okay, look," he says, settling in his chair and inhaling deeply, lowering his gaze before lifting it to mine. "You want to raise the price? I understand that. It's not like I'm asking you for something small. You're fucking a great piece of a guy. Not everyone gets this lucky. It shouldn't be hard for a nice piece of ass like you to slip into his bed. Anyway, if you do this, I promise you'll have enough money to pay for your mother's clinic for at least a year...plus all the other bills and hospital bills. In other words, I don't think your economic problem has exactly disappeared, right?"

Nausea takes over my stomach so fast I find it difficult to swallow the bite of a sandwich I took a few seconds ago. I don't know if I'm more scared that he knows the amount of my debts—and that I don't even have medical insurance—or that he thinks I would really prostitute myself to give him the scoop he wants.

"Let me understand. Since when have you become a pimp

who places prostitutes in clients' beds? Because I think this is what you're proposing."

The sneer on his face is nothing short of creepy. "Don't act like a saint with me. I know you need money, and a fuck is no big deal." His insult isn't even remotely veiled.

I tilt my head to the side and smile coldly. So much so that for a moment, I surprise him and his facade falters for a second before recomposing. "Let's get one thing clear here, Ron. I've already told you I don't know them, but even if I did, they're not for sale. My ethics aren't for sale. My mother is not for sale. And don't you dare use your filthy mouth to talk about her again. Have I been clear? Go crawl back into the sewer hole you came out of," I hiss with a coldness that is the complete opposite of the hot anger I feel.

Ron looks at me for a few seconds, then leans slightly on the table and stares into my eyes. "Remember that you are no one. Even if your blog does have all those visits, it's not because of your mediocre writing, it's because someone famous who wants to get into your pants took the easy way to get your legs open. You're in debt. Sooner or later, you're going to come back to me on your knees, and then I'm going to dictate the rules and the price, and I'm not going to be as generous as I've been now," he slithers in my ear as he gets up to leave the café.

The exact moment I see him turning the corner, I start breathing again. My hands begin to tremble with tension, and his words ring in my ears. I'm not mediocre. I put my body and soul into my blog, and I know I'm doing it right. I have studied, I have committed, I take care of it down to the smallest detail. I am not who Ron says I am.

I turn to Ian, motioning that I need a paper bag. He gives it to me with a smile. I put my unfinished lunch inside and head toward the subway as fast as my legs will take me.

*

Sitting on the steps leading up to my apartment is Thomas. He's looking down, clenching his fists. I don't know what he's doing here, but something's wrong, and after meeting Ron an hour ago, nausea rises in my stomach even before I know what the hell happened. His driver, leaning against the car with the darkened glass parked a few meters ahead, seems ready to take off just in case. It's all wrong, and my heart sinks deeper and deeper into guilt and fear of losing him.

"Is it true?" he asks as soon as I reach him. His expression and posture are serious as he gets up and walks toward me, but not close enough to touch me.

We've never been able to stay physically apart since the first day we met. This couple of feet separating us is like a stab wound to the heart. "What?"

"Did you sell Michael's pictures to that newspaper? Did you take them?"

His voice is broken with anger, and I can't breathe. "How the hell did you know?" Right now, no reasonable question can find its way to my lips.

"So it is true... The editor of the newspaper called Evan less than an hour ago. Giving your name. Was it really you?" he hisses again, increasingly impatient.

Ron. He wanted me to pay after our meeting, and he did it in the worst way. I didn't think he'd burn me at the stake—he must have known more than I thought. That meeting was just confirmation to test my reaction. How stupid I was; he doesn't need me anymore if I start protecting the people I should be photographing instead. I knew when Thomas found out he'd get angry, but to discover I was the one who almost lost them their careers was the coup de grace. What the hell did I expect? That this story would end well?

"Yes." Lying again would be like stabbing him in the back, and I'm tired of hurting him. I can't live hiding who I really am from him anymore.

Thomas releases half a laugh in disbelief. "Are you a paparazzo?"

"Yes," I whisper.

He stares at me for a few seconds, then bursts into laughter and runs his fingers through his hair, clutching them hard in fists full of rage. "So you only slept with me because you needed a few juicy shots to sell? For Christ's sake! I trusted you. I told you private things about my life that I don't tell strangers. I even suggested you sell your photos to get more money!"

"Let me explain..." My voice is broken by the tears stuck in my throat that are now about to fall.

"No. I don't want any explanation from you. I want you to stay away from me, or I'll have you arrested."

I don't even see him turn around and get in the car because tears cloud my eyesight, and sobs shake my chest so much it hurts. Or maybe what I'm feeling is my heart breaking because, deep down, I was hoping I had found my fairy tale.

*

Emily looks at me, worried, as I sip the coffee she made and try to stop the constant flow of tears from falling. She ran to my apartment as soon as I texted her about Thomas. I tell her what I know. "Ron must have called Thomas's manager and told him I'm a paparazzo."

Emily clenches her fists in an angry ball. "That son of a bitch. If I ever see him again, I swear I'm going to hurt him. I'm assuming Thomas didn't take it very well."

I shake my head, thinking again of his disappointed expression. The worst was seeing the pain of betrayal in his eyes.

"Maybe when he realizes that despite having many chances, you've never sold a picture of him, he'll realize you're not like the rest of those paparazzi." Her voice is uncertain. Not even she believes what she's saying.

"Ron told him I sold him the pictures of Michael."

"Oh…" The sorrow on her face tells me it's finally dawning on her—there's nothing I can do to remedy this mess.

"I knew sooner or later he'd find out. It was just a matter of time. How could I expect to keep playing this game? I've been telling him lies since I met him. Michael was just the icing on the cake."

"Yes, but that time it wasn't your fault. Michael doesn't need to be doing that shit in a public parking lot."

An almost hysterical laugh escapes my lips. "I know you're trying to make me feel less guilty, but it was all my fault. That parking lot is private. It's for the residents of that building and for the valet parking service of the club. I snuck in there by jumping a railing! And even if it was a public place, I had no right to capture Michael's vulnerable moment on camera for all the gossip magazines to post. There's no excuse for what I did."

Emily's silent for a while. "What do you think will happen now?"

I shrug and look down at my cup of coffee. "I don't know. The interview with the Red Velvet Curtains will fall through, I assume. Then the day after tomorrow, I'm going to have to see him parade in front of the Met for the Christmas event. He had invited me. But just now he told me that if I approach him, he'll have me arrested... I just hope he doesn't keep his promise at the gala."

"You think he'll follow through with it, for real? And maybe the interview won't fall through. Maybe they'll decide to do it anyway. After all, they're two different bands."

I glance at her, and the grimace on her face tells me she doesn't believe what she just said either. I inhale deeply and stare at my cup in silence. This is the mess I feared would happen from the first day I met him. What I didn't imagine was how bad it would feel to have Thomas disappear from my life.

CHAPTER 15
Iris

I'm not sure if I ended up in front of the Metropolitan Museum today or in the middle of a Christmas fairy tale. The stairway, covered by a vast white marquee that shelters the entrance, is covered with a pristine red carpet, despite people walking over it. But what makes the décor so spectacular are the giant Nutcracker characters that surround the staircase. Guards who look carved in ten-foot-tall wood stand beside Christmas balls the size of an armchair. Fake snow covers the entire area, giving the bright red and dazzling silver tones a magical, otherworldly feel.

The glitz has been meticulously displayed to make guests feel like they've stepped into a magical world. Tonight, high society's most famous people on the globe, slipping into elegant, uncomfortable clothes in which they will freeze, come here to cough up considerable amounts of money. Everything will be done to make their evening beyond enjoyable—to let them know that large amounts of money have been spent on their entertainment so they'll be more likely to open their designer wallets and sign fat checks.

But this is not a fairy tale, as the raw reality of the bitter cold air penetrates my bones. Despite being covered in countless layers of clothes, standing here waiting for the first guests to arrive has been like taking a bath in a frozen lake. Until a few days ago, I was supposed to be on the other side of the barricade, and now I'm groveling with all the nobodies, as if proving to Thomas what I really am. Just thinking about him makes my heart tighten in a grip.

Standing here for ten hours in front of the stairs to get an interview with the Red Velvet Curtains wasn't a great idea. After Thomas's outburst the other day, I thought the meeting would fall through. I was sure I'd get an email withdrawing the offer, and honestly, I expected it. I'm still stunned by our last meeting, unable to process the information that his 'I don't want to have anything to do with you anymore' entails. I was used to seeing him pop over to my home at the most random moments, and my heart still hopes a little, despite reality.

My feet hurt, I'm tired, the barricades press against my ribs under the pressure of dozens of paparazzi squeezed up against them at the top of the red carpet. I'm not an official photographer for this event, entitled to a designated position on the stairway, so I've had to stand here since this morning with dozens of other second-class photographers who don't have a pass. It's been an hour since the minor stars came through, the ones for whom few flashes are unleashed but who are usually also the funniest to watch as they try to attract attention. A wave of shoves hit my back and ribs when Alicia arrived—the first big name to show up and a bad sign for an actress struggling to re-emerge after a scandal. Next year, she risks arriving completely unnoticed during the first hour of the red carpet, between the less famous stars or those who have fallen out of favor.

After that came a couple of well-known singers, but the big

crush I'm feeling now is because the Jailbirds are here. The first limousine unloaded Thomas, Simon, and Michael, who waited as the second limousine with Damian and Lilly pulled up. As soon as the photographers realize who arrives, chaos erupts and they push against me until I'm out of breath, putting their cameras on my shoulders to take as many photos as possible. Guests at the gala don't stop in front of us, so we have to take as many photos as possible as they walk by. I notice Lilly looking at us almost shyly and, when her gaze rests on mine for a fraction of a second, a slight smile appears on her lips. It's a fleeting gesture, it lasts a few seconds, but it's enough for me to lower my camera and look at her dumbfounded. I move my gaze to Thomas, and my heart skips a beat. With the black tuxedo fitting him like a glove, he looks like a model on a catwalk. Tall, slender, haughty-looking with a slight smile on his lips, he is the most handsome man I've ever seen in my life. The memory of what we had and what I threw away weighs like a boulder on my chest, and I find it difficult to swallow.

I'm so caught off guard seeing Lilly and Thomas, who doesn't even look back at me, I don't realize that paparazzi are pressing harder than usual, and the barrier on my rib is vibrating abnormally. The buzz of the cameras covers any other noise as one of the legs of the barrier gives way and takes away my only support.

It all happens in a matter of seconds which, to me, feel like hours. I'm shoved to the ground, trampled by the crowd behind me that falls with me when the front barrier collapses. With one arm stretched out, I try to stop the fall. With the other, I try to protect the camera and lens that cost me so much sweat and fatigue—my only source of livelihood. Unfortunately, I can't hold the dozens of people rushing forward to escape the chaos behind them and I get trampled. The metal barrier presses into my side with a force that takes my breath away. The shoulder I tried to support myself with has crumpled under my weight, and the camera lens is jabbing into my side. In the confusion, I see several faces around me, including a worried Lilly trying to come to my rescue but being restrained by Damian. Then security makes its way among photographers who no longer know where to seek shelter. The last thing I see is the square face embedded on the big neck of a security guy wearing an earpiece. Then someone stumbles, kicking me in the face, between my nose and cheek, while another shoves a knee in my side, knocking what little air that was left in me out of my lungs. At this point, my body decides it's had enough, and darkness falls over my eyes.

*

I open my eyelids and realize I'm in the emergency room. Overhead, neon lights blind and annoy me. To the side, I am greeted by a green curtain that divides the beds. I notice my clothes and camera, not in the best condition, in the chair. The lens dangles from the camera's body, where I can see a thick crack in the plastic. I don't who's more banged up, the camera or me.

I try to sit up but the pain in my ribs and shoulder almost makes me cry out. "Great." An annoyed hiss escapes my lips when I realize the damage could be severe.

"Where do you think you're going?" asks a young, cute doctor, with dark, messy hair and two hazelnut eyes so wide he looks like I've just threatened him with a gun.

"Home," I announce when I finally manage to sit up and

realize that this damn hospital gown they put me in is open from behind.

"I don't think so. You have a mild concussion, two cracked ribs, and a dislocated shoulder. We're keeping you here for the night," he announces as he waves a chart in front of my eyes.

I know he's just doing his job, but he's wasting my time. "And you found out all of this how?"

He frowns and studies me, perplexed for a few seconds. "With an MRI," he says, like it's obvious and I'm behaving like a crazy person.

"Perfect! How much will this cost me? Let's see…fourteen hundred just for the ambulance ride, then twenty-five hundred for the MRI, a thousand for the X-rays, and I don't know what other tests you've done on me. I'm leaving here with a bill of almost five thousand dollars already and I have news for you: I don't have medical insurance, and staying here tonight costs me more than a room at the Ritz. So, unless I'm about to die any minute, please let me sign the damn discharge papers and stop wasting my time as well as yours?" I know I'm being rude, but I want to make it clear right away that I have no intention of being hospitalized.

"I can talk to the administrative office. They can set you up on a payment plan. There are other options you can consider…" His voice is almost imploring.

I watch him for a few seconds, and I realize he's young— only a few years older than me, probably an intern who hasn't seen a bed in at least twenty-four hours and likely working a weekend shift because he has no family. He's seen mostly drunks and people stabbed in brawls, probably had to call security at least three times last night, and he doesn't know what to do with a madwoman determined to get out of here as soon as possible.

I smile at him, get out of bed and rest a hand on his shoulder. "I have so many 'installments' to pay, I'd be paying thirty dollars a month for the next forty years to be able to afford to stay here tonight. I know you're just doing your job, and I can assure you, I won't be causing any problems. Just let me sign those papers and give me some painkillers. I know whenever the effect of what you gave me wears off, it'll hurt like hell."

He looks at me for a few seconds, then turns around without saying anything and approaches the nurses' counter to talk to a blonde ponytailed woman in her fifties, undoubtedly his supervisor. He says something to her, pointing at me, and the woman throws a glance at me. They exchange a few more words then she spreads her arms and raises her shoulders. The young doctor lowers his defeated gaze and walks away to the nurses' room.

The wait is endless, and I have now lost hope that they will let me sign those damn papers. I walk around the bed and start grabbing my stuff to get dressed, determined to get out of here with or without permission. It's not easy with one arm hanging around my neck in a sling.

"Does the doctor know you're leaving?" A woman's voice startles me back to reality. She's a dark-haired nurse in her forties with a slender figure.

I smile at her and nod. "I made him angry because I wanted to sign out and get discharged."

She studies me for a few seconds, looking undecided about whether to help me.

"I don't have insurance, and I can't afford to stay at the

Grand Hotel. I'm not dying. I just have a few cracked ribs and a dislocated shoulder. Nothing's going to happen to me," I explain, avoiding mentioning the concussion, the main reason they want to keep me here tonight.

The nurse looks doubtful for a long moment that seems like an hour, but then she approaches to help me, which I thank her for because I can't seem to manage it alone.

"Take a couple of these if your shoulder hurts, but never more than six a day and at least four hours apart," the doctor, who has finally returned, tells me, handing me an orange bottle with my name on it and some pills inside. "These are the papers you need to sign. This is a prescription for more pills if you need them."

I sign and grab the papers and put them in my pocket. "Thank you." I say, approaching the chair to get my camera back.

"Promise me that if you feel sick, if you experience nausea or vomiting, or severe dizziness, you will immediately come back here? Even a strong headache…or if you have trouble speaking or maintaining your balance," he begs me as I'm about to leave.

"Yes, of course." The sarcasm in my voice is so obvious both he and the nurse look worried.

I wave goodbye and fly out the door before he changes his mind about my discharge. I walk through the emergency room as fast as my condition allows, which is somewhere between a limp and a marathon runner on the last mile. This place goes on forever and it takes way too long for me to get through it.

When I finally get to the entrance, then across the street to where I can find a taxi, I realize it's now midnight. Four hours I was locked up in Lennox Hill Hospital, five minutes by car from the Met, two by ambulance. Most expensive drive in the history of the Big Apple—I could've walked and saved fourteen hundred dollars! In the car, I allow myself to breathe a sigh of relief, though not too big, given the pain in my rib. I pull out my phone to look at the latest news, as the Met event seems to have continued smoothly after clearing up the red carpet accident. When I get to my emails, one immediately stands out. Lilly asks me how I am. I smile and reply that I'm home now and the interview can go on as planned.

My heart sinks when I realize Thomas hasn't even tried to contact me. I could have died in that hospital bed, and he went on with his evening like nothing happened. Maybe it's too much to hope for a visit to the emergency room, but at least a message on social media, some kind of sign that before I ruined everything, he cared about me.

*

The following morning my body feels traumatized. Not a single bone or muscle isn't sore. I open my eyes and realize I'm in the same position I fell asleep in. This time, though, Dexter is next to me and hasn't even started in on his dose of dry food.

"Then you're not always an asshole." I smile at him as I carefully get out of bed and start getting ready for the interview.

With everything that happened, I didn't even have time to get anxious about it. Normally, I would have spent the night awake thinking up an excuse to cancel the interview. As soon as I get to my computer, I see a new email from Lilly confirming their location and telling me to feel free to cancel if I'm not well.

In the bathroom mirror, I see I might have a legitimate reason to back out. The left side of my face, where someone kicked me, is purple under the eye and on the side of my nose. I look closely at my face and immediately realize I will not be able to wear makeup to cover it, nor will I even be able to dress decently with my arm in this sling. So I opt for the runaway look: I slip my head and healthy arm into a wide sweater, leaving the hurt one tucked inside, then put on a pair of tracksuit pants and rubber boots without laces or socks. I'm going to get blisters, but it's better than the pain of putting on socks.

I give Dexter the dry food, slip on a beanie, leave my windbreaker open in the front, and look for a scarf big enough to cover the rest of me. I grab my notepad and phone and put them in my bag, not bothering to look at the camera as the fall broke both the lens and the body. When I put my bag on my good shoulder, I have to lean on the coffee table to catch my breath. My legs tremble with exhaustion.

I arrive at my usual café and find the band at a secluded table waiting for me. Emily closed off public access with a rope normally used to close the bathrooms during cleaning. Emily tries to stop me to ask me what happened, but I motion that I'll tell her later and approach the table.

Martin is the first to notice me and his eyes widen. "Holy cow, I didn't think it was that bad," he says, drawing the attention of the others who have more or less the same reaction to my appearance.

"Are you sure you're okay?" Lilly asks worriedly.

I smile and sit down, starting to pull out my notepad with the questions. "It looks worse than it is," I say, trying to play it down.

Luke studies me for a few seconds. "Is that why you're moving like Robocop?" he teases gently, making the others laugh too.

"Don't worry, I'm fine. Shall we start? I don't want to take up too much of your time." I try to change the subject in a hurry. This interview is making me nervous.

The band doesn't seem bothered by the change of subject and immediately gets comfortable. I start with the early days of their career—the concerts they did in Brooklyn clubs, their relationship with the fans—and I notice their surprise at the amount of research I've done. They laugh when I ask about a few anecdotes I found on their Instagram page and launch into new ones, joking like it happened right then and there. The hour passes pleasantly, and I slowly relax too.

"Do you mind if I take some photos with my phone to put on the blog?" I ask, wrapping it up. "Unfortunately, my camera is not usable at the moment."

"Are you serious? No questions about the Jailbirds?' Martin asks, puzzled as Lilly tenses next to him and throws him a look that could kill.

"No, why should there be? It's your interview. I want to know about you, not about them."

Luke smiles at me, and the others seem flattered. Even Lilly struggles to hide a smile.

"I like you, girl," Luke says, satisfied.

"Usually, half of our interviews are about the Jailbirds," Taylor explains.

"Because the journalists who interview you are idiots," I say without thinking, and they burst out laughing.

When we're done, the guys get up to order something to eat and have a chat with Emily, who seems more than ecstatic. Only Lilly stays at the table and helps me put my stuff away. "Can I ask you a question?"

I expected this moment to come, but I'm still nervous about what she's going to ask. I nod, holding my breath in fear.

"What were you doing on the fire escape near our apartment that day?"

She's straightforward, just like I expected. I smile at her and lean back in the chair I'm sitting in. "The truth? I was hoping to get some pictures of you and Damian that could earn me some money. But don't worry, I couldn't see inside your apartment from that location. I didn't shoot anything compromising. And I would never sell something that could ruin your personal life or your career," I admit with sincerity.

Something about Lilly seems genuine, and my natural response in her presence is to be honest in return.

"Why should I trust you? You sold Michael's pictures. How do I know you won't sell more when you need money?"

"You can't be sure. You can only trust me. When I sold those photos, I was desperate. But as soon as I saw what happened, I made a promise to myself to never do it again, even if I'm starving. I know it's not a great guarantee, but it's the only one I can give you. All I can do is be honest with you."

"Why do you even do this job? You don't look like a person who enjoys hurting people," she asks.

"Many of us do it because we need money. In my case, even if I had three good jobs, I wouldn't be able to earn the same level of compensation," I answer ashamedly.

Lilly frowns and studies me for a few seconds. "Are you in

trouble? Is that why you need so much cash?"

I burst out laughing, and then grimace in pain when my ribs remind me that certain things have not yet been able to heal. "No, I'm not in trouble. Not everyone who needs money is in trouble...sometimes, life just puts you in situations where you have no choice. Or rather, you can only choose between bad and worse. I'm not a bad person, you have to believe me, and I never hung out with Thomas for personal profit. I turned down giving him my phone number several times, for Christ's sake, because I didn't want to mess up our relationship. I realize I don't have the luxury of having a normal relationship with someone like him. I know it could never work. But I took the chance to dream about it for a while and paid the consequences."

Lilly struggles to find the words to respond to my solemn little speech and I feel embarrassed confessing all of those things to her. "But you don't have to worry about me and my work anymore. I can't afford to do it now, given the condition of my camera." I try to downplay it, but I'm sure my smile comes out like a bitter grimace.

"Is it that damaged?" she probes.

"It's literally trashed, I have to throw it away," I tell her, saying a quick goodbye and getting up to leave before the thought of a camera I don't have the money to replace makes me burst into tears.

The air that hits me when I'm outside cools my cheeks, leaving a wet wake where the tears are coming down. The shop window next door is illuminated with the decorative lights of a Christmas tree. A smiling reindeer attracts customers with his red nose and a festive attitude that electrifies the season. But not for me. As much as I've always tried to be strong in life, this time, I don't know how I'm going to get through it. That camera was how I survived. With the hospital bills looming, the idea of prostitution doesn't seem all that crazy to me anymore.

CHAPTER 16
Thomas

Michael is the only one of us who never decided to buy a house here in New York. While Simon, Damian, and I needed something of our own—a retreat where we could stay when we're in town—Michael prefers the perks and convenience of a hotel: presidential suites, room service, and discretion. He's lived for a while at the Four Seasons, The Mandarin Oriental, and even the Plaza, but the tourists those places attract have made him opt for the Royal Suite at the Park Hyatt during the last few months.

I tip the guy who brought me through the private elevator, and I enter his living room, hoping Michael isn't naked with a woman somewhere. Everyone in the band, including Evan, is on the guest list with access at any time, but I'm regretting not calling him before showing up. In all honesty, since Iris's story exploded like a bomb in our lives, I've avoided him. I feel guilty about seeing her because I still have vivid memories of the photos of Michael unconscious inside the car in the underground parking lot: the model collapsed next to him, the coke strips on the dashboard. I remember the rush to the hospital like it was yesterday, with the model almost dying and the subsequent months in rehab for Michael. It was the worst time not only in our career as a band, but in our lives, when we, as his friends, didn't realize how serious his addiction was. We always believed him. We always closed our eyes at his vices, thinking it was "rock star" life, but we didn't fully understand how deep he was in it. Guilt has devoured me for months, and it came back after Iris's betrayal.

"Michael, are you naked? Do I have to cover my eyes?" I shout when I don't see him in the living room.

"I'm getting dressed! Damian's the one who has to show off his dick every time he gets the chance, not me," he jokes from the other room.

He joins me a few minutes later, wearing sweat pants and a short sleeve t-shirt, and sits on the couch in front of me. "Do you want a beer or whisky?"

"It's ten o'clock in the morning. Better make it a soda." I raise an eyebrow scolding him as he stands again and approaches the bar. I'll never get used to the unbridled luxury Michael loves to surround himself with.

"So why have you been avoiding me for three days? Is it because of the paparazzo thing? Iris?" he asks, handing me a Dr. Pepper.

"Can't say you don't get straight to the point."

"Cut the bullshit and tell me why you're here with that puppy-dog face." One thing you can say about Michael, for better or for worse: he never beats around the bush. He's a straight shooter and demands the same from you.

"I wanted to apologize for sleeping with Iris," I admit.

"Was the sex so bad you felt the need to apologize even to me?" he teases me with a laugh.

"Come on, man. Be serious for once. I screwed up, and I'm apologizing."

He looks at me with a puzzled gaze, as if he's trying but can't discern my intentions. "Because you sleep with a paparazzo? Unless she photographed your dick and sent it to every media outlet, I don't see what the problem is, really."

"She's the one who took and sold the pictures of you and Kim in the garage. She's not just any paparazzo. She hurt you and almost ruined our career!" Incredibly, I have to clarify these things with him.

Michael bursts out laughing, and the reaction both confuses me and makes me angry. "I know who Iris is, and when I meet her, I want to thank her."

I'm dumbfounded, waiting for him to say more. Is he crazy?

"The one who risked ruining our career was me, not her. I started doing coke, and I crossed the line with that model. If Iris hadn't been in that garage, if she hadn't taken the pictures and then called the ambulance, I'd have died in that car. By selling those pictures, putting them in those magazines, she opened my eyes and slammed reality in my face. I thought I had the situation under control. I thought I could stop whenever I wanted, like I did with alcohol, but that wasn't the case. I could never have gotten myself out of that shit I was in. Iris actually saved my life, and now that I have a face to go with the person I think of as my guardian angel, I want to thank her. And I should have had the balls to apologize to you for the mess I made."

His confession leaves me stunned. I spent years hating the faceless paparazzo who took those pictures—and the whole group of them in general—and now he tells me it was all for nothing? "Do you know what happened to my family?" I ask him.

"You never told me."

"Three days after the sentence that sent me to jail, my father died of a heart attack. He fought so hard to get me out of trouble that, when he couldn't, his heart literally gave out by breaking in two. My mother let herself go that day. Within a week, she had lost her son and husband, and in a couple of months, she fell ill with cancer. Maybe that would have happened anyway, but she didn't fight it. She let herself die while I was in prison, when I couldn't do anything. My sister stood by her when I couldn't. She died a year later. I couldn't even go to her funeral. When I got out of prison, I found out my sister had completely disowned me. After years and an avalanche of money in private investigators, I discovered she had moved to Australia, changing her name and setting up a family, never letting me meet any of her children. I have three nieces or nephews, and I will never see them grow. I don't even think they know I exist."

"Wow, you never told me all of this," Michael whispers.

"Women have never been sincere with me. They always took something from me—never gave me anything."

"That's bullshit."

I turn to my friend and glare at him.

"Don't look at me like that. You know it's not true. Rita took everything you had. She only wanted to use you. But Iris is the exact opposite: she tried to stay away from you because she didn't want you to think she was using you. Iris gave me my life back, and she gave you back a friend you'd been losing over time. And honestly, she also gave you some happiness that you never had. Have you even paused to think about how happy you've been lately? Everyone can see it!"

I look at him without being able to say a word. Some of the assumptions I've had for years begin to vanish, taking with them some of the anger and hatred that was tearing me up inside.

*

"So, she does it because she needs money?" I ask Lilly.

She's just called me after doing the interview with Iris. At first, I was mad at her for still wanting to do it despite knowing the truth, but I finally gave in when I realized she wanted to find out why Iris was in the alley outside their house.

"Yes, she was candid with me. She is simply a girl who decided to be a paparazzo instead of becoming an escort. From what I understand, she needs a lot more money than a normal job pays, and she chose this path. She seems like a really nice girl. Imagine, during the interview, she made no reference to the Jailbirds. Luke, Martin, and Taylor are crazy about her."

"Really?" My surprise is so evident that Lilly chuckles amusedly.

"I'm serious. She was very professional, and it was delightful to talk to her."

The guilt that assaults me for the way I treated her almost makes me faint, forcing me to move away from the window where I'm admiring Manhattan to sit in the armchair that looks like the Space Shuttle. Iris is a paparazzo. She's the one who sold out Michael. She's the one who climbed a fire escape to take pictures of my friends and then sell them. I've always hated paparazzi. I've always hated what they did to Michael, what *she* did to Michael. This awareness has been tearing my heart apart for three days, trampling over any other feelings

I've had for her. I shouldn't feel guilty. I shouldn't feel like a jerk for not going to see how she's doing. I shouldn't have felt so scared when I saw her crushed by dozens of people.

"That doesn't change the fact that she lied to me." I become defensive, and I hate myself for it.

Lilly inhales deeply, and I'm sure if she was here instead of on the phone, she'd have punched me already. "Thomas, think about before you found out. Do you really think she wanted to exploit you? She didn't even give you her phone number. You followed her, remember that. And now she can't possibly take any pictures of you because her camera is destroyed. I don't think she has the money to buy another one. She walked out of the café crying when we spoke about it. I think that's really the only job that keeps her alive."

The sigh I let out expresses all the guilt invading my stomach and brain. "All you need is a cell phone to take a picture." I continue with my idiotic defense like a kid who no longer has an argument to stand on.

"Thomas, don't make me come over and kick your ass. Don't be an asshole. She doesn't deserve that." Lilly's voice is annoyed and amused at the same time.

"I know, I know. You don't need to scold me."

"Then don't act like an idiot."

I smile and shake my head. Since this girl entered our lives, it's been like a breath of fresh air. "Alright, go back to Damian. We spent so much time on the phone it's going to be him kicking my ass. And I'm sorry to say I'm a lot more scared of that." She hates it when I tell her she wouldn't hurt a fly.

Lilly snorts and, in response, hangs up without even saying goodbye. I smile and look out the window, partly relieved, partly weighed down by guilt. On top of that, I'm worried because Lilly said Iris was in really bad shape this morning. Last night, after seeing her get trampled by all those people and then transported to the hospital unconscious, I spent the evening glued to the news for fear that she was seriously hurt or even dead. For the first time I have no idea what happened at an event—and not because I was drunk.

I turn to the kitchen and see the mountain of cookies I baked after my conversation with Michael. I've already decorated about fifty of them, and I haven't even made a dent in the pile. "Claire is gonna kill me this time," I whisper to myself thinking about the mess I've made.

'Claire, I have a few dozen cookies to donate,' I text her.

She answers right away: 'I had to take the last ones to New Jersey because no one in Manhattan wants them anymore. Please stop! I'll pay for your therapy but stop baking cookies!'

I burst out laughing because I can just see her, grandchildren in tow, bringing cookies to all the homeless shelters on the East Coast, muttering like a grandmother who no longer knows how to rein in her grandson.

I grab my laptop and check out the location of electronics stores in Manhattan. To my surprise, I find one not too far from here. I call Max and, when he gets here, I ask him to drive me there.

*

I walk to the door of her building, noticing one of the bars in the window has been damaged in an attempt to force it. The more I spend time in this neighborhood, the more I realize it's a long way from the safe streets I'm used to living in.

The usual smell of urine welcomes me in the lobby, making

my nose wrinkle. The blankets near the stairs where Charlie sleeps prove that he, in fact, lives here, among the cockroaches and dirt, he's not just passing by. He's even got a small suitcase in the corner with his stuff in it. No building with a decent property manager would have allowed such a thing. Making my way up to the third floor, I peek down the other hallways. Garbage in the corners, a bicycle without wheels resting on a wall, and an eviction notice on one of the doors. Only if you're desperate to save money would you look for a roof over your head in this place. I'm a perfect idiot. How did I not notice? How did it not occur to me that someone who lives in a dump like this does not have any money? After all, when we were just out of prison, without a penny, we lived in places like this too.

I breathe deeply. I take courage and knock on Iris's door. I hear the sound of the latch, then the door opens a few inches until the chain strains.

"What the hell are you doing here?"

The answer dies on my lips when I see the tension on her face, like she's not particularly happy to see me. I certainly can't blame her. The last time I spoke to her, I was extremely rude and told her I would have her arrested. I look down at the floor, shaking my head, and exhale a disappointed sigh. The moment she closes the door, my heart sinks into my stomach. I almost turn around to leave when I hear the sound of the latch, and she appears wrapped up in a jumble of clothing. Holy cow! Her face is bruised and swollen, and her shoulder is in a sling. Lilly told me she had obvious bruises, but I had no idea the extent of her injuries until now.

"Can I come in?" I ask ashamedly.

Iris hesitates for a second, then she steps aside and lets me walk in, closing the door behind us.

Dexter catches up with me and rubs on my pants, purring. "And how are you?" I ask him, lowering and scratching his back.

Iris beckons me to sit on one of the two stools, and I gladly accept. Better than standing like a jerk in the middle of her house.

"Do you want coffee?" she asks, pointing to the machine.

I gladly accept. I notice her tampering with the pot, grumbling, exasperated when she can't turn on the faucet. I get up and help her. At first, she stiffens but then makes room for me by pointing to the cupboard where I find the coffee I bought her a few days ago. I take a few seconds to look in the cabinet and see only the stuff I bought her. How could I not notice that basic things like food are missing in this house? I was so focused on her I didn't see anything else.

Iris looks at me from a distance. Neither of us talk and, while we wait for the hot liquid to fill the pot, I observe my surroundings. Most of her stuff looks like discarded objects which she painstakingly restored. Iris has done a great job of making it all look presentable, but when you look a little closer, you see the curtains are worn and ripped in some places, the bookshelves are made of old vegetable boxes held together by metal wire. Most of the containers are nothing more than boxes of food cleaned and used for other purposes, like storing brushes. Or canned food tins used as pots for plants. Nothing in this place is new.

"You never told me what you're doing here," she says when we finally both sit at the table.

I scratch my neck and take a deep breath. "I was really worried about you when I saw them take you away in an ambulance the other night," I admit with sincerity.

Iris smiles and shakes her head slightly. "Really? Because I must have missed your messages asking me how I'm doing," she reproaches, irritated.

I'm ashamed because I deserve it, but I can't tell her. "I couldn't text because I don't have your number."

A smile slips from her lips as she lowers her gaze and shakes her head annoyed. "Lilly didn't either, yet she found a way to message me not even half an hour after the accident. Try another excuse."

I look down because I don't know what to answer. I know I was an asshole, but I was pissed off. I felt betrayed, and these are things I can't get over by snapping my fingers.

I feel her inhale with difficulty and, when I look up, she seems less angry. She seems almost resigned. "Did you come here just for this? You could have asked Lilly."

"I spoke to her, but she didn't reassure me much. I wanted to see with my own eyes how you are. Anyway, I didn't come here just to find out about your condition. I also have this," I tell her, raising the bag I'd brought and put aside when I got here. I place it on the table in front of us.

Iris peeks in it and, after a puzzled moment, widens her eyes as if diamonds were inside. "Beautiful, is it yours?"

I frown, surprised. "No, it's for you. I know yours broke. I thought you'd like to have another one."

Iris looks up sternly at me, and I see she's not pleasantly impressed by my gesture. "I don't want your charity. What is it with you? You think I live like Charlie in the basement? With a filthy blanket and clothes that smell like urine?" She gets up and goes to the sink and spills her cup out, then turns and leans on the counter, annoyed. I expected anything but this reaction.

"It's not charity. It's just that I thought you'd like it. You work with your camera, and I thought... I don't know, I guess it's my way of telling you that I accept what you do. I talked to Michael, and he opened my eyes about what happened. I've been harboring anger for so many years, and maybe that wasn't the only feeling I had to carry. But until he showed me the situation from another perspective, I was mad at you, period. So I'm apologizing," I snap, annoyed by her reaction to a gesture that was meant to be positive.

"Not everyone needs a superstar to give them gifts. People can survive without the help of ridiculously rich people's charity. I don't want your pity. What am I? Your new social project?" She continues angrily as if she hadn't heard a word I said.

"No, you're not my new project!" I get angry too, more hurt than annoyed. "I just wanted to do something nice."

"You got mad because I lied to you, but who are you? The sweet and caring Thomas I knew until three days ago or the ruthless man who threatened me in front of my house and didn't let me explain?" she screams angrily, and her tone pisses me off.

I burst into exasperated laughter. "Are you really reducing it to this level? Do we want to compare who's done the most damage? Because I'd like to point out that you're no saint either. And as much as you need money, what you did was petty, even if the consequences worked out well for everyone. And you know what? Hell, if you want that camera, good. Otherwise, throw it away, sell it, do whatever you want!"

I stand up furiously and stomp out the door, slamming it behind me.

PRESS *Review*

Red Velvet Curtains Interview!

Hi, Roadies!

The wait is over. Finally, you're going to know what the Red Velvet Curtains confessed to me during our interview. We covered some powerful topics, some of them inspiring their most meaningful songs.

Q: Your song, "I Will Rise Stronger," that we heard at the festival, talks about bullying. As you shared yourself from that same stage, it's based on your personal experience with this topic. Is this a commentary about the society in which we live?

A (Lilly): More than commentary, it's the desperate cry of a victim who can no longer bear to be crushed. The experience I had when I was only fifteen years old has marked me deeply. Bullying is something that changes your life and transforms you. It can make you stronger, but it can also make you slide into a deep state of depression. I needed to channel my emotions and suffering in the only way I had to express myself at the time: music. We found that this song helped many people to process their own pain and we're pleased about that.

Q: This aggressive bullying, nowadays, is channeled mainly through social media. What's your relationship to it?

A: (Luke): Love and hate (laughs). Sometimes we're still amazed at how inclined people are to confess deeply personal things to us through social media. We get the impression, reading specific messages, that people think they know us. They make assumptions, give us advice, or, in great detail, confess to us what they would not dare to say to people close to them. While it flatters us, it scares us to death. Because some get very insistent and ask very personal questions that we don't want to answer. We always walk the thin line between not answering and giving the impression of agreeing or answering and starting an uproar because we disagree with them.

Q: I assume "I Will Rise Stronger" will be included on the new album. How far along are you? Are you finished with it? The record company has not yet announced a release date.

A: (Martin) We finally have a final list of songs that will end up on the first album (laughs). I swear before I signed with the record company, I had no idea it was a problem to have too many tracks. It was hard to decide which ones made the list and which didn't; each of us has songs we're attached to that didn't make the cut. But now we can go ahead with the promotion and then launch it.

Roadies, there's more to the interview, but if you want to read it and see new exclusive photos, subscribe to my newsletter. You'll get more content about the up-and-coming band of the year!

Be kind and Rock'n'Roll,
Iris
381720 Likes 20784 Tweets 22698 Shares 5682 Comments

CHAPTER 17
Iris

I'm an idiot. Here he came back, despite my lies, and I managed to make him angry again with my refusal to accept help. I peek into the bag again. The camera is top of the line. I could never afford it, even if I saved for the next hundred years.

I walk to the door and thrust it open, ready to chase Thomas down the street, but I'm surprised to find him in front of me. "Sorry...I shouldn't have treated you like that." My voice sounds uncertain.

"And I shouldn't have left like a little kid. Let's start this conversation again and pretend I never brought you that camera?"

I invite him to come in, and he doesn't think twice. He grabs Dexter, who seems invigorated by his presence, and takes him to his chest, cuddling him. He sits at the table, and I sit in front of him.

"I owe you an explanation." I start.

"Yes, you owe me a lot of them." His voice is not angry, it's more like an observation.

"Do you want to ask me questions? I don't know what you know about me."

"Why are you doing this job?"

"Because I need money. More than just what it costs to live

in Manhattan."

"Do you have a drug problem or something?"

I burst out laughing, the pain in my ribs flaring up, but I hide the groan that closes my throat. "No, nothing illegal. Believe me."

"Did you call the ambulance when you found Michael?"

I didn't expect that question. I didn't think anyone knew I did it. "Yes, when I realized the situation was serious, I left the garage and called the ambulance. I waited outside until they arrived and guided them to the floor where Michael was. When I saw the foam coming out of the girl's mouth, I realized they didn't just fall asleep in the car. She overdosed."

"Why didn't you take pictures of her in those conditions?"

"I took a lot of pictures, believe me, but I didn't sell them. I was desperate, but I have a limit, too. I thought about what a mother would feel to see her daughter overdosed on the front pages of all the newspapers."

"You had to be close to see those details."

I see him tightening his jaw. He's testing me, he wants to know the truth, and I owe him the truth this time. "I was next to their car door, but I decided to sell only those from afar with some reflections of the glass... I didn't want the world to see that scene up close. Michael would never have survived the scandal after those photos."

"Can you show them to me?"

I hesitate for a moment. I would never want to see pictures like that of someone I love.

"I'm sure," he insists, noticing my hesitancy.

I get my laptop, access folders protected by two different passwords, and look for pictures of Michael. Thomas brings his hand to his mouth as he scrolls through dozens of photos I took but never sold. They're raw, desperate, of two people who look like they're dead. I see his eyes watering, and I can hear him clearing his throat before closing my laptop.

"Thank you," he whispers.

I don't know if he's thanking me for showing him the pictures or not selling them. He is particularly shaken, and I prefer not to probe any further.

"Why don't you move somewhere less expensive to live?"

"Because famous people live here, and I need this job."

"Can't you move to a city where the cost of living is lower? Where you can do a normal job and get a decent apartment without having to climb over drunk people to get to the front door?" The irritation in his voice is almost palpable.

"No, I can't do that," I snap at his insistence.

"Why? That's what I can't understand. Is it because you like New York clubs, the good life?"

"Because there are other people who depend on me and the money I bring home!" I reply angrily.

The silence that follows is tense. "Explain," he whispers almost in prayer.

"I can't explain it to you. I have to show you."

"Really?"

"If you want to see it...understand why..."

"You told me it's nothing illegal, so yes, of course, I want to understand." His tone is almost sweet, as if he were clinging to this explanation to have a reason for our existence.

"You're a rock star. Shouldn't you be the one who always lives on the edge? The one who feels the thrill of living on the verge of lawlessness and transgression?" I tease him to lighten the heavy atmosphere, but I immediately regret it because, for a second, I see pain veiling his eyes before he tries to bring back a tired smile.

"The life of the rock star is not that exciting, trust me. It's all tours without a moment to take a breath. After that, you go to the studio to record an album, then you start with promotional parties where you don't have fun at all. Then you go on a new tour to promote the album. It's an endless wheel spinning, spinning, spinning, and we're the hamsters running inside it, desperate not to be fired out like missiles. That's why Michael succumbed to cocaine at first."

"Have you all done it?" I'm terrified at the idea of him doing drugs.

"No. Just Michael, but he's been clean for years now."

I nod and smile, getting off the stool and grabbing my jacket. "I thought your life was more exciting. Sounds to me like it's not exactly a life I'd want."

Thomas gets up and puts Dexter down, who meows disappointedly, and helps me slip on the jacket. "Don't get me wrong, I like the life I have. I love being on tour because the guys are like brothers, and we have a lot of fun. I love making music, and I don't think I can do anything else in life. But you always have to be focused, present, active, deal with everyone. It's not like you can be a rock star and say, 'Okay, I don't want to do anything today, I'm going to stay in bed all day,' because that'll be the day there are at least ten people who depend on you, on your commitments, on your decisions. That's all."

The glossy, over-the-top image presented in the media and on stage is nothing like the serious, laid-back, sweet guy who fills this apartment with his humble presence. "Okay, you're making me want to write a documentary blog post about the real life of a rock star," I admit with sincerity.

He smiles and nods. "We can talk to Evan about it. Why not? It might be interesting," he suggests, and I'm worried he may think I brought it up to get a successful article out of it, not because I'm really interested in his life.

"I don't want to take advantage of this. I'm sorry," I look down, ashamed.

Thomas gently rests a finger under my chin and makes me lift my head until I meet his big, blue, sweet eyes that make my legs tremble. "I know you didn't say it to take advantage of this conversation. If you wanted to exploit me, you'd have done it already. I know you didn't approach me to get a story. I honestly thought of at least twenty occasions when you could have used your position to your advantage, but you didn't. I said it because it really could be an interesting idea to explore and you're a great journalist, never underestimate that. And don't tell me you're just a blogger simply because some of your articles don't get published in the papers."

"I've never majored in journalism."

"Why is that?"

"I was able to get into Columbia and New York University, but they cost too much, and I couldn't take on hundreds of thousands of dollars in loans, besides the ones I already have."

"For what it's worth, I think you're much more qualified than many journalists who write important articles every day. Those schools lost a great student."

His words, so sincere and completely unexpected, make me blush and look away from embarrassment.

"Are you ready to go? I have to call Max to pick us up."

Thomas changes the topic, and I appreciate the fact that he didn't press me any further.

"I thought I'd take the subway. It's only a few stops from here," I suggest, puzzled.

Thomas lowers his gaze, tucking his hands into his jean pockets and nervously rocking from his heels to his toes. "Well, one thing someone with my fame can't do, if he doesn't want to be assaulted by fans, is take public transport," he explains with a half-smile.

"Oh," is the only sound that comes out of my mouth like a perfect idiot. I had not considered such an eventuality at all.

"I know, I didn't think about it at first either and went about my business, driving Dave—our head of security, and Max, our driver—crazy. They had to come and pick me up from the most stressful situations," he chuckles while he texts a message.

"Like what?" I'm as curious as a kid with a gift she can't open.

"Like the time they fished me out from under a mountain of diaper packages and toilet paper because I went alone one night to get milk and cookies at the supermarket. Some of the clients recognized me, and I found myself running away from a small crowd who wanted photos and autographs." He laughs at the memory, and I laugh with him.

"Milk and cookies? I thought at least a six-pack of beer or a bottle of whiskey," I tease him.

"Are you kidding? I can't sleep if I haven't finished my day with a hot cup of milk and cookies," he says, pretending to be shocked.

I burst out laughing when I realize that, in our own way,

we're working things out.

"Not a rock star, you have the lifestyle of a Teletubby," I tease, and he rolls his eyes, nodding toward the door.

"Come on, let's go meet Max before you kill my dignity completely."

*

I climb into the black Range Rover with darkened glass parked in front of my house, and immediately I am met by Max's greeting and smile.

I tell him the address, and he flashes his gray eyes in the rearview mirror to seek the silent approval of Thomas, who gives him a slight nod of his head. He starts the car and heads into the light traffic of my street before diving into the chaos of the rest of the city.

We exchange a few jokes on light topics in the car, perhaps because even Thomas can sense the nervousness that begins to churn in my stomach and makes me silent.

"Do you know what surprises me the most right now?" I ask, looking away from the city out the window and turning toward his smile that beckons me with a nod of his head. "That I have been coming to this place for years, but I have no idea what the city around it is like, the neighborhoods nearby. I've always reached it by subway. I know every detail of the stations where it stops, but I have no idea what's on the surface."

Thomas smiles at me and nods. "I know, and maybe that's the beauty of New York, Manhattan in particular. Though you've been living here for years, it'll always surprise you by showing you a corner you've never seen or slightly changing some place you haven't been in a long time. The great thing, though, is that it always manages to make you feel at home, even though it's never the same."

I know the feeling. I've lived all my life in New York, and I think I could never call anywhere else home. Strangely, when I walk here, I always meet people I've never met before, but I feel like I know them. Eight and a half million people, and it still seems like everyone is part of a large neighborhood.

"We're here." Max's voice recalls us to reality, and when I look out the window, I realize that the gates have opened and we are slowly entering the parking lot that I never use, despite being entitled to it.

I turn to Thomas and notice the attentive and perhaps even worried look when he realizes where we are. We get out of the car, and I tell him to follow me into the clinic. When I look at the nurse behind the counter, she looks up, and immediately her worried gaze rests on me.

"Oh, honey, are you okay? I saw on the news what happened at the Gala, and I was scared to death." The concern is heartfelt in her voice and on her face.

"I'm fine, really, just a little pain in my shoulder but nothing more." I try to minimize it when I feel Thomas's eyes on me.

She rounds the counter, takes my chin between two fingers, and moves my head to look at my bruises more carefully. Her serious glance, from my face to the arm stuck to my chest, makes me realize that I couldn't convince her.

"You know that if you need physical therapy, you can come to us, right? We can find room in Liam's schedule, and you don't need to pay," she adds when she notices how slowly I sign the register.

I smile and nod, then turn to Thomas and look at him doubtfully. "Is it a problem for you to sign the guest register? They don't let anyone in without a signature." Maybe he doesn't want his name on a long-term illness clinic list.

"Of course, no worries." He approaches the desk, smiles, and takes the pen from my hands, short-circuiting my brain when our fingers touch.

We greet the nurse at the entrance—who lingers longer than necessary on Thomas's slender figure—and reach the cream-colored room where my mother is sitting alone in her usual armchair in front of the window overlooking the garden.

"Hi, Mom, how are you today?" I whisper to her as I go to gently kiss her head, pressing my lips to her hair that smells of vanilla and baby powder.

Out of the corner of my eye, I see Thomas carefully following my every move, his eyes glued to me, to my hands as I untie the braid that keeps her long hair gathered and start brushing it. I beckon him to approach, and he does so slowly, weighing every gesture with sweetness as if he could somehow disturb the stillness of this place. I see him inhale deeply and hold his breath. His eyes are glistening and he can't hide the pain on his face. I wasn't prepared for his reaction—it's as though he's suffering physically at what he's seeing, at meeting her for the first time. When he sees me watching him, he tries to recompose himself and gives me a half-smile, but his eyes can't hide the pain he seems to be feeling since entering this room.

"This is Thomas, the guy I told you about. The one whose arms I literally fell into. Do you remember that?"

Thomas smiles.

"She hasn't answered me in years, but I like to keep her up to date on my life," I explain.

He nods with a smile more confident than before and warmth in his eyes.

"He's a famous drummer. I know you only consider the drum noise, but he's definitely good."

I can hear Thomas chuckling as he sits in a nearby chair. "What happened to her? If you don't mind me asking."

I place the brush on the bedside table, and I go back to braiding her hair. "Senile dementia."

"Really? I thought she wasn't...I mean, your mom looks young to me."

I nod and smile. It seems impossible to me, too, that she's in this condition. "Apparently, you can get it even at forty-five, and when it takes you so young, it's very aggressive. It's a rare case, but it can happen. Her brain stopped working properly; the disease has a complicated name, but the reality is straight-forward: she's shutting down. She needs someone to assist her twenty-four hours a day, seven days a week. At first, I tried to take care of her, but it's almost impossible on my own. Now, you see her catatonic in front of this window, but sometimes she wakes up in a confused state, doesn't recognize anyone, and gets very upset. I can't stay with her all the time. I once found her wandering the neighborhood streets just in her robe at six in the evening on my way home from work. It was a struggle to drag her back into the house," I explain without ever looking him in the eye.

"Can I ask what happened to your father?" he says almost in a whisper.

I look up and find tears threatening to fall down his face. It leaves me breathless and suddenly I want to wrap my arms around his neck.

"He left us almost seven years ago. He said my mother was crazy and he couldn't be with her anymore. In a way, it was true. The first signs of dementia were already showing up. Sometimes she would scold me because I hadn't done something she'd never really told me to do. In hindsight, I understand why he left. Anyway, I never had a great relationship with my dad. The first few summers, I went to visit him on vacation in Florida, but then he started a new family, and I stopped going. I felt unwelcome. He doesn't even know my mother's like this."

"Why don't you tell him? Maybe he can help you."

My bitter smile makes him frown. "Because he's not doing well, either. He's always given me about two hundred dollars a month to help with expenses, which he still does, even though I'm twenty-four years old and don't need it. I know how much effort it is for him to get that money out, and yet he's always on time for payments. At Christmas and on my birthday, he gives me a hundred more. He has never missed a date or anniversary. He's not a bad person, he just never realized that my mother's condition was due to illness and not because she had changed from the woman he fell in love with. It can be really exhausting to live with someone who has this condition. It wears you down, day after day, little by little, until all your energy is gone."

Thomas nods but says nothing. He seems lost in his thoughts as he glances between my mother and me, perhaps realizing how much we look alike. Or wondering if one day I'll get as sick as her. I've often wondered it, too, but I resigned myself to the belief that I can't control it. I'll think about it if and when it happens to me.

"Scared?"

He raises his blue eyes and gives me a reassuring smile. "No, I was thinking about how much a place like this must cost."

"A lot, trust me. I have some assistance from the state and some charities that help with elderly care, but the remaining tuition is still really expensive. That's why I do the work I do."

He barely nods, his eyes fixed on my mother's profile and his gaze earnest, as if he's considering how to miraculously heal her from this state. Despite my lies, despite what I do for a living, he's here, with me, and trying to understand my world, choices, and difficulties. I'm glad Ron told him everything because he lifted a weight off my chest. I was exhausted from the lies and secrecy, living in a limbo between happiness and fear.

*

We walk into my apartment, and Thomas helps me take off my windbreaker, careful not to hurt me.

"Have you been able to eat since you ended up in the hospital, or are you fasting?" he asks, halfway between worried and scolding.

I smile and look down guiltily. "Sometimes I order out, sometimes Emily brings me something from the café."

"But more often than not, you don't eat, do you?" I don't answer. It's impossible to hide the truth when your stomach grumbled all afternoon. "Sit. I'll cook something."

I watch him tinker with eggs, bacon, cheese, butter, and bread. He is the perfect mix of sweet and sexy that makes my heart melt so much I have a ridiculous smile on my face. So this is what it feels like when you're genuinely happy.

When he turns to me with the two plates of sandwiches he

has prepared, he looks puzzled. "What?"

"No, nothing, you're just perfect. A rock star, good in the kitchen, great in bed... So, where do I sign on the dotted line?" I joke, trying to lighten the heavy day we've had.

He shrugs and smiles, embarrassed. "I'm not that perfect, trust me, but I like to take care of you. I know you're independent, and you're doing great on your own, but making dinner makes me feel useful."

I'm not used to this attention, but I can put aside my pride for at least one sandwich. "Okay, alright, you're not perfect, but this sandwich is amazing. Just saying." I devour the two slices of toasted bread and butter with little grace and I'm stuffed.

"You also said I'm great in bed, don't forget that part." He winks at me and smiles.

"Damn it, I was hoping you missed that!" I laugh as I finish the last of my dinner and wash it down with a sip of water.

Thomas gets up, catching me by surprise, and puts his arm under my knees and behind my shoulders to lift me up. He walks to the bed and carefully sets me down as if I were a fragile package. Dexter, napping on the pillows, gets up, jumps out of bed, and takes refuge in the bathroom, looking annoyed.

"Let me remind you how good I am even away from the stove," he whispers in my ear and then kneels in front of me to take off the shoes that I struggled to put on this morning.

The comfortable mood of our dinner changes, unleashing an electricity that usually sparks just before we end up between the sheets. Thomas keeps undressing me: first my socks, pants, panties, and then my sweater and t-shirt, leaving me naked in front of him. He helps me lie down, then undresses without ever taking his eyes off mine and lays down next to me, covering us with the warm quilt. He comes closer and kisses me softly, taking his time, sliding his hands over my bare skin, stroking me with the delicacy of a feather, igniting my desire.

He's a different Thomas than the passionate one I've gotten used to, but no less sensual. He kisses the skin of my neck and then descends to my breasts, leaving a glowing trail on my body. Butterflies spring from my belly when, with light kisses, he slowly approaches the center of my pleasure. I want to tell him that I need to feel him inside me, to feel him move in me to feed my mounting pleasure that needs release, but my voice doesn't come out—it's stopped by my lack of breath and my brain wrapped in oblivion.

He slips his tongue between my legs and awakens my desire. He kisses me, taking care of my pleasure with a slowness that both tortures me and makes me shiver with pleasure. He takes me almost to the apex, with kisses and light touches. Then he stands up, and, after sticking on a condom he finds on my bedside table, gets on his knees between my legs and sinks into me slowly, savoring the moment and throwing back his head with closed eyes, lost in the sensation. I watch him as, with slow movements, he sinks deeper and deeper into me, filling me with his presence and persistence. Thrust after thrust, though careful not to disturb my sore shoulder, he takes both of us to a deep orgasm that leaves me exhausted.

I look at him, getting lost in his blue eyes gazing at me, still intoxicated with pleasure. It's a vision I'd like to imprint in my mind and relive every day of my life, but my eyelids get heavy, and as Thomas kisses me and snuggles closer to me, I close my eyes and sink into a serene sleep.

In the morning when I open my eyes, his side of the bed is empty. Last night I felt a kiss on my forehead, then the front door closing soundlessly. I thought I dreamed of it, but I realize Thomas is gone. My heart sinks into my chest when it occurs to me that maybe he regrets our reconciliation and doesn't want anything to do with me anymore.

I sit up and find a note on the nightstand: 'I couldn't stay. I've already made coffee. Just turn on the machine. Have an awesome day!' And I smile.

CHAPTER 18

Thomas

I've been staring at the ceiling for hours since waking up in the middle of the night. I can't stop thinking about Iris and what she's doing for her mother. The thought of my sister looking after our sick mother while I was in prison haunts me more than ever. My sister, who hasn't spoken to me since my mother died, who moved to the other side of the world, started a family, and never once contacted me. Not even through the lawyers who reached out to her, making sure she was doing well.

I deserve it. I deserve all the indifference the people I love the most are showing me. I ruined my life, theirs, and all those who loved me and tried to help me—the ones I dragged with me into the abyss because I didn't open my eyes in time.

The way Iris takes care of her mother reminds me that I've never been there for mine, that I slowly killed her, that I killed my father. The fact that she opened up to me, showing me the most vulnerable side of her family, while I don't know if I'll ever be able to do the same, makes me feel even worse. The thought scares me, makes my stomach twist, and as much as I know I'm being deceptive, I still hide behind a thousand excuses not to work up the courage to do what's right.

I look at the alarm clock. It's a decent time to get up and make some phone calls. When I reach the kitchen and make myself coffee, the first thing I do is call my lawyer and financial advisor and make an appointment related to the management of my estate.

"Hi, do you have time to take a ride with me to Brooklyn this morning?"

The resulting silence, long and full of unspoken words, makes me realize he's swearing softly. I'm always coming up with absurd demands. "Yes, of course, I can find the time."

This is an emergency, and, given the number of zeros behind my bank account numbers, I can afford to put some pressure on him. "Perfect, what time can I pick you up?"

"Ten o'clock will be fine."

I hang up and go back to sipping my coffee, then head to the pantry and grab the pack of vanilla cookies that always put a smile on my face. If I couldn't do something for my mom, I can always do something good for Iris's mother. That way she can breathe and focus on what she really loves to do in life: photography and writing.

I've always tried not to open my heart to anyone anymore. But now, here I am, obsessed like I'm thirteen and I don't even know how I got here. Because the reality is that I've fallen in love with Iris, and there's no point in me trying to hide it or make up other explanations. When you worry about someone, when you get mad because she disappoints you, when you want to see her and protect her twenty-four hours a day, you're completely smitten. There's no other explanation. I know what it means. Even though I was just a kid, I was in love with Rita. It was an undeveloped, immature love, almost adoration, but no less sincere and profound. What I feel for Iris is different, more settled and sure, but just as impulsive.

When my lawyer gets in the car with a tired smile three hours after our conversation, he's surprised to see me with coffee for both of us and the excitement of a kid who skipped school.

"Are we going on a road trip?" he asks, accepting the coffee with puzzlement, like Snow White taking the poisoned apple.

"More or less," I reply vaguely, watching out the window as Max dives into the heavy traffic of south Manhattan.

I can sense him tensing next to me, but I don't want to explain anything to him before I get there. I already know he's going to tell me to verify who Iris is, to check her past, to see if what she told me is true or not. All indisputable precautions for someone at risk of fraud, given my financial status, but I don't want to hear them now. He doesn't know her the way I do, and maybe I'll look presumptuous and a little crazy, but I don't see any dishonesty or premeditation in that girl. Since finding out about her work, I've spent hours retracing every single moment we've been together, and I can't recall a single one where I got the impression that she was taking advantage of me.

When we arrive at the clinic, my lawyer gets even more restless and starts to interrogate me, sweating like a lamb at Easter. "Do you have something to tell me? Are you in trouble? You know everything's confidential between us—you can tell me anything …"

"Calm down. It's not about me, okay?" I try to reassure him while I stifle a chuckle.

Looking in the rearview mirror, I see Max struggling to hold back a smile. He's so used to dealing with our craziness he's no longer scandalized, even at the most absurd requests.

When we enter the clinic, I notice there's a different nurse than yesterday, and I immediately give her my most disarming smile. Sometimes I feel guilty about using my looks so shamelessly to get what I want. The day will come when I no longer have this face and then I'll pay for all the times I took this shortcut to achieve my goals.

"Hello, is it possible to talk to the manager, please?"

Her brows furrow worriedly. "Is something wrong? Can I help you in any way?"

The agitation in her voice tells me that maybe I was a little too straightforward. "No, absolutely no problem. I would like to settle the bill for one of your patients, and I would like to talk to someone."

As she breaks in a gorgeous smile that lights up her face, my lawyer rubs his eyes and sighs with frustration.

"You need to talk to the administration. I'll call right away to check if they can see you."

In less than five minutes, I find myself at the door of a small but cute office with a large window that faces the garden and the same cream-colored decor that characterize this clinic. The only pop of color is the bright pink floral dress on the statuesque woman with chocolate-colored hair who gets up and firmly shakes my hand. I smile as soon as I see her, then take a seat on one of the armchairs in front of her desk. My lawyer, next to me, looks as happy as a serial killer waiting for the electric chair. I feel almost guilty for dragging him into this mess without mentioning anything to him.

"So, Mr. Simons, what can I do for you?"

"I would like to settle the bill for one of the patients in this clinic," I announce, getting right to the point.

"Someone who has died or is planning to change clinics?" She is puzzled.

"Oh, no, she's still alive and staying here. I just want to... pay the bill." I realize that the request may seem a little strange.

The woman clasps her hands in front of her on the desk. My lawyer keeps fidgeting in his chair restlessly. "Do you have a date of death, so I can better calculate how much you owe us?" she asks me, raising an eyebrow.

I frown and stare at her with less enthusiasm than before. I don't like it when people make fun of me, and she's clearly making fun of me. My lawyer, meanwhile, has sunk into the chair and is covering his entire face with his hand.

"No...I hope later, down the road."

"Can I at least have the patient's name? Maybe we can find their payment agreement." She tries to accommodate my total ignorance.

"The room number is 108. She has a daughter named Iris," I tell her, losing confidence with every passing minute.

"You don't even know her name?" my exasperated my lawyer exclaims. I don't dare look him in the eyes.

"Do you know the daughter's last name?" she asks, and I shake my head like a little boy who doesn't have the answer to a test question.

"Not even that, Thomas?" This time I look at my lawyer, who I assume is going to be my former lawyer before the end of the day, and the disbelief on his face is nothing short of comical.

The woman begins to look for information on her computer, then she smiles and turns to me again in less than a minute. "Do you want to make arrangements to contribute to the payment?"

"If that's the only thing I can do, yes."

"We have to call Iris, but if there's no problem with her, I'll prepare the necessary documents."

Panic creeps in and squeezes my stomach, making my blood freeze. "Is that necessary? Can't I make an anonymous donation?"

The woman's forehead creases as my lawyer leans over to look me in the face, wide-eyed. "Does she even know you're here?" he asks.

"Not exactly?"

"Yes or no?" he insists.

"No," I reply in a faint voice, but then I regain my courage looking at the woman. "Is it not possible to do something anonymously?"

The woman inhales deeply and seems to be searching for the words to make me feel more idiotic than I already feel. "Mr. Simons, it doesn't work like in the movies. You can't come in here and pay for someone without the person responsible for them knowing anything about it. You can make an anonymous donation to the clinic, but you can't pay for a patient."

Anger begins to make its way into my chest at these stupid rules. "But I'm trying to pay *for* someone. I'm not adding debt to her bill."

My explanation is met with silence until the woman picks up the phone and dials a number. "I'm calling Iris, so we can solve this problem right away, okay?"

The woman turns her chair around for some privacy, and in the meantime, my lawyer seems to be trying to find the right words to tell me what an imbecile I am. "You know this epic gesture you're making could cost you a fortune, right?" His expression is almost compassionate, as if he understands something I haven't realized yet and feels pity for me.

"I'm not poor...so it's really not an epic gesture. I'm just trying to help her."

He has no time to reply because the woman in front of me attracts our attention. "You're lucky. Iris is here, visiting her mom. We can straighten up these details right away."

Except I don't feel lucky at all right now, especially not when Iris enters the room in a rampage. "What is your problem?"

She doesn't even give me time to say hello or react. Even my lawyer shrinks at the fury of this redhead in the room. Her face has become the color of her hair, covering up any freckles that give her the appearance of a young girl. The woman in front of me right now scares me.

"I didn't bring you here yesterday so you'd pay the bill! I brought you here to let you know why I do that job."

"I just want to help you. First, you refuse the camera, but you accept the groceries. Now you reject this. How do I know what the hell you want? Why can't I help you?"

Iris looks at me with an incredulous expression on her face. I forgot there are other people around us. "You really don't understand, Thomas? Seriously, it doesn't occur to you why I can accept the groceries but not the rest?"

"No, really. I have no idea why you're so stubborn all the time. I always feel like I'm walking on eggshells when I'm with you."

Iris seems dumbfounded by my words. She shakes her head, taking a deep breath, then turns her gaze toward the woman behind the desk. "Please don't let this braggart pay my mother's bill.

It's clear that his ego is so huge he can't see anyone but himself," she says calmly before leaving.

The seconds of silence that follow seem to stretch until they seem like hours. When I turn again to the woman in front of me, unsure what to do, she looks at me with a sympathetic smile. "Now do you understand why we don't allow payments anonymously, and without the consent of the family?"

No, I don't understand it, just as I don't understand Iris's outrageous behavior. She can't refuse to help her mother simply out of pride.

*

"What did you do this time?" Lilly greets me with a scolding gaze and her arms crossed.

I walk into her apartment when she steps aside, and I find Damian sitting on the couch with a notepad on his knees, a pen in his hand, and an amused smile as he looks at me.

"Nothing, why should I always be the one who does something wrong?" My answer reflects all the irritation I still feel since fighting with Iris at the clinic.

Lilly motions for me to sit on the sofa next to her boyfriend, then she fills a cup with coffee that she hands to me, and I gladly accept. I couldn't be more nervous right now. A little more caffeine won't make a difference.

"Because you came here to talk, and your face is halfway between a furious man and a beaten dog. You've definitely done something."

I inhale deeply and take a long sip from my cup then start telling them what just happened. As I get on with the story,

Lilly's face looks increasingly disbelieving and Damian starts laughing his head off. They are not helping right now. I need comfort.

"Have you become stupid overnight, or were you born that way?" Lilly's incredulous question makes me even more irritated.

"Look, I didn't do anything wrong. I just wanted to help, and I don't understand why she got so angry. At the end of the day, she accepted the groceries. It's not that different from the camera or the fact that I can pay for the clinic. I can afford it. It's not like it's a sacrifice for me."

Lilly shakes her head as Damian watches me, amused. She tries to explain: "Thomas, the groceries you bought her were a bit like you took her out to dinner and decided to pay. She accepted because she knows that if you go out again, she can pay for you. It's the game of dating, getting to know each other. You pay, then she pays, but you're playing on equal terms, there's no difference between you and her. Give her a camera or pay for the clinic...that's something she can never reciprocate. You're not on the same playing field. Jesus, you're not even playing the same game."

Damian defends me: "He, however, can afford it...and he didn't do it to flaunt his money. It's Thomas we're talking about, the most generous and selfless person I know."

I thank him for that. I need someone on my side.

Lilly smiles and watches us both, shaking her head. "I know you didn't intend to bully her, but the result is the same—she felt inferior to you. Maybe she thinks you see her as weak and helpless, unable to take care of herself."

"But that's not the case. I just wanted to help by making her life easier," I protest.

Lilly smiles and rests a hand on my leg. "How would you feel if someone did something like that for you when you were in trouble?"

"I would have accepted! I'm not that stupid."

Damian bursts out laughing. "But you did insist that we starve like beggars when Joe offered us leftovers when the kitchen was already closed, and we didn't have the money to pay for it," the traitor recalls.

Lilly turns to me and smiles lovingly. "Thomas, not all women need to be saved. Many can make it on their own without a man coming in and solving their problems."

"I know that. I've never considered women the weaker sex. In fact, I think it's the opposite. You can stand everything that's thrown at you...we don't know which way to turn when you leave us. I wasn't trying to be the hero here."

"Thomas, I know you're not doing this for Iris. You're doing it to save yourself for not being able to do something for your family. But she doesn't know that. She only sees the egotistical, arrogant star who tries to solves everything with a swipe of a credit card."

Lilly's words hit me like a punch in the stomach. It's disarming how this woman can read me. When she gets up to wrap her arms around my neck, I feel my eyes burning with emotion.

"Go and apologize to her, because you'll never find a woman like that again."

I don't answer her. I just nod, holding onto her in a hug that gives me courage.

CHAPTER 19
Iris

The hot water flowing down my skin erases the tension I've accumulated over the last few hours. When I think of Thomas's arrogance, anger still squeezes my stomach, making me almost nauseous. How dare he to treat me like I'm his property? Like I can't take care of myself and my mother. I lower my head and let the hot spray ease away that last knot of tension that has gripped my shoulders.

I turn off the water, get out of the shower and approach the mirror now covered with droplets of steam. With my good hand, I rub the mirror with my towel and see my reflection, then I grimace. The bruise on my dislocated shoulder has gone from intense purple to a light blue surrounded by shades of greenish yellow. It's horrible to look at, and even more horrific is the fact that I haven't recovered the mobility or strength in my arm yet, preventing me from doing even the most basic things. My face is a little better than the day after the fall, but the bruises are still visible, if fading slightly.

I struggle to get my bathrobe on just in time to hear someone knocking on the door. I breathe deeply, trying to calm the tension that never really went away. Looks like my apartment has become very busy lately. The fact that I already know who's at the door makes my stomach twist in a vice—partly pleasant, mostly nervous. I know it can't be Emily. She would have used the spare key I gave her a long time ago.

I take a deep breath and open it. In front of me, Thomas holds a cup of coffee and a red velvet cupcake that I know he got from Emily. She's the only one who knows that sweets can turn even my worst moods around for the better.

"Truce?" he pleads in an unsteady voice.

I let him in and, when I close the door and turn around, find him looking at me as if the vision has somehow destabilized him. I realize I'm only wearing a short bathrobe and I feel embarrassed, remembering what it feels like to have his hands and lips on me. The thought makes some of my anger fade, giving way to the desire to undress him and taste every inch of that perfect body.

"I'm sorry, I'm going to change," I say, collecting something in my closet and taking refuge in the bathroom.

I breathe deeply and look in the mirror, seeing my flushed cheeks and a smile on my lips. I slip into a comfortable pair of sweat pants, then look at the t-shirt I grabbed and realize I can't wear a bra, as it is white, see-through and hangs too low under my arms.

"Damn," I hiss between my teeth, realizing I haven't been wearing one for days because I can't fasten it. Still, I grab it from the bathroom shelf and put my arms through, but when I try and fasten it, a tearful pain almost makes me burst into tears. I take deep breaths until the pain returns to a reasonable level. Then I hold the bra with one hand and cover my breasts, even though he's already seen them on several occasions. But this time I'm angry with him and I want him to stay focused on my pissed-off mood, not my nipples. I slowly open the door and find him playing with Dexter, sitting on the edge of the bed. I'm increasingly sure that my cat gets replaced by a more friendly version of himself whenever that guy walks in through the door. There's no other explanation.

"Thomas?" I call in a hoarse voice.

He raises his head and wrinkles crease his perplexed forehead.

"Could you help me out? I still have a hard time fastening it," I say, embarrassed and pointing to my bra.

Thomas seems a little dumbfounded, then gets up from the bed, pissing off my cat, who tries to grab his hand, and approaches slowly. I turn around and give him my back, feeling his fingers move my hair aside, touching my skin, making me shudder. His gestures are slow, almost like he's paralyzed at the idea of touching me, as he grabs the bra straps and calmly joins them, barely grazing me. He gently rests his hands on my back once finished, then he slips a finger under my right shoulder strap and sets it right, sliding along the fabric, touching my shoulder with his knuckle, leaving a glowing trail on my skin. I don't see him, but I can feel his breath quickening on my neck, raising the hair there with shivers of pleasure. My heart bounces in my chest, pounding furiously, and all of a sudden, I realize I'm holding my breath.

"It's okay," he whispers near my ear in a hoarse voice.

His mouth is so close I raise my head, my gaze with his, losing myself in his big blue eyes that, at this moment, look like a stormy sea. Memories of last night, when we made love, come back to mind. The delicacy with which he took care of me, the attention he paid to my bruises, pleasuring me so sweetly, every gesture infused with affection. It wasn't just about sex.

It was about feelings.

"Thank you," I whisper in a faint voice and walk one step toward the bathroom at the same time he steps back.

When I close the door behind me, my legs almost give way, making me slide to the floor. I breathe deeply, trying to get my temperature back to normal and my heart rate to a decent pace. I find it a little difficult to slip on my shirt but, when I finally succeed, I have become more or less presentable. I grab the handle and walk out confident, smiling when I see Thomas snuggled up to my cat, who is licking his cheek.

"It's not what you think," he says thoughtfully, making me smile.

"Yes, of course, that's what they all say."

"I swear he came here and snuggled. I tried to resist him, but he's really too insistent. Basically, I'm a man with a weak heart and will."

I burst out laughing and approach the kitchen. "Do you want some coffee?" I ask, sipping mine and nibbling at the cupcake.

"Yes, thank you."

I notice him coming up behind me as I fill the machine with water.

"Look...forgive me for the way I behaved earlier at the clinic. Believe me, I didn't mean to offend you in any way or put pressure on you. I just wanted to help, but I realize now I was wrong," he admits in a miserable voice, which almost makes me feel tender toward him.

I turn to find him looking down at his toes.

"Did you understand it for yourself, or did your friends have to explain it to you?" I tease him good-naturedly, keeping my voice and my expression light.

Thomas bursts into embarrassed laughter, scratching behind his neck and wreaking havoc on the dark curls that are usually unkempt with meticulous care.

"Okay, they explained it to me because I couldn't figure it out by myself. I swear I wanted to help you, and I didn't understand until Lilly practically made me a drawing to get it into my head."

That makes me laugh out loud, and suddenly, all the anger I had toward him evaporates. I have to admit, I like this side of Thomas, the one who knows how to apologize.

"I appreciate your sincerity." I smile at him, giving him a cup of coffee.

"I just want to help you. I know what it's like to have trouble getting to the end of the month... my mother used to eat half her portion of dinner to give my sister and me a decent meal. Now, I have so much money I could never spend it in a lifetime, so it's no trouble helping people. After all, it's just money. I have enough to live my whole life without struggling, and a safe retirement fund. What do I need with all this extra money?"

It's disarming how he can worry so genuinely and without a trace of selfishness about my life. Money is a bit of a touchy subject for me. I don't like to talk about it, or what I have to do to get to the end of the week without starving. I still get angry because I couldn't go to college, even though I managed to get into New York University and Columbia. Money is a topic I don't want to address, especially with someone who's interested in me.

"Do you have a sister?" I ask incredulously, realizing that

I know practically nothing about this man, apart from the fact that he is one of the most famous drummers in the world. In fact, there is an air of mystery around all the band members that no one has ever managed to dispel.

Thomas bursts out laughing, but I can see he's nervous. "Is that the only detail you picked up in all this talk?"

"No, but that's what stood out. Not much is known about you and your private life."

"It's part of our charm," he says winking at me, and I melt a little, but I realize that he hasn't answered my question.

"Yes, I guess so."

"Promise me that if you need it, you'll ask for my help? I will no longer offer to give you money unless you ask me for it yourself."

I roll my eyes and beckon him to sit at the coffee table. "Yes, I promise that if I need help, I will ask you," I confirm, at least after I have tried everything else by myself.

If there's one thing I've learned growing up, it's that you're on your own, always. You can't count on others because people have their own problems, and their lives are just as messed up as yours. They may be kind people wanting to help you, but at the end of the day, you have to deal with the decisions you make and the consequences of your choices. Others can only give you support, a word of comfort, but they can't solve your problems.

I grab the coffee pot and pour more into Thomas's cup, but since it's my left hand, I spill some of it on the table, swearing softly in exasperation. He grabs the sponge to clean up.

"Does it still hurt?" he asks me worriedly.

I nod and breathe deeply. "Yes. I'm not supposed to use it

for a few weeks and then do physical therapy, but I live alone, and I can't do that. Everything requires two hands, and that only makes my shoulder worse. I hope it will hurt less at some point, but I'm starting to doubt it." My small smile, combined with my confession, does nothing to help calm his worry.

"So you can't even work like this. Or can you?"

I shake my head while I finish my coffee. "No, the camera weighs too much to even think about lifting it and going around taking pictures," I admit. I can't hide my disappointment. "Let's put it this way, I have more time to work on the blog," I smile, but he seems engrossed in his own thoughts.

"What do you have to do to get really good money for your photos?" he asks me. There is no scolding in his voice, just curiosity.

I study him for a few seconds to see if he's serious. I'm surprised when I can't find any sign of humor on his face. "Do you really want to know the truth?" I raise an eyebrow.

He nods and sips from his cup as if this were a typical conversation between two work colleagues.

"Lilly and Damian are worth a lot. They're the golden couple right now. Any public scandal about them would earn me top dollar. You have no idea what Ron is like, the slimy way he manipulates the information he's given. He could mount a scandalous campaign about the Pope if I brought him the right picture. Someone like him could make a picture of two people who love each other seem sketchy, or worse—indecent."

My confession doesn't seem to bother him much. It's almost like we're discussing strategies for my next job.

"It makes sense," he says with such serenity that it puzzles me. I thought he'd jump at my throat, look for a thousand reasons to make me realize that this is wrong, that my job ruins people's lives, that they're human beings, not just superstars. All things that I repeat to myself every day when I get up in the morning, grab my camera, and go out to capture private moments of celebrities. Instead, he is thoughtful, as if he's trying to evaluate alternatives to this situation, but none come to mind.

"Aren't you angry about this?"

"No, I made my peace with your work. After all, it's my problem, how I feel about paparazzi. You just make a living. I get it...and I also realized that you never once reached out to me to get a story to sell."

Thomas eliminates the distance between us by reaching out his hand to stroke my cheek.

"Where the hell did you come from? You're an amazing musician, a world-famous rock star, to-die-for sexy, and on top of all that, you are also one of the most generous and honest people I have ever met. Even in romance novels, the main characters aren't as perfect as you are."

He bursts out laughing at my genuine confession. "They're anything but perfect, trust me. But I try to be a good person, that's all."

He kisses me gently on the lips and in my stomach, those butterflies that I have pretended to ignore until now come to life. Despite everything, including my lies, he's still here, and while I'm in seventh heaven, I'm also terrified. Because while he and I have chemistry in bed, it's in everyday life that we get along perfectly, without any effort. I've learned to expect the worst from life, to be ready for whatever blow comes at me, but I'm afraid this time I won't be able to take it if this happiness is torn from me.

I grab him with my good hand by the shirt and draw him to me, raising my face to look for his lips. His hands cup my cheeks in such a sweet squeeze that he drives away all my fear. It's the most tender kiss anyone has ever given me, and so full of promises that I'm afraid to find out if they'll be kept. But right now, I don't care because Thomas is taking off the very shirt and bra that he fastened a few minutes ago. He's stripping me again like he did last time, his hands feeling their way all over my skin.

His eyes are glued on mine, enjoying every nuance of my pleasure when with one hand, he slips between my legs and finds me ready to welcome his fingers.

"Thomas," a whisper escapes my lips as I close my eyes and enjoy his expert touch.

With one hand, I unbutton his pants while I kiss his chest after his sweater falls to the floor. I slowly savor his skin while my breathing becomes faster and faster. He puts a hand in my hair and draws me to himself. I can feel him tightening my hair in his fingers as if he's afraid I'll slip away from him.

"Get off the stool," he whispers, keeping me steady on my feet while he strips off my pants, leaving a trail of kisses on my thighs while he does so.

"It's not fair that I'm naked and you're not." I smile as I point out his freshly unbuttoned pants and boxers still in place.

Thomas gives me a sly smile and lets his pants and boxers slip to the floor, kicking off his shoes. When he makes me sit on the stool again and positions himself between my legs, he doesn't move his gaze from mine as he sinks into me, keeping me in an iron grip that makes me feel protected.

With my legs curled around his hips, I follow the slow pace of his breathing until I feel the pleasure mount to a crescendo and emotions exploding in my chest as Thomas chokes my moans with a kiss that leaves me breathless.

I stand panting in his arms, feeling him inhale deep into my hair, and when he moves away just enough to look me in the face, a serene smile greets me.

"I didn't hurt you, did I?"

It takes a few seconds to realize he's talking about my battered shoulder. And I shake my head.

"Hurt is not a term I would apply to this situation."

Thomas chuckles as he grabs me by the butt and lifts me from the stool, leading me to the bed, still unmade since this morning. We slip under the blankets, and he wraps me in a hug that seems to melt our two souls into one.

"I wish I could stay here with you for the rest of my life," he whispers in my ear.

I hold on to him and feel my heart explode with happiness.

"Me too," I reply, whispering too, for fear that this magic will end.

CHAPTER 20
Thomas

"You're completely out of your mind."

Michael's voice is the first sound we hear following the silence that falls in Evan's office after I speak. I asked our manager to gather the guys here so I could explain a plan I was excited about sharing with them, but given their faces, I'm not so sure anymore. Even Simon, who's back from Connecticut, is looking at me with wide eyes.

"What the hell did I miss in the month I've been away from New York?" our bassist asks.

Lilly responds for me, the only non-Jailbird member present but naturally involved because she is Damian's girlfriend. "He fell in love with a penniless paparazzo, and now he's trying to save her ass," she chuckles, finding it both amusing and romantic.

"I'm not in love."

"Yes, of course, we all believe you," Michael jokes. "You're proposing we make up a fake story to give her the photos she needs. And, at this point, you'll take the pictures for her because her shoulder still hurts—but you're telling me that you're not in love? I hope she's at least a great fuck."

I expected all of this from him; what I didn't expect is that he would accept Iris. Every day he surprises me more. When I look down and start playing with the ripped hem of my shirt, he bursts into loud laughter.

"Oh, now you don't want to talk about sex? You're worse off than Damian."

"Hey, I'm not that bad," Damian replies half-heartedly, while making sweet eyes at his girlfriend.

I glare at Michael, expecting better from him because he understands what's going through my head right now. If I really didn't care, I'd be making jokes right along with him, not getting pissed off at him.

"You're really in love, aren't you?" My non-answer is enough to make him see the truth of the situation. "For Christ's sake, you're worse off than I imagined," he adds, rubbing his pained face like I'd just told him I was going back to prison. I can't quite read what's in the half-smile he's wearing.

"Okay, so why do we have to come up with a plan for her to make more money? Can't you just give it to her? You're loaded," Simon says pragmatically.

I throw an exasperated glance at him at the exact moment Lilly makes an equally exasperated and annoying sound. "Why the hell do you men have this thing about paying to get us out of trouble?" she asks to no one in particular. Damian's hand rests on her arm. It's strange to see how he's changed so radically in just a few months. I wonder if I'm going to end up the same way, given this room full of people I've gathered for an utterly absurd reason.

"Maybe we're more practical than you women who stir up drama over everything?" replies Simon honestly, and I kind of relate to him.

"I refuse to have this conversation with you too," Lilly says, and on the one hand, I can't blame her. We men are really knuckleheads when it comes to women: pulling these stunts we think are heroic but that probably just make us look like idiots.

Evan gets up and wanders around the desk, leaning against the edge with his arms across his chest and a serious look. He seems to be considering helping me with this crazy plan, and he's trying to figure out how much I am sure of what I'm doing.

"And you know why she needs that money? Are you sure she's an honest person? Does she have a drug problem?" he asks me, and Michael bursts out laughing.

"It's not like drugs are a big deal among rock stars. It wouldn't be the first time," he blurts out amusedly, and I wish I was as cheerful as he is right now. He's not helping me with Evan and, this time, I have to have our manager on my side. I can't go off on my own like I've been doing lately. If something goes wrong, we'll end up in all the newspapers looking like idiots or, worse, manipulators or even swindlers. Not to mention, Iris could get into serious trouble.

"Her mother suffers from an early form of senile dementia. She needs assistance all day, every day, and Iris has no other choice but to put her in a long-term clinic because she can't do it alone. Those clinics cost a lot, and it's hard to find the money," I explain, feeling a little guilty. This is Iris's business, I shouldn't blab about it to all of them, but my band is like my family: what's being said in this room will never leave here, not even under torture.

"Okay, my question is still valid: why not just give her the money?" asks Simon, increasingly puzzled.

"I tried, and she almost ripped my eyes out. Trust me, that girl scares me when she gets angry."

"No, I give up. I don't even want to try to understand how women think," Simon says when it becomes clear that a month out of town was enough to shake up the quiet state he'd left us in.

"Enough with the bullshit. How do we come up with it?" asks Michael.

"I have an idea, but I don't know if you'll like it," Lilly suggests as we all turn and look at her. She's got that enthusiastic, persuasive smile on her face that almost makes my skin crawl. That girl, behind the sweet and innocent facade, could drag you into anything. Lucky for Damian—and us too—there's not a shred of evil in her. Compared to us, she's a lamb in a pack of lions.

*

How Evan agreed to this, I don't know. I think he's with our press office right now writing a press release to try and save Damian and Lilly from what they volunteered to do for me. I'm in front of Iris's door, my heart pumping furiously in my chest, and I feel the urge to get out of here quickly. I'm worried this isn't such a good idea anymore. I'm afraid this time she really will kick me out of her apartment and call the police. I have no time to change my mind because the door to her apartment suddenly opens before I can even knock.

"You're getting creepier and creepier, you know that?" she

says with a half-smile at my dazed face.

"How the hell did you know I was here? I didn't knock... did I?" I ask for confirmation with a puzzled raised eyebrow.

Iris's lips widen into an amused smile. "No, you didn't knock." It reassures me somewhat to hear these words. "I noticed Dexter nervously pacing back and forth in front of the door. I came to look through the peephole, and I found you with a terrified expression," she explains.

"I don't look terrified," I say, pretending to be shocked.

Iris lets me in while she giggles. "Yes, I can assure you that you look terrified, and you're usually like this when you have to tell me something I won't like." She crosses her arms on her chest and raises an inquisitory eyebrow.

I never knew what performance anxiety was until I met this woman. "This time, I'm sure you'll like it."

Her non-answer, and the eyebrow that arches even more, weakens my confidence, so I hasten to add an explanation. "I won't offer you money or try to pay for something you don't want."

"But?" she's too smart to believe it's that simple.

"But you *can* make a lot of money from it," I explain proudly, realizing that, given Iris's perplexed face, I didn't explain anything at all.

She sits at the table stool in the center of the kitchen and looks at me carefully. "Why is it every time you come up with one of your ideas, I get the feeling that I'm going to get mad at you?" Her question is slightly mocking, but she doesn't seem particularly angry.

"No, I swear that this time it is organized well and thought out. I can give you the story you're looking for on Damian and Lilly."

I get her full attention, her face lighting up with hope, concern, perplexity. "And you would sell your friends out like that?" she asks doubtfully.

I smile and shake my head. "Actually, it was Lilly's idea," I admit almost proudly because this time, I didn't act impulsively or alone; I ran it by my friends before I offered it to her or did it behind her back. I'm getting better, given my record.

"Okay, this thing is getting more and more surreal. Who's involved, exactly?" she asks me halfway between incredulous and amused.

"All my bandmates, Lilly and even Evan, who's working with the press office," I say as if it were the greatest idea ever, and I take in Iris's face, first amused, then puzzled, then incredulous.

"So you involved everyone?" her tone is almost shrill.

"I called a meeting tonight. Simon even came back from Connecticut."

"You're completely out of your mind," she says with a smile that makes me hope she's not mad. She's not going to kick me out of her apartment, or attack me screaming like she did at the clinic. It's a huge step forward.

Iris inhales deeply as if she's undecided about what to say. "Well, what is it? You haven't explained it to me yet."

"You'll find out when we get there. You have to get your camera and come with me."

Iris's face darkens. "I can't take pictures with this shoulder."

I smile at her and pound a hand on my chest. "That's why you have an assistant. You tell me what to do, and I shoot in silence," I say as she bursts into laughter.

"I knew you were crazy, but I didn't think you were this crazy. You've completely lost it."

She's right, and what makes me the most nervous is that I've never done anything like this, not since I got out of prison, at least. Since keeping on the straight and narrow, I've become someone who never lets himself get carried away by emotions, who thinks before he acts, who calculates every move. Now, I'm feeling like a little boy on his first adventure.

"So you're in?" I ask for confirmation.

"At this point, I'm curious to know just how far you've gone," she confesses before turning around and going to get her camera bag which I offer to carry.

*

We're stationed behind a six-foot hedge at the park in front of Lilly and Damian's house. When we have a nice view of their stairs and entrance, I position the camera and pull out my phone to send a message to my friends.

"So what? What are we going to do?" Iris asks, the curiosity obviously consuming her.

"Wait, they should be in sight soon."

As if summoned by Iris's question, Damian and Lilly walk out the door. They look around to make sure there aren't too many people around but, thankfully, at eleven o'clock on a Tuesday night, there's not much going on in a residential, private street in this part of Manhattan. The show begins: they pretend to shout at each other, to fight furiously like two crazy people in the middle of the street. They look like mimes gesticulating, pointing an accusing finger at the other, but not making a sound. As I begin to shoot, I feel Iris beside me, struggling to hold back a laugh. The grand finale comes when Lilly pushes Damian on the chest, he staggers slightly back, then she goes back inside, banging the door behind her, or at least pretending to. Meanwhile, my friend sits on the steps, elbows on his knees and hands digging into his long dark hair. When the scene ends, he gets up, gives us the thumbs up, then goes back inside the building laughing like a madman.

Iris turns to me. "You are completely insane. Can you imagine if anyone had seen them shouting like two idiots without making a sound? They'd take them for two fools! Or call the police!"

I laugh and put the camera away. "They would've called the police if they'd really been fighting furiously in the middle of the street. Damian's voice isn't meek and mild...and trust me, Lilly can screech like an eagle. I've only heard her a couple of times, but I had to run before my eardrums pierced."

Iris smiles at my story then lowers her gaze, shyly. "Thank you," she whispers.

I don't know what to say. I'd do anything for her, she doesn't have to thank me. But I suspect that if I say that, she'd think I'm a fool, so I stretch my hand out until I grab hers and squeeze it.

"Come on, they're waiting for us."

Iris looks at me with her wide eyes, and I have to bite my tongue to resist the temptation to lean in and kiss her right here, in the middle of the street. "Who?"

"Damian and Lilly. Do you really think they did that whole scene without wanting to see the pictures? Those two are so picky that, if they didn't come out well, they'd make us stand in the middle of these bushes until we shoot something decent," I explain, and I hear her giggling as I drag her across the street and up the stairs leading to the apartment.

I can sense her amusement but she hesitates as we reach their door and I squeeze her hand. I know she's nervous, and, in a way, so am I.

When Lilly opens the door, she wraps Iris in a hug that leaves her almost disoriented. I see her wide her eyes, caught off guard, while Damian laughs at his girlfriend's affectionate gesture.

"So? How did they come out?" Lilly asks when she finally frees Iris from her grip.

"I don't know. We haven't seen them yet," Iris admits in a somewhat uncertain voice.

"We're here to look at them together," I explain as the hosts guide us to the sofa.

Iris sits down and pulls out her camera. While Damian hands a beer to each of us, I watch Iris laugh at Lilly's words, the light-heartedness on her face. It's a moment that catches me off guard. I could spend my whole life like this, with my best friend laughing and joking along with his girlfriend and the girl I love. The realization comes so sharp, so sudden, that I can't help but feel almost short of breath with happiness, and at the same time, fear. The only time I loved a woman, I gave her everything and ended up in prison, and the feeling that memory elicits scares me and at the same time excites me. I realize I don't have the slightest control over my emotions, and I feel lost.

"What are you doing? What are you waiting for?' Lilly's voice seems to come from afar as my mind is tormented by thoughts overlapping with each other. How the hell am I going to tell Iris about my past without ruining everything? How can I continue keeping her in the dark about a part of my life that has profoundly changed me? The fear that all this may end as soon as my past comes knocking at my door tightens my stomach in a cold vice. I feel like I might faint.

CHAPTER 21

Iris

Sitting on the subway, I smile like an idiot when I think back to last night. The hours I spent laughing and joking with Thomas, Damian, and Lilly, then him taking me home and wishing me goodnight with a sweet kiss at my door. A kiss that became two, then three, and finally a night between the sheets—the memory makes me blush.

I've always wondered what rock stars were really like. I've made a thousand guesses about their personalities over the years, but I never expected Thomas to be such a sweet, at times insecure, generous person who's usually utterly oblivious to how the female universe works.

The lady next to me chuckles as she steals glances at me. I must really be smiling like crazy if I managed to cheer her up. When I arrive at my stop and get off, I wave my hand, and she reciprocates good naturedly. I give some spare change to the homeless man huddled with his dog just outside the entrance to the subway, and walk at a quick pace toward the café where I usually meet Ron.

For the first time in my life, I'm meeting him without the weight of guilt on my conscience, without feeling like I'm losing part of my soul by selling the photos. I called Agata, the editor of a competing newspaper—the other shark in this tank—who has no qualms about running gossip stories. There was a period, between 1990 and 2000, when the paparazzo profession was at its most profitable. Some of those celebrity photographers became famous for their shots and their reckless behavior. The newspapers went out of their way to go after photos, until it got to a point where people were put in life-threatening situations. Celebrities were forced to flee from photographers at top-speeds, and at all hours of the day or night, endangering ordinary people who happened to be in their way.

Photographers and newspaper editors came together and honored their consciences, took a step back, and put a limit on what was allowed. Since then, the decline of the paparazzo profession and its earnings has been slow but steady. Everyone in the media was at that meeting, but Ron and Agata were clearly elsewhere. Although they stick to this non-harassment agreement by buying most of their photos from the agencies, they still pay generously under the counter for great shots. To raise your fee, you just have to involve both of them, and the bid rises with each phone call. Thanks to editors like them, I sometimes manage to get prices that compete with the golden years of our profession.

For what I'm going to sell to Ron, Agata has offered me seven thousand dollars. I've never received such a large proposal. With him, I can play the game of buy low sell high. Worst case scenario, I can go back to that despicable woman, though I was almost tempted to raise the price on her to avoid coming here. I also considered accepting her money and not contacting Ron so I didn't have to see his face. But then I thought back to the satisfaction I'd feel getting the money for a job that's nothing more than a setup. It won't hurt Damian, Lilly, or the Jailbirds' career—they're just fake photos.

I enter the café, and the aroma immediately makes my mouth water. I notice Ron at a table in the corner waving at me, but I take my time, letting him sit on pins and needles. I approach the counter where a new girl smiles and asks me what I want. I order a coffee and a piece of cake, enjoying the luxury of eating more, since I'll be leaving here decidedly richer than when I entered.

"Take your time. It's not like anyone has work to do," Ron says as I sit down, the irritation in his voice making me sneer, satisfied.

"I'm working. Aren't you?"

"Don't come in here and play Miss Know-it-All with me. Let me see what you have," he demands, his tone implying this had better be good. I move slowly on purpose, pulling out my old, run-down iPad with the photos, and slide it in front of his eyes.

His eyes immediately light up like a child at Christmas time, but he quickly recomposes his poker face to hide his true reaction. He's been doing this for so long he probably can't even recognize his own emotions in front of the mirror anymore.

"I'll give you five thousand for those."

His voice has no particular tone, impassive. He's in bargaining mode.

The laugh that escapes my lips is so genuine it surprises him. "Honey, Agatha offered seven thousand. And you know she's stingy, too. Go ahead, call her," I challenge, because I know he's quivering with curiosity to see if what I told him is true.

After five seconds of hesitation, he sends a text. The reply doesn't give him much pleasure because his face looks like he's just swallowed a sour lemon. "Eight."

"She would've offered me at least ten if I hadn't mentioned coming to you."

"Eleven."

"You can do better than that," I venture, knowing he desperately wants them.

"Twelve. I'm never going to get to fifteen, and you know that."

I smile and nod. I know fifteen would make him look weak. I'm okay with twelve thousand dollars for twenty photos. With that money, I can breathe for a couple of months and pay the bills I owe.

"I'll upload them to the site. As soon as I get the money, you can automatically download them," I remind him, because if I don't charge him in advance, he "forgets" to pay.

His bitter laugh is almost gruesome. "What's this? Now that you're fucking the drummer, you snub your nose at me and don't trust old friends anymore?"

I decide not to go into the details of my relationship with Thomas. "You've already screwed me enough times when I was a naïve little girl. I just learned who my friends really are and who I can't trust." My voice is calm, as I'd hoped, despite the anger mounting inside me.

Ron gets up and looks at me with his usual arrogance before moving closer, icily whispering to me: "Remember that you are still a whore. You sold yourself to the drummer to get close to them and take these photos. You just earned twelve thousand dollars sleeping with him."

"Look, these photos exist because of your phone call to Thomas that detonated a bomb in the band. Don't blame me for something I didn't do," I hiss between my teeth.

"Exactly. My phone call revealed that you opened your legs to get something in return...in this case, twelve thousand dollars. How does it feel selling yourself to get what you want? Are you really different from a street whore? At least they're honest about their profession," he shoots at me before walking out the door.

He would've almost convinced me if I didn't remember that Thomas helped me plan this whole thing. If there's one thing Ron can do right, it's get into your head and use your insecurities to get what he wants. But not this time.

Not even five minutes after he leaves, I get a notification that the money has been sent. I immediately transfer it to my personal account and breathe a huge sigh of relief. I'll be able to pay the hospital bill, the monthly fee I owe at my mother's clinic, and maybe even start paying back the thousand dollars Emily lent me almost a year ago. For once in my life, I leave this café with a smile on my lips and the prospect of a bright future ahead of me.

*

I enter the small restaurant in the Tribeca area, and with its rustic wooden coffee tables and red and white checked table-cloths, I feel like I'm in a parallel world, outside the glittering, modern buildings of Manhattan's financial district. The clientele amazes me: casually dressed customers sitting next to businessmen poured into ridiculously expensive suits. No bulky backpacks or Macy's bags scattered everywhere. These are no tourists.

I spot Thomas at one of the tables near the back, under a pergola of fake bougainvillea next to a red brick wall. I've never been to Tuscany, but the rustic wood, flowers, and other outdoor décor mimic a farmhouse in the hills, and it makes me smile. When Thomas sees me, his face opens up in a sincere smile that illuminates his face in a way that makes me almost faint. He stands up, kisses me on the cheek, and with his hand lightly touching my lower back, seats me across from him at the small table. A bottle of red wine is already open and has been poured into two glasses.

"How long have you been waiting?" I ask him.

Thomas smiles and shakes his head. "Not long, but the waiter suggested I pour the wine because it has to 'breathe.' I have no idea what that means," he chuckles as he sniffs the contents and furrows his forehead.

"Don't ask me," I say, shaking my head.

Thomas studies me for a few seconds, then inhales deeply and, while he hands me the menu, asks me the question that is obviously nagging at him "So? Did you sell the photos?" There's no scolding in his voice.

"Twelve thousand dollars," I answer as I smile behind my glass of wine.

Thomas's eyes widen, surprised, then his forehead creases, as though he's puzzled. "I just realized I have no idea if that's a good price or not," he chuckles amusedly, and I echo him.

"I'm happy with it. Ron has never paid me that much," I admit, ashamed of it. After all, those pictures aren't even genuine.

"I'm glad. Lilly will be thrilled by the news." He smiles amusedly but his expression shows his tenderness. She must really be special to him. I noticed it last night when the three of them were so in sync they finished each other's sentences.

"That girl is crazy. Who would've thought of a fake fight?" I admit with a laugh.

Thomas nods vigorously. "She must be. Otherwise, she couldn't be with someone like Damian. As much as I love him like a brother, you'd have to have an infinite amount of patience and madness to put up with him."

I'd like to ask him more, how they met, what they did before they became famous, but fear of sounding like I'm investigating holds me back. I'm always afraid he'll think I'm with him just to get a story, rather than the pleasure of spending time together.

"What do you want to eat?" I ask, looking at the menu, whetting my appetite.

"They have an excellent Sicilian pasta with eggplant and mozzarella," he says. "What sounds good to you?"

"I think I'm going to have the Gnocchi Sorrento," I smile, thinking about when he made me the pesto gnocchi that day he brought me groceries.

Thomas looks up and smiles at me triumphantly. "Then I impressed you with that dish!" He puffs his chest out in a way I've come to recognize.

I smile and nod, giving him this well-deserved victory. "A man who cooks always impresses. If he cooks a fantastic dish, he gets even more points."

When he looks at the menu again, I steal a glance at him. He's comfortable being in a public place with me, at the risk of people thinking we're a couple. Suddenly, I realize how important this moment is, for me, for him, for what we are together. He could have chosen anywhere far from the prying eyes of strangers: my apartment, his, even the record company offices. But he decided I'm important enough to show me to the world, and the fact that he came back, after he knew I had lied, gives me confirmation that Thomas has no intention of pretending that our relationship is only about the sex. The warmth that invades my chest, the irrepressible joy that overwhelms me, makes me smile and, when he looks up at me again, I see in his eyes the feeling is mutual.

*

Yesterday's scenario seems to be repeating today: he's in front of my door, calling on me like a true gentleman and kissing me on the cheek. I smile shyly, though I must have a puzzled look on my face because he stands there staring at me with one eyebrow raised.

"Did I do something?" His question is hesitant, like he doesn't know what to expect for an answer.

"No, absolutely not. In fact, you're a perfect knight," I reply candidly.

"But?" he presses me, and I feel my cheeks burning. I didn't want the conversation to veer off into this topic.

"No buts, I swear...it's just...I don't know... Usually, the guys I go out with don't even give me time to shut the door before they've already jumped on me. But you kiss me on the cheek and wait for me to make the next move... I'm not used to this." I'm stuttering in embarrassment. He'll think I'm a teenager with zero experience. He's probably used to confident women who don't have a problem jumping *him* while I'm here waiting for a kiss on the cheek.

The frown on his face almost worries me. "Rule number

one: never talk about the guys you went out with the one that takes you back to the door. Our egos are very fragile...I don't want to have to go and smash someone's face in."

"Are you jealous?" I want to make a joke, but he seems to be taking it very seriously.

For a few endless seconds with his forehead crinkled, Thomas observes me, then bursts into amused laughter. When he looks at me again, I see an infinite number of emotions I can't decipher. I don't have the time anyway, because his lips are immediately on mine in a frantic, sensual kiss full of affection that I didn't think he could feel. His hands wrap my face as his body gently pushes me into the apartment, closing the door with a slight kick.

"This is the first time in my life that I've gone out with a woman, taken her home after a date, and not even thought about sex. I don't know how to behave. I feel like an idiot sometimes," he whispers to my lips as he pushes me toward the bed, lifting my hips to meet his.

I smile when I feel his hands under my skirt, stroking the skin of my thighs between the stockings and panties; his lips trace the skin of my neck as he gently strips me. Alone in this apartment, our sighs and groans blend together and fill the air as our bodies merge in perfect harmony. Making love to Thomas is a mixture of sensuality and sweetness that inebriates me to the point of near madness. His rock-star confidence disappears in an unceasing pursuit of our pleasure. When he sinks between my legs, we're pushed to the brink of an ecstasy that consumes us until we whisper each other's names. He has me lie on the bed while with his hands, he grabs my legs and rests them on his shoulders, taking the liberty of sinking more into me, making me reach that pleasure peak that makes me tremble.

"Thomas," his name slips from my lips a moment before I steal a kiss that leaves him breathless.

I feel him sinking into his own pleasure while making sure not to crush my body underneath him. This is Thomas: protective and vulnerable at the same time.

"I don't know how to woo a woman, take her out, entertain her, but I swear I'm working on it..." he whispers breathlessly as he lays beside me.

I put a finger on his lips before he can say anything else. "You're perfect just how you are." I kiss him as he grabs a blanket and wraps us in a warm cocoon that feels like home.

CHAPTER 22
Thomas

I wake up with something tapping on my face. It takes me a minute to open my eyes and understand that Dexter is sitting on my chest, pressing his paw on my face. I stretch my arm out looking for Iris's perfect body, but I can't find her. My heart sinks a little, wondering if maybe I was too honest yesterday and she got scared.

I sink my fingers into Dexter's fur and stroke him so he will stop torturing me with his paw and he immediately begins to purr.

"I'm glad to see that he doesn't just wake *me* up." Iris's voice makes me raise my head just enough to see her sitting at the kitchen table, her laptop in front of her and a smile plastered on her face.

I get lost gazing at her beauty, studying how perfect her face is even in the morning when she's just woken up—even more than usual. There's something about this time of day that makes her particularly radiant.

I sit up despite Dexter's protests—he'd spend the whole morning on my chest—and I feel her eyes on me. I slip on my boxers and look for my shirt, but I can't find it anywhere, even in this small apartment.

"I think you're looking for this…" Her words make me

look up, and I realize what happened to the t-shirt. It's so sexy on her that I struggle to hide an erection.

"Keep it. It looks better on you than me." I smile as I approach her and grab her by the waist, lean against her back, and kiss her on the neck.

"Would you like to have breakfast? I haven't cooked anything yet," she asks hesitantly.

Does she really think I'd leave without looking for an excuse to spend as much time with her as possible? The thought almost frightens me. Since when have I been so attached to a woman that I'm looking for an excuse to stay? Usually, it's the opposite: I make up the most absurd stories to be out of their bed as soon as I'm done.

"What do you want me to cook for you?" I whisper in her ear as I deeply inhale the scent of her hair.

"You don't have to do anything. I can do it." I can't tell if there's any irritation or mockery in her voice, so I decide to split the tasks between us.

"Make the coffee while I look at what's in the fridge?"

She nods, jumping down from her chair and freeing herself from my embrace. It feels like she peeled off a layer of my skin and left me exposed.

"Sweet or salty?" I ask as I stick my nose in the refrigerator, which thankfully has been filled since I was here last time.

"Salty is fine."

I take out the eggs, bacon, and sliced bread and find the pots on the kitchen shelves. I spot the dishes and cutlery and realize how natural it is to move around this apartment with her as she hands me a cup of steaming coffee and the eggs start to fry in the pan. It's a routine I never thought I'd do with anyone, and it's both reassuring and terrifying. It doesn't come naturally to me. I wasn't born to trust people. But she's like a drug—I tried her once, and she sucked me into addiction. Like all drugs, though, in the corner of my mind, I know she's going to kill me someday. I can't shake the thought, despite feeling extremely happy with her. Maybe it's because the only time I've ever been this happy is when I was a kid. I forgot how it feels.

I put our breakfast on the table, and she follows me, carrying the cups of coffee.

"How does a paparazzo's life work? Do you go hang out in certain places looking for famous people?" I ask, genuinely curious.

Iris shrugs and makes a slight guttural sound of pleasure as she tastes a bite of the food. It takes considerable effort for me not to pull her into my lap and make love to her for the fourth time in less than twenty-four hours.

"No, not always. I usually take my laptop to one of the cafés in an area where celebrities are known to frequent, then I start searching online for the various accounts that report spotting celebrities. People who hang out on the streets, using social media to report someone's presence. There's usually five or six of us working the same area. I have friends that I trust, and we alert each other in a chat when we hear about celebrity sightings. When a restaurant waits for a high-end customer, there's more frenzy. Often their assistants will call ahead to make sure everything's in order. This gets everyone all excited: waiters are reassigned, tables are freed and reserved... Basically, clues that something is happening. And some of our friends are waiters or drivers who call us with tips."

"Really? What restaurants? Can you tell me?'

She bursts out laughing, clearly amused. "Do you want a tip about where you should never show up?"

"I'm just curious."

"The Mandalay is full of waiters who would easily sell other people's private lives."

"Is that why I met you there a few weeks ago?"

She nods blushing, like she's embarrassed for lying to me. "But I wasn't there to photograph you. Ron called me, saying Alicia was going to be there with her new boytoy. Sometimes, very often lately, it's these people's managers who tip us off."

"If Evan did something like that, I'd punch him in the face," I say with a smile on my lips and seriousness in my voice.

"That night you caught me outside the Mandalay, Alicia played her part and so did the kid. They took their time getting in that car, and they didn't particularly hide themselves from the shots. We were there for major national news outlets—in fact, the next day, the photos came out in the three largest print magazines in the United States."

I feel a little relieved hearing this. "Do you work only for Ron or for other magazines?"

"I don't work for anyone. Photos are usually uploaded to agency websites where magazines pay a monthly subscription. Ron and Agata are the only two people unscrupulous enough to get photos under the table that agencies would never touch—either because they were illegally obtained or too raw to be published without warning the reader. Michael's pictures would never have passed an agency's guidelines, but Ron would sell his own mother for something like that."

"It's absurd how morbidly attracted people are to this kind

of news."

My statement is mostly me thinking out loud, but I see Iris nodding. "I feel sorry for Alicia. Really. She's the one who found herself with an unfaithful husband and a marriage that was falling apart. But the news is so perverted they made it about him running away with a man. What difference does his sexuality make? If he'd run away with a woman, it would have been no different: Alicia's the victim in this case. And yet she gets massacred by the media. People are attracted to what they think is the most scandalous, and the media gives them what they want. They know exactly how many times a link is clicked on their site, what topic attracts the most readers, and what keeps them glued to the page. So–it's more of a scandal in America if you're gay than a cheater."

From her tone and the two small wrinkles that form between her eyebrows, I get how annoyed she is by this, and it's all the more reason I can't understand how she does this job. It's clear that she doesn't want to hurt people; following them and taking pictures like this without feeling something for them is not in her nature.

"But what do you like to do? What does a musician do when he's not on tour?" she asks, smiling, lightening the heavy mood that my questioning brought on.

"We're now at the stage where...we have nothing to do," I admit, chuckling.

"Nothing? Don't you have an album coming out?"

"Yes, but we've finished recording, we're just making the final tweaks, and the marketing staff, along with the press office, has been preparing for the launch for months. In a few weeks, the promotional campaign will start with radio, television, newspaper interviews...basically, we'll be targeted day and night. At its most intense, right around the release date, we'll be doing three or four television appearances a day."

"It must be stressful. The fact that you can't stretch out the promotional appearances over time, I mean."

"It's just a crazy time. Over the years, I've learned to completely trust the people around us who organize our every move. Basically, we do nothing, just show up where we're told. The assistants are the ones who have the worst life." I smile, embarrassed, because we sound like spoiled children.

Iris, however, seems fascinated by this topic and nods. "So, you don't even know which interviews or appearances you'll be doing?"

"No, to be honest, we approved that list months ago. We have the last say in everything we do, but the list is given to us months in advance. When the appointments come up, the assistants get going to keep up. Do you want me to have Evan contact you for an interview on your blog?"

Iris's gaze snaps on mine, and I almost regret proposing it. "My blog isn't at the level of your band."

I smile and watch her mouth settle into a stiff grimace. "If you mean the fact that it doesn't have as many followers as other blogs that are more famous than yours, yes, you're right. But if you mean it's not as professional as the others, you're wrong. It's one of the best music blogs I've seen in recent years and is as good as the most famous magazines or websites in the industry."

She seems to relax at my statement and even blush a little.

"Look, I'll speak to Evan, but he's not the one to decide either. It's going to be the press office."

"Okay." She seems more convinced than before, as she brings the dish to the sink, and I follow her.

I put my hands on the kitchen cabinet, trapping her in my arms, and when she turns, she rests her fingers on my chest, a shy smile appearing on her lips. She tiptoes to kiss me on the mouth, a light gesture, not at all mischievous.

"Thank you for making breakfast."

I smile at her, put my hands on her hips, and lift her up until she sits on the cabinet behind her. "Don't thank me, I had ulterior motives," I tease, sinking my head into the hollow of her neck, kissing her, and pushing my erection between her thighs.

She giggles and, with one hand, stretches to one side of the counter where there is a new box of condoms. Seeing her struggling to move her dislocated shoulder, I wonder if she should be seen by a doctor before she does more damage. Still, I'll need to bring it up calmly, suggesting something that doesn't make her feel embarrassed. I can't do it now anyway, with my brain clouded by her hands exploring my body.

In less than five seconds, my boxers are on the floor and her fingers are sticking a condom on me with a delicacy I'm not used to. When I finally get between her legs, I move her panties to the side and sink into her with a slow movement, enjoying every moment she wraps me with her warm body.

Like last night, we take our time, enjoying each other, and when we finally get to the peak of our pleasure, I feel her sink her teeth into my shoulder gently, making me shudder. I don't think I'll ever get enough of her. Despite panting and almost out of strength, I want to start over, get lost in her like I've never done with a woman. Enjoy her breath, her hair falling on her forehead partly covering her eyes, wide open and full of pleasure, her small and perfect breasts that rise with each of my breaths, becoming swollen against my chest. I wish I could hug her like this for the rest of our lives, and that thought terrifies me to death.

*

The sense of discomfort seizes me when I leave Iris's apartment, and I walk quickly toward Max's car waiting for me. I need to breathe fresh air, talk to someone.

"Can you take me to Michael's?" I ask Max as he opens the door for me.

He looks a little perplexed and maybe even worried, but he doesn't say anything. He just gets in the car and slips into traffic, casting a few glances in the rearview mirror every now and then. I need to talk to my cynical, realistic friend. He can help put my feelings into perspective. Damian and Lilly would only make it worse. Those two, since they met, have been on an eternal honeymoon. I shudder at the thought.

Max takes me to Michael, who is on the roof of a building by the Hudson River playing golf. I didn't even know there was such a place in Manhattan, let alone on a rooftop, but the fake grass and protective nets contrast wonderfully with the view of New Jersey across the river. The practice cubicles are practically empty since it's morning on a work day in the middle of winter, with a cold that penetrates your bones.

"Since when do you play golf?" I ask him amusedly.

Michael throws a glance my way before hitting the ball with the golf club in a swing I wouldn't exactly call elegant. "Playing isn't quite the word. It's more like hitting those poor balls without having any idea how to do it," he chuckles, teeing up another ball and hitting it worse than before, sending it only a few feet in front of him.

I watch him, amused, and sit in the chair a safe distance away. "So I see."

"It's relaxing. I found that hitting a ball in a purely mechanical way loosens my tension."

"I need to try it too."

"Isn't it enough to be fucking the redhead?" He raises an eyebrow and then sits next to me, following my gaze toward the river.

"I think she makes me more tense."

"Because she isn't good at fucking or because you've decided to do it exclusively with her?" he jokes in his usual irreverent way.

"The latter, definitely the latter." I rub my face and try to put my thoughts together.

"It's not a bad thing, I don't think. I mean, look at Damian. He looks happy with the same woman. I'd go crazy, but you two seem like normal people." He shrugs.

I look at him, shocked. I didn't expect this. I thought he'd say I should go out and fuck the line of women waiting for me in the Manhattan clubs. "I've never wanted a relationship, and now I find myself so deep in it I'm scared to death."

Michael can't hold back a laugh. "It's pretty clear that you're in up to your neck. But can you tell me why? Is it still about that story and my pictures? That's all water under the bridge for me, I swear."

"No, I made my peace with her job. If you say it's not a problem, it certainly isn't for me."

"Then what is it? That shit about you not trusting women? You already know how I feel about that."

"This morning I woke up at her house, she was at her computer, wearing my shirt. It all seemed so perfect: I got up to make breakfast and talked about our day like it was the most natural thing in the world. And that's what terrifies me."

"Don't you like her enough to consider living together? I don't get it."

"I'm too happy."

Michael stops fiddling with the ball in his hand and turns to me with a confused look. "And is that a problem?"

"No, it's just that happiness never lasts for me, and I'm afraid one of these days I'll get up, and it'll all be over. I've taken her home for two nights now, and when I'm at her door, I don't know what to do. I kiss her on the cheek. Can you believe that? I kiss her on the cheek, and I stand there like an idiot, wondering if it's too much to suggest going inside. She's the one who makes a move every time. I have no idea how to be in a relationship, and every time I think about it, I wish I could ask my mom or my sister, who's married with three kids, but I can't. I've lost the only women my life, the most important ones, and it's been my own fault. I'm afraid of repeating the same mistake."

Michael smiles and I expect him to make a joke, like he always does when the topic of women comes up between us. He leans toward me and remains silent for a moment, thinking carefully about what I just told him. "Do you remember when Evan offered to represent us, and you were hesitant at first? You said we shouldn't delude ourselves because, in this industry, fame comes and goes, that it's not a guarantee. Even then, you were terrified, you just tried not to show it with that know-it-all attitude. You were afraid our good fortune would suddenly disappear overnight...but it didn't. We worked hard, sweat blood, but we're still here. Fuck, we even managed to get over my cocaine bullshit. Are you telling me you won't be able to keep a relationship together with a good woman?"

"What if I fuck it up?"

"You will work on it until it's fixed. You've already done the worst shit in your life and you've paid for it, you're not going to repeat the same mistake."

"What if she doesn't want to be with someone who ended up in prison?"

"More likely, she won't want to be with someone who lies to her to the altar. My advice is to tell her."

I know the longer I wait, the harder it will be, but is there ever an easy time to drop a bomb like that? Maybe waiting for her to fall in love with me, the actual me, who I am now, without being influenced by my past, will help her accept what I've done.

"Since when did you become so wise?" I grin, looking him in the eye.

"I've always been, it's just easier to be the clown than to be the confidant of desperate lovers like you."

"I'm not desperate!"

"But you are in love."

"Yes."

Michael pats me on the shoulder, clutching it slightly before getting up again. For him, that's as much as a hug, and I'm comforted by this rare show of affection as I watch him go back to hitting golf balls.

CHAPTER 23
Iris

When I go out for lunch at Emily's café, I'm grinning from ear to ear, looking as ditzy as a teenager in her first crush, but I honestly don't care. I've never been someone who's desperate to be in a relationship. I've been single for a while, but that doesn't mean I don't enjoy someone's company, and, in this case, I enjoy everything about Thomas. He's intelligent, kind, handsome as hell, and he knows how to drive a woman crazy in bed. Plus, I have to admit, the fact that he's a famous musician who actually makes music for a living intrigues me. Everything about him makes me believe that fairy tales maybe do exist, and I happen to be right in the middle of one of them.

As soon as I enter the café, Emily sees me and, throwing her apron in her co-worker Chris's face, she shouts that it's time for a break. Less than five seconds later, we're sitting next to each other on the most remote sofa in the place and she's looking at me like I'm her new favorite toy.

"That smile on your face makes me jealous, you know that, right? Why didn't you come for breakfast this morning? I was waiting for you." She raises an inquiring eyebrow.

I can't hold back an even bigger smile that betrays all my unholy thoughts about last night…and part of this morning. "I was busy."

"Did you do the nasty with him?"

"Yes, he came over last night." I like to keep her on pins and needles.

Emily sighs dreamily. "And he stayed until almost at lunch? Did you have breakfast together? So it's not just sex anymore...I mean, you're trying to keep him around for more than a few stunts in bed?" She teases me.

"I don't know what it is, but it's definitely not like a few weeks ago. I don't know how to explain it, but he made me breakfast, we talked about us...it was nice, but it felt really natural. Like we've been doing this for years."

"So now that you've been to the Mt. Olympus of rock musicians, do you think you're going to start living it up like they do? A different guy every night?" She laughs amusedly.

"Absolutely not. I'm already messed up with one, forget taking on others."

"Do you think there's any way to have a monogamous relationship with him? On both sides, I mean."

It's her way of asking me if we're a couple and, to be honest, I have no idea. I don't know where we are, and I certainly won't ask him. I've never been good at these things and, with someone as famous as Thomas, I'm afraid of seeming like a desperate fan looking for a chance to frame him.

I can't answer her because we're interrupted suddenly by Ron, who sits in front of us on the couch. We both turn to him, surprised. In my case, with my heart beating in my throat: how much did he hear of our conversation, exactly?

"What the hell are you doing here?" I hiss, annoyed by his invasion of my favorite place.

"A source told me that someone who looks a lot like the Jailbirds' drummer came out of your house this morning. I knew you had opened your legs for him and, apparently, you're still doing it. What can you tell me? Any juicy news about it? You must have had a conversation, I assume. With what I paid you for those photos, you owe me at least that," he says with his usual lousy fake smile.

"How the hell did you get here so fast? Did you send someone, or did you spy on me in person?" I ask, and I realize that the latter assumption is the correct one. Otherwise, how did he get here exactly five minutes after me? Even if he had someone stationed down here, he could never have arrived so fast. The realization floors me—if he went to the trouble of hiding in my garage, then he knows much more than he's letting on, and I may end up in that damn magazine of his soon.

"Don't be difficult. I know you're opening your legs for money. Do think I'm stupid? At least use that little body of yours to get me more details. Where does he come from? What did he do before he became famous? You've never wondered why there's no information about those guys? There's not a single piece of news about their past. It's like they materialized here ten years ago and became rock stars instantly. You've never been curious to know who you're really sleeping with?"

His sneer is so smug that I'm rendered speechless by his insinuations. Emily's the one who rescues me. "Look, piece of shit, get out of my cafè or I'm going to call the police. In fact, I'm going to do more. I'm going to start making a scene right here, complete with tears and accusations. You won't be able to show your face around Manhattan anymore."

"Do you really think you're scaring me? Everyone sues me. But don't worry, if you two don't collaborate, surely your friend will know how to help me."

Emily and I look perplexed, and the sneer it brings to Ron's face almost makes me shudder. He's got something up his sleeve that I'm missing and it worries me. I get the feeling he's not one but ten steps ahead of me, and all my happiness from a few minutes ago vanishes.

"Think about it, honey. Do you really think this fairy tale will last? He's going to get tired of you and dump you like every girl he's had. I, on the other hand, am always here, ready to shower you with money. Decide who you want to make an effort for."

He turns around and leaves the cafè, followed by numerous intrigued and annoyed glances. His act of humiliating me did not go unnoticed.

"You okay?" Emily whispers.

"Yes...I was just thinking. What the hell did Ron mean 'my friend'? Who the hell could he ask for help? Besides you and Albert, no one knows about us..." The uncertainty in my voice reflects the fear creeping into my stomach right now.

"In the last few days, Albert's been asking questions about Thomas: if I know anything about him, if you're together or something," Emily says, frowning. "I thought he was just jealous because he's had a crush on you for years, but after what Ron said... Didn't he seem sure he knows something we don't? Or is it just me?"

"Way too confident. What did you say to Albert? What was he asking for in particular?"

Emily shrugs and thinks about it for a few seconds. "If you're sure what you're doing. If you know anything about Thomas. The same things he asked on pizza night at your house. He was hoping to get some more information, I think, but I couldn't give him much. First, because it's none of his business, and secondly, because I don't know much more about Thomas. Do you think I messed up?"

"Albert hasn't been around since the day after our pizza night, and now I'm wondering if there's something I missed about that night."

"I remember you wanted to know if he had asked questions. Do you think we forgot about something we talked about because we were too drunk?"

"I don't know. I have vague memories of that evening, but I distinctly remember he did not touch the tequila. Before we got drunk, you passed him the bottle. He sniffed it but made a face without touching it. I remember thinking: What a loser, he can't even hold his liquor."

"Do you think he got us drunk on purpose to make you talk about Thomas? It's Albert. That seems to be a pretty elaborate plan even for him," she asks me doubtfully, and it nags at me.

"Maybe he didn't come over for that purpose, but he took advantage of the situation. I mean, he certainly put his nose in my laptop, but why clear the history and then leave the outgoing e-mails, with the tickets he forwarded to his personal e-mail? Why hide his research but not the fact that he was stealing my tickets?" I can't put the puzzle together, and it irritates me almost physically.

"Do you think he's hiding something from you?" Emily's face gets serious and worried. "Or trying to protect you? Maybe he's worried because you're seeing someone you don't know anything about because, to be honest, you don't know much about Thomas and, from what you say, he seems too good to be true."

Emily's words awaken a thought that I've tried to silence several times: I always found it strange that no one knew anything about the band even before I knew him. We live in the age of the Internet, where if you're famous, you can't even go to the bathroom without half the world knowing. There's something strange about not finding any information about their past.

"I don't know, I don't have a logical explanation for that evening, and it bothers me... Maybe it's just me being paranoid because Ron's staking out my house. When that slimeball's around, I can't even think clearly."

"Do you think Ron found out that the photos you gave him were fake? Maybe he wants to make you pay."

I raise my healthy shoulder and breathe deeply. "I don't know. The Jailbirds' manager issued a press release denying the breakup and as far as I know, the matter ended there."

"Maybe he just wanted to scare you." She tries to encourage me, but her voice doesn't sound convinced.

Yes, maybe he just wanted me to capitulate, but it's never that simple with Ron, and the doubt he insinuated starts digging into my brain and heart, making me worry. I grab the phone and try to call Albert, but he's not answering. I have to deal with him and get some answers.

*

Not even an hour after seeing Ron, I'm back home with a notebook and a list of things about Thomas that I know from our conversations but never gave much thought to. I stare at a Google search page with a growing sense of guilt, even though I haven't started digging for news about him yet. It annoys me to death because I want our relationship to be normal—to the extent that we have a relationship—but I need to know what information Ron can get even without my help. Thinking back to that night we got drunk, I could kick myself for telling Albert what I knew about Thomas just to get him to stop talking.

As I type keywords into the search window, I keep telling myself that I'm doing it to keep Thomas from any trouble with Ron, but I don't feel less guilty about sticking my nose in his private life. He decided to share just a few things with me, as in any normal relationship. Using my experience as a journalist to find out more about him makes me feel slimier than when I was walking around looking for photo opportunities.

After two hours of searching, I'm back at square one. There's nothing about Thomas in New York. His name doesn't appear in any school yearbook in the city. I look at my notebook and realize how stupid I am: he once told me that his mother married her neighbor and that they never left the small town where they lived. She never visited Italy, or Manhattan, which was just a step away. The realization makes my legs go weak. Everything public about the Jailbirds, or at least Thomas, seems artfully staged.

I look for all the small towns around New York City, and I notice there are a lot in New Jersey. In the end, it doesn't take long to figure out what it might be. I eliminate places where there are no Simons and where there are a few, I check and see that they clearly have nothing to do with Thomas. I'm left with a couple of cities, but too many families that could be false leads.

I start pacing in my tiny apartment with Dexter watching me, bored. I don't have the energy to do more research. I'm stuck, and while part of me breathes a sigh of relief that there's nothing questionable about him, I'm now a bundle of nerves because there's no information at all. Ron knows this—he clearly said that the band seems to have materialized a few years ago. He's not stupid. On the contrary, he is brilliant, and the fact that he does not own a moral compass makes him dangerous. The Jailbirds have been careful not to divulge news about their private lives, but Thomas confided in me. I'm the weak link in the whole chain, and I've been stupid enough to get drunk with the only person who has the means to dig deep, given the new confidential information he has.

I don't remember much about that night, but if I blurted everything I know about Thomas, the problem could be huge. I grab my jacket and open the door, my heart threatening to leap into my throat.

*

Standing in front of the building of the most famous newspaper in New York City, I look up and feel a pang of guilt nipping at my heels. It's my last chance to see if I've done any damage and whether I have an opportunity to fix it or even stop it. Albert has always been very loyal to me, he's helped me whenever I needed him, but his disgust with my relationship with Thomas makes my toes curl. It's over the top, and since my conversation with Ron, his persistence has taken on alarming connotations. How long has Ron been following me, and how did he get in touch with Albert?

I take the elevator that brings me to the newsroom and, with my heart slamming in my chest, I approach his desk.

"I hate it when you have that look. It means you have to scold me, or you're mad at me," Albert whispers, so others don't hear. There's so much noise in this place that if I hadn't leaned in, I wouldn't have heard anything either, but we're still in a newsroom, and there are ears where you least expect them.

"Good morning to you, too. It's a pleasure to see you. How are you?"

Albert rolls his eyes at my sarcastic response and then smiles. "What do you want? Really." His face is suspicious, but I think mine is more so. I think my guilt is turning into paranoia, and I'm looking for any sign that helps me understand where this conversation is going.

"Did Ron try to contact you?" I ask, not beating around the bush. After all, Albert wants to be a journalist. It's his job to be wary of everything.

Albert's lips tighten in a fine line and his jaw contracts, letting me know I'm on the right track. "Why would you care about that?"

"Because he's just been to the café where Emily works and threatened me. I'd like to know how many people are trying to stab me in the back." What the hell am I thinking taking up the challenge of this idiot?

"Do you really think I'm the problem? You sleep with someone you don't know anything about, but the problem is who I talk to when I'm at work? Do you realize how crazy that sounds?"

The fact that the focus has shifted from Ron to the person I'm sleeping with makes me nervous, and I'd like to take the stapler on his desk and shut his mouth. "First, it's none of your business who I sleep with. Second, I don't know what Ron promised you, but if you try to use what I told you to get him a story, I swear I'll destroy you."

"What are you afraid of? Finding out something you don't want to know about your precious Thomas?"

"No, I'm not worried about that. My problem is that Ron spreads lies to make money and then ruins people's lives."

"That's funny, I thought you were the one who sold Michael's pictures."

I give him the evil eye. "Do you really think you can scare me? Believe me, honey, I can handle much worse."

A colleague stands up in the cubicle next to us and throws us a worried look. Albert sees it, and this seems to cool him down somewhat. "I didn't say anything to Ron. I swear... Besides, I have nothing to give him."

His answer encourages me, but not much. He hasn't yet done his research, but sooner or later, he will. "There you go, good. Quit while you're ahead."

"I'm a journalist, Iris. You can't expect me to shut up and watch when I have a potential story on my hands."

"First, you're an apprentice, you're not yet a journalist, and the information came to you from an untrusted source, from the assumptions and speculations of a paparazzo. I wouldn't play this card if I were you. You know credibility is everything in this job, and I have a thousand ways to disprove everything you're going to reveal," I threaten him, perhaps more vehemently than I should, and he pulls his chair back to put a little distance between us.

"I understand, don't worry. It's not like I work for a gossip magazine. I still have nothing to write. And Ron's a slimeball if he thinks he can buy me with a piece of candy. Like I'm his dog," he snorts, trying to change his approach.

I don't trust him. Not Albert, not Ron. I don't trust anyone in this situation, but I can't do anything because I don't know how far he's gone in his investigating. My only hope is that I didn't tell him everything that night, that some details were lost due to my level of alcohol intoxication, and that Albert was at least a little tipsy.

I should tell Thomas so he can alert the press office to catch the damage. But what damage? I don't know anything about Thomas, I don't know anything about what Albert is aware of, and I don't know if he'll talk to Ron. What exactly should they worry about? I should be relieved—if Albert had anything to use against Thomas, he would have done it—but I'm afraid this is more serious than I suspect. I'm afraid Thomas will lose whatever trust he put in me after he forgave me. How many times can you forgive a person who constantly makes the same mistake?

CHAPTER 24
Thomas

Iris looks around at my living room in wide-eyed wonder, like a child in a museum—the museum of science and technology, to be exact. It's so different from her apartment she might as well be on another planet.

"Is that a chair?" she points at the Space Shuttle.

I smile, amused, and nod. "Yes. If you sit on it and turn fast enough, it shoots you into orbit."

She laughs and does it, playing like a little girl. "It's true. If you stop suddenly, you find yourself splattered against the window. But you get a fantastic view of Central Park."

I approach her and sit in the other chair, which, thankfully, remains stationary, anchored to the floor. "Right. It's the only thing I like about this apartment," I admit with sincerity.

"Why do you live here, then, if you don't like it?" Her question is straightforward, curious.

"Because it's a good investment. I saw the pictures, it was in a good location, I bought it."

"You never saw it before you bought it?" she asks me incredulously.

I laugh and shake my head. I guess for her, and for any normal person, that sounds absurd. A few years ago, I would have thought so, too, but now I understand what matters most in life, and this apartment is without a doubt an investment, and that's it.

"I didn't care, it was a property that would gain value over time, and my consultant told me it was a great decision to buy it."

"So you didn't choose this furniture." More than a question, it sounded like a statement, and she's relieved when I shake my head no.

"I found it this way. I've been wanting to furnish it more to my taste, but in the few weeks I'm home, doing nothing, honestly, I don't have the energy to take it all apart. I keep putting it off so it's stayed exactly as it was when I bought it. I swear, some things I just haven't figured out yet."

Iris listens intently, like I'm telling her the secrets of the universe, and I'm starting to get embarrassed. I'm like a kid babbling on about random things in front of his first crush, and with horror, I realize it isn't the first time this thought has crossed my mind.

"Don't you want it to feel like it's yours? Like a home?"

I shrug and think about it. "For me, a house is the people who live there, the love that's created inside the walls, not the walls themselves. Any place is home when the people I love are with me."

"The Jailbirds," she whispers.

I don't respond. This is a minefield; sooner or later, she'll ask about my past, and I don't know if I'm ready to go into detail with her.

I try to change the topic with a bad joke that might make her smile. "But how come you didn't want to go out to dinner tonight? Not that I mind making you dinner, trying to get into your panties by showing off my cooking skills, but you see-med pretty tense when I texted. You didn't even want me to send Max to pick you up." Her eyes don't light up at my light tone like they usually do, and it worries me.

"You know Ron? The man I sold Lilly and Damian's pictures to? The other night he stationed himself in my garage and saw you leave my apartment. He's definitely realized there's something going on, and even though I've denied it, I'm afraid he's going to send some of his people to stalk us. I'm sorry I dragged you into this," she admits miserably, as if it was her fault.

I can't help but burst into laughter. "You dragged me?"

"If I didn't work with Ron, he would've never figured it out. I'm no one special in Manhattan. He only found out because he keeps an eye on me."

"Trust me, every step I take is monitored. You should know that. If you hadn't worked for Ron, do you think our date would have gone unnoticed?"

"If we were careful, probably, yes."

"The places I'm used to going, waiters would sell their souls to the devil—or Ron, in this case, for a story. It's part of the game, and if it doesn't bother you, it's not a problem for me. Does it make you uncomfortable to go out with me?" I ask her when doubt assaults me.

Now it's her turn to laugh, and I find myself getting lost in the melodious sound that sends shivers down my back.

"No, how could it bother me? I'm certainly not used to the attention since I'm usually on the other side of the lens. But that didn't stop me from meeting someone I really care about."

Her confession makes me happy and scared all at once.

Soon, she's going to want to know more about me, and I won't know how to answer her. "Good, because tonight you will experience my famous lasagna...and no, don't make that face, that's not an analogy for sex." She laughs, and I get up to go check on the oven.

"What are these? Why do you have hundreds of decorated cookie packages?" she asks, puzzled when she sees the boxes on the couch.

I feel embarrassed. I forgot to hide them in the guest room before she arrived. I don't want her to react like Lilly when she discovered Michael likes to carve wood. "I made them," I admit.

She looks at me dumbfounded for a moment, as if expecting me to tell her it's a joke, but then she picks up a box and looks at them carefully.

"Did you really make them? Even the decorations? They look professionally made—like at a bakery!" she exclaims, impressed, and my chest swells with a bit of pride.

"When I was a kid, I used to make them with my mother. She taught me how to make the icing, and I always had a certain artistic side to me, so I took to it easily. I usually make them when I need to blow off some steam. Staying focused on decorating distracts my mind from my problems...like a fight with the girl I like," I admit sheepishly.

"Oh...then it's my fault that your house has turned into a pastry shop."

I laugh. "You helped make the holidays much sweeter for all the homeless people in the city."

"What about those?" she asks, pointing to more cookies sitting in front of the stove where I'm busy cooking.

"Claire, my assistant, packed them up to donate them to a charity that raises money for a foster home in Queens. They need a new roof, and they're running out of cash."

"Wow. They'll have a line out of the store when they know they're your cookies."

"No one knows they're mine. Not even my friends. It's something I do anonymously...something that only Claire, and now you, know about."

Her blushing rosy cheeks almost make me melt. "And I thought you couldn't get any more perfect." She looks at me with a dreamy glint in her eyes.

And now I'm blushing, but in shame. I'm anything but perfect and, even though she keeps saying it, I can't hide the guilt I feel for deceiving her.

*

"It's amazing. Did you really make it?" she asks me, her eyes wide.

I smile and nod while I pour another glass of wine for her. "Yep, do you really like it?"

She nods and takes another bite as if it's the best thing she's ever tasted. "Did your mother cook this too, besides gnocchi?" she asks, and I shake my head, happy to have an anecdote about the Jailbirds instead of my biological family.

"Actually, no. During our first European tour, the band finished our gigs in Italy and, since we didn't have the obligation of more shows, we stayed on for a two-week vacation. I fell in love with the cuisine and lifestyle there. The flavors were spectacular! And it seems like my taste buds have a mind of their own because sometimes I'll remember eating something there and my brain shouts at me to cook it instantly." I laugh at my twisted explanation.

"I think your taste buds are right, and I also think you'll have to cook for me more often because these are the best dishes I've ever tasted in my life." She laughs and it's contagious. I find myself watching her cleaning that perfect mouth with the napkin, and I just want to kiss her.

And that's what I do. I lean over the table and kiss her on the lips, savoring the taste of the sip of wine she just drank. "I'm sorry, I couldn't resist."

Iris smiles as she looks down. When it comes to my displays of affection, I find her blushing, like a young girl, incredibly sexy. "Don't apologize. I'm glad."

"What's your specialty?" I ask. "What do you make when you have to win someone over with your cooking?"

Iris thinks about it for a second. "I think cottage pie." She nods like that's the right answer.

"Really? How come? It's not a very American dish."

Iris shrugs and takes another sip of wine. "My mother is Irish. She moved here when she met my father and then they got married. It's a dish from her childhood; she used to make it for me a lot when I was a little girl. I'd cook it for her when she started showing the first signs of dementia because it seemed to trigger some memories. Maybe, as you say, taste buds have memories that activate the brain. Unfortunately, that trick hasn't worked for years." Her smile is melancholy.

"That explains your complexion," I say without thinking.

"What?" She frowns.

"Your pale skin, red hair, green eyes, freckles…it's all very Irish or Scottish."

"Oh, right. My dad didn't give me much from a genetic

point of view. I don't look like him at all." She laughs amusedly, and I can't even imagine what her father could be like. "And you? Who do you look the most like? Does your sister look like you?" she asks as panic begins to take over. What the hell do I tell her?

I inhale deeply and then put a massive bite of lasagna in my mouth to buy some time. Her eyes are on me, expecting an answer. I take a sip of wine. "I have my mother's eyes, but otherwise, I look like my father. My sister...I don't know if I look like my sister." I stop short. The last time I saw her, I was just a kid. We've both changed a lot. At least, I know I've changed a lot, physically and otherwise. I'm sure she has, too, since she's a mother of three children I'll never know.

"Don't you know if you look like your sister?" she asks, puzzled.

Iris isn't an idiot. She knows this story of mine has holes all over the place, and she's probably annoyed that I haven't told her everything, though you couldn't tell it from her expression. This is why I never wanted to be in a relationship—sooner or later, you get to know each other beyond the sex, and I have nothing to say. I have a history that I want to keep in the past, for my own sanity, and therefore have nothing to offer anyone but lies and evasion. The problem is that with Iris, I'm beginning to think this "us" thing could work, and as much as I tell myself to stay away, it's just impossible to do that.

"We don't call each other very often, and I don't see her much. She doesn't live in New York."
My answer is nowhere near complete.

"Where does she live? In the same town where your family is?" She sips some wine casually and rests her gaze on me. I feel suffocated.

"No, in Australia. She moved there ten years ago."

"It must be hard to live so far away...even if you've never been particularly close," she points out, and I can't tell if she's saying it because she knows it's breaking my heart in two or if she's trying to find a way to make me smile again after noticing my jaw tighten.

"Are you finished? Do you want more?"

Iris seems caught off guard by my change of topic. "No, thank you. It's delicious, but if I eat any more, I'll explode." She smiles, massaging her stomach.

I grab the dishes and take them to the sink, rinsing them before putting them in the dishwasher. She follows me, bringing the two glasses of wine still half full.

"Thomas, you know there's nothing in your past that you should be ashamed of, right? That I would never judge you... Jesus, I'm the last person who has a right to judge anyone. I want you to know that you can trust me," she says earnestly.

I can't take my eyes off what I'm doing. I know if I look at her right now, I'll lose it. All my resistance would melt. But I can't do it. With this whole situation, it's not just me I'm protecting but also the three guys who have been with me for years. Before I blurt out, "We've been in prison," the least I can do is ask them for permission to share our secret with her.

She's not the problem. It's me, my past, that I can't make peace with. So far, I've simply ignored it. I changed my life. I changed my name. It's like I erased that night over ten years ago, and that stupid kid who thought he was so tough was just someone I met when I was a teenager and lost sight of.

"Yes, I know. I do trust you. I just have a hard time talking about myself. I haven't done it in a long time, and I have to get my confidence back with all of this." I tell her a partial truth.

Iris nods and slips the glass of wine into my hands. I drink some and watch a sincere smile appear on her lips before she sips from her glass. "Okay, so if you trust me, do you want to tell me the real story about how you ended up in the middle of a pile of diapers and toilet paper when you were just buying milk and cookies? Or about the half-pants at the festival, if you like."

I burst into laughter, grateful she wants to steer the conversation toward a completely safe subject. "Have you ever had hot milk and cookies? Really, it's the basis for every happy evening. Sofa, TV, and hot milk and cookies. There's nothing better."

"Lucky for you I didn't eat any more lasagna, so you can give me a live demonstration."

Her proposal is so simple and disarming that I feel the air leave my lungs and return with difficulty. Sleeping together is one thing, preparing her dinner, a little more private but certainly not intimate like spending the evening watching a movie on the couch eating milk and cookies. That tastes like home, feels like family, something I lost years ago.

"Go pick the movie on Netflix while I prepare the meal of the gods."

Iris laughs as she walks away from the kitchen, and I'm glad she didn't hear the panic in my voice. I grab the phone as soon as she's out of earshot and try to call Michael. He's the only one who can reason with me and make the panic that's settling into my stomach disappear. His phone goes directly to voicemail.

"Shit!" I whisper, setting mine on the kitchen counter.

*

I enter the dark living room, illuminated only by the moon. Iris is in the bedroom, sleeping, but I couldn't fall asleep. The evening slipped between the warmth of a blanket, a cheesy movie, and the comfort of something I did as a child with my family. Sharing such a heartwarming moment with Iris brought me closer to her in a way that I didn't think possible. In my heart, it feels like this red-haired girl, with her sarcastic humor, has been in my life since I was a kid. Back when I was happy. Sharing this piece of happiness with her was so natural it frightened me. Because Iris is now a fundamental part of my heart, she helped transform my survival into a joyful existence, and I wish I could savor this joy with my family. I can make love to Iris as many times as I want, but sex with a woman can never fill that void that family fills.

I sit in the spinning chair and look at the darkness that is Central Park right now, hoping to make sense of the thoughts that crowd my mind. I look at my phone, and without thinking about it, I start scrolling through the names. I get to "S" for Sarah, a name that no longer exists in the registry, but will always be the one I said a million times when I was little. My sister is now called Margaret, a name I never liked and will never be able to accept.

The temptation to press the call button, hear her voice again, is strong. I haven't done it in the last ten years. At least not personally; I've always pushed my lawyers forward, and I've always found a wall on the other side. Again, like every other time, I turn off the phone before I can change my mind.

It will soon be Christmas and, like every year, I'll find myself wandering around FAO Schwarz on Fifth Avenue among thousands of toys I'd like to buy, and I'll eventually leave empty-handed. I don't know anything about my nieces or nephews: their age, their names, their tastes. Every now and then, I wonder if they look like me, if they like music, if they've ever listened to anything of mine. We're famous worldwide, even in Australia, but I don't know if my sister has ever told them about me. I wonder if she changes stations when they hear our song on the radio.

Iris brought back a flood of feelings that I can't handle. Memories I want to forget, wounds that have never healed. It was hard watching the movie with her tonight because she snuggled up by my side, eating milk and cookies, like I used to do with my sister when we were kids. We watched Christmas movies, and she was always angry because I thought they were stupid. I basically liked them, but I wouldn't admit it out loud. There are so many things I've never said to her, like 'I love you' or 'Thank you for taking care of Mom.' As a child, I was ashamed to say certain things. Now, I wish I could shout them from the window of this building, so loud it would reach her on the other side of the world.

I'm staring into Central Park as tears cloud my sight, then fall down on my cheeks and turn into sobs that shake me until I'm trembling in this chair.

"Hey," Iris's whisper almost sounds like a cry at this time of night.

I'm so surprised to see her here that a sob dies in my throat. She rests a hand on my shoulder as I wipe tears on my arm.

"Do you want me to help you bake cookies?" She smiles as she sits on my legs, wrapped only in a light blanket she found at the foot of the bed.

I smile at her attempt to save me from embarrassment and make me feel better. "No, Claire will kill me if I bake another batch." A half laugh escapes my lips as Iris caresses my hair, kissing my head and making my sadness slip away.

I grab her hips and scoot her further into my lap, resting my head on her shoulder and holding her tight, chasing away the fears that grip my chest.

Iris puts two fingers under my chin and forces me to raise my head and look her in the eye. She lowers toward me and, with light kisses, wipes the tears from my cheeks. My hands slip under the blanket to caress the soft skin of her hips and the curves of her butt.

Her lips rest on mine, and what begins as a chaste kiss soon turns into a clash of tongues and desire that awakens every part of my body. My fingers sink into her flesh, pulling her against my erection in an almost primordial need. Her lips blend with mine in a kiss that leaves us breathless.

When I caress her opening with my fingers, I find her ready to welcome me, releasing a guttural groan that makes my chest ache. Iris slips her fingers into my hair and, with a decisive gesture, pulls me toward her bare breasts while the blanket falls on the floor at my feet. I rush to the pale skin of her breasts, her nipples, teasing them until she gasps and, when I sense that neither of us can wait any longer, I lower my boxers just enough to free my erection and sink into her with a single decisive movement.

A cry slips from her lips while, helped by the movement of the armchair, Iris moves sinuously on me, dictating a rhythm that leaves me no choice but to follow. She doesn't feel like playing, pausing, and prolonging the pleasant agony; her movements are determined and make me sink into her like never before. She is the first to orgasm, with her eyes closed and her lips open in an expression of pleasure so sensual I plunge with even more vigor until I explode.

Panting, she slumps on my shoulder, her breasts against my bare chest. I wrap her in a hug and hold her tightly, thanking her in silence for not asking me more about my tears, for not forcing me to confess something I wasn't ready for.

I get up from the chair with Iris in my arms and, taking her back to the bedroom, I lie next to her, clutching her to my body until we both fall asleep.

CHAPTER 25

Iris

I open my eyes, and for a moment, I'm lost. I'm not in my room, and only after a few seconds do I remember sleeping at Thomas's. It wasn't planned, but after making love twice, I wasn't physically able to stand up, get dressed and take a twenty-minute taxi ride back to the apartment. When I reach out my hand, I feel only the cold sheets. He must have gotten up a while ago.

I get up and use the master bathroom, with a shower so large my entire bathroom could fit in it. Hell, my whole apartment would fit inside this room. I smile at the idea as I wash my face and get dressed.

When I get to the kitchen, I find Thomas drinking a cup of coffee while reading the newspaper, shirtless except for a pair of basketball shorts. His back is toward me, and I could spend all day admiring that perfect body full of muscles, those arms and shoulders defined by years as a drummer. I feel like nibbling on that perfect body while I stick a hand down those shorts.

"Do you like what you see?" he asks without turning around, a smile in his voice.

I blush violently at getting caught staring at him. "Yes, definitely." It's useless to try and act demure after two out-of-control orgasms in his bed last night.

Thomas turns around, giggling, reaches out, kisses me on the lips, then goes to the coffee maker and pours me a cup, adding two tablespoons of sugar the way I like it. "I took the liberty of baking some croissants," he says as he beckons me to the lit oven.

I give him a wide-eyed stare and shake my head. His culinary ability is getting downright overwhelming. "Did you make those too?" I ask, astounded.

Thomas laughs and shakes his head. "No, that would be a little over the top. I became friends with the pastry chef of a cafè I love here in Manhattan, so I convinced him to make croissants and freeze them before baking them so I can take them home and put them in the oven whenever I feel like it."

"The perks of being famous," I tease him, raising an eyebrow and folding my arms across my chest.

"If I don't take advantage of these things, what's the point of being a rock star?" He raises his hands innocently.

I can't help but smile and approach him, kissing his chest before peeking into the oven. "How many of us are there for breakfast, exactly?"

"Just the two of us, why?"

"There are six rolls in here!" I point, stunned.

Thomas smiles and drinks some of his coffee. "I didn't know what kind you like, so I made two of each: berry, cream, and chocolate."

My mouth is already watering. As I expected, breakfast is nothing short of fantastic, relaxing, and a glimpse into a routine that I could get used to very willingly. That's why I'm particularly annoyed when the phone vibrates in my pocket insistently and, when I pull it out, my heart stops for more than a beat. Albert's name flashes menacingly on the screen. I get up and move away just enough not to be heard by Thomas.

"What?" I answer briskly.

"I have information for you. It's big, huge, apocalyptic."

The excitement in his voice makes my legs tremble. It must be bad news, at least as far as my relationship with Thomas is concerned. "I told you to let it go," I reply in a low voice, hoping Thomas won't notice anything strange. I look at him, but I see him intent on reading the paper.

"I suggest meeting in person. I can't talk about this on the phone, trust me. I'll text you the location of the coffeeshop I'm at."

My stomach tightens in a vice. I want to yell at him that he's a complete idiot, but then I'd have to explain to Thomas what the hell I did. "I'm coming," I tell Albert in a choked tone, and the panic overtakes me. I should scream at him that he didn't have to do any research, that I didn't ask for it, that he should have listened when I told him to stop, but who am I fooling? I knew he would do it, I was just hoping he wouldn't be able to find anything out, given the little information he had.

When I get back to the table with Thomas, I put on a fake, tight smile.

"Everything okay?" he asks.

"Yes...no...it was Emily. She said she stopped by my apartment, and Dexter made a mess with the litter. I have to go back before the little devil decides to destroy my house." I'm surprised at how easily I'm able to lie to him.

Thomas chuckles while he gets up and takes away our now empty plates. "I love that cat."

I should smile, or at least make some sarcastic joke, but I'm paralyzed on the spot, my heart pounding in my chest and the bile rising up my throat. The reasonable thing would be to tell Thomas that a friend of mine has some "bombshell news" about him, so he can unleash his lawyers and his press office, but I'm still hoping to persuade Albert to keep his mouth shut. I'm going to have to sweat to convince him, use his feelings for me to get what I want, but I can't tell Thomas I betrayed his trust again. This time he could never forgive me.

*

I enter the café feeling like I'm going to throw up. It's one of the big chains where everyone has a MacBook, and no one really drinks coffee. I immediately spot Albert in the corner and make a considerable effort not to punch him. I told him not to snoop. And at the same time, I know this is my fault. That nausea I feel isn't anger at Albert it's my own guilt. I realize now that I was colossally wrong to be so casual about the information Thomas shared with me in confidence. I'm terrified the situation is getting out of hand, and I don't know how to fix it. To silence my brain, which was trying to piece together information that didn't make sense, I planted suspicion in a person I no longer trust and who scares me. I don't know how bad the news is, but if Albert wants to see me, it must be huge.

"I told you to let it go," I hiss in a desperate attempt to make him feel guilty.

"Do you really think that after you come in making a scene at my office over someone like him, I'd be good to stand by and watch while you earn thousands of dollars? I need whatever source of income I can get. Honest or not."

I used to think he was an ethical guy and, a few years ago,

maybe he was. But he probably discovered that morals don't pay the bills, and quickly learned how to work the system. I'm not entirely convinced, however, that he only did it for the money. I think he's angry because I'm sleeping with Thomas.

"Let me see what you found." I decide to get to the point. It makes no sense to beat around the bush now, better to know immediately how serious the situation is and manage the damage.

Albert hands me a court document with names and addresses crossed out with a black marker. He runs his fingers between his ash-colored curls, and I notice behind those thick-framed, huge glasses, his pale brown eyes look almost fiery. I have to reread it three times before my brain can process the information in front of me. Panic begins to invade my stomach.

"It's just partial information. I went looking in various school yearbooks. Apparently, your boyfriend now uses his middle name and his mother's last name. He's got a sister who doesn't live here anymore, and his parents are dead... I had to make several phone calls to some friends in the police department and ask for favors, but I managed to get this in the end. I'm not one hundred percent sure it's him, he's almost completely erased his previous life, but it seems your friend was in jail when he was a teenager."

His explanation is confusing, but it becomes more than evident in my head as I'm reading. The tone Albert's using confirms this is not about the money. His arrogant expression reveals all the satisfaction he feels rubbing in my face the fact that I sleep with someone who, in his eyes, is just a convict. Someone you'd never bring home to meet your family, someone who's worthless.

The names are deleted because he was still a minor, but it appears from the documents that he was convicted of drug trafficking. That information doesn't match the picture I have of Thomas. He's a sweet, kind, caring guy who loves to cook. How could he have been convicted of drug trafficking? For crying out loud, the man bakes cookies to donate to charity! That's not a criminal pastime. Trafficking isn't dealing. It means he was some kind of drug courier, caught carrying large amounts of that crap back and forth.

"It's not the same person. It can't be...I know him. It can't be." My words come out weak, and the chuckle from Albert confirms he doesn't believe what I'm saying either.

"Are you serious? Look at the rest of these papers I printed out. Birth certificates, his parents' marriage certificates. This information is worth thousands of dollars, and I want my share. You either sell it to that magazine piece of shit you work for or directly to the Jailbirds in exchange for keeping it quiet, but I want half. Ironic that they're called Jailbirds, don't you think?"

"I'll give you ten thousand dollars to keep this to yourself," I spit out all in one breath, not knowing what else to do.

Albert widens his eyes at my proposal, studies me for what feels like forever, and then smiles, almost amused. "You know this information is gold. Think about my proposal, I expect your call by tonight with the amount, or I'll find someone myself who can use it and make it pay off."

Helpless rage almost makes me jump up and punch him. "Why didn't you just do it yourself? Why did you come to me?"

"Because unlike you, I have an honest job. If rumors fly

about me and my unprofessional conduct, they'll fire me, and no other newspaper in the state would hire me,"

I find myself wishing with all my heart that it will go exactly like this while I watch him walk out of this place, barely hiding the mocking smile planted on his face once he realizes he has me where he wants me.

Another wave of nausea hits me and I run to the bathroom to empty my stomach of the incredible breakfast I had less than an hour ago with the man I'm about to ruin.

*

I'm out of breath from running to Thomas's apartment, and now that I'm out front, I lose the courage to ask the concierge for permission to go up to Thomas's apartment. But I have to. I have to warn him of the mess I made before Albert starts contacting the papers. Before this shit hits the Jailbirds like a tsunami. I feel mean, dirty. How the hell did I get myself into this when Lilly and Damian went out of their way to help me? How could I be so ungrateful?

The concierge looks up and immediately recognizes me, since I just left here less than two hours ago. He looks a little perplexed at my distressed expression when I ask to talk to Thomas. But he calls him, and immediately walks me to the elevator where he slides the magnetic card before punching the apartment code. The ride seems both endless and too short. When the doors open to Thomas's smile, it occurs to me that this will be the last time I'll see it.

"I made a huge mess," I blurt out as he comes to hug me, and his arms stop in mid-air.

"Okay..." his answer is almost a question, perhaps even a little suspicious.

"Before you get mad, know that I didn't do it for the money. I was drunk, and I caused a disaster of catastrophic proportions."

My choice of words is terrible, because he looks at me suspiciously, not even inviting me in, leaving me to stare at the windows on the other side of this immense entryway.

"Explain." His voice is hard, icy.

I don't even know where to start. "That time you met Emily and Albert in my apartment for pizza night, at the end of the evening we got drunk... Albert was being an asshole, accusing me of sleeping with you, and I didn't even know you... I mean, fueled by alcohol, I said something about you...maybe too much...and he used the information." The more I try to explain what I did, the more I realize it was because of my stupid desire to prove something. Not knowing how to continue, I simply take out the court documents that Albert gave me and hand them to him.

Thomas grabs it, and his expression is all the confirmation I need to know it's all true. The warmth leaves his face and is replaced by a tall, impenetrable wall. Anger flashes in his eyes.

"Did you sleep with me just to find out information about me?" he hisses with such fury he's scaring me. Not physically, but the distance his rage puts between us is so vast I know nothing can ever bring us together again.

"No, I swear. I realize I screwed up, but I would never do something like that on purpose, I swear," I stammer one pathetic excuse after another.

Thomas laughs, a laugh so bitter and full of sarcasm it makes my blood freeze in my veins. "Oh, so you just stumbled across this information? You didn't ask your friend to find out more? You just happened to trip over my feet and end up with your legs wide open? How long were you waiting on that fire escape to fall down into my arms?"

The venom that permeates his words makes me feel small, very small. "I..."

"Shut up. I don't even want to hear your pathetic excuses. I don't want to see your fake sad puppy-dog face anymore. You're dead to me!" he shouts while he types the code to open the elevator with one hand, and takes me by the arm and pushes me inside with the other.

I don't dare say anything. Tears fall down my cheeks until my neck and the scarf I'm wearing are soaked. When I stumble outdoors, I'm so lost I don't even know where to go. All I can do is pull out my cell phone and call Emily. "I screwed up. You have no idea what a mess I've made,"
I babble, sobbing and sliding down the wall to the ground, oblivious to the strange looks I'm getting from passersby.

PRESS *Review*

People:

Shocking news from the Jailbirds. Sources report that Thomas Simons, the band's drummer, spent his teenage years in prison for drug trafficking. The documents have been sealed because he was a minor at the time, but as you can see from the photos, the evidence is overwhelming. Is this the downfall of the world's most famous band? Not only is their career at risk, but their record company could drag them to court and claim damages for millions of dollars, leaving them penniless. And how will their fans react? A lie that has lasted for ten long years is hard to swallow and forgive.

Gossip Now!

Thomas Simons is a former inmate! You read that right. The Jailbirds' drummer spent his adolescence in prison for a serious offense: drug trafficking. The famous musician has deceived everyone for years, pretending to be a good guy when he actually has a dark past that fans will not appreciate. It is unclear whether their record company—or the band itself—knew about this, but we are confident that his career has come to an end. In all probability, he will be replaced shortly, and someone has already started naming names.

Rock Now:

The recent story that has shaken newsrooms across the country is one that no one expected. Thomas Simons of the Jailbirds spent his teenage years locked up in a juvenile prison for drug trafficking. No statement has yet been released by the record company or the band's manager, but we are sure that more details will be released in the next few hours. If the information turns out to be true, we'll have to expect repercussions on the drummer's career and his bandmates—there are rumors the record company could drop them.

@jailfreakingbirds I'm speechless. No. You shouldn't have done this to me, Thomas.

@jailbirds_groupie I don't believe it. I was at the listening party for the single, and he didn't seem like a prison scumbag.

@wannabe_rockstar Now we know who gets Michael the drugs.

CHAPTER 26

Thomas

We're all in my apartment when the news hits the tabloids. Evan, Damian, Michael, Simon, and even Lilly, because this thing will turn her life upside down as well.

"Wow, we're all here. I hope at least she got good money out of this so she can take care of her mother for a few years." Michael's voice is so sarcastic I don't even want to object. "And to think I wanted to thank her for opening my eyes. She screwed me too, that bitch."

"Don't be a moron."

It's Lilly's voice that scolds him, and I look over at her tense face. She's the only one who didn't believe Iris could do such a thing, and when the news first appeared in Ron's paper, her face twisted into a grimace of pain. I wished I could hate Iris for it, because she hurt not only me but all my friends as well. I don't care about my life, but I care about them, and seeing them so knocked down makes me sick.

Evan has been walking back and forth in the corner of the room, not far from us, on the phone since Iris left my apartment this morning, and I called him. His face is tense, focused. He smiles in front of us, he says everything will be okay, but this is a big thing even for him. It's no longer about paying people who ask too many questions, covering scholarships for the children of those involved in our old lives, or tricks like that. This time it's a matter of trying to stop the flood of bad news all over the United States, and worse, the whole world. It's no longer just Manhattan, New York, or the States. There are articles in Chinese and Japanese posted with our worst photos.

"Don't be a moron? She sold Thomas out after fucking him. She doesn't deserve any respect from the world. I trusted her, I liked her, and this is the result." Michael is mad, more than the others who took it like a punch in the stomach.

"You don't even know for sure it was her," Lilly says in an attempt to defend Iris. I have no idea why she cares so much about Iris. I suspect she caught a glimpse of a potential friend in her, a girl to confide in amid all the testosterone around her, and it pisses me off even more because Lilly is a good person and doesn't deserve to be betrayed this way.

"She came here this morning and told me that her friend had researched me. What other proof do you need?" I ask irritated, earning a nasty look from Damian that I decide to ignore.

"Confessing that her friend did research and selling herself what he discovered to the papers are two completely different things. What reason would she have had to come here and warn you? Do you even know the name of this friend who helped her? Did you wonder what the hell of a role he had in this whole thing?" Lilly is livid, and it pains me to look at the suffering in her eyes.

"Lilly." Damian's whisper is sweet but firm as he wraps his arm around her shoulders and pulls her to his side. A simple gesture that hurts me. Only this morning, I did the exact same thing with a person I thought I could trust, and now I'm here rethinking her every gesture in an entirely negative way. I wonder why she kissed me with passion and sweetness, why she caressed me like she was exploring something new or precious, why she allowed me to enter her and sink into her most intimate parts, letting me know her like few people have.

Evan comes back to the conversation and sits on the couch. "We're getting to the bottom of it to see who actually released the information and how much he got for it. That document she gave you comes from the court records, so whoever found that information had to ask for a favor from someone who had a legal responsibility not to reveal sensitive information about a minor. In addition to losing his job, he also risks a felony charge."

I'm surprised to notice I sincerely hope that person is not Iris. After all that's happened, after even more proof that women cannot be trusted, I find myself wishing that she's not involved, proving once again that there is something profoundly wrong with me.

"What the hell is there to get to the bottom of? It was Iris, and that's it," Michael snaps, standing up and throwing his laptop on the couch he was sitting on.

"Michael. If no one had given you the chance to explain and give you a second chance, you would still be cleaning toilets at Joe's bar," Evan harshly scolds, turning everyone's eyes on him. "I know you don't want to hear this, but I'm not going to slaughter someone in court if I don't have proof that she's really involved. So, I ask you to be patient until I get to the bottom of it. In the meantime, we all have to move to the hotel. The paparazzi are starting to arrive in front of your house. Max, Dave, and a couple of other drivers are already in the garage with four cars ready. We're going to Connecticut."

Evan's words cut the air like a reprimand and an order. At this point, I understand how much we need someone like him to manage our lives better, because they'll no longer be the same after tonight.

*

The drive to Connecticut is a string of confusing images running past the window and as many equally confusing ideas flowing through my mind.

I relive every single moment I spent with Iris: every single conversation we had, every single moment of intimacy and shared breath. Not one moment did she seem insincere or even ambiguous, not even when I found out she's a paparazzo. She took me to the clinic to meet her mother, refused any financial help I offered her, and I can't help but wonder if it was all a grand plan designed to get more information about me. But I don't understand why. Why invest so much energy in something that could easily earn her nothing? At the end of the day, dozens of bands have a boring and monotonous life. Ours could have been too. Maybe she enjoyed the sex? Was that what she got out of this? If so, she could have given in earlier and enjoyed the roller coaster. Instead, she pushed me away for a long time, almost like she was trying to protect me.

When Peter, one of our drivers, opens the door for me, I realize I'm in front of a cottage in the middle of nowhere. It's probably one that Evan rented at the last minute to avoid paparazzi.

"This way," he points me to a side door from which I can see Evan and Damian with Lilly.

I go into the house without taking too much notice of my

surroundings. I reach the kitchen and, when I meet Lilly's gaze, I see she's been crying, though she tries to give me a comforting smile that actually never reaches her eyes. I inhale thoroughly to not freak out and approach the small wine refrigerator next to the counter.

"I had the pantry filled as soon as I booked this place two hours ago. I don't know what they have, but I hope you can find something you like," Evan suggests in a calm tone.

Michael and Simon have yet to arrive, and the atmosphere is much more peaceful. It almost seems like the negative energy melted away the moment we left Manhattan. The anger didn't last, because it wasn't the worst of it. I feel betrayed, emptied, terrified of what will happen; the anger left a void in my chest that is almost suffocating.

In the fridge are cheeses, fruit, and sliced bread, as well as eggs. I don't want to cook. The last time I did was this morning, now yesterday morning, for Iris, in a completely different world when I thought I might have a future with her. What's so ironic is that I was always hesitant about what I wanted from her when there was no threat of losing her. Now that I don't have her anymore, I realize there was really nothing to be undecided about. In the corner of my brain, very far from my reason, I had already established that she might be my future.

I start laughing out of the blue. A laugh that makes me bend in two and slump on the floor, hysterical, out-of-control laughter. Damian reaches out. Lilly clings to his arm. She doesn't know whether to stop him or to hide behind him for protection. No one touches me. No one dares to get closer. They just stare, not knowing what to do.

I laugh until the tears come, until I almost stop breathing. I laugh until I sob, until I can't hold back anymore. I tighten my knees close to my chest, wrap them with my arms and sink my head between them to hide. Only I can't hide from the others. My crying is so raw, so desperate that I couldn't disguise it if I tried. I miss my father, my mother, my sister. This story brought back memories that pierce my heart like that first day I got out of prison. I can't push them to the corner of my heart anymore, the heart I managed to seal shut in order to survive.

I feel Damian's sturdy body sitting down next to me, wrapping his arms around me and drawing my head against his chest. I let myself be taken into my friend's embrace. I let myself be held together by his strength, because this time I don't know if I can keep from falling apart.

*

We're all sitting on the deckchairs on the back porch—I've got a beer in one hand and a cigarette in the other. I'm not crying anymore, but my eyes are still swollen. I don't care. My friends have seen the worst of me; crying certainly won't change their opinion of me.

"What do you think they're going to say at tomorrow's meeting? Do you think they're going to dump us?" Simon breaks the silence with a question we've all asked ourselves.

The record company has called an emergency meeting. They know our situation, of course, but I don't know how they're going to react to the wave of criticism they're getting right now. Some of it for keeping quiet, some for making criminals famous. There are too many ways this could end up, and we don't come out well in most of them. We still can't quantify the damage. It will take time. We'll find out with the next album just how badly this shit has affected our career.

"I don't know, I don't think they can let go of a band with millions in sales and a new album ready to come out because of a scandal that could actually be to their advantage," explains Damian.

"Especially knowing that every small record company would go into debt to offer us a contract," adds Michael.

I don't know whether the silence that follows is good or bad. It's too dark to read their expressions to see if they really believe these things or if they're just trying to bolster themselves for the morning ahead in a few hours. It's the bitter cold of winter and you can see our breath in the air, but the icy cold that fills my chest is not because of the season. What if this is really the end of our career? I could never forgive myself for ruining the lives of these four.

"In case they decide to drop us, I'm leaving the band. I don't want to drag you into this shit. At the end of the day, it's just me under attack. They don't know anything about you yet," I say and I mean it. They can stay afloat and keep what's theirs.

I get a punch from Damian on my shoulder as he laughs. "Do you really think our bullshit isn't going to come out? It's only a matter of time. And by the way, we were together in that prison, we got out together, and we're going to face this together, too. Don't even think about getting rid of us," he reassures me.

A chorus of "yep" and "exactly, well-said" comes from Michael and Simon, and I don't need to see their faces to hear the sincerity in their voices. That's what has always united us, and got us through everything, until now.

CHAPTER 27

Iris

Never before had I thought my job could ruin my life. The photos I've taken of celebrities have always been to earn money. I knew they would create problems for people, but I always thought that a well-paid press office could fix them. I never dwelled on what the people in the photos might be going through because of me: they were strangers, and I never saw the direct consequences of my actions on their lives. At least not until now. Because of me, my carelessness, I have a front-row seat to how much damage those magazines can do. They are doing it to Thomas—he's completely crushed by this news and media attack—and also to me. I've lost the only man who has ever loved me, in spite of the lies I told him and the weight of my family obligation. A fantastic man who does not deserve to be lynched in a public square for what happened in the past. Gossip magazines, media, the fans, even parents' associations are lashing out at him and the band.

"Hey, you have to eat something." Emily pushes the plate in front of the computer I've been obsessively checking since last night.

She came to my house as soon as she got the call, and she never left, not even when I didn't mention going to sleep and stayed up all night searching for a way to stem the damage.

"I'm not hungry." Right now, I couldn't get even the head of a pin in my stomach without vomiting.

"I know, but you also threw up the only thing you ate yesterday morning. You have to make an effort."

"He hates me." It's a simple observation that comes out in a desperate whisper.

"Probably." Her sincerity is what I appreciate most about her, even if it sometimes hurts like hell. Right now, though, I deserve to feel sick. I deserve to suffer, even if it will never be as much as he's suffering right now.

"I don't know how to clean up the shitstorm I've created. I don't know how to help him."

The despair in my voice reflects what I feel in the middle of my chest. I've been thinking all night about what I could do, but I'm nobody. I don't have a reputation big enough to overshadow voices from all over the world. I'm a tiny drop in the middle of the ocean.

"I don't know either. I don't think anything can be done at this point. But you have to go tell him it wasn't you that sold the information."

"What difference does it make?" I look up and find her looking as tired and worried as I feel.

"It makes all the difference in the world. As wrong as you were, you didn't intentionally hurt him. He may not want to talk to you anymore, but he needs to know you didn't throw him under the bus on purpose. You owe it to him, and you owe it to yourself. Do you think he's ever going to trust a woman again, after you pull something like that? He'll never get close to anyone in his life again, and no one deserves to spend their whole life alone. If you want to do something for him, that's the one thing you can do."

Her reasoning opens a glimmer of hope in this situation that I hadn't considered. I've thought several times about insisting on explaining to him how things went, but I've only thought about how it would make me feel. Now that Emily points out how he must have felt, I feel guilty for being so utterly selfish.

"Will you come with me?" I beg her. I don't know if I can even stand in front of him.

*

The record company building is under siege by paparazzi. I recognize the faces of half the people who are crammed behind the barricade, hoping to get some pictures of the Jailbirds. I know they'll be here for a meeting today. Everyone in the industry knows this. I've received at least five texts from different people asking me if I'll be here today. Last night, the Jailbirds disappeared. None of them stayed in their own homes and were not seen anywhere in Manhattan. I wouldn't be surprised if they were put on a private jet and flown to the other side of the world.

"We'll never get in," I tell Emily, who seems as puzzled as I am.

She seems to think about it, then takes me by the hand and drags me to one of the security guards at the entrance, a guy with a shaved head who's so big he could hide another person under his jacket. His earpiece makes him look like an automaton, a robot that could destroy anyone trying to get past him with his bare hands.

"You can't go in. Move behind the barriers like everyone else."

The man motions us to go back while spreading his arms

in a protective stance toward those inside. I admire his determination. I'm sure that if this whole horde of paparazzi and journalists decides to break in, he'll singlehandedly be able to stop them.

"She's the one who sold the information that created this mess."

I feel Emily's words, strong and direct, like a punch to my stomach knocking out all the air in my lungs. What the hell is she thinking? Throwing me under the bus is not the best way to tell Thomas I didn't sell that information. I look up at the man, who seems to study me resentfully, and I immediately understand where his loyalty lies.

He beckons his colleague to approach, says something to his ear, and receives a nod of consent. If I hadn't been focused on their faces, I wouldn't even have noticed his head move. He rests a hand on our shoulders, opens the door, and with his head beckons us to enter and follows us. He passes us and approaches the blonde receptionist who is probably a few years younger than me. I see her look up at us, then grab the phone and start talking fast to someone on the other end. Less than two minutes later, the elevator doors across the white, ultra-modern entrance open, letting out a middle-aged, grizzled, tall man in a dark blue suit that makes him look menacing. His square jaw clenches, his gray eyes slice through me like blades. He knows exactly who I am, and it makes my legs tremble.

"You can't stay here." His voice is calm and authoritarian at the same time. I wouldn't be surprised if he opened his jacket and showed us a weapon under his fancy suit.

My voice, by comparison, comes out as uncertain as a little

girl who knows she screwed up. "I just want to talk to Thomas, help him fix this mess. I can deny it, say I made it all up. Tell him that I'm sorry and that if I could go back, I wouldn't fall like a fool into Albert's trap."

The man studies me for a few seconds, almost seems to weigh an answer, then opens his mouth, dropping the bomb on me calmly and impassively. "Mr. Simons' lawyers will contact you, and you'll have the opportunity to explain everything to them. Now you have to leave," he says, nodding to the closest guard to approach.

His words penetrate my skin and freeze my blood. Until now, I hadn't thought about the legal aspect of this, only the emotional. I'm numbed by the realization. The blood pulses in my ears, my mouth dries up, and I'm not sure I'm breathing regularly. My eyes are fixed on the white carpet under my feet; I haven't blinked in I don't know how long.

Emily's voice brings me back to reality. "He's literally in front of us. She only needs less than a minute."

She's begging the man. When I look up, in front of me I see the Jailbirds walking quickly to the elevator. It's been two days since all hell broke loose, and Thomas seems unrecognizable. All of their faces are gloomy, but Thomas's almost makes my legs give out. His eyes are reddened as if he's cried or drunk to the point of exhaustion, and the dark circles around them show he hasn't slept at all. His gray and sunken face behind the curls has never looked worse.

They ignore me, all of them. I'm sure they saw me because we're the only people in the middle of the all-white entrance, but they're walking fast to the elevator as the photographers behind us go wild. I can see flashes penetrating through the windows.

"It wasn't me." It comes out as a whisper that barely reaches my ears. I'm so paralyzed, I can't even scream. But Emily's doing it for me.

"Thomas, it wasn't Iris who sold the information!" she shouts as the doors are closing, and I see him lowering his head with his eyes fixed on the floor.

The guard grabs us both by the elbow with a light but decisive gesture and escorts us out the door, where another rapid sequence of flashes hits us, and people start asking us questions about why we were in there. We don't answer, walking quickly to the building corner and slipping into a side street.

"Are you okay?" Emily asks me worriedly.

I don't know if I could faint or throw up right now. "I have to find myself a lawyer," I whisper, looking at my hands visibly shaking.

"Yes, I think so. I can ask around if there's anyone who can help you."

I nod without really thinking about her words, though I do notice my friend seems to have lost her characteristic enthusiasm and positivity.

*

I enter the editorial room of Ron's magazine, invigorated by anger. Emily is behind me, just as angry as I am. By their looks, I'm sure people are thinking I'm crazy as I walk like a bulldozer among the desks, glaring at anything and anyone in my path. I see Ron's office behind the glass across the room and, when I furiously open the door, he gives me a look that's at first surprised, then amused.

"Good morning, sunshine," he teases me.

I grab the papers lying on his desk and throw them across the room, but he barely registers a reaction.

"You have to clean up this mess!" I shout angrily "Post a denial, do something, but you can't ruin people's lives this way."

Ron starts laughing, and I feel Emily's hand on my shoulder, preventing me from jumping over his desk and punching him. "Are you kidding me? I've never had so many ad requests. The site is exploding with visits, and people are literally going crazy over this story. I've never been so rich," he says with such simplicity that I'm almost caught by surprise.

"And you don't care that you're ruining people's lives?" My voice is shrill. I almost don't recognize it—my throat is so hoarse from screaming.

"Thomas ruined his own life when he decided to become a drug courier. I didn't do that."

I can't even argue. He's so out of his mind that I have no answer for him. "Albert came to you asking for money. How much did you give him?" I hiss between my teeth.

Ron laughs again, this time surprising me. "Do you really think that kid would have the balls to come to me?" I'm taken aback by this statement. "I paid someone to be on you when I started having my suspicions. I knew you were fucking Thomas, but I didn't want just the average sex story. I wanted something that would blow up. I knew sooner or later you'd make a mistake, and I went straight to the source. I contacted him and gave him money for his research."

"So, his threat to make me blackmail the Jailbirds and give him half the money was all a joke? Just your sick game to see if I would give in?" I ask, so horrified that I almost vomit on his desk.

Ron laughs again, and I'm grateful Emily's on me because I'd gladly smash his face in right now. "No, that was his attempt to get more money, put his conscience at ease, and, perhaps, also save his job and face."

I see red. I fell into Ron's trap like a complete idiot, did precisely what he wanted, and was crushed by his lowdown tactics. Enraged, I grab the MacBook on his desk and throw it against the window behind me.

The gesture is so sudden and violent it shatters the window, causing shouts of alarm from the the editorial room on the other side. Looking at Ron's horrified face, I walk to the door, slamming it open, find the laptop a couple of feet from his office and stomp on it until it's shattered. When I turn around, I'm met with Emily's shocked face and Ron running his hands through his hair.

I point a finger at him. "Don't think this is over. I swear, I'm going to make your life so miserable you'd wish you never met me," I hiss, then march out of the newsroom with my friend following behind.

Back outside, I rest my hands on my knees to keep from passing out and inhale deeply.

"You scared me to death! But I've never seen a more epic scene. I felt like I was in a movie." Emily bursts out laughing and, when I straighten up, meeting her wild gaze, I can't help but laugh too, feeling the fear, adrenaline, and tension slipping away from my body until I'm empty.

CHAPTER 28
Thomas

The cottage in Connecticut, where we returned, right after meeting with the record label, is a hidden treasure within a vast park surrounded by trees. It is warm and welcoming, an ideal place to raise a family. Ironically, as much as it would be a perfect place for me, I have no one to share it with.

I look out my bedroom window. It's Christmas morning. We should all be gathered around the fireplace at Damian and Lilly's house. Instead, the world seems suspended in a limbo between reality and hell, where there's no celebrating. I admire the manicured garden and the trees at the far end of the yard, past the pool, and a bitter smile forms on my lips. Every time I thought about having more than a one-night stand with someone, a future, maybe a couple of brats, I'd regret it, feeling stupid for hoping I could have more than a life of solitude. Not that I thought of having children when I was thirteen, but I distinctly remember feeling that with Rita, it would never end. At the time, it was mostly irrational certainty: Rita would never leave me because I would never let her go. I didn't accept the end of our story, even as I shared the room with three other guys who beat me almost to the point of death at least twice a week. I kept hoping she'd be waiting for me when I got out, with a suitcase full of clothes and a place to stay, since I no longer had a family. It was the prison psychologist—the one who helped the four of us get into the recovery program—who made me realize that I was just one of the many victims of the only woman I've ever loved...at least until Iris.

Because ultimately, whether I want to believe it or not, I wanted more than just sex with Iris. Why do I trust these women who end up betraying me? It's clear as day that I don't have a clue about their intentions. I can handle an entire room of malicious journalists. I can face a battalion of music industry people who just want to squeeze as much money as possible out of me. But I can't discern sincerity in a woman's eyes.

Emily's words in the lobby of the record company office ring in my head. She told me it wasn't her, and part of me wants to believe it. It doesn't make sense—Iris, who always turned down my money, sold that information? Am I so repulsive that she'd rather sell me out than be with me? Was it all just a charade to make me fall in love with her? To earn my trust? I've been thinking about it for hours, and I still can't figure it out.

An insistent knock on my bedroom door startles me. Someone tries to open it, but I had the foresight to lock it. I don't want to see anyone. Our career is in jeopardy because of me. The record company has been clear: if this story negatively affects the sales of the next album, we're out. No matter how many millions we've brought in over the years, they're not willing to risk losing sales of the other artists on their label. That's why I don't dare look my friends in the face. Not so much because we could end up living on the streets, but because music is what pulled us out of the shit we were in. It literally saved our lives, gave us a new chance, and thinking that we can no longer do it is a possibility I can't even consider.

"Open this fucking door, Thomas. We need to show you something." Damian's voice thunders on the other side of the dark wood, and, with a huge sigh, I go and open it. Something in the tone of his voice tells me it's best to do as he says before he takes down the door.

"I don't want to argue again, okay?" I say when I see them all enter the room.

Damian, Lilly, Simon, Michael, and Evan enter quickly into the space that has become a bit tight. My best friend's girlfriend rests her laptop on the dark mahogany desk and opens an internet page.

"You have to see this," she says as she loads a page.

"That's Iris's blog. I don't want to see anything on there."

"Trust me, you want to see this." Michael puts a hand on my shoulder, makes me sit on the bed, and hands me the laptop.

I start the video, and immediately I see Iris, sitting calmly on her bed, her eyes red from crying, her posture rigid, her expression tight and tired. I feel bad seeing her like this. She clears her throat and I hold my breath until she starts talking.

"Hi, everyone. This is probably going to be the last post on this blog, but I need to tell you something I did, and I realized it was the worst decision of my life."

Last post? What the hell is she talking about? She lives for that blog. My hands start shaking, and my stomach tightens in a vice I've never felt before.

"I made up the whole story about Thomas Simons of the Jailbirds. I sold the information to Ron, the newspaper editor that first published the story, but none of what I sold him is true. I used Photoshop to create the documents, and I edited the story to make it sound real. As you can see, I downloaded a sample legal document from a law school website, and then I changed some things and added a signature at the bottom. The names are deleted not because Thomas was a minor, which the story claims, but because there was no name written on it. I needed credible evidence, and I went so far as to make him look like the worst of criminals."

I feel like I'm dying. She's digging the pit herself. No one in this room is talking. They're not even moving. I don't think they're even breathing, and neither am I. Iris's voice is the only sound we hear.

"I did it because I needed money. Ron paid me well for this information. I went to him because I knew he wouldn't check my sources. He never does. He just needed a scandal, so he could sell the ad space on his site at a higher price. I don't really know Thomas. I only had the opportunity to meet him once. He was nice and very kind. I thought he might be up for sex, but when I propositioned him, he kindly declined my invitation. I felt rejected, so when I needed money, I thought this was the best way to make him pay. I made a mistake, I know. That's why I made this video, to clarify the situation and to apologize to him. I'm really sorry I created all this mess. I'm sorry I used the fame of the Jailbirds to get money. I know I can never be forgiven for something like this, but I'm asking all of you not to go after them. They're innocent parties in this whole thing."

When the screen turns black at the end of the video, tears flow down my cheeks, and I can't even think. What she did is absurd. She committed professional suicide to silence the rumors.

It's Evan who speaks first: "I got to the bottom of this, and she didn't sell that story," he explains. "The guy she inadvertently gave the information to did it himself. I went with the lawyers to talk to him. He explained how he got her drunk to hound her with questions...she was not lucid that evening. Iris doesn't even remember that night. He also said he tried to sift through her computer files, hoping to find something juicier, but he didn't find anything about you or the Jailbirds. He used some contacts in the justice and police departments to fill in the blanks of what he managed to snatch from Iris that night. For God's sake, he made his living verifying sources for journalists. His job was digging up information... He's already been fired, and he's probably never going to find work as a journalist. He's lost his career, but she hasn't done anything wrong."

"She confided to others what I told her. None of this would have happened if she hadn't done that." Words come out of my mouth before I can think. I've wondered if she tried to find out more about my past, and I never got an explanation. And the reason is that she didn't. She even told me, but I didn't believe her.

"Are you serious? She was drunk!" Michael points out. "Just a few days ago you told me what happened to your parents—after more than ten years of knowing each other. You're not exactly someone who trusts others. You never talk about yourself. Never. You never told her anything about your real past. You never let her know it was important for her to keep quiet. If you had told her everything, she would never have blurted it out, even under the influence of alcohol." He's telling the truth. I haven't always been like that. Life has made me closed off and wary of people. It's not a justification, but it's still difficult to change.

"Why the hell would she make that video? It's professional suicide," I ask my friends.

"Are you serious?" Lilly's voice is incredulous. "She's in love with you, you idiot. Do you want me to spell it out for you? And besides, it's not just professional suicide. It's also personal. The comments below the post are slaughtering her. Literally, some fan of yours has threatened her with death several times. I've never seen such hatred against a person."

I look down at my screen and start scrolling through the comments. They're chilling, to say the least. Someone calling her a whore is the kindest. Others say her mother should have aborted that abomination. The anger bubbling in my veins feels like corrosive acid.

"We have to have this video taken off the site before it goes viral. It will ruin her life," I say as soon as I realize it, but the expression on the others' faces stops my breath. They look like they're going to a funeral, Iris's, to be exact.

"The record company pushed it out and made it go viral. There's no way to stop the spread at this point," Evan says, and from the disgust on the faces of others, I know they're on my side, too.

"What the hell are we going to do?" I whisper, defeated.

"I think I have a solution, but I don't know if you're going to like it," Simon proposes with his hands tucked into his pockets and a sheepish look on his face.

Simon does not speak much, tends to stand aside, and keep to himself. He gardens to relax, and he certainly doesn't look like the bassist of the most famous band in the world. When he has something to say, it's usually profoundly life-changing. From the expression on his face right now, I'm imagining it will pull the earth out from under us. Considering my world is already completely turned upside down, I'd say I'm ready to hear what he has to tell us. Almost.

"Do we need alcohol for what you're about to say?" I ask with a sigh as I put the laptop on the bed.

"Yes, I think a whisky, maybe a double, is in order," he admits, glancing furtively at Evan.

"I'll need an antacid if I don't want to be hospitalized with an ulcer," our manager whispers as he exits the room.

I admire Evan and his ability to handle the thorniest situations with an enviable calm. We leave my room and I notice Lilly clasp Damian's hand, and he reciprocates by gently massaging the back of it with his thumb. My mind goes to Iris. I wonder how she's coping with the disaster that has come with her video, and I wish I could hold her hand to give her the strength she needs in this moment. Since meeting her for the first time, I finally understand why she never accepted my help. She never wanted me to solve her problems because she knows how to solve them very well on her own. She doesn't need anyone. She has the strength to navigate her own life. Her shoulders are strong enough to sustain the weight of the consequences.

I wish I was there with her—to tell her she'll get through this, too, that we're going to get out of this. I wish I was there to hold her hand and telling her everything's going to be okay, to reassure her that she's not alone in this battle like she's been her whole life. I wish I could make the journalists who stormed her building disappear, along with the fans stationed under her windows like vultures ready to pick on her carcass. Because when she exposed herself publicly for me, she opened herself up to the morbid hatred and curiosity of everyone. All of a sudden, the miles that separate us weigh like a boulder. I have to go to her, but I don't know how to do it without being assaulted by the press.

PRESS *Review*

People:

The Thomas Simons case has developed some new twists and turns. Apparently, a stalker of the band created fake documents to get the attention of the drummer who had previously turned down her sexual advances. Just how dangerous this person is and whether she has tried to approach Thomas Simons on other occasions is unknown, but we are waiting for a press conference to shed more light on the matter. It is unclear whether the band has issued restraining orders against either the woman or the newspaper that published the news without verifying its sources.

Gossip Now!

What would you do to get the attention of your idol? Surely, Iris has created an unprecedented media sensation, attracting the attention not only of Thomas Simons—the object of her obsession—but also of the rest of the world. This blogger with a modest following managed to catalyze the collective hatred of the band's fans and gain thousands of followers of her own in a matter of just a few hours. Was it just a bad publicity stunt to position herself as a new social media star?

@jailfreakingbirds You must die, ugly bitch! #IrisYou-HaveToDie

@jailbirds_groupie You're the most disgusting person I've ever met. I hope you die, ugly bitch. #IrisYouHaveToDie

@wannabe_rockstar She wrote a review of their new music without even listening to it. She wasn't even in the room with us! This one's completely crazy.

CHAPTER 29

Iris

Dexter snuggles by my side. Since uploading the video two days ago, my life has become hell, and even my cat has realized there's no need to beat this dead horse. Maybe he sees me walking around like a zombie—I haven't changed or showered for more than forty-eight hours—and feels sorry for me.

A soft knock on the door is the only sound in my apartment, and I can't even handle that. "Go away, Emily. Pretend I disappeared from the face of the earth, okay? I don't need to eat, drink, do anything. I just want to stay under my blanket, okay?" I shout without moving.

I'm tired of seeing the concern on her face. She's stuck by me through this whole situation, and I really appreciate it, but I need to be alone, figure out what I want to do with my life now that I've destroyed everything. I'm not usually one to give up hope. I'll fight to the end with the knife between my teeth. But this is too much even for me, I need a few days to gather my strength to get back on my feet, and I don't know what I'm going to do then.

The exact moment Thomas's past was revealed, I realized I would lose him forever, and it broke me. Because the worst of it is that I really cared about him. I wanted to find out where this relationship could go. I told him about my mother. I showed him my most vulnerable side, and he treated it with a kindness I didn't think was possible. He didn't run away, didn't look for excuses to leave like all the others I dated. He even stuck with me when he found out my work was something that could ultimately damage him. He's the only person Dexter loves unconditionally. That alone has to be worth something.

"It's Thomas. Can I come in?"

For a moment, I think I hear wrong. The voice on the other side of the door can't be his. He's furious with me, and he has every right to be. I ruined his life and career. It can't be him.

"Iris, please open this door," he repeats with a bit of exasperation in his voice.

"Go away, please. It's full of reporters and crazy fans down there. Do you really want to get caught here with me?" How the hell did he get in the building without being recognized?

I hear him inhale and, perhaps, chuckle. I'm not sure. "Look, Iris, you know how insistent I can be. Open this door and don't make me sit on this mat all night, please?"

His voice doesn't sound angry. He sounds almost tired, exasperated by the situation. I get up and sit down. I'm a mess. My pajamas are stained with I don't know what food, and my hair is all mangy. Even Dexter looks at me as if to ask: Are you really going to open the door looking like this? I suck, and I'm ashamed of it.

I put my feet on the ground and realize I'm still wearing my socks with the floppy rabbit ears. They're pink, and they're horrible. I consider taking them off, but that would only be worse, so I throw on my robe with the unicorn hood, complete with a lavender-colored mane flowing down my back, and pull my unruly hair into a rubber band. The result is no improvement, but I can't leave him out there while I take a shower.

When I open the door, I find him leaning against the jamb with a tired face and a tight smile. He's wearing a pair of dirty, stained gray sweatpants, a hoodie of the same filthy color, and an old windbreaker that looks like it came out of a dumpster. On his feet are a pair of torn canvas sneakers and no laces. The beard tells me that he, too, isn't faring so well, and I feel guilty. My frown must be obvious because he throws me an embarrassed half-smile.

"I figured to get in here unnoticed, I'd have to dress like Charlie."

"Ah. Makes sense."

Once I let him in and close the door, I notice the disaster that is my house. There are pizza and Chinese takeout boxes everywhere and scattered used Kleenex I didn't have the energy to throw away. "Sorry for the mess...and the way I look. I'm not a pretty sight, I know."

Thomas looks at me and shrugs like he doesn't even notice. "Have you seen my beard and the bags under my eyes?" He grins.

I look down and feel guilty. It's because of me he looks like a truck hit him in the face. Two fingers gently lift my chin, forcing me to look up. There is no anger in his expression, only exhaustion, and I don't know how to interpret this gesture. After the way he kicked me out of his apartment, I thought I'd never see these blue eyes up close anymore. They make me forget everything else.

"We have to talk." I nod and open my mouth, not sure where to start, but he lays a finger on my lips. "Can I explain?" he asks me with imploring eyes.

"You don't have to explain anything. I'm the one who screwed up. I have to pay for this. I'm sorry. I'm really sorry because I shouldn't have asked about your private life. I should have known Albert had ulterior motives and was going to cause trouble. Big trouble. Huge, immense trouble... I should have shut up, waited. Instead..." He won't let me finish my rant because he puts his finger on my lips again.

"You had every right to do so."

I gasp a couple of times, trying to find words, but I can't. I'm confused, and he knows it. He motions for me to sit on the bed and then snuggles up next to me, leaving no room between the two of us. He grabs my hands, weaves our fingers as if he needs all the support in the world, and then inhales deeply.

"If you hadn't asked about my past, I wouldn't have told you anything. I've been doing this for ten years—avoiding getting close to anyone—so I don't have to feel the heavy weight of my past. It's easier for me just to run away and pretend I don't feel anything than to deal with it."

My heart sinks into my stomach as Thomas tells me his story. It's so full of suffering and despair that tears flow down my cheeks. I feel sadness for that little boy who lost his whole family because of one mistake. I feel immense sadness for the man who's always kept everyone at a distance and has never known true peace or happiness. His story is long, detailed, full of a depth of feeling I didn't think was possible. He tells me about how he met Damian, Michael, and Simon in prison, how the psychologist rescued them from the streets, giving them a purpose in life, making music. When the silence returns, I realize Dexter has snuggled between us as if undecided as to which of us is suffering most right now.

"So, you have no idea what your nieces or nephews are like?" I ask in a whisper.

"I don't even know what my sister's face looks like. She was a teenager the last time I saw her. Now she's a woman, a mother...I'm sure she's changed a lot."

My heart squeezes to hear him say all of this and, when I lift my eyes toward him, I find tears falling down his cheeks. With one hand, I try to wipe them away without pulling back the other that's in a grip so tight it feels like it won't ever loosen.

"I'm sorry. I'm so sorry. I wish I hadn't put your suffering on display for the whole world, believe me. Thank you for sharing your story with me. I know how much it cost you."

Thomas looks at me and smiles as if I'm the only one in the world who matters to him. "After what you did for me with that video, it's the least I can do."

"I didn't do anything special. I don't even know if it helped." I shrug, downplaying the whole situation.

"It worked. People are starting to wonder what's true and what's not. Plus, they started sifting through Ron's newspaper and pointing out every time he published fake or made-up news... Like, for example, the fight between Damian and Lilly." He smiles at me, and it lifts the weight from my chest a little. Not entirely, because my life is ruined regardless, but maybe he could get his back on track.

"Well, I'm glad."

"Now we need your help to change the direction of our future."

I turn to look at his face, surprised. He doesn't seem worried, his face looks more hopeful than anything, and it catches me off guard. When I woke up this morning, I certainly didn't think my day would take a turn out like this. I'm not sure what he's about to propose, or if I'm going to like it, but I do want to help him. And maybe it will silence my conscience, or at least in part.

"I'm listening."

Thomas shakes his head and smiles at me. "It's Simon's idea. They're waiting for us at the cottage in Connecticut to discuss it with you."

"Oh...so I assume I have to get out of this bed and shower."

Thomas smiles and helps me out of bed. "I'm going to help you take a shower. I imagine you're still having a hard time washing your hair with that shoulder." It's not a question, it's a simple observation and, for the first time in my life, I let someone take care of me. I have to resign myself to the idea that sometimes in my life, I need help, and Thomas needs to take care someone, like he couldn't do for his family. We're depending on each other, and it doesn't feel as bad as I thought it would.

He helps me undress and washes my hair so gently that when I close my eyes and let him lather it up, for a moment, I'm taken back to my childhood and feel my mother's hands washing my hair. It feels natural, and the memory is a pleasant one of scents, colors, and laughter that I haven't had in a long time. Thomas is waking up a part of me that I thought died forever, and when he towels my hair after helping me get dressed, I feel like the entire weight of the world has been lifted. When he presses his lips on mine, all my fears slip away, leaving me with only the tenderness and affection he manages to convey. His tongue touches mine, dispelling any fears that I'd lost him, reinforcing my resolve to face this difficult moment together, like a real couple, two lovers trusting each other.

*

When Thomas said it was a cottage in Connecticut, I thought he meant a little mountain cottage in the woods. Nothing could be further from reality; this villa has at least ten bedrooms and, as I discover, a library for our meeting. An actual library bigger than my entire apartment.

"Thank you for coming." The man introducing himself as Evan, their manager, motions for me to sit in a chair among the others who wave their hands. They all seem very quiet, though I don't get the feeling they want to rip me apart. "You know the guys, I guess...so let's skip the pleasantries?"

I take a quick look at Lilly, who's watching me with a smile, and she seems almost excited about what they're going to tell me. I don't know what to think. "Yes, I'm not particularly good with apologies, and I feel like a complete idiot right now."

Damian and Michael laugh as Lilly slaps her partner and Simon smiles shyly. Thomas extends a hand toward me, and I grab it firmly, regardless of whether everyone can see the gesture.

"Thomas, do you want to explain it?" asks Evan.

"Oh, no, sweetheart. I've already told you how she's going to answer, you deal with her."

Everybody laughs, and I'm not sure Thomas is on my side anymore. I give him the stink-eye, and in response, he smiles sweetly and lightly kisses my fingers.

Simon speaks up: "We want to do an exclusive interview on your blog, explaining the truth about our past, how we met, and what unites us: prison. We believe it's time to take this step, that is, if you want to help us out. We're tired of living secretive half-lives just to keep our past hidden. It's time to grow up and accept our responsibilities." As he's talking, I remember Thomas telling me this was his idea. I didn't expect that, nor their offer.

"Okay, I appreciate it, but don't you want to do it in a more reputable newspaper like…I don't know, the *New York Times*? After that video, I don't think my blog has much credibility. Plus, how would your record label react?" I ask, puzzled. I feel like there are too many holes in this sinking ship, and a little tape isn't going to fix it.

"That leads us to the second part of our proposal," says Evan, throwing a look at Thomas that I can't decipher. "The band's contract with the label ends after this upcoming album is released. We've decided not to renew with them, or rather, we're sure they're going to dump us. They'll use the damaged reputation clause to get rid of their obligation to do five more albums—in addition to the four already produced. It's in their contract renewal and has to be signed by the two parties. We could find another record company, maybe smaller than this one, and we'll be thinking about those options in the next few days. However, we want to manage the public relations ourselves, be much more transparent, and above all, move our media presence to social media rather than traditional channels like print and television. I did an estimate of the value of your blog, considering the growth you had from Thomas's tweet, and we'd like to buy it and hire you. The blog would be the only official communication channel of the Jailbirds," he says, wrapping up his speech and handing me a piece of paper with numbers. "The amount we're offering is at the bottom of the page in bold."

I'm literally stunned. I don't know how to respond to this proposal, let alone how to read this number. I place the paper on the coffee table in front of me and bend over to count the zeros. I do it four times, but I can't figure it out. They all look at me, grinning.

"Does anyone have a pen?"

Evan is puzzled but handles me one. I look at the number again and realize it's at least two hundred dollars. I group the zeros, count them three more times and then look up at Evan. "Are you crazy? I don't even want to consider it," I blurt out, stunned.

Everyone bursts out laughing, and I look around, resting my eyes on Thomas. He raises his hands innocently. "I told them you'd answer like that. Don't blame me."

"A million dollars for my blog? Who gave you the estimate? Roger Rabbit?' I ask Evan, astounded.

He smiles and shakes his head. "The experts I hired. Your current blog's value with the projections of the first year after merging the two brands, yours and the Jailbirds. Plus, you'd get a paycheck as an employee."

That number seems impossibly high, but Evan seems to be someone who's more concerned about doing good business for his clients—the four band members I have in front of me—rather than doing me a favor.

"But I won't be able to write whatever I want about music anymore. If it's your blog, I'll have to follow your rules. I'll be bound by what you want to communicate. I've always refused to run ads precisely because I didn't want to feel obligated to anyone," I say skeptically.

Evan shakes his head again. "Your blog works because

you're honest. We want you to keep writing your reviews and articles, but we also want you to reserve a regular space for the band. No censorship from us. You decide the content."

I think about it. This is surreal. Getting paid for what I love to do? It feels like a dream. "I currently have zero funds to run this blog, so I'm making do with what I have. Can I have access to an annual budget to produce content?" I ask with what I hope is bravado in my voice. I don't know how much I can pull strings.

"Absolutely, yes. The biggest expenses will have to be approved by the accountants, of course, but you can manage the funds as you see fit."

I feel all their eyes on me, and I don't realize how anxious they are until I accept their proposal and see them smiling and relaxing. Lilly and Damian seem immersed in their bubble of happiness, whispering between smiles and caresses. Simon suddenly looks ten years younger, and I'm assuming it's relief because their secret had become too big to carry. Michael is studying Thomas with a frown and a half-smirk, like an older brother: happy, and at the same time, worried. Evan watches them all, sitting on those couches, with the concerned face of a father watching his children make a complicated and risky decision, and the pride of knowing they're doing the right thing.

Thomas, though, only has eyes for me and what I read into them are happiness and determination. I've never been as proud of him as I am at this moment. They're thrilled that I'm on board with this risky, potentially career-destroying idea.

CHAPTER 30
Iris

I open my eyes to Dexter's rear end pointed straight at my face. His tail is raised, revealing all the intimate parts. "Gross. Can't you at least turn the other way? I prefer your dry-food breath," I complain aloud.

Next to me, a chuckle makes me turn to find Thomas's amused face. He grabs my cat and snuggles him on his chest to caress him. The traitor furball immediately begins to purr.

"Of course you two are plotting against me. I'm surprised you haven't killed me in my sleep yet." I roll my eyes and try to get up, but Thomas holds me back.

"Not even a good morning kiss?" he asks, sticking out his lower lip like a kid.

"You don't deserve it," I reply, irritated.

Thomas gets Dexter out of bed, then makes me lie down again by rolling over me and tucking between my legs. He presses his morning wood against my most sensitive parts, re-igniting my lower belly that has barely slept since last night when we relieved our stress as intimately as possible. Afterwards, I slept like a log in his arms. Since the streets around my apartment are still crawling with journalists and fans who don't show any sign of leaving, when we got in from Connecticut yesterday, he was forced to spend the night, and I didn't complain.

"Are you sure?" he whispers in my ear as he gently kisses my neck and sends a shiver of pleasure down my body that makes my back arch, seeking more contact.

"When you put it that way, I think I can make an exception," I reply as I stick a hand in his boxers.

"Uh, no, miss. We have to get up and take a shower, or we'll be late for the interview." He chuckles as he gets up and fixes his boxers, giving me a full view of his perfectly sculpted chest, and then heads to the kitchen to make coffee.

I let out a frustrated puff and get up. "You are going to pay for this." I point my finger at him as I lock myself in the bathroom.

When I get out, Thomas has cooked breakfast, fed Dexter, and brought the dishes to the table. With such a sexy man in the kitchen, I could consider living together. The thought makes me blush.

"What?" Thomas's eyebrow perks up.

"Nothing, I was just thinking how sexy you are when you're walking around in my kitchen half-naked...even dressed, actually," I admit with a chuckle.

Thomas approaches me, kisses me passionately, leaving me breathless, and the taste of coffee on his lip awakens my senses. "You're damn sexy all the time, even when you sleep."

I doubt this is true since I snore worse than a train, but I accept his compliment blushing. "Are you ready for the interview?" I ask as I sink my fork into the eggs and enjoy a mouthful of the delicious breakfast he has prepared.

He shrugs and sips his coffee, washing down the piece of toast. "Yes, as much as you can be prepared to tell the world that you've been to prison," he admits honestly.

"Do you want to think about it? I don't think the others would blame you."

"No, I need to say it and put my life in order. We've had enough years to prove to everyone that we've really changed. If anyone has something to say, it's their problem."

I really admire him for what he's doing. I appreciate his strength in facing life so decisively, even though it has brought him to his knees in a brutal way. He got up, healed his scars, and put the pieces back together masterfully. I respect him for that.

"Do you think your sister will talk to you after the interview?" I know this is the most important part for him.

He shrugs as he chews a piece of bacon. "I don't know. I hope so, but I have no illusions. She decided to cut off all contact with me and stuck to it even after I clearly proved that I had moved beyond it. I don't think this great gesture of mine will make things any better between us."

I don't say anything, but I hope with all my heart that his sister will change her mind because I didn't meet Thomas when he was a kid, but I know for a fact that the man in front of me is worth reconnecting with. He's loving, he cares about the people in his life, he's got his life back on track, and he's living it to the fullest. There's nothing about him that would make me give up on bringing him into my kids' lives, and I hope his sister realizes that.

*

"These are the questions I have prepared. Tell me if you don't want to answer something or if you want to add more," I explain as I put the camera on the tripod in the living room of Damian and Lilly's house, the place they chose for the interview. It is a familiar, welcoming environment where they feel comfortable and can speak freely without being interrupted.

The guys read the questions carefully while Lilly is in the kitchen talking to Evan. This is an aspect of Damian's life that will also affect her life and career. While the Jailbirds have finished their fourth album under contract, the Red Velvet Curtains have yet to release their first and, if the record label got angry, they could stall forever in getting it out, which would destroy their career. I admire her for never having a doubt about supporting her partner at this challenging time. And to think that at first, no one believed in their relationship, given Damian's history with women.

Evan is smiling at her, but his rigid posture reveals he's tense for this interview, although years of working in this industry have led him to mask his feelings well. Right now, his entire career is at stake, along with the Jailbirds. Many of his clients may decide to change managers. In this industry, reputation is everything, and he's dancing on the razor's edge with this interview. The way he manages this emergency will determine his future career.

"I think they're perfect." Damian catches my attention and makes me look back at the sofa where all four of them are already sitting with their microphones on.

Thomas is studying me curiously. It's not the first time he's done it during an interview, but it's the first time he's been on the other side of the camera. Now he's also my boss, since I signed the contract to work with them almost two days ago.

I turn on the camera and motion that we're ready. They smile at me, and I start with the first question. "You chose Jailbirds as the name of the band. Why?"

Damian takes the lead in an utterly convincing way. He seems almost relaxed, leaning against the back of the sofa in his house, no hesitation in his voice: "The four of us met when we were only sixteen years old, in a juvenile detention center. We all ended up there for crimes that weren't dangerous but serious enough to land us in jail for a couple of years. We were four scared kids fighting to survive in an environment far from suitable for our young, impressionable minds. We had no hope, no one had confidence in us, and we didn't know what else to do but get into fights. Prison guards called us 'jailbirds.' In prison jargon, they're the ones without a future, who spend their lives going in and out of prison. We were seen as hopeless and treated as such. Little criminals with no futures, hence the name for the band."

"But things turned out differently. We've all seen it," I continue with my interview. Ironically, my voice is the least confident.

Thomas takes the floor now, and the intense look he gives me almost makes my legs tremble.

"In prison, a psychologist ran a program which tried to rehabilitate boys with less serious crimes. The four of us were her pet project, proof that kids shouldn't be thrown away, that there was still hope. She was the only one who believed in us, to see us as more than just thugs. She suggested we form a band and we did, having two hours of practice every day under the supervision of the guards. That's what saved us those two years. It kept us sane and able to drown out the voices of those who told us we were worth nothing. When we got out of there, we were lost, confused. No one wanted to give us a job, but we had our music. We started playing in the clubs that didn't require references. Then we met Evan, who believed in us more than anyone and took us all the way to the largest record label in the country." Thomas's words enter me as if he's telling me directly and not the whole world. I have to look down and read the next question to ease the tension a little.

"Did Evan and the record company know about your past?"

It's Michael's turn to respond. "Yes, but while all of us wanted to be up front about who we were right away, the label thought it would tarnish their image. They said the world wasn't ready for a band of ex-convicts, that we'd be remembered just for that. We wanted to lose that stigma, show the world that we were more than just the mistakes of our past, and we fucking did. But when we became famous enough to prove it, we had already signed a confidentiality agreement with the record company."

"What has changed now? Why did you decide to speak up now after almost eight years into your career?"

This time Simon responds, and even though I already know the answer to this question, I can't help but feel a squeeze in my stomach as I hear it. This is the decision that will completely change their lives, their careers, their future.

"Because our contract with the record company included four albums. The fourth will be released soon and when it is, our relationship with them will end, we'll be free from the contract, and we've decided not to continue with them. We don't care if this album does well or not. We couldn't care less if we put more money into the record company's pockets... hell, if you want to download it illegally, do it, as long as you talk to your friends about it. It's not about money. It's about the honesty and respect we're going to earn with our fans. We're already working on the fifth album and we're going to do a tour once it's finished. If we don't fill stadiums like before, that's fine with us. It's the music that matters to us. It saved us once. It's going to save us again."

His honesty and enthusiasm are so contagious that the serious tone that's permeated the interview so far seems to lighten. You can see it in their eyes—they're finally free from a burden that they've been carrying for too long. They can breathe now like they never were able to before.

"So, for now, you're without a record company?"

"Yes, if anyone wants to volunteer..." Damian laughs as he runs a hand through his hair. It's not as nervous a gesture as I would have expected.

The interview continues with other slightly lighter questions that focus on their intentions for the future and, when I finally turn off the camera, their enthusiasm turns to joy. Evan and Lilly bring out beer for everyone and we all take a moment to process what we just did, sipping the cold liquid silently while we gather our thoughts.

*

We're still at Lilly and Damian's place when I finish editing the video and loading it onto the blog site. We gather around the screen to read the comments. It's as though people had been waiting for this their entire life. Aside from the usual toxic ones who spread negativity online like it's their job, most are words of encouragement. Some people admire their decision to change, others tell their story, very similar to that of the Jailbirds only without the same happy ending, and some wish them continued success. Unexpectedly, their confession seems to have worked out quite favorably for the Jailbirds—at least for the immediate future.

Evan's phone starts blowing up. We all anticipate a verdict, something that reveals how industry insiders took the news. "Pretty much every TV station in the country wants an interview with you. There are already a couple of record companies asking for a meeting..." He smiles, a gesture that seems relaxed but that no one has any idea how to interpret.

"Is that a good thing?" Damian gives voice to what we're all thinking.

"It's very positive at the moment. It's publicity for you. I'm going to have to work overtime to handle all this attention. Hell, I'm not going to sleep for weeks." He laughs as he runs a hand over immaculate hair.

"Do you need help? Because I know a person who would like to do exactly this job and would do it for free."

Thomas looks at me, puzzled. "Who the hell would that be?"

"Emily."

"Oh! Yeah, and that woman has the balls to handle it," Thomas admits with such seriousness everyone bursts out laughing.

"It seems like she's already kicked your ass once," Michael jokes.

"Twice, actually," Thomas admits, joining in the laughter.

"Call her immediately. I want her here in less than an hour." Evan points his finger at me as he turns to answer an email.

"Really? Do you really want me to call her?"

"Do I look like I'm joking?"

I raise my hands in surrender and pull out my phone. It seems that life is about to change for everyone, not just the Jailbirds.

PRESS *Review*

People:

We expected denial from the Jailbirds, especially after the video posted by the blogger. Instead, they completely floored us with a confession that made the walls of every news room tremble. The Jailbirds didn't randomly choose their name, they met in a juvenile prison. The confession has provoked reactions all over the music world. Most offer their support, while others turn their noses up, sensing a publicity stunt. However, the band will undoubtedly need as much publicity as it can get. Their record label has confirmed their contract with the Jailbirds has come to an end and will not be renewed. Now we'll wait and see how the fans will react and whether they will continue to support the band after hiding the truth for so long.

Rock Now!

Breaking news we did not expect: confirmation that the Jailbirds have served time in prison has been discovered in a video posted on the blog site, *Rocking in New York*. We've always wondered about the mysterious past of the most famous band in the world, and now we have the answer—from their own voices. Damian, Thomas, Michael, and Simon met in a juvenile prison and played music together to survive a situation that threatened a somewhat dark future. Words of support flooded in from several major bands, as well as admiration from all over the world, for what these four guys managed to do, proving that it is possible to redeem themselves and change a seemingly hopeless future. It's a profound example of how kids who make mistakes can become thriving, successful adults. Their confession is further confirmation that this band has integrity, and not just musically. We'll surely be hearing from them for a long time to come, despite the fact that their record company decided to cut ties with them.

Gossip Now!
Sexy, famous musicians *and* bad guys with a past in prison? Where do we sign up to have one of the Jailbirds delivered directly to our house?

@jailfreakingbirds How sweet are they all together on that couch? No matter what your past is, we will always be by your side.

@jailbirds_groupie Can we talk about that video? They're the best. But I don't understand why they used that Iris blog after what she did to Thomas.

@wannabe_rockstar I knew it! I sensed something was up when I met them to listen to their single!

@Thomas_Jailbirds Thank you all for the support you are giving us at this particular time in our lives. Remember that the only official and reliable information about us is found at

Rocking in New York.

@Damian_Jailbirds Our fans are the best. I've always said that. Thank you all for your support.

@Michael_Jailbirds You're the best! And remember, the only blog that doesn't bullshit you about us is Iris's official blog.

@Simon_Jailbirds You're the best fans in the world. Thank you for not abandoning us at this difficult time. We've been wanting to tell you our story for a while. We finally got to do it.

EPILOGUE
Thomas

I watch Iris asleep in her bed, peaceful, as Dexter walks around my legs, waiting for me to fill his bowl with food while I make coffee. I've been living in this house for a month now, and the routine is reassuring. Although, I have to say, it's inconvenient to have all my stuff at my house. There's not enough space in here for a pin, it's crammed to every corner. I open the fridge and take out the bowl with the pancake mix I made last night. Iris teased me for two hours because she said I'm doing too much, but I know she's starting to appreciate the fact that I take care of her. It's therapeutic for both of us, I can finally let go of my guilt about the past, and she's learning that allowing people into her life and getting help isn't all that bad.

Dexter starts meowing, so I feed him before he goes to wake up Iris. As I pour the coffee in the cups and put them on the table, out of the corner of my eye I see Iris sitting up and rubbing her fingers through her unruly red mane. I still can't figure out how she can tame that hair. During the night, I'm almost strangled sometimes by that mass of hair that seems to have a life of its own.

"Is that coffee that I smell?" Her voice is still croaking, and it is the most beautiful sound I have ever heard.

"Hot the way you like it," I say as I pour a spoonful of the pancake mix into the pan.

Iris comes close, wearing my blue t-shirt she put on after we made love. It's huge on her but makes her look sexy as hell. Her small arms wrap me from behind, and she sticks her head between my side and my arm to peek at what I'm doing.

"This thing you do where you make the mix the night before, I'm starting to like it."

"Really? I'll remember that when you make fun of me next time. In fact, wait a second, I'll get my phone and record you repeating that."

Iris giggles and gives me a hand pulling out dishes and forks for breakfast. I love the perfect way we fit together in the kitchen without getting in each other's way, splitting the housework without even talking.

"I don't make fun of you, I just like it when you're in my kitchen. Like when you're stressed, and you make cookies for an entire army."

"If you've noticed, I haven't done that in a long time. You relax me. I don't need to decorate cookies to ease the tension." I kiss her on the neck, making her sigh.

"Then we'll have to find some other excuse to bake them because I like it when you focus on creating the perfect design. We should make it a fun ritual, like you did with your mom as a kid."

My heart swells with happiness. It's beautiful how she tries to make my past less painful, even just reminding me that baking cookies was a source of joy for me, not just a way to ease my frustration. I kiss her on the lips and get lost in her smile.

"I'd like to call the security company today, to come take a look at the locks on the door and windows. Is that okay with you?" I ask her as we sit at the table to eat.

Iris frowns and looks at me, tilting her head to the side. "Still with the idea of armoring my apartment?"

We've discussed this until we were exhausted, but I need to put some security between me and the outside world if I spend most of my nights here. Unfortunately, there are a lot of lunatics out there and, having doors and windows that look like tissue paper is dangerous for both her and me. All it would take is one rabid fan of the Jailbirds to get in here and put her in danger.

"If I keep spending my nights here, yes, it's necessary. It's not an option that our head of security is willing to put off any longer."

Iris inhales deeply and seems to be thinking for a long time about what she's going to tell me. It kind of unsettles me because I'm always afraid she'll get tired of me and ask me to leave. "I've been thinking about something lately. Since I no longer have any particular money problems with the new job, I was considering moving into a building without a homeless person to feed in the lobby. I love this apartment, and I don't mind feeding Charlie, Bill...Jack, or whatever he calls himself this week, but I'd like a little bigger place, one where I can have a desk and an office. Does that make sense?" she asks, and I feel a boulder lifting off my chest.

I nod and chug quickly to swallow down the bite of pancakes. "Okay...I might have a proposal
for you, but feel free to refuse, alright?"

"Should I be worried?" One investigating eyebrow pops up and terrifies me like few things in this world.

I burst out laughing, even though my stomach is in knots

over what her reaction might be. "No, I just want to know if you'd like to go into business with me."

Iris looks at me with an expression that seems more worried than angry, and I breathe a sigh of relief.

*

We enter the gates that lead to the private garden in the courtyard of the building on the Upper Eastside. Iris looks around with wide eyes, just like I did the first time I set foot in here. It feels like a parallel world. A house with a private garden that occupies the entire length of a neighborhood in the middle of Manhattan seems impossible.

"Exactly what are we doing in front of a six-story building under renovation?" She's puzzled as we get out of the car and the iron gates closed behind us.

"It's actually seven floors, one is underground...but that's not the point. I was thinking of buying it."

Iris looks at me and her green eyes seem to pop from her orbits. "What the hell do you do with a seven-story building? You'd get lost in it!" she points out.

I smile and nod. I know this space is huge, but I thought I'd put it to good use by setting up our business in it. Since we left the label, the band has decided not to sign with another one and to start our own. We called it Jail Records, just to show the snobs in the music industry that we can do whatever we want. We hired two friends of Iris's who have a small recording studio in a Brooklyn garage. But since we can't put our headquarters there, I thought, why not live where I'll spend most of my days working?

"In the basement, we could build two recording studios for Jail Records, on the ground floor there would be offices, while the three floors above could be transformed into my home... furnished the way I want, this time." I chuckle as I nervously run my hand across my neck. I explained the easiest part, the hardest part is coming.

"And the top floor?"

"That's where you'd become my partner in this business," I say in one breath.

Iris's eyebrows rise, and her eyes shine with a light I've never seen before. Perhaps the situation is not so tragic. "Explain."

"On the top floor, there is an independent apartment. It has a kitchen, a living room, a bedroom, a bathroom, a covered patio area that can be turned into an office, and a small balcony. I would sell it to you for about two hundred and fifty thousand dollars, for about another hundred thousand, you could furnish it however you want. I know how much you care about your independence, so I propose you buy it as an investment for your future. If things don't work out between us, I could always buy it back, and you'd have the money to buy elsewhere. At first, I thought I'd make an apartment for the guys if they want to stay late...but since you talked this morning about looking for something else...this would be better than renting, right?" The explanation comes out a bit confused and in a hurry.

The silence that follows is infinite and gives me the cold sweats. Iris has had her eyes fixed on the building since I started talking, and for a moment, I'm afraid I said it all in my head and not out loud. The world feels like it's going to collapse on me when she finally turns to me with a smile.

"Can I see my investment?" she asks, struggling to keep the happiness confined to her eyes.

I put my hands in my pocket and pull out the bunch of keys.

Iris laughs, amused. "You've already bought this place, haven't you?"

I pass a hand again across the back of my neck and smile. "I talked to the guys about it. They thought it was a great idea to start with the record company, so I signed last week before they could go on with the reconstruction. We'll split the costs of the label by five. Otherwise, it's up to you and me if you accept the proposal."

"Five?"

"Yes, Evan decided to go into business with us. Apparently, the way he handled our situation brought him a lot more clients than expected, and he decided to invest in a project that couldn't have existed without him. I think that, in addition to hiring Emily, he's going to expand his staff to a couple more agents by the end of the year. From a simple manager, basically, he can set up an agency. His only artists would be us and someone big, like the Red Velvet Curtains. He would leave the smaller acts to the new agents."

"Wouldn't his part in the label be a bit of a conflict with his job as a manager?"

"Not if he keeps the interests of his clients foremost as a manager. He's always been an honest and trustworthy person. If another record company offers a better contract to his clients than ours, he'll advise them to sign with them."

Iris seems impressed when we enter the house, although it is actually still an open construction site with walls to build and floors to redo. We go up the stairs to the top floor and when we enter, I'm sure I've won her over. The living room view is spectacular, with an entire glass wall and ceiling. She's entranced, approaching almost tentatively toward the part of the balcony that overlooks the garden and this small, happy island in the middle of a chaotic city. She inhales deeply, closing her eyes. She looks happy.

"Where do I sign?" she asks, laughing, and all my fears slip away.

"I'm so relieved you like the place and accepted my proposal, because now you can be closer to Dexter. Obviously, your cat loves me more and will come and live in my apartment."

"That's for sure," she says, locking her arms around my waist.

She stands on tiptoes to gently kiss me on the lips. I pull her in and deepen the sweet kiss with all the affection and love I feel for her. I hope she can feel it. It's a kiss that leaves me breathless, with my head spinning and my legs weak. That's what Iris does to me: she takes the earth from under my feet and makes it disappear, letting me fall into my emotions. The only anchor I have to reality are those two big green eyes and mass of red hair that fell on me, literally, months ago and that I will no longer be able to live without.

She walks to one of the concrete bags piled up along a wall and grabs the permanent black marker sitting on it. Then, she takes my arm and pulls up my sleeve, her face concentrated as she writes something on it. "Here, that's my number. Call me when you have a contract ready for me to sign. I like the neighborhood, I've decided to take it," she says, winking.

I burst into laughter. "And now I can finally tell you what really happened that time I walked out on stage with only half of my jeans."

Iris wraps her arms around my waist and rests her head on

my chest. "No, not now. I want you to do it when we're an old couple, and you have to tell me the story of when we met, so I won't forget it."

I hold her in a hug. "I promise I will never let you forget us."

Want to get more FREE from Erika?

Sign up for the author's New Releases mailing list and get a free copy of the short story "Eliot." You will periodically receive free short stories and unique chapters.

Click here to get started:
https://www.erikavanzin.com/newsletter.html

Acknowledgements

A heartfelt thank you to all those who read Backstage and chose to give Paparazzi a chance. You are the reason I can continue to write stories I love. I am grateful to you all.

About the author

At the age of eight, Erika asked Santa for a typewriter. That was when her parents, quite surprised, realized that she was not like all the other children. However, when she received her first heavy, professional and brand new "Olivetti Letter 35" that Christmas, it was love at first sight. She immediately started writing the words that soon became her first short story. Over time she bought a much more efficient computer, but that typewriter will always have a special place in her heart: it was her first love.

Erika was born on December 6, 1979 in Valdobbiadene in the province of Treviso, a small village at the foot of the Prealps. Both her parents were born and raised in the same town where they still live today. Erika moved to Padua at 18 to attended university, and after graduation, she did not return to Valdobbiadene but followed her heart and traveled worldwide, living in Los Angeles, Vancouver, and London and visiting North America and Europe.

It was at Nicolò Bocassino primary school where she met the teacher who made her fall in love with books, writing, and studies in general, encouraging her creativity and eventually starting her on the path toward being a writer.

Made in the USA
Middletown, DE
24 September 2021